The Last of A Dying Breed

The Last of A Dying Breed

Carl Michaelsen

Boxhead Books

A Novel by Carl Michaelsen

Cover Designs by Taylor Piggott

Edited by Ryan Schuetz

Proofread by Kathy Michaelsen

Published by Boxhead Books

First Printing, 2022

Prologue

The sound of gunfire, screeching tires, and terrified screams from pedestrians were all that Noah could hear. His ears were ringing something awful, giving him a pounding headache. He dove behind a blue United States Postal Service Box and reloaded his AR-style assault rifle. His mask was filled with sweat; he ripped off the rubber clown mask and sucked in as much oxygen as he could before throwing the sweaty mask back on.

"They're flooding in through the back alley!" Cooper screamed, the fear present in his high-pitched voice. Like Noah, he was wearing a clown mask. Cooper gripped the duffle bag stuffed with money and ran across the street, shooting wildly from his machine gun. He ducked behind a parked car as the police began returning fire, bombing rounds all over the road.

Noah gripped his gun but stayed behind the metal box, flinching every single time a gunshot rang out. This was not at all what he had signed up for. The sirens from close to fifteen LAPD squad cars were blaring so loudly that Noah could feel the vibration in his chest. That, combined with the incessant gunfire, was disorientating.

"Noah! Get your ass up, now!" Jake Tell roared, grabbing Noah by the collar and hauling him to his feet. Jake had ditched his mask a long time ago. His face was gushing blood from a wound on his cheek; a bullet had scorched him, taking a chunk of his face with it. "Miles, cover fire!"

Miles came barreling after Jake and Noah, blasting off an entire 30-round magazine at the blockade of cops behind them; he swapped in a fresh magazine as he ran. The officers were attempting to close the road in front of them in hopes of blockading the four men, leaving them no escape route.

"Cooper! Do you copy?" Jake yelled into the mic clipped to his shirt.

"Yeah!" Cooper's voice came back.

"Meet at the truck! We need to get out of here before they close the road!" Jake answered.

Before Cooper could respond, a pair of cop cars came around the corner. Jake threw Noah down and leveled his weapon, squeezing the trigger. Miles swung around and also engaged, firing at both cruisers. The cops inside didn't stand a chance; their bodies were riddled with bullets before they even knew what was happening. Jake adjusted his aim and blasted off the rest of the magazine at the blockade of cops in front of them - the gunfire forced them to seek cover, giving Jake, Miles, and Noah a chance to run. They could see their black SUV just down the next block, parked on the street in front of a pharmacy.

"Joe, you better have the truck ready, we're coming in hot!" Jake said into his mic.

"Yeah, I know. Hurry the fuck up!" Joe shot back.

"Where's Cooper?" Miles asked, breathing heavily through his mask.

"Cooper, what's your location?" Jake asked, coming to a stop and ducking into an alley. He reloaded his rifle as Noah and Miles sought cover in the alley as well. It still sounded like gunfire was all around them. "Cooper, where are you?"

There was still no answer.

Jake Tell shook his head and cursed. He looked at Noah and Miles sadly.

"This is really not how I thought this was gonna go," he admitted. "We'd been doing so well..."

"We're almost there, man," Miles responded, lifting his mask up.

"Cooper's got the money," Jake muttered. "And without that, we're dead anyway..."

Jake gripped his rifle and took a deep breath.

"You two get back to the truck, I'll be back."

"Jake..." Noah said in protest. Jake put his hand up.

"I don't want to hear it. Just go," Jake ordered. "Go!"

Miles grabbed Noah by the shoulder and they started running toward the truck. Jake broke from cover and sprinted back the way he'd come - right back into the gunfire. Noah watched Jake raise his rifle and re-engage the police officers as he moved across the street, hoping to find Cooper and the money.

"This is so fucked up," Miles muttered, letting go of Noah as they ran.

"I didn't agree to any of this," Noah responded.

"You think I did?" Miles shot back, clearly upset with the situation. "I've got a wife and kid at home!"

Jake Tell saw Cooper leaning against a bus stop vestibule, a pool of blood around him. The police officers were slowly starting to approach him; their gunfire had lulled for the time being. Keeping low and moving fast, Jake managed to avoid detection as he made his way to Cooper's side. Cooper barely acknowledged Jake; he was holding onto his life by a thread. There were at least four gunshot wounds in Cooper's chest and stomach, blood pouring out of the bullet holes.

"I'm sorry, Coop," Jake whispered, gently taking the duffle bag full of money from Cooper's grasp. Cooper mumbled something incoherently before his head slumped forward, and he took his last breath.

Grabbing the bag of money, Jake peered over the vestibule and saw a group of officers less than twenty feet away - their guns at the ready. He made sure his rifle was fully loaded before darting back toward the escape vehicle.

Miles and Noah paused as the gunfire erupted once again. Something terrible had to have happened; there was no other explanation for that amount of shooting.

"Go," Miles grumbled, checking his rifle. "I'm not leaving Jake out there."

"Come on, dude. Let's just get out of here!" Noah insisted.

"I said get the fuck out of here!" Miles screamed, sprinting toward the gunfire. "You and Joe gotta make this right, it can't be for nothing."

"Miles, you're gonna get killed!" Noah yelled back at him. "Let's just go!"

"I need help!" Jake Tell's voice suddenly came through their radios. "I've got the money!"

Noah was frozen. He didn't want to just let Jake die, but he wanted to live. More than anything, Noah wanted to live. Miles was about to round the corner back onto the road where Jake and Cooper were when his body jerked suddenly - blood spattered onto the ground. He stood still for a moment before falling over onto his side. There was nothing left for Noah to do. Jake and Miles and Cooper had made their choice. And now Noah was making his. Switching his radio to a different frequency, Noah started jogging toward the truck.

"Joe, you copy?" Noah asked.
"Go ahead," Joe answered, sounding numb.
"I'm heading back to you."
"Alone?"
"Alone."
"Copy that."

The gun battle on the next street raged on as Noah turned his back on it. He could envision Jake Tell trying to fight his way through a horde of police officers. Every gunshot that rang out made Noah flinch. Joe suddenly pulled up in front of Noah and threw the passenger door open for him.

"Get in, we need to get outta here. Now!"

Noah leapt inside. Joe slammed on the gas and drove down an alley before making a hard left and driving away from the gunfire.

Part One: The Prodigal Son

"You need not fear it, but you always must bear in mind that the past is never quite as finished with you as you think you are with it" - Kathryn Kennish; Author

1

The two paramedics looked at the wound and shook their heads, knowing he was lying. He sat in the back of the parked ambulance, bleeding steadily from a nasty gash on the side of his face. The cut ran from his eyebrow down to the middle of his cheek; his face was covered in blood, and his right eye was swollen shut. His jeans and collared shirt were already stained red, making the injury look a lot worse. The blood had even dripped onto his Timberland boots.

"So," the taller of the two paramedics said, kneeling down next to the man, "did you fall on a knife?"

"Something like that," the man muttered, wincing in pain. The paramedic chuckled softly to himself and went to work tending the wound.

"This is going to sting a little," he warned before he started cleaning the cut. As expected, the man shuddered in pain. "We should really take you to the hospital."

"I thought you said you could stitch me up here?" the man countered.

"I said I *think* I can," the paramedic responded, not hiding his annoyance. "But it would be easier if we could do this at the hospital. You need to make sure there was no damage done to your eye."

The man sighed loudly and cursed under his breath.

"Alright, fine," he relented. The paramedic smiled.

"Great! Let's go."

"I need my phone," the man grunted, standing up. Both paramedics yelled in protest, but the man ignored them, walking back to his black pickup truck and retrieving his cell phone from the cup holder.

There were two police cruisers parked around his vehicle; the cops were eyeing him just as skeptically as the paramedics were. They didn't believe his story either. And they shouldn't have. It was a bad cover story. And he knew it. But what was the alternative? Not like he could tell them the truth about what happened. He was a 6'5 200 pound male and doubted they'd believe him anyway. It wasn't worth the hassle or embarrassment.

"Mr. Riordan," one of the police officers said, walking over to him. She was holding a clipboard. "How're you feeling?"

"Wonderful," the man grunted, trying to smile at the officer. His face was throbbing, and truth be told, he couldn't wait to get to the hospital. They'd have painkillers.

"Are you sure you don't want to press charges?" the officer asked, lowering her voice significantly. The man met her eyes, staring at her intense blue eyes. She was a kind-looking woman, which felt surprising to him since she was a cop. Several piercings lined her ears, including an industrial piercing in her left ear. Her dirty-blonde hair was tied back in a loose ponytail, exposing a small tattoo she had behind her ear, although he couldn't make out what it was.

"No, I don't want to press charges," the man said. "I already told you, I fell getting out of my truck."

The cop looked him up and down and shook her head. She sighed and reached into her back pocket, pulling out her wallet. Producing a card, the officer handed it to the man.

"If you change your mind, my number is on there," she said with a soft smile. "I'm sorry, Mr. Riordan. I wish you'd let me help you."

"Please stop with the Mr. Riordan," the man grunted, hundreds of horrid memories flooding through his mind. "Just call me Noah."

"Well, alright Noah," the officer said. "You give me a call if you think of anything."

"Will do," Noah nodded, turning to walk back to the ambulance. He flipped the card over to read the name on it.

Police Officer Jackie Walsh
Los Angeles Police Department

Noah tucked the card into the breast pocket of his shirt and finally let the paramedics do their job, helping him into the stretcher in the back of the ambulance. Less than a minute later, they were on their way to the hospital, sirens and lights blaring. The taller paramedic was driving, leaving the shorter one in the back with Noah. The man looked too young to be a paramedic, but Noah wasn't one to make assumptions; Noah knew he looked younger himself.

"How long have you been an EMT?" Noah asked, uncomfortable with the silence. The man smirked at Noah.

"First night."

"Oh god," Noah blurted.

"Ha! I'm just screwing with you, I've been doing this for a few years now," the EMT laughed. "I'm Danny."

"Noah."

"What do you do for work?" Danny asked as he pressed another bandage to Noah's face.

"Construction," Noah mumbled, his voice slightly muffled from the bandage. "I'm a foreman for Omicron."

"Ok, yeah I've seen your guys' trucks all over the 101," Danny said, referring to L.A.'s busiest highway.

"That's where I'm working right now," Noah admitted. "Been there for months."

"That's been torn up for a while," Danny remarked.

"And it's not getting finished anytime soon," Noah grunted, getting a small chuckle out of Danny.

It was true, the project to demolish and expand parts of the 101 was plagued with delays and red tape. Noah's job was almost impossible, constantly getting berated by his boss for lack of productivity from his crew while at the same time getting stonewalled anytime they made progress. Omicron LLC was a multi-million dollar enterprise handling large-scale civil construction projects. Anything from highways, skyscrapers, and arenas fell under Omicron's umbrella of expertise. Noah was paid fairly for his position but not nearly enough to be living comfortably in Los Angeles. It was an issue that affected everyone on his crew and something they talked about frequently.

"So why won't you tell us what really happened?" Danny finally asked.

"I have," Noah mumbled. "Plenty of times."

“No offense, Noah, but we both know you didn’t fall. Someone hit you, and they got you pretty good. My guess is they were wearing a ring or used some type of small object.”

Noah didn’t say anything, or even look at Danny. He was smart and observant. And he was right. But Noah wasn’t about to give him the satisfaction of knowing that. The rest of the ride to the hospital came and went in silence. As soon as they arrived, the EMTs hurried Noah into the Emergency Room and turned him over to the proper doctors. The doctor put Noah under almost immediately and went to work repairing the side of his face.

When Noah regained consciousness the next morning, he was surprised that he’d only needed half a dozen stitches to sew up the wound. His eye was still going to be swollen due to some damage to the eye socket, but other than that, he was good as new. Until the eye was fully healed, the doctor warned Noah about going to work. As much as he hated to admit it, the doctor was right. To do his job, Noah obviously needed both of his eyes functioning. Just to save his own ass from certain discontent from his superior, Noah had the doctor write a note to Omicron.

Twelve hours later, Noah was back at his small house, cleaning the blood from his pickup truck. The truck didn’t even belong to him; it was a work vehicle - the Omicron LLC logo displayed on both doors. He tried not to think of the previous night's events, knowing it would just continue to bother him. He was confused, his pride was damaged, but most of all, he was hurt. Hurt in a way that he was not accustomed to. Ever since he was a child, Noah felt like he’d been missing something. He yearned for the kind of connection he saw in those stupid Rom-Com movies his mother would watch. But in his 28 years, he had little to show for it in terms of meaningful relationships. And if recent events were any indicator, he'd just hit rock bottom.

2

The truck was finally clean. Or at least free from any bloodstains. Noah didn't think the truck would ever be considered 'clean'. It was a work truck, after all, and was supposed to be dirty. The tires, mudflaps, and undercarriage of the truck were caked with dried mud, concrete, and dirt. The sides of the truck were equally dirty. But it was still a good-looking truck, and Noah took pride in that.

It was a white Ford F-350 diesel, a monster truck in its own right. Noah's truck was outfitted with a grill guard and orange light system. He'd installed a Weatherguard toolbox for the bed of the truck as well. All of the Omicron fleet vehicles were white Ford pickups, but the models varied from 150s, 250s, and 350s. Before being given the truck, Noah's only mode of transportation was his motorcycle - a blue and black Suzuki GSX-R750 that he'd bought when he first moved out to California with his mom just about ten years ago. Despite being an older model, the bike still ran perfectly, and Noah took impeccable care of it, much like the truck.

Wiping his hands on a rag on his belt, Noah closed the door to his truck and headed back into his small house a half-hour outside of Los Angeles. It wasn't anything special, but it was home, and Noah had done his best to make it feel like a home. The living room was decorated with movie posters and comic book memorabilia; Noah was an avid film enthusiast and reader of comics. A large TV sat in the corner, atop a beautiful display case that Noah had built himself. His living room was the highlight of the home, the rest was pretty standard; a kitchen, two bathrooms, and two bedrooms. Contrary to the living room, the rest of the house was nowhere near as decorated.

As soon as Noah opened the door to his house, the big dog came running over from her bed in the kitchen. She was a golden retriever and one of Noah's best friends in the entire world. A few years back, he and his crew had been building a parking garage when the small pup trotted onto the site, malnourished and badly beaten. A couple of different guys on his crew had tried to pet her, but she'd cowered and hid every time someone came near her. Noah had jumped out of his excavator almost immediately and went over to the terrified pup. Surprisingly, she allowed Noah to pet her, and he ended up scooping the dog up in his arms. She spent the rest of the day on his lap or on the floor of the excavator, curled up on his work boots. After contacting a few local shelters and learning that no one had reported a missing dog, Noah brought the puppy home with him. It took a while for him to decide, but Noah landed on the name 'Ivy' - her red fur reminded him of the DC character Poison Ivy.

"How you doing, girlie?" Noah asked as the dog jumped up on her hind legs to greet him. He scratched behind her ears and pet her all over until she calmed down. No matter how long he'd been gone, as soon as Noah entered the house, Ivy could barely contain her excitement. Noah kicked off his boots and looked at himself in the mirror mounted right next to his front door. Noah Riordan wasn't arrogant by any means, but he knew he was a good-looking man. He stood tall at six and a half feet and weighed just under 200 pounds. Although he didn't work out nearly as much as he used to, Noah was still in decent shape and had most of the muscle definition in his arms, shoulders, and chest from his more athletic days. His brown hair was always cut short, nearly bald on the sides and back, and combed over on top. Although he always received grief from his mother for his unkempt look, he kept a rather long beard as well.

He went to the fridge to grab a beer and refill Ivy's water bowl. Cracking the beer open, he took a gulp and opened his phone. He smiled when he saw he had missed a call; he redialed and put the phone up to his ear.

"I was starting to get worried," a woman answered. "It's Saturday, and I know your 'work on the truck and drink beer all day' ritual is in full swing."

"Only on my first beer," Noah laughed.

"What, you get a late start?"

"Something like that," Noah muttered, taking another sip of beer and flopping down on his couch. Ivy leapt up onto the couch, resting her head on his knee. "Ivy says hi."

"Tell my girl I love her," the woman said. Noah could tell she was smiling. Tayler Palmer was one of those people who just always seemed to be smiling. "Well, how'd it go? I can't believe I haven't heard from you. I've been waiting on pins and needles."

Noah fell silent immediately. He hadn't talked about it to anyone. Normally there would have been some talk with the guys on his crew, but he'd stayed home from work the rest of the week. Reluctantly, at that.

"Noah, are you ok?" Tayler asked after a few seconds of silence.

"Uh, yeah," Noah lied. He sighed loudly. "Well, no, not really."
"Do you wanna talk?" Tayler offered.

It was one of the most loaded questions someone could ask another person, especially when they knew that person as well as Tayler knew Noah. Of course, he wanted to talk about it. He needed to talk about it. But at the same time, the last thing he wanted to do was talk about it. Talking about it made it real.

"Yeah, I think that's probably a good idea," Noah admitted.
"Meet me at Lucky's around seven?" Tayler suggested. Noah looked over to the clock on his oven.
"Yeah, that sounds good."
"See you there," Tayler said, hanging up.

Noah sighed and finished off the rest of the beer before setting it on the small table next to his couch. He set a timer on his phone and closed his eyes, cuddling up next to Ivy. Sensing that he needed her affection, Ivy curled up around Noah and licked his face.
"I don't know what I'd do without you," Noah muttered, dozing off to sleep a few minutes later.

****

Lucky's was busy as usual, packed with its stereotypical younger customer base of Californians. It was a relatively new restaurant to the area but had already established a name for itself with its cheap drinks, good food, and open mic nights. Noah sat in a booth at the back of the restaurant, still wearing sunglasses and an Omicron baseball hat. The stitches were still raw, and the wound was looking particularly ghastly. He already hated the attention it was bringing. A trip to the grocery store had him feeling like an attraction at the circus.

Noah looked up toward the door and instantly smiled as he saw Tayler Palmer walking in. She was a year older than him, 29 to be exact, and was a truly beautiful woman. Her long, blonde hair, combined with her bright smile and kind eyes could light up the darkest room. After graduating from USC, Tayler got a Master's in art education and was currently teaching graphic design at a private high school. When she wasn't teaching, Tayler coached the girls softball team and spent time with her own two dogs. As soon as she entered, Noah held up his glass in her direction. She spotted him, waved, and headed over to the booth. He stood up and smiled brightly.

"Tayler," Noah grinned, giving her a warm hug. "Good to see you."

"You too!" Tayler said, hugging him back. She slid into the booth across from him. "What're you drinking?"

"Long Island," Noah shrugged, taking a big sip. "It sounded good."

"That sounds awesome," Tayler agreed, ordering herself one as soon as the waiter came over. "Dude, what's with the sunglasses? Battling a hangover or something?"

"Or something..." Noah muttered. Slowly, he took his sunglasses off and put them on top of his hat. Tayler's eyes widened when she saw the wound and covered her mouth with her hand.

"Oh my god, Noah!" she gasped. "What happened to you?"

Noah lowered his head slightly, embarrassed, despite knowing there was no need to be. He and Tayler had been friends for most of their adult lives, having met while attending the University of Southern California.

When Noah had first met her, he developed a massive crush on her almost instantly. During his college career, Noah had gotten passionate about writing his own comic book series - a hobby that manifested from seemingly nowhere. During that same time, Tayler had been marketing herself as a freelance artist, hoping to earn a job as a graphic designer or digital artist. The two met during a class and discovered their artistic abilities a few months into the class. By then, Noah had finished the story for his comic but lacked the artistic ability to bring the panels to life. He mentioned it to Tayler one day during class and was surprised with her enthusiasm to work on the project. With Tayler's beautiful drawings bringing the story to life, Noah was able to submit the comic for publishing a few months later. Although it had started because of a mutual interest in creating, Noah and Tayler had become close friends over the years, staying in touch years after they both left college. There wasn't much about Noah that Tayler didn't know and vice-versa. Aside from Ivy and his mother, there wasn't another person in the world that Noah trusted more than Tayler. He thought Paris would've made that list for a while, but not anymore.

"That bad, huh?" Noah said quietly, trying to make light of the situation. "I think it makes me look a little bit more rugged."

"You were rugged-looking enough without the mess on your face," Tayler responded, still gaping at the wound. "Seriously, Noah. What the hell happened?"

"You're not gonna like it..." Noah warned.

"I'm sure I'm not," Tayler folded her arms. Noah smirked and shook his head.

"You know, you're always right," Noah admitted.

"I know," Tayler nodded. "Now spill."

"I picked her up and took her to dinner, like we planned," Noah began, taking his hat and sunglasses off and setting them on the table. He took a sip of his drink and Tayler took the opportunity to take a sip as well. "We went to Perch, and I had to sell my liver just to afford a drink, but that's beside the point."

"I thought I told you to take her somewhere normal," Tayler narrowed her eyes. Noah rolled his eyes and sighed.

"I know, I know, but that's where she wanted to go."

"Already don't like this," Tayler said, sipping her drink.

"Continue."

"I had the ring in my pocket, I had it all planned out perfectly," Noah continued on. "Dinner went great, we were having a great time. And she goes to the bathroom, leaving her phone on the table."

"No!" Tayler groaned, already seeing where this was going. "Please tell me you didn't look. You're never supposed to look! You know what happens when you go looking for trouble?"

"I couldn't help it," Noah shook his head. "I know it was wrong, and I shouldn't have, but as soon as she left, it started buzzing. I got curious, she hadn't really been on her phone at all. But yeah, I saw a few texts on there from Billy."

"You're kidding me?" Tayler exclaimed, her mouth open. Tayler knew who Billy was, she'd spent many hours on the phone talking to Noah about him. He was the ever-annoying ex-boyfriend. Ever since Noah had started going out with Paris Brady, Billy Evans had been a constant issue for them. As far as Tayler knew, which was only what she heard second-hand from Noah, Paris and Billy had been engaged at one point. But they had still been teenagers at the time, and it never amounted to anything more than that. They had been high school sweethearts, and Noah had stumbled into the middle of a very complicated relationship.

"Well, what did the texts say?" Tayler asked, feeling slightly ashamed that she was so excited to hear. The one good thing about Noah's relationship with Paris was the stories Noah always had. That was the *only* thing Paris was good for, in Tayler's opinion. Paris Brady was *that* girl and was good at it. Tall, skinny, fake boobs, and long, wavy brown hair. She had a reputation for being quite promiscuous, which was how Tayler knew who she was when Noah started talking about her. Tayler had been suspecting that Paris had been cheating on Noah for some time, again, only from things that Noah had said. It was mind-numbingly frustrating that he never seemed to hear himself talk.

"They were not good," Noah cracked a sad smile. "Pretty graphic."

"What does that mean?"

"Come on, don't make me say it," Noah groaned. Tayler's eyes widened, and then she looked repulsed.

"Seriously? When she's out with her boyfriend?"

"Oh Tayler, I looked through their convo, she sent him stuff before we left. Sounded like they were going to meet up after dinner," Noah admitted. He fell quiet and finished the rest of his drink. "And I was going to propose to her..."

"Anyway, she came back from the bathroom, and I waited until she checked her phone before I asked her about it. As expected, she denied it vehemently. I finally just told her I know she's been talking to Billy and that I saw everything," Noah said.

He paused his story when the waiter came back over, excited to share the specials with them. Tayler and Noah both ordered another drink, along with their entrees. Once the waiter was done taking their order, Tayler turned all attention back to Noah.

"Did she still try to deny it?" Tayler asked. Noah shook his head.

"Nah, she just got super quiet, and as soon as the waitress came back, she paid for her drinks and food and started to leave," Noah shrugged. "I don't know, I kinda felt bad, and I just wanted to talk things out with her,"

"Let me get this straight, she cheats on you, and you feel bad?" Tayler clarified. Noah shrugged. "Ok, that makes a lot of sense. Continue."

"I mean, she was staying with me for a few days, so I wasn't exactly sure where she was going to go, but I didn't want to be pushing her right into his arms. You know what I mean?" Noah sighed heavily. "But anyway, we were driving back to the house and got into it again. I just wanted to know why, like what was I doing wrong, that she felt the need to start talking to him and sleeping with him again."

Tayler fought the urge to slap Noah upside the head for that comment but let him continue talking. She knew from experience that it was better to just let him talk and figure it out for himself instead of trying to point out everything wrong with how he was looking at the situation. It was maddening, most of the time, though. Noah was one of the most down-to-earth guys Tayler had ever known. He was sweet, kind, handsome, and hardworking - all essential qualities for a guy to have. Tayler couldn't get over how he always found himself with a woman who was just no damn good. For years, she'd heard about girl after girl who treated him poorly. Yes, it was maddening.

"But yeah, she didn't like that," Noah smirked. "And I said something about her not even apologizing, and she lost it. Hit me pretty good with that damn ring of hers," Noah gestured to the wound on his face. "Shattered part of my eye socket,"

"Noah. Sweetie," Tayler said, reaching across the table and grabbing Noah's strong hands. "I mean this with all of the love in the world. If you talk to her again or even look at her, I will punt you across the city. Do I make myself clear?"

Noah hung his head and laughed, squeezing Tayler's hands. He smiled at her but understood that she was dead serious. She was right, as usual. Tayler was always right. More often than not, Noah's life would've been much easier if he had just let Tayler make all of the important decisions. He had affectionately dubbed her his 'life coach' many years ago.

"Yes ma'am," Noah nodded. "I read you loud and clear."

"Good," Tayler said, satisfied. "I hope I never see her, I can't imagine what I would do to her if I did."

"You wouldn't do anything," Noah said, rolling his eyes. Tayler gasped, offended.

"I could take her and you know it," Tayler snapped. "Those fake boobs and her fake ass wouldn't do her much good in a real fight where she's not sucker-punching someone. No offense."

"None taken," Noah said with a smile. "I'll give you that her chest is fake, but her ass is all real, trust me."

"I hate you so much."

****

Noah rolled back into his driveway, exhausted and slightly intoxicated. One more Long Island, and he'd have had to call an Uber. But thankfully, he was only slightly buzzed and not enough to affect his driving in the slightest. The evening with Tayler had been a much-needed good time once they were done talking about Paris. Tayler shared stories from school, and they argued over the uncertainty of the Los Angeles Rams playoff hopes. Both of them were major football fans, which was another reason why they got along so well.

Walking up to his front door, Noah stopped dead in his tracks when he saw the woman sitting on his front step. She was wearing sweatpants, a sweatshirt, and those cute Ugg boots that Noah had bought her for Christmas last year.

"Paris..." Noah muttered, looking at her. She looked at him sadly and slowly stood up.

"I probably should have called..." she said, looking at her boots. "Working late?"

"Sure, something like that," Noah shook his head. She was the last person he wanted to see or speak to right now. "Um, what are you doing here?"

Paris stepped off the front porch and walked to meet Noah halfway. When she saw the full extent of his injury, she put her hands over her mouth and started crying. Noah stood there, watching her cry. He was unsure exactly how to handle the situation. Initially, Noah thought about trying to comfort her. But the stitches in his face, courtesy of her, made him rethink that idea. So, he stood there, hands in his pockets, and watched her cry.

"I'm so sorry!" Paris cried in between sobs. "I didn't mean to, you have to believe me. I didn't mean to hurt you. I could never hurt you."

"You could never hurt me?" Noah asked, the sarcasm unmistakable in his tone. "So what do you think you were doing when you cheated on me and smashed my face in? That wasn't hurting me?"

"Noah, please, you have to let me explain," Paris begged. Her makeup and eyeliner were a complete mess, making her look a little bit more unstable than she probably intended. In a different situation, Noah would have found it almost comical.

"No, Paris," Noah shook his head. "I don't think I do. Do you even know why I was so excited to take you out for dinner?"

"What do you mean?" Paris asked, wiping her eyes and trying to compose herself a little bit. Noah sighed and reached into the inside pocket of his Carhartt jacket. He pulled out the small box and popped it open, showing Paris the ring. She took a step forward, eyes wide.

"I was going to ask you to marry me, Paris Brady. I was going to get down on one knee and ask you to spend the rest of your life with me," Noah spoke in a quiet voice.

He couldn't hide or disguise his sadness. Actually, sadness wasn't the right word. Noah was heartbroken. For the longest time, Noah had envisioned a life with Paris. And he had been excited about that future. She was everything he thought he wanted in a significant other. Their first year together was, in a word, perfect. Paris and Noah had been a great couple and brought out the best in each other. It was what Noah had always hoped for from a relationship, as his previous ones had been pretty terrible. But slowly, Paris began to change. She got more and more demanding, expecting more from him each and every day. When Noah got promoted to Foreman and suddenly took on more responsibility, Paris was proud or happy for him, rather annoyed that more of his time would be taken up focusing on things that weren't her. Deep down, Noah knew that Paris was a good person. But she had been raised by her father and had never been told no. The result was an extremely selfish and demanding woman. When you took all of that into consideration, it wasn't shocking that she hadn't been faithful to Noah.

"It's beautiful," Paris whispered. And it was. The ring was a work of art, Noah had paid a small fortune for it.

"Yeah, it is," Noah muttered, snapping the box shut and stuffing it back in his pocket. "It'll look great back in the display case."

"Noah, I'm sorry!" Paris cried. "I don't want to lose you."

"Well, what do you want me to say, Paris?" Noah asked, throwing his hands up in annoyance. "Am I supposed to just ignore that you broke my fucking face and cheated on me? Honestly, I could forgive the whole cheating thing, but this..." Noah gestured to his face. "No, I have nothing left to say to you."

"Noah, please."

Noah brushed past her and unlocked his front door. Ivy was at the door in an instant, wagging her tail and yipping with excitement.

"Go home, Paris," Noah said, stepping into his house.

Paris Brady, makeup streaking down her face, hung her head and walked back to her car. She got into the driver's seat and started sobbing. Noah watched from behind his front door, feeling surprisingly conflicted.

3

The sun was just starting to peek over the horizon as Noah Riordan swung the cab of his excavator back toward the pile of rubble behind him. Large spotlights on the construction site and the lights on his excavator allowed Noah to see reasonably well in the early morning haze. The engine of the Caterpillar 329F Hydraulic Excavator roared loudly as Noah expertly lowered the boom and swung the stick out. Working the controls smoothly, Noah scooped up another full bucket of broken concrete. He pushed the joystick, and the machine rotated back around toward the dump truck; he dumped the bucket full of rock into the back of the truck, the concrete crashing onto the metallic bed.

Behind Noah's 329 was a trail of destruction that used to be the off-ramp for the 101. The previous two days, Noah's crew had been working on demolishing the existing ramp and clearing it away in preparation for the new and improved ramp to be constructed. It had to be done in phases to avoid any dangerous collapses. Normally, Noah would be on the ground directing his crew, but they were severely shorthanded, so Noah had been operating one of the excavators. The excavator boasted a 240 horsepower engine, an operating weight of just over 68,000 pounds, and a maximum digging depth of 25 feet. Omicron had a fleet of fully-operational 329F excavators. It was the perfect size for their large-scale projects. The wide array of attachments for the machine - jackhammers, pulverizers, shears, or grapples - made it irreplaceable. The inside of the cab was fully Climate Controlled and comfortable enough for Noah to never feel cramped. Like all of Omicron's machines, the excavator had its logo and name on the side of the machine.

Noah dumped another bucket full of rubble into the back of the dump truck and pulled back on the boom and stick, leveling out the load as best he could. He pressed the button on his joystick, honking the horn to signal the driver he was done loading him. Within a few seconds, the truck lurched forward and drove away. Noah swung the excavator back toward the rubble and reached for his radio with his opposite hand.

"EJ, you got a copy?" Noah asked, setting the bucket down on the ground in front of the machine.

"Copy," EJ answered a few seconds later.

"Bring the dozer over here and push some of this shit towards me," Noah said. "I want to get this done today, we're already falling behind."

"Be over in a few minutes, just fueling her up right now."

"10-4," Noah muttered, tossing the radio back into the cupholder.

Turning the throttle down to idle, Noah popped open the door and climbed out of the cab. It was an unseasonably cold morning in Los Angeles, especially in September. The sun would bring more warmth, but they had at least another thirty minutes of dawn. Noah reached back into the cab and grabbed his extra-large cup of Dunkin; he took a long sip and watched the construction site. Several different machines and companies were working on other parts of the highway. From the outside, it looked chaotic, but it was far from that. Everything was as organized as could be. Omicron was only in charge of the demolition, excavation, and concrete. The other contractors on the job handled everything else, which made Noah's job much easier.

Unzipping his neon green Hi-Vis jacket, Noah pulled his phone out and tapped the screen to check his notifications. The only new notification was a missed call from Paris. It had been almost two weeks since he ended things with her, and he hadn't heard a word from her since then. Noah couldn't think of any reason for Paris to be calling him, especially at 6:15 in the morning.

"Ah, damnit," Noah grumbled to himself, tapping on the notification to call her back. He put the phone to his ear and waited.

"Noah?" Paris said sleepily.

"Yeah," Noah grunted. "What's up?"

"I miss you, Noah," Paris said quietly. "Please, I just want to talk. I'm... I'm a mess over this."

"I'm at work," Noah said shortly. "I'll have to call you back."

"No, Noah, wait!" Paris cried. "Please, can I buy you a drink or something after work tonight? I just want to talk. Please."

Noah shook his head and rolled his eyes. It was way too early in the morning to be dealing with Paris. Plus, he only had a few sips of coffee in his system. Noah sighed and relented despite every part of his brain telling him to hang up on her.

"Alright, fine," Noah said. "I'll meet you for a drink after I'm done."

"Thank you," Paris said, sounding relieved. "Where would be easiest for you?"

"I'll text you when I get off," Noah muttered.

"Sounds good. Have a good day, Noah."

"Yeah, you too."

Noah hung up and stuffed his phone back into his jacket, wishing instantly that he hadn't even checked his phone. Shaking any thoughts of Paris from his head. The familiar sound of clanking treads was getting louder and louder. Noah looked up to see two machines rolling towards him - a CAT D9 bulldozer and a CAT 272D3 skid steer loader. Both machines were monsters in their own respect. The dozer, sporting a 452 horsepower engine and an operating weight of 110,225 pounds, was outfitted with a standard blade and a ripper on the back. While the dozer was more of a brute and could push material better than any other machine in Omicron's fleet, the skid steer was quick and precise. Both machines were essential to a large scale construction project like the 101 job.

The duo of machines came to a stop, and the two operators jumped out of their respective machines. Edward 'EJ' James climbed down from the dozer, looking more tired than usual. His long black hair was tied back in a sloppy man-bun, and his equally long beard was controlled by a rubber band. He had several visible tattoos on his neck and hands, along with a few piercings in his nose and lip. At 41, EJ was a little bit past his prime, and a consistent knee issue constantly sidelined him from work.

Behind the controls of the skid steer was Chandler Bannington, who was a year younger than Noah, and one of the new hires at Omicron. Being the new guy had earned him a substantial amount of hazing, but once the other guys got to know him, they respected him. Chandler was different from most of the guys who worked at Omicron. At the age of 18, he got married a few days after his graduation to his high school sweetheart, Lyla. They had been married for all of two years before she was diagnosed with lymphoma. And since then, she had been fighting the horrid disease with the grit of a boxer. Chandler worked at least two jobs to pay for the constant medical bills. Getting hired at Omicron was a dream come true for him. Their wages were significantly higher than what anyone else was offering in the area and getting unionized gave him access to better health care for Lyla. There was no one on Noah's crew who worked harder than Chandler Bannington.

Noah bumped fists with EJ and Chandler, meeting them halfway. EJ lit up a cigarette, offering one to both Chandler and Noah. They declined.

"EJ, take the dozer up to the top of the ramp and just start pushing shit towards me. Chandler can work down here with me to load up trucks, I'll have Scott start sending two at a time. We need this area completely clear by the end of the day. I do not want to have to remove rock tomorrow."

"Sounds good to me," Chandler said and climbed back into the skid steer, where it was no doubt warmer than it was outside. EJ continued puffing on the cigarette, looking at Noah strangely.

"What?" Noah asked. EJ hesitated a few times, debating whether or not to speak on his concerns.

"Do you know if we're getting any overtime soon?" EJ asked. Noah narrowed his eyes slightly.

"Why do you ask?"

"Nothing, nothing, it's just..." EJ took another puff from the cigarette. "Mel is on my ass about child support. I'm a little behind."

"EJ, come on, man," Noah sighed, rubbing his forehead. EJ had been on Noah's crew for almost two years, and the man seemed to be allergic to paying child support on time. "How behind are you?"

"A lot," EJ muttered, tossing the smoke on the ground and stepping on it with his dirt-caked boot. "I can't afford it man, it's ridiculous. I barely make enough to live on, and I have to pay her every month. She doesn't even work, just lives off of me."

"We'll talk about this later, ok?" Noah felt bad about having to cut him off, but two empty dump trucks were driving toward them. Part of being the boss was knowing when to listen and when it was time to suck it up and get to work.

EJ grumbled under his breath and went back to his machine. Noah liked EJ well enough, but the man was unreliable at best. As expected, Chandler was already hard at work, piling up debris to streamline the loading process. If anyone at Omicron deserved the overtime, it was Chandler. As both trucks came to a stop, Noah hopped back into his backhoe and throttled it all the way up. With EJ pushing material towards the hoe, Noah went to work loading the trucks with clean-up assistance from Chandler.

****

The hours came and went, taking the sun with them. In the blink of an eye, the entire day had gone by. Yawning loudly, Noah swung the excavator back to face the ramp. EJ pushed the last remaining bit of rubble towards Noah's excavator. Noah scooped up a full bucket of concrete, turned back to the dump truck, and emptied the bucket into the bed, honking the horn as he turned back toward the ramp. The last truck of the day rumbled to life and drove off. As Noah went to drag more rubble toward the pile, Noah saw the blue-red F-350 SuperDuty truck pull up and park alongside the highway next to the rest of the trucks and cars. Noah smiled to himself and gently lowered the bucket until it was on the ground. He turned the throttle down on the excavator and popped open the door to the cab. Corey Riordan, one of the Construction Superintendents at Omicron and Noah's direct boss, jumped out of the truck and strode through the site toward Noah. Noah climbed down from the cab and met Corey halfway.

"How's it goin?" Corey asked, flashing a smile at Noah. Corey's blue jeans and tan boots were caked in a thick layer of dirt and concrete.

"Almost done for the day," Noah said, peeling off his Los Angeles Rams hat and wiping the sweat from his brow. "How's everything else going?"

"Well, we poured concrete at the bank today. Builders are showing up tomorrow to start. Dave unloaded equipment at that Lamp bar in Montebello, and once the electricians are done there, I'm gonna have you handle that job," Corey rattled off. "I know you're in the middle of this one, but I don't have another foreman for that job.

"The Lamp? Really?" Noah asked, smiling a little. "I take the guys there every week for drinks."

"Yeah, we're just doing some concrete work for them," Corey said.

"Ok, that should be a quick one," Noah nodded. "When do you think you'll need me over there?"

"Probably next week, if we're being optimistic," Corey said with a small shrug. "Just depends on the electrical guys."

"I get it," Noah muttered. He was slightly annoyed that Corey was pulling him off the 101, but the small sidewalk job in downtown Los Angeles wouldn't take Noah more than a few days to complete.

Corey had always been one of the few people Noah trusted regardless of anything; they were related after all. Noah's mom was Corey's older sister and was the reason that Noah had gotten hired. He was almost 50, married, and had two kids in college. Corey Riordan was built solidly, coming in at 200 pounds and just under 6 feet tall. His brown hair was always cut short, and his beard and mustache were well maintained. On miserably hot days, he wore t-shirts that showed off his muscular arms and tattooed biceps. He pretty much always wore a hard hat, no matter what they were doing, and most definitely always had chewing tobacco in his lip.

"When's the last time you saw the old man?" Corey asked, spitting into the dirt. Noah cocked his head and looked behind him at what remained of the ramp. He put his hands on his hips.

"Well, it's been a while," Noah admitted. "I've been pretty busy."

"Do me a favor, go see him, ok?" Corey said. "I saw him last night at your mom's house, and he's not doing so well."

"Ah, shit," Noah grunted. "Yeah, I'll go see him and my mom tonight."

"They'd like that, I'm sure," Corey smiled and patted Noah's shoulder. "I love you, kid."

"Love you too," Noah said with a smile.

"Well listen, I'm on my way home, so have a good night. Please go see them and get some rest, you look awful."

"Yeah, I know," Noah chuckled. "It's been a rough few weeks."

"Your mom told me about what happened with Paris," Corey said. "Sorry about that."

"Eh, don't worry about it," Noah brushed it off.

"Go home. Get some rest," Corey ordered.

"I will!" Noah said, laughing. "We're done for the night, just gotta tuck the girls in."

"Go home, Noah!"

"Goodnight, Corey," Noah waved as Corey jumped back into the pickup truck. Turning on his heels, Noah climbed back into the 329 and shut the machine down for the night. He climbed back out, swung the door shut, and locked it. Noah double-checked the door was locked before putting his keys in his back pocket and heading for his white truck parked on the shoulder of the highway. EJ and Chandler were leaning against the hood of EJ's Dodge Ram, parked in front of Noah's truck, and talking quietly amongst themselves.

"You guys gossiping about me again?" Noah asked, opening the door to his truck and tossing his hard hat and Hi-Vis vest inside. He pulled out his phone and sent a quick text to Paris, asking her to meet him at a bar closer to his house.

"Nah, we were just saying that we haven't heard from Darren. He never made it in today, and EJ and I both texted him," Chandler said. "I hope he hasn't gone off the deep end again."

Darren Lock was the youngest guy on the crew. He was a college dropout with a bad gambling addiction and a girlfriend with a worse drug addiction. He was unreliable at best and a complete liability at worst. But, he had some sort of familial connections to the upper management at Omicron, which prevented Noah from firing him. The last thing he wanted to be thinking about was Darren.

"Give him a few days," Noah shrugged. "Not the first time he's gone M.I.A. for a while. If y'all still don't hear from him by Friday, let me know."

"Any word about overtime?" EJ asked. Noah internalized his annoyance.

"No, nothing yet," Noah answered quickly. "Look, I know you guys are tired, and I know you're waiting for some OT, but I can't control that. That's up to guys who make a lot more money than me. As soon as I hear anything, I'll let you know."

"Sure," EJ grunted, obviously agitated. He jumped in his truck and drove off, a little too fast.

"Don't let him get to you," Chandler said. "He's just stressed."

"We're all stressed, Chandler," Noah muttered. "How's Lyla doing?"

"She starts chemo again next week," Chandler admitted, stuffing his hands in his pockets. "I could use the overtime too man, bills are piling up."

"I know, I know," Noah shook his head. "I'll talk to Corey and see what we can come back with. I'll let you and EJ know if I hear of any side jobs. It's the best I can do at this point, I'm sorry."

"Nah, don't be sorry, I know it's not your fault," Chandler said. "It's just annoying. They used to be pretty generous with overtime. Now, you work a minute over 40 hours and they're on our asses."

"Times have changed, my man," Noah turned his truck on, letting it warm up. "Alright, I'm out. Have a good night."

"You too," Chandler and Noah bumped fists and climbed into their respective trucks.

****

She was already sitting at the bar by the time Noah walked in. He spotted her from a mile away. Despite the circumstances, Noah couldn't deny that Paris Brady was still one of the most beautiful women in the world. Everywhere she went, people tended to take notice. Noah took a deep breath and walked over to her, sliding into the barstool next to her.

"Hey."

"Hey! I'm so glad you came," Paris said with a smile. "I ordered a margarita, would you like one too? It's on me."

"Sure, that sounds good," Noah smirked. Paris called the bartender over and ordered a second margarita.

"How was work?"

"Oh, you know," Noah shrugged. "We're overworked, underpaid, and behind schedule. So, the usual."

"Still on the 101?"

"Yeah, yeah. Major pain in the ass," Noah said. "How's work for you?"

"It's fine, I guess," Paris said. "Long hours and stuff, we're pretty understaffed too."

Paris worked at a Southern California tech company in sales. She didn't really care much about the job, but the high paying salary allowed her to shop and spend money on her appearance, which were her two favorite hobbies.

"Yeah, same with us," Noah agreed. "Hard to find workers anywhere, I guess."

"Yeah."

The bartender set two bright and colorful margaritas in front of them. Paris clinked her glass against Noah's and took a sip. It was the perfect combination of the sweet mixer and tequila.

"So, what did you want to talk about?" Noah asked, setting his drink down on a coaster after taking a sip.

"Us," Paris said. She looked very serious all of a sudden. "Noah, I cannot even begin to understand how you feel or how you must think of me. I hate myself right now, and I know you might not believe me, but I am truly sorry. I don't know what came over me that night, and I know that's no excuse... I'm just sorry and I want you to know that."

"Alright..." Noah said quietly.

"I need you to know that I never cheated on you," Paris said. Noah cocked his head slightly.

"Dude, I saw your phone..."

"We were just texting," Paris continued. "But I did not cheat on you with him. I swear I didn't. I got a little drunk and we were sexting a little bit, but that was it. Yeah, we were talking about doing stuff, but we didn't. It was just a moment of weakness on my end."

"Do you really expect me to believe that?" Noah asked, taking another sip of his drink. "Look, if all you wanna do is feed me lies like that, I'm gonna walk out of here real fast."

"Noah, I am not lying to you," Paris said, grabbing his arm. "I swear to you, I did not sleep with him or do anything like that. It was just the texts, that was it."

Noah looked at her, trying to find any indication in her eyes or face that she was lying. Normally, Noah was pretty good at telling when people were or were not telling him the truth. His laborers loved to give him crazy excuses why they were late to work or missed a day, and he sniffed it out almost instantly every single time. But with Paris, his abilities had always been hindered. Maybe it was because he had been so crazily in love with her that he just wanted to believe everything she said, even if it didn't make sense. If she was telling the truth, it did make Noah feel a little better about the whole situation.

"I don't expect you to forgive me or want to get back together or anything, but I just need you to know that," Paris kept on talking. "I love you, Noah. I want to be with you and only you,"

"I love you too, Paris..." Noah whispered. He looked at her sadly, remembering just a few short weeks ago how excited he'd been at the possibility of spending the rest of his life with her. "I'm not saying never, but right now I need some space. Just to kind of think about everything. You have to understand that seeing those texts and then your reaction to me confronting you about them doesn't exactly scream 'we weren't doing anything'. And you still rocked my ass."

"I know, I know, and I'm sorry," Paris said. "I didn't mean to hurt me - I mean you. I promise I didn't. I just wasn't thinking, I don't know what else to say."

"You've got a hell of a right hook," Noah muttered, sipping his margarita. He looked at Paris's confused face and knew she couldn't tell if he was joking or being serious. He couldn't help but laugh. "Lighten up, I'm gonna make jokes about it. I'm fine, all things considered."

"That's not funny," Paris crossed her arms, but she was smiling. Things felt less awkward between them, and that was good.

Noah and Paris finished off their drinks and decided to call it a night. Paris paid the tab, as she said she would, and the two left the bar together.

"Where'd you park?" Noah asked, shivering slightly from the cold.

"Just down there," Paris pointed down the street. "I'll be ok, don't worry."

"You know me," Noah huffed and started walking with her toward her car. He put his arm around her shoulder when he saw her shivering. Feeling the warmth of him, Paris couldn't help but smile. Noah was one of a kind.

"Thank you," Paris said, holding onto his arm tightly. They got to her car and she quickly unlocked the door and turned her car on, cranking the heat on. "I had a nice night, it was good to see you."

"Yeah, I had a nice time too," Noah admitted. He smiled at her and turned to leave.

"Noah..." Paris called.

"Yeah?" Noah turned around. Without another word, Paris threw her arms around his neck and kissed him. It caught Noah slightly off guard, but he didn't pull away. Noah gently touched Paris's cheek and kissed her back. He couldn't explain the rush of sudden emotions, but the heat between them was just as prevalent now as their first night together. Slowly, Paris broke away, looking up at him and grinning.

"Wow," she whispered. Noah chuckled, feeling his cheeks getting red.

"That's one word for it," he said.

"Take care of yourself, Noah," Paris grinned, getting into her car. Noah waved and jogged back to his truck, jumping inside and turning it on as fast as he could.

****

Noah opened the passenger door to his truck, and Ivy leaped out, darting for the front door of the house in Thousand Oaks. She sat down on her haunches on the front porch and barked.

"Ivy, wait for me!" Noah called, hurrying up the perfectly manicured lawn to the door. He bounded up the stairs and rang the doorbell. Ivy wagged her tail impatiently, panting heavily from all the excitement. The door opened, and Ivy rushed over to greet the 50-year-old woman.

"Hi!" the woman exclaimed, dropping down to pet Ivy. Rolling onto her back, Ivy's rear leg started kicking wildly as the woman scratched her belly.

"I swear she doesn't get that excited to see anyone else," Noah said.

"Well, I'd certainly hope not," the woman said, getting up and giving Noah a warm hug. "It's good to see you."

"You too, ma," Noah said, hugging his mom back.

Noah's mom led the way into the house, closing the door behind them. Ivy calmed down and took her place on the large dog bed next to the fireplace. After a few minutes, her head was buried in her paws, snoring softly.

The kitchen smelled of freshly baked chocolate chip cookies, and Noah was instantly reminded of his childhood. It was a double-edged sword for Noah, thinking about his upbringing.

Noah Riordan, born Noah Carter, grew up in Northern California in a suburb of San Francisco. His earliest memories involved running around with his older brother and playing football. He'd been a gifted athlete as a kid and started his high school varsity team at the quarterback position. When considering going to college, Noah had been offered a few scholarships to play football but ultimately ended up deciding to join the Local 12 International Union of Operating Engineers. Many factors played a part in that decision, most of which were not good.

When he was 16 years old, Noah and his mother, Amy, moved away from their home and headed south, leaving behind Noah's older brother and father. Noah's older brother, who was 21 at the time, decided to stay behind with their dad, which Noah didn't understand and probably never would. Noah didn't hate as a rule of life; it was too much of a burden on him. But he hated his father. The man had been a ruthless drunk and was an absolute nightmare to live with. For years, Noah had prayed for some kind of relief from the horrid living situation. When his mother came to him and said they were leaving, Noah didn't hesitate. He packed up all of his clothes, comic books, and other belongings eagerly. As soon as he turned 18, Noah legally changed his name to Noah Riordan - his mother's maiden name. It had been twelve years since Noah had spoken to his father or his older brother. On the other hand, Noah's mom had some semblance of a relationship with her first-born son. Their relationship had improved over the years, but that did nothing to repair the damage done between him and Noah. Both brothers thought the other had abandoned them and that was not something easily gotten over. Football had been something Noah's father and older brother had lived and breathed. Once he graduated high school, Noah never played another down of organized football. The union job was intriguing, the pay was decent, and there was opportunity for growth. In ten years, Noah had already worked his way up to Foreman.

"You mind helping out with dinner?" Noah's mom asked, already working in the kitchen. "BLTs tonight."

"Oh my, it must be a special occasion if we're having the famous BLTs," Noah smiled, washing his hands at the sink. "Where's the old man at?"

"He's in the den watching TV, probably asleep on the couch," his mom answered. "I'll get him before dinner. Figured I let him rest until then."

"How's he been? I saw Corey today, he didn't seem to think he was doing so hot."

"Corey overreacts about everything. He's doing fine, actually a little better, if you ask me."

"Good to hear, it'll be nice to see him," Noah said. His mom handed him three tomatoes, a cutting board, and a knife. He went to work cleaning and slicing the vegetables.

"He asks about you all the time," his mom said, going to work on frying the bacon on the stove. "I wish you'd come around a little more."

"I know, I'm sorry," Noah said quietly. "Work has just been so insane and everything with Paris... I just haven't felt very social."

"You haven't seen her, right?" his mom asked, looking over her shoulder at Noah.

"No," Noah said almost immediately.

Noah was aware of his mother's sentiments toward Paris. He found no enjoyment in lying to her but knew it was easier than explaining their current situation. Amy Riordan was fiercely protective of her son and had gone ballistic when Noah told her what had happened. He'd called her from the hospital, unable to drive himself back after his eye had been stitched up. The entire drive home, Amy had lectured him relentlessly about ceasing any and all contact with Paris. No matter how old Noah got, the motherly lectures never ended. But as he got older, he grew to appreciate them much more than he did in his teenage years. At the end of the day, Noah and Amy had a trusting, open relationship. They talked all of the time, and there wasn't much that the other didn't know.

"Have you seen Taylor recently?" Noah's mom asked, knowing it was a good idea to switch the subject of conversation away from Paris.

"Actually, yeah," Noah smiled. "A few nights ago, we had dinner."

"And how is Taylor doing?" she asked, opening up a loaf of white bread while continuing to cook the bacon. "I love that girl."

"She's doing good," Noah smiled. "Yeah, she's the best."

"You should ask her out," Amy suggested. Noah laughed and shook his head. He tossed the tomato slices onto a plate and slid it across the counter to his mom.

"We're just friends," Noah said.

"Whatever you say," Amy popped four slices of bread into the toaster. "Why don't you go get him, and we'll eat."

"Yes, ma'am."

Noah walked down the small hallway toward the room at the end. The TV was on quietly, an old Stallone movie flashed across the screen. He leaned against the door frame and folded his arms, a smile spread across his face.

"How are you doing, pop?" he asked. The old man lying in the recliner looked up, and a huge smile formed.

"Noah! I didn't know you were coming," he exclaimed. It took a couple of beats, but he got up from the chair and hobbled over to his grandson. They shook hands before embracing.

Ron Riordan was 82 years old but looked at least ten years younger. For his age, he was still fairly active, playing golf at least twice a week with some friends from his days in the Army. Ron was a veteran of the Vietnam War and still kept in close contact with the guys from his platoon. After finishing his service, Ron and his wife, Jane, opened up a restaurant near Reno, Nevada. For years, Vet's was an extremely popular place, pulling in customers from all over the country. Its military-themed decor and menu brought in a ton of current and former servicemen. But once they got too old to run the place anymore, Ron made the tough decision to sell to a group of three younger veteran entrepreneurs. They had done an excellent job of honoring Ron's wishes for the restaurant and opened several more locations in California, Arizona, and New

Mexico. With the money from the buyout, Ron and Jane retired to Palm Springs, where they intended to live out their days. But as is so often the case, life had other plans. Jane had been killed in a freak car accident less than a year after retiring. It was one of those life-altering events that changed Ron, and he was never the same man after that. Once his heart started giving him issues, Corey and Amy encouraged him to move to Los Angeles to be closer to them. He ended up moving in with Amy, and the rest was history.

Dinner was just as good as Noah had hoped, and he filled his stomach with half a dozen of his mother's sandwiches and a handful of her chocolate chip cookies. Just due to his hectic and exhausting work schedule, Noah rarely got to indulge in food anymore. He made a mental note to stop by his mom's more often. The food and the company were perfect. Ivy sauntered over to the kitchen table, licking up a few crumbs she found. Although Noah usually just fed her dog food, she'd been known to enjoy an occasional meal with her human friends, especially if there was steak involved. After putting his dishes in the sink, Ron opened a cabinet in the living room and pulled out a slim cigar box; he looked at Noah and smiled. Noah returned the smile and immediately jumped up, knowing the routine. He fetched a six-pack of Corona from the fridge and found a bowl of perfectly sliced limes.

"Close the door before you two clowns light those things," Amy warned. "I hate the smell."

"You got it," Noah said, giving his mom a quick hug before throwing on his jacket and stepping onto the front porch; Ivy followed close behind. Ron was already sitting in his rocking chair, an ashtray set up on the small glass table between the two chairs. Ivy plopped down by his feet, and Noah sat in the unoccupied chair.

“Macanoodles,” Ron said, using his own terminology for the cigars. Noah chuckled and took one of the cigars from the box, cutting it and popping it into his mouth. Noah and Ron lit up their cigars using the matches in the box, puffing enthusiastically.

“Ah, that’s a good cigar,” Ron sighed, propping his leg up on his knee. Noah cracked open two Coronas and handed one to his grandfather.

“Cheers, pop,” Noah said.

“So, how’s work?” Ron asked, taking a swig from the bottle. “Still on the highway?”

“Yeah, yeah,” Noah nodded, puffing on the cigar. “It’s getting a little tougher, we’re getting delayed almost every day.”

“Damn bureaucrats,” Ron scoffed. “Same as it was back in ‘Nam. You make a little progress, and then the higher-ups make you fight with your hands tied behind your back.”

“Yeah, just like ‘Nam,” Noah laughed. Ron laughed too.

“So, what happened to your face?” Ron asked, gesturing to the nasty scar on Noah’s face. Noah’s hand instinctively shot up to touch the wound.

“I fell getting into a hoe at work,” Noah lied, using the cover story he’d been using for a few weeks now. Ron didn’t say anything. He took a puff from the cigar and killed the rest of his beer, helping himself to another one.

“Really? You fell at work?” he asked. From the old man’s tone, Noah knew that he didn’t believe him for a second.

“Yeah, just took a nasty slip,” Noah said, avoiding eye contact. Ron chuckled softly.

“Son, I been around a long damn time. And if there’s one thing I know, it’s how to tell when someone is lying to me,” Ron grumbled. “I’m old and feeble, but I sure as shit ain’t stupid. Something happened with Paris, seeing as I haven't gotten an engagement announcement or anything like that. And my guess is that gash on your face has something to do with it. So spit it out son, I ain't got all night."

"Yeah, something did happen with her," Noah mumbled, flicking the ash on the end of his cigar into the tray. He popped the Macanudo back into his mouth and puffed, enjoying the taste of the cigar. "I don't know man, we got into this fight, one thing led to another, and yeah... She got me pretty good."

"Women who hit hard are not to be trifled with," Ron shook his head. "Not gonna pretend I didn't learn that the hard way either."

"It's complicated, you know?" Noah said, debating telling him that he'd seen Paris mere hours before. "It's not like I don't love her anymore, but I can't really go back to her after that, right?"

"Life is complicated. Always has been, always will be," Ron looked out at the front lawn and smiled. "But you know what shouldn't ever be complicated? Loving the right person. Your grandmother and I had our hard times. What couple doesn't? But through it all, we never questioned if we were supposed to be together or not. The best decision I ever made was asking her to marry me. It's a shame how it ended, but I'm forever grateful for the time we had together."

"Amen to that," Noah said, holding his bottle out toward Ron. They cheered and took a gulp of beer.

"I'll tell you the same thing I told your mother when she got engaged to your asshole of a father," Ron grunted. "I am not a fan. I wasn't a fan of his, and I wasn't a fan of Paris."

This was news to Noah. He valued his mother's and his grandpa's opinion very much, and as far as he knew, Ron had liked Paris. To hear him say otherwise was surprising.

"How come you never said anything?" Noah asked. "You were always so polite to her."

"It's not my place to have any influence over what you do with your life. Same with your mom. What was I going to do? Forbid her from marrying the man? She was old enough to make her own decisions, and if I tried to stop her, that would've just pushed her away even more."

"That must've been hard," Noah muttered. Ron scoffed.

"It was. Your father is a real asshole."

"I know."

"Look, son, can you live without this girl?"

"Huh?"

"Paris. Can you live without her?" Ron asked, now all of his attention on Noah.

It was a question that Noah had given much thought to over the last few days. He would've said no if he'd been asked that a month ago. But now, if he was being honest with himself, the answer had changed. Too much had happened, and at the end of the day, he couldn't trust her anymore.

"Yeah, I can," Noah admitted quietly. "I don't think I can spend the rest of my life with her."

"Well, then there's your answer."

The two finished off their cigars in relative silence. After a while, Ron got up and clapped Noah on the shoulder; Noah patted his grandfather's hand.

"Good to see you, kid," Ron said, going back into the house.

"You too, pop. You too."

4

The hydraulic jackhammer pounded into the concrete repeatedly, breaking off bits of material as it dug deeper and deeper into the ground. Dust kicked up all around while the hammer relentlessly beat into the pavement. Behind the controls of the Caterpillar 305E2 mini-excavator, Noah Riordan forced the hammer further into the ground until it maxed out. Like with all excavators, the 305 could swap out its standard bucket for a jackhammer attachment, which Noah was currently utilizing. Noah had a Caterpillar 262D skid steer loader parked alongside the sidewalk as well; the loader was fitted with a standard bucket, but he also had a beak attachment for ripping out larger chunks of concrete. Together, both machines made a job like this a piece of cake. In Noah's mind, having the right tools for the job was a concept that remained true across all walks of life.

Noah pulled up on the boom and swung the hammer over about a foot before attacking the concrete once more. Behind him was a path of destruction along the sidewalk he was breaking up; rebar and chunks of concrete littered the destroyed sidewalk. He was ripping out the sidewalk in front of The Lamp - a popular bar in Los Angeles. The concrete contractors would be arriving in two days, giving Noah a tight window to dig up the concrete, remove it, dig the new foundation, and then backfill with gravel. It was a hotspot for union guys and white-collar guys alike. The Lamp was not a five-star establishment by any stretch of the imagination, but it boasted a wait staff of scantily clad young women, which brought in the customers. After finishing a job or passing a significant stage of the massive 101 job, Noah would treat his crew to drinks at The Lamp.

For the last two days, Noah worked at the site by himself. It was relatively easy work, and Noah was experienced enough to handle it by himself. To devote more than a single operator to the job would've been a waste of time and money. Noah enjoyed working by himself; it was oddly peaceful compared to the high-stress highway project. Unfortunately, Noah found it incredibly hard to focus on his job. Ever since he and Paris had gone out, he hadn't heard a word from her. It was a double-edged sword because Noah knew he probably had to break up with her, but not hearing from her was equally anxiety-inducing. It was driving him nuts that he kept checking his phone, waiting for any kind of communication from her.

After seeing no new notifications, Noah sighed and tossed his phone back into the cupholder in the cab of the small machine. After nearly three hours of nonstop hammering, Noah crawled the excavator back toward the skid steer. He swung the cab of the excavator around and placed the hammer on the ground horizontally. Turning the throttle down, Noah used the control screen in the cab to disengage the lock pin on the hydraulic coupler. Slowly, Noah curled the coupler and carefully removed the hammer; he expertly swung the cab around and lowered the boom, picking up the regular bucket with the connector. Once again, he tapped the button on the screen, and the pin locked into place, securing the bucket to the stick. The process only took a few minutes but was still annoying, especially on a job where Noah constantly had to switch attachments.

He unclipped his radio from his belt and flipped it to the second channel.

"Scottie, you got a copy?" Noah asked, climbing out of the excavator, the engine idling.

"Go ahead, Noah," Scott answered a few seconds later.

"Bring the truck over, I'm ready to start loading it up."

"Copy, I'm on my way. Traffic is pretty tight, give me about a half-hour."

"You're good. See you soon."

Noah slipped the radio back onto his belt and walked toward his truck, which was parked in the customer parking lot for The Lamp. He climbed into his truck, unscrewed his thermos, and sipped his iced coffee. Waiting was another annoying part of his job, especially when he had a deadline to meet. No matter how the foremen and superintendents managed the projects, one constant was having to wait for a dump truck.

Forty-five minutes later, Noah saw the red dump truck pull around the corner, carefully moving alongside the ripped-up sidewalk. Scott threw the truck in park and turned it off, climbing down from the cab.

"Sorry, traffic was a mess," Scott groaned.

Scott was 60 years old, had unruly gray hair, and was in pretty good shape for an older man. He'd been married happily for forty years and always talked about his wife, kids, and grandkids. Noah thought of Scott as the ultimate family man; hardworking, generous, and kind. No matter how much Scott could annoy Noah with his slow driving and overly-enthusiastic personality, Noah liked working with Scott quite a bit.

"No worries, bud," Noah waved. "We'll start at that end, work our way back toward the skid steer."

"Sounds good," Scott nodded. He climbed back up into the cab of his truck and fetched a shovel.

Noah hustled back over to the mini-ex and locked the door open. He climbed back into the 305 and fired it up. The machine roared to life, and Noah maneuvered back over to the start of the sidewalk, parallel to the dump truck. He went right to work, scooping up chunks of concrete and rebar and dumping them into the truck. Scott shoveled chunks that missed the truck back into the path of the excavator, trying to keep the rest of the sidewalk and street clean.

Noah swung the cab back around after dumping a bucket full of material and spotted a couple standing a little too close to the sidewalk for Noah's comfort. The woman was walking toward The Lamp, probably an employee. They looked to be having some kind of an argument, the man was getting extremely animated. The man was much larger than Noah; he looked like a bodybuilder and was wearing a tank top with a pair of shorts that Noah deemed a little too short for a guy. He had tribal tattoos up and down his arms and wore a backward hat. It was also cold, so the entire outfit made no sense. It took Noah Riordan about half of a nanosecond to classify the man as a 'douchebag'.

The woman, however, was a different story. She was clearly smarter, as she was wearing baggy sweatpants, an old Blue Moon sweatshirt, and she had glasses. Her hair was blonde but had highlights through it. Noah couldn't tell if they were purple or red. Again, it took Noah Riordan less than a second to categorize her as way too good for the gorilla she was arguing with. There was just something about the way she carried herself that instantly made Noah feel concerned. She looked uncomfortable, even scared. They both were paying little attention to their surroundings, the woman nearly stumbled over a chunk of concrete.

"Jesus," Noah groaned as he set the bucket down in the rubble before turning the throttle down on the excavator. "Scott, you see these idiots? I guess the tape and barricades weren't enough fucking clues to not walk there?"

"Guess not," Scott laughed. "Want me to say something?"

"Nah, just leave it. Hopefully, they get the idea once I work my way back over to them," Noah sighed, not having the energy to deal with stupid people at the moment.

"You got it, my man," Scott gave Noah a thumbs-up.

Noah turned the throttle back up and went back to work. He kept glancing in his mirrors, watching the couple intently as he continued throwing concrete into the truck's bed. The argument didn't appear to be going well, with the man pointing his finger at the woman and appearing to yell at her repeatedly. She tried, poorly it seemed, to defend herself. Stepping on the pedals of the machine, Noah walked the excavator back about ten feet, having cleared out the first area of rubble; Scott slowly moved the truck into position, keeping in line with the 305. The woman saw the excavator and truck getting closer.

Looking past her male companion, the woman eyed Noah as he dumped another bucket of rubble into the back of the truck and swung back around to take another chunk of rubble away. There came a point whenever Noah was operating where he hit a rhythm, where he felt like the machine had become a part of him. When that happened, it was incredibly difficult for Noah to stop until he absolutely had to, for one reason or another.

This time, his reason for stopping was the woman. He swung around to start scooping material from behind the excavator and made direct eye contact with the woman. Pausing for half a second, Noah raised his hand and gestured for her to back away. The woman nodded and tried to pull the man away from the sidewalk, but he swiped her hand away and started yelling louder. Noah couldn't hear a word of what he was saying, but he clearly wasn't happy. He entertained the idea of saying something but decided against it. It wasn't his business, and if they wanted to make a scene, then that was their choice. But that sentiment flipped on a dime when the man pushed the woman to the ground. Noah had been raised by a woman, and he had been taught from a young age that you never, ever put your hands on a woman. There weren't many things that got Noah riled up, but seeing that was one of those things that just enraged him.

Slamming the bucket down on the ground, Noah shut the machine off and leapt out of the cab. He grabbed a large torque wrench from under the operator seat and jogged over to the couple, ducking under the yellow tape.

"Noah, wait!" Scott yelled, hurrying after him, shovel still in hand.

The woman was still on the ground when Noah approached. The gorilla-man barely had time to notice him before Noah swung the wrench into the man's gut. It didn't matter how much you could bench press, a torque wrench to the abdomen would subdue anyone. As expected, the man doubled over in pain, his face turning purple. Noah jerked his knee up, hitting the man square in the face. He fell back in a heap, completely stunned. Noah put his dirt-covered boot over the man's throat and leaned down so he could see his face. Before the man could do anything in retaliation, Noah spotted the man's wallet on the ground next to him. He picked it up and thumbed the driver's license out of the wallet. With the man still wheezing for air beneath him, Noah snapped a picture of the ID and dropped it and the wallet on the man's face.

"Now I know you," Noah growled. "Don't ever put your hands on a woman."

Noah turned around to the woman, still sitting on the ground, looking at him in shock. Seeing her up close, Noah saw she was younger than he'd thought, probably closer to 23 or 24. Her striking blue eyes were wet with tears that hadn't fallen yet. Dropping to a knee, Noah looked at her seriously.

"Are you ok?" he asked. She nodded, lowering her gaze away from Noah's glare. "Good."

"Everything ok?" Scott asked, panting heavily. He put his hands on his knees and bent over, sucking in air. "Ugh, I'm too old for this shit."

"I'm fine," Noah said, not taking his eyes off the young girl. He stood up and offered her his hand. Reluctantly, she took it and let him help her up.

"Thank you," she said quietly, finally looking at Noah.

"Don't mention it," Noah muttered, wiping his hands on his jeans. "You work here?"

"Yeah, I have to start in a few minutes," she said. "I'm sorry, I didn't mean to cause a scene."

"Nothing to apologize for," Noah responded.

The man finally got up to his feet, glaring at Noah with a face of blank rage. Noah stared back, unimpressed with the macho posturing. Scott stood up to his full height and gripped the shovel.

"Fuck you," the man spat. His nose was bleeding steadily.

"Get the hell outta here," Noah growled, flexing his hand around the torque wrench for emphasis. Shaking his head, the man turned and walked back to his car. The woman watched him leave the parking lot before heading into the bar.

"Thank you again," she said, wiping her eyes.

"Don't mention it. Go have a good day," Noah waved, smiling at her. She waved back and stepped into the bar.

"Well, you tuned that guy up," Scott said, fighting back laughter. Noah looked at him with a wry grin.

Scott and Noah shared a laugh and bumped fists. They walked back over to their equipment; Noah hopped back into the mini-excavator. Noah throttled the CAT 305 back up and got back to work, topping off the dump truck as fast as he could. As much as Noah had wanted to, he couldn't quite fit the entire sidewalk in the truck. He and Scott would have to come back tomorrow to finish up, which was not a huge deal to either of them. After digging up the rest of the sidewalk, Noah would still have to dig about a foot deeper and level everything off for the new sidewalk to be constructed on a level foundation.

"Alright, I'm out," Scott said, climbing back into his truck. He checked his cheap wristwatch. "I gotta get to the quarry before they close."

"I'm just gonna finish up here, and I'm on my way," Noah shrugged. "Be back here tomorrow morning, early. I want to finish this up so I can bring the machines back over to the 101."

"Got it. Have a good night," Scott waved and drove away, blowing diesel smoke out the stacks on either side of the cab.

Noah parked the excavator next to the skid steer and slammed the door shut. He locked the doors on both machines and roped them off with bright yellow caution tape before heading for his truck, just in time to see an Omicron LLC truck and a black Chevy Suburban pulling up in front of his own pickup. Two men that Noah recognized instantly hopped out of the vehicles. He froze in his tracks and glared at them, his fists instinctively balling into fists, finding himself wishing for the torque wrench he'd just locked in the mini-ex.

"Hey Noah," the bald man driving the Omicron LLC truck said. He was wearing jeans, work boots, and a flannel shirt. His name was Brian Tyler, and he was the Chief Executive Officer of Omicron LLC. The man standing next to him was wearing black pants, a blue dress shirt, and a sport coat that was more than likely concealing a pistol. He was Stan Simmons, a Business Agent for the Local 12 Union.

"What do you want?" Noah asked quietly.

"We need you to come with us," Stan said, adjusting his belt.

"Nope," Noah shook his head. "Not a chance."

"Noah, we can do this the easy way or the hard way," Stan said, putting his hands on his hips. Slowly, he pulled his sport coat back enough to reveal the grip of a Glock handgun in a holster on his hip. "I'd rather do this like gentlemen."

Noah lowered his head, cursing under his breath. He had plenty of experience dealing with these two men, and it was never good. Anytime they came to fetch him, Noah got a horrible sinking feeling in his gut. That same feeling was coursing through him as he stood before them. And he was already having such an exciting day.

"Fine," Noah grumbled. "I'll follow you guys."
"No," Stan shook his head. "You'll ride with me."
"Great," Noah muttered.

****

The International Union of Operating Engineers Local 12 headquarters was located in Pasadena, California. A sprawling red brick building with beautiful courtyards surrounding it, the Local 12 represented over 18,000 men and women in the Southern California and Southern Nevada area. The top floor of the Headquarters was dedicated to the top-ranking officers of the Local 12 - President Thomas Swaney and Vice President Larry Trudeau. Both men sat in President Swaney's spacious office overlooking Pasadena. Brian Tyler and Stan Simmons sat across from them on a long couch. And Noah Riordan sat in an armchair, with all four men staring at him.

Noah had been in this situation before, with four of the most influential men in the state of California staring into his soul. Most people assumed that the politicians or celebrities were more influential, but they were sadly wrong. Thomas Swaney had his hands in several politicians' pockets and was well-connected all the way up to the state representatives and senators. There wasn't much that went on in California that he didn't know about. Larry Trudeau was Thomas's Vice President and right-hand man. Stan Simmons, on the other hand, was an enforcer disguised as a Business Agent.

"How's work going, Mr. Riordan?" Thomas asked with an emotionless smile. "I understand you're off the 101 job for this week."

"It's going fine, sir," Noah said, rubbing his sweaty palms on his jeans. Even though he had no respect for Thomas Swaney, Noah had no desire to be on his bad side.

"Noah's our best foreman by a long shot," Brian Tyler chimed in, giving a respectful nod toward Noah. Although Brian was essentially a puppet for Thomas and Larry, Noah still liked him well enough. He was a good man who had gotten wrapped up in a bad situation. Noah understood that.

"I'm aware of that," Thomas said. "Noah has a bright future with us. My guess is he'd have more than enough votes to secure a Business Agent position,"

"I appreciate that," Noah responded. "All due respect, but can we please get to why I'm here."

The four men looked at each other apprehensively. Thomas stood up and walked over to his desk. He picked up a manila folder and sat back down next to Larry.

"We are in need of your services again," Thomas said, choosing his words extremely carefully.

"What kind of services?"

"The acquisition kind," Thomas narrowed his eyes on Noah.

"No," Noah blurted out. He got up and started walking for the door.

Stan Simmons stood up and blocked the doorway with his massive presence. Noah stared him down.

"Move," Noah snarled. "Or I'll move you myself."

"Noah, please sit down," Brian tried to reason with him. "We just want to talk."

"I have nothing to say," Noah said, not taking his focus from Stan.

"Then just listen," Brian responded. "Please."

Closing his eyes and taking a deep breath, Noah turned around and sat back down in the chair.

"Just us," Noah said, looking at Brian and Thomas.

"Leave us," Thomas grunted. Larry and Stan filed out of the room quickly, always at the mercy of Thomas's orders.

"Just listen," Brian insisted, moving closer to Noah and Thomas once the door closed behind the other two men.

"The Union is bleeding money right now, Noah," Thomas began, opening up the manila folder. "We've got a dozen lawsuits on our hands, we're losing operators to retirement on a daily basis, and there's just not enough applicants for the Apprenticeship program. Omicron is our top-earning signatory..."

"And we're struggling too," Brian said. "We need a cash influx, desperately."

"Look, I already saved this union and this company once before," Noah kept his voice low. "And I barely got away with my life. You can't ask me to do that again."

"We're not asking, Noah," Thomas answered. "We need you to do this for us."

"I know you're the big bad President, but fuck you," Noah spat. "I already put my life on the line for you two. The others did too, and where are they? Six feet underground. That won't be me, I'm not going out that way. You got 20,000 members, pick one of them to do it."

"You are the only one who has done this before. Do you really think I'd grab some moron off a site and tell him to go rob a bank?" Thomas asked incredulously.

"Last time you threatened my girlfriend, my mother, my grandfather, my fucking dog," Noah felt his blood boiling.

"And that was not right," Thomas put his hand up. "And I am sorry. We would never hurt anyone you care about, I swear."

"Guys, I can't do this again. I won't do it again," Noah shook his head. "I'm sorry, but I already did this. You guys don't get it, you get to sit in your offices and pencil-push. You've never walked into a bank or up to an armored truck and aimed a gun at someone. You've got no right to ask me to do that again."

The room fell quiet, and Brian hung his head. Noah could tell he was remorseful, at least more so than Thomas. He hadn't known what to expect when Brian and Stan showed up earlier that day, but this was far from anything he would've suspected. It was making Noah sick to his stomach just thinking about it.

"Noah, I don't want to have to persuade you in a different way," Thomas said ominously.

"What happened to not threatening me?" Noah shot back. Thomas smirked.

"Drastic times call for drastic measures, my friend."

"Yeah."

"Would you just listen to the jobs before you say no?" Brian asked. "Please, Noah. We wouldn't be asking you if it wasn't dire."

"Fine. What is it?" Noah relented. He couldn't deny, he was slightly curious about what Thomas had cooked up this time. The last time, Noah had been surprised with the amount of planning and detail that Thomas had dedicated to the jobs. Thomas was a smart man and a brilliant strategist, but Noah was the only one he trusted enough to pull off the jobs. And Noah knew that.

"Two trucks and one bank," Thomas explained. "All within a four-week time period. You'd need a crew. Three, maybe four guys total. You would have access to whatever hardware you need, all you have to do is say the word."

"The trucks are easy. Banks are damn-near impossible nowadays, and the payout isn't going to be nearly what it was the first time around. People have adapted, security is tougher to beat, and the cops' response times are going to be faster. You want to do trucks, not banks."

"I realize you have more experience than we do," Brian said, always trying to be polite, even in tense situations. "But based on our information, these specific ones will be enough for us to stop the bleeding. All the money will go through Omicron before going to the Union,"

"How much are we talking about?" Noah asked, genuinely curious.

"The bank is only going to haul about $200,000," Thomas said. Noah scoffed and shook his head.

"200 grand is not worth the risk," Noah said flatly. "It just isn't."

"The bank is not for the money," Thomas responded, refusing any more details. "The trucks are for the money. Two trucks at the end of their shifts before unloading at the depot. According to my information, each truck will be hauling anywhere from 500 million to 600 million."

"Holy crap," Noah gasped, running his hands through his hair. "That's a lot of money."

"An armored truck can carry anywhere from four to six pallets of money. These two should be filled to capacity, so we're estimating closer to 600."

"Be that as it may, you run into a whole new set of issues dealing with that kind of cash," Noah said. "No way to move that kind of money."

"With the right equipment, it's doable," Thomas countered.

"What's in it for me?" Noah asked, hating himself for asking, but he had to know. That amount of money was life-altering.

"If you do this, I'll make you my partner," Brian said. "You and I would each own 50% of Omicron, and your salary would reflect that instantly."

"Additionally, I'm prepared to offer a generous retirement and college fund should you choose to have kids someday. If not, you can take the money and do what you want," Thomas continued.

"How much?"

"75 million," Thomas answered immediately. Noah kept his face neutral, he'd mastered the art of a convincing poker face a long time ago, especially when dealing with Thomas Swaney.

"What about the crew?" Noah asked.

"Five each," Thomas said. "More money than most of our operators could even dream of. It's fair."

"I'm not saying yes..." Noah said quietly. "But I'd want to pick the guys myself. And they're going to need a reason to do it. A good one."

"We can arrange some lay-offs," Brian offered. "Do you have people in mind?"

"Yeah, I think I might," Noah looked at both men and shook his head. "If either one of you screws me over, I will not hesitate to come down here and put a bullet in each of you."

"Understood," Thomas smiled. He stood up and stuck out his hand. "Do we have a deal?"

Noah's mind was made up, and he hated himself for it. But, the truth was he had made a deal with the devil years ago. He'd already done this job, and he'd done it to perfection, at least in Thomas's mind. There was no decision. With that kind of money, Noah's mom would never have to work again. His grandpa could spend his last years on Earth doing whatever he wanted. And Noah's future would be secure, Union or no Union.

He stood up and shook Thomas Swaney's hand.

"Deal."

5

It was mere minutes past six in the morning when Noah Riordan turned into The Lamp. After finishing the sidewalk demolition and backfill, Noah had been instructed to rip up part of the parking lot to expose a sewer line that had been damaged. It was funny how a supposed quick job was turning into a major pain in his ass. Instead of driving his truck, Noah was behind the wheel of a massive Peterbilt 389, which Omicron LLC used strictly for hauling equipment. Today, Noah had the Talbert Lowboy trailer hooked up to the semi and was towing a CAT 328D LCR Hydraulic Excavator. Although Noah preferred to use a slightly bigger machine like the 329, the 328 was a better fit for working in a parking lot with heavy traffic. Coming in at just over 73,000 pounds, the 328 was significantly heavier than the 329, but more compact. The beauty of the 328 came in its small cab and engine configuration and zero tail swing, meaning it could operate in extremely tight places.

Noah slowed down and parked alongside the empty lot, the perimeter of which had been roped off by the Department of Water and Power. Because of the limited space, Noah would have to haul away the material as he dug into the ground. Scott, the dump truck driver, would be on-site in an hour, giving Noah a tight window to unload the machine and get to work. He threw the truck in park and jumped out, pulling his Hi-Vis vest over his gray hoodie. Noah put on his hard hat, adorned with several Local 12 stickers, and went to work disassembling the trailer from the truck and unchaining the excavator.

20 minutes later, Noah had the 328 crawling toward the back of the parking lot. The spray-painted lines outlined the perimeter of the soon-to-be exposed sewer line. He positioned the machine and set the bucket on the ground next to the orange lines. Shockingly ahead of schedule, Scott came rumbling into the lot. He expertly backed the truck over the curb and into the lot, parking it feet away from the excavator. He tipped the dumper back slightly and shut the truck off. Noah cranked the throttle up and got to work digging, carefully maneuvering around the damaged sewer line.

By midday, Noah had almost completed half of the dig; everything was neat, square, and sound. The plumbers would have to climb down and inspect everything before starting repairs; Noah had to make sure the walls of the hole wouldn't cave in. Scott had been driving like a madman, taking the full loads of dirt to the quarry, dumping them, and racing back. He'd told Noah before his last trip he was stopping for lunch. Noah set the bucket down next to the hole and shut the excavator off. Resting on the floor of the cab was Noah's grey-blue lunch box and cooler. He unzipped the box and produced a tinfoil-covered sandwich. Reaching into the cooler, Noah grabbed a bottle of Gatorade and water.

As he ate his lunch, Noah couldn't help but notice The Lamp was already filling up with patrons. It always made him question what people did for a living that allowed them to go to a bar before noon. Clearly, he had gotten into the wrong profession.

There were plenty of reasons for Noah to be distracted. Noah and his entire crew would be formally laid off by Omicron at the end of the week. It would come as a major shock to everyone except Noah. The timing had actually been perfect; they would have had to lay off his crew anyway for the next few weeks while inspections took place on the 101. There was just not enough work to warrant sending them to another site. Noah would have to wait at least a week before pitching the idea to his crew, but he was hopeful. He figured EJ was an easy yes. But Chandler was still a wildcard. Noah wasn't sure what his reaction would be. However, Noah figured he had the upper hand. Chandler needed money for Lyla's procedures desperately. Desperate men do desperate things, and Noah could exploit that. It didn't make him feel good at all, he liked Chandler quite a bit, but Noah needed the bodies. If they followed his lead, Noah was confident they could pull off these jobs. Then, he could get out from under the thumb of Thomas Swaney.

His mind was filled with conflicting thoughts as he tossed his garbage into the dirt he was yet to dig out. Noah opened the door to the 328, and climbed back into the seat and fired the excavator back up, cranking the throttle up. Using the foot pedals, Noah moved the excavator closer to The Lamp so he could finish up the backside of the dig. He swung the cab around and lowered the boom, driving the teeth of the bucket deep into the loose dirt. Noah curled the bucket in and scooped up a full load of dirt; he swung the machine around and dumped the dirt off to the side. By now, the sun was blocked by the clouds, driving the temperature down. He cranked the heating up before rotating back and digging up another scoop of dirt.

Once Scott returned from lunch, Noah wasted no time filling the bed of the truck with dirt. He used the teeth of the bucket to level out the load in the truck before signaling to Scott that he was good to go. Scott slammed on the gas and drove away. Noah swung the machine back around and began grading the bottom of the hole, smoothing out the area around the pipe as best he could. He glanced over at The Lamp and spotted a young girl walking in to work. It was the same girl he'd met last week. She looked at him and smiled, turning on a dime to walk toward him. Noah throttled the machine down and set the bucket on the ground before climbing out.

"Hey," she said, smiling softly at him. She was clearly a little shy, in an adorable kind of way.

"How's it going?" Noah asked, smiling back at her.

"It's going," she shrugged. "I broke up with Duke."

"His name was Duke?" Noah said, his face breaking into a grin. "Seriously? Is he a real American hero too?"

"Ha!" the girl laughed, getting the reference to the classic G.I. Joe character. "That's funny."

"That's a dumb name, I'm sorry. Don't think I could ever date someone with a stupid name like that," Noah shrugged.

"I should've known then," she shook her head, laughing.

"Yeah, seriously," Noah agreed. He wiped his hand on his pants and stuck it out towards her. "I'm Noah."

"Nice to meet you," the girl said, shaking Noah's hand. "I'm Jessica, Jess for short."

"Pleasure," Noah smiled. "Are you working today?"

"Yep, that's why I'm here."

"Same," Noah said, gesturing to the idling machine and piles of dirt and asphalt behind him.

A small white car pulled into the parking lot and stopped closer to where Noah and Jessica were chatting. A young brunette jumped out and walked over to them; she was dressed similarly to Jessica in black yoga pants and a baggy hoodie.

"Hey girlie," the woman said to Jessica, giving her a hug. She looked at Noah before looking back at Jessica. "Is this the guy?"

"Shut up!" Jessica hissed, blushing instantly. The woman laughed and looked at Noah.

"I've heard about you, you're pretty popular now," she said. "I'm Maggie, by the way."

"Noah," he introduced. "And how am I so popular?"

"Anyone who protects my girl is popular with me," Maggie said, putting her arm around Jessica. "I've known her my entire life. Since first grade, we've been best friends."

"It's true, "Jessica said. "Can't tell you what I'd do without her."

"Aren't you guys cute?" Noah said with a hint of sarcasm. Maggie rolled her eyes.

"It is pretty cool watching you do all that, though," Jessica said, changing the subject. She gestured to the idling machine. "What do you call that exactly?"

"The machine?" Noah asked, cocking his thumb behind him. Jessica nodded. "Well, technically, it's an excavator. But different people call it different things; backhoe, trackhoe, etcetera," Noah said. He liked how Jessica seemed genuinely interested in what he was saying instead of pretending to listen, as Paris had done so often.

"That's so cool," Jessica commented. "Duke could never do anything like this."

"What? Hold a job?" Maggie snickered, giving Noah a wink.

"Very funny," Jessica rolled her eyes. "I just mean he's not one for getting his hands dirty. So how does it work?"

"How does what work?"

"The excavator!" Jessica said, pointing to the machine. Noah smiled inwardly.

"Come on, I'll show you," Noah said, offering Jessica his hand.

"Is that ok?" Jessica asked. "I don't want to get you in trouble or anything."

"Do you see anyone else around here?" Noah laughed. "Come on. Maggie, you want to try too?"

"I'll just watch!" Maggie said. Jessica took Noah's hand as he carefully led her under the yellow tape to the excavator.

"Watch your step," Noah said, kicking some sharp stones away from them. Jessica was smiling ear to ear as they came to the massive machine. "Alright, climb up in there," Noah said. Carefully, Jessica climbed onto the treads and then into the cab, sitting down in the operator's seat. She looked around the cab and smiled back at Noah; he climbed up onto the treads and crouched next to her. Maggie already had her phone out and was snapping pictures.

"See that dial on your right-hand side?"

"Yeah!"

"That's your throttle," Noah instructed. Jessica turned the knob, and the engine roared to life.

"It's so loud!" Jessica yelled.

"Yeah, I know," Noah said, reaching over to turn it back down. "Ok, your controls are the two joysticks," Noah pointed to each of the sticks. Jessica gripped them like a proper operator. Noah smiled. "The machine won't run right now, I've got the master break on. Once I leave, throw this lever down," Noah said, tapping the yellow lever on the left side of the seat.

“Ok, got it,” Jessica said.

“Alright, the right joystick is your bucket and boom. Push forward, you’ll lower the boom. Pull back, you’ll raise the boom. Tilt it right, you’ll open the bucket. Tilt it left, you’ll close the bucket. Left joystick is your stick and swing. Push forward and you’ll stick out, pull back and you’ll stick in. Tilting it left or right will swing the machine in that direction. Got it?” Noah asked.

“Uh, I think so,” Jessica said. “Can I give it a shot?”

“Hell no,” Noah laughed. “Sorry, but I had to do a four year apprenticeship to run these things. Once you do that, I’ll be happy to let you run it anytime you want,”

“Fair enough,” Jessica climbed down from the machine. “Thanks for showing me, though. Kind of cool,”

“It’s very cool,” Noah said. He heard the horn of the dump truck and saw Scott driving toward them. “Alright, give me a few minutes,”

“I’m not going anywhere,” Jessica responded.

As the dump truck came to a stop alongside the excavator, Noah climbed over the treads and up into the cab. He quickly swung the machine around and went right to work, digging like a madman. He worked both joysticks simultaneously, operating the machine at a very fast pace. The 328 was a quick machine by design. With the right operator, it was impressively fast. Noah honked the horn and watched as Scott slowly pulled the dump truck away for what would be his final trip to the quarry. He opened the door and winked at Jessica. Noah shut down the excavator and climbed down; he locked the door shut for the day before turning back around to Jessica.

“Well, I hope you have a good shift.”

“You’re done?”

"I'll be back early tomorrow," Noah said, gesturing to the remaining piles of dirt and asphalt. "Should be done at the end of the day tomorrow."

"I'm sure you have plans, but if you don't, would you want to come sit in my section and have dinner? I feel like the least I can do is buy your dinner, I owe you."

"You don't owe me anything," Noah smiled. "Some food sounds great, but I'm paying. You're not buying me anything."

"Give me ten minutes, and then come in!" Jessica smiled. She hugged Noah before walking into the bar with Maggie.

****

After inhaling a sandwich and a couple of beers, Noah sat back in his booth and sighed, ready to go to bed. The drive back to his house was at least a half-hour, probably more with traffic. He was not looking forward to that in the slightest. The Lamp was busy, especially for a Wednesday night - not exactly a popular night to go out drinking. Noah was happy to be by himself off in a corner, away from the crowd by the bartop.

"Hey, hey," Jessica said, appearing in front of Noah's booth. "Can I get you anything else?"

"Nah, I'm good," Noah smiled up at her. "I gotta get home. Early morning tomorrow and all."

"Yeah, I feel that," Jessica said, sitting in the booth across from Noah. "I'll be here until close."

"When's that at?" Noah asked.

"Two. Which means I probably won't get home until three or three-thirty," Jessica rolled her eyes.

"That actually sounds kind of awful," Noah said. "I normally get up around then."

"Now, that sounds awful," Jessica responded. "I could never get up that early!"

"Eh, you get used to it," Noah shrugged. "Even on the weekends, I'm normally up by five or six."

"God, what is wrong with you?" Jessica laughed. Noah smirked.

"Oh, more than you know."

Jessica set Noah's receipt and a pen in front of him.

"Write your number down for me," Jessica said, blushing a little bit. "I'll text you."

The request caught Noah slightly off guard. Noah Riordan wasn't a bad-looking guy by any stretch of the imagination, but he was humble and never saw himself in that light. The number of times a woman had asked him for his number could be counted with one finger - Paris. But she still had yet to reach back out to Noah, and he had gotten sick of wondering if she ever would. That was pointless, waiting for a possible chance with someone he didn't see a future with. There was nothing there anymore; Paris Brady was a thing of the past. He sat up a little straighter and wrote his cell phone number on the receipt.

"I'd like that," Noah said, pushing the receipt and pen back toward Jessica. She smiled and folded the receipt, slipping it into the pouch on her belt.

"Thanks for coming in, Noah," she said. "It was great to chat with you."

"Yeah, it was," Noah agreed.

****

When Noah rolled over at exactly 4:15AM the next morning, he checked his phone, squinting as his eyes adjusted to sudden bright lights. The first thing he saw was the text notification from a number he didn't recognize. Sliding his thumb over the message, Noah opened it to read.

Hey, it's Jessica! Thanks for coming in last night, it was great to get to talk to you. Let me know what you're up to this week, I'd love to see you again <3

Noah smiled and could feel himself blush a little bit. Jessica was interesting to him, and the thought of going out with her was nerve-wracking and exciting. Paris had been the only girl he'd ever seriously dated. As much as he wanted to text her back immediately and set up a date or something, more pressing matters were at hand. The lay-off was happening in a few days, and Noah's crew would turn to him for help and guidance. EJ would be mad, Chandler would most likely get desperate, and who knew what Darren would do. The only good thing about the situation was that they all had reasons and motivations for needing extra money. The easiest part would be getting EJ and Darren to go along with the plan. Chandler, however, would definitely need to be convinced. He absolutely hated exploiting his crew's personal lives for a man like Thomas Swaney, but Noah wasn't left with much of a choice. If he didn't, Noah was positive that Stan Simmons would pay everyone he cared about a visit, and that was not something Noah was willing to risk.

****

Just as Noah got into his truck and began driving to the job site, his phone began ringing. Slightly annoyed that anyone would be calling him so early in the morning, Noah groaned loudly before answering the phone - not bothering to see who it was beforehand.

"This is Noah," he answered, taking a sip of coffee from his large thermos.

"Hey Noah, how's it going," Brian Tyler said. Noah shook his head, wondering what in the world Brian could want. There was really no bad blood between them, but Noah found Brian to be a lot to deal with, especially when there were a ton of things going on. Brian had a tendency to overreact and put a ton of pressure on his foremen when they got behind schedule. But most of the time, Brian was a good guy. Noah knew he was married and had a couple of kids, one of which had just started working at Omicron; he couldn't remember if it was Brian's son or daughter. Generally speaking, Brian took care of his employees and was generous with bonuses when the Union allowed him to give them out, that is.

"Driving to The Lamp, what's with the early call?" Noah asked. "I figured you're never up this early anymore."

"You'd be surprised," Brian chuckled. "Listen man, I don't think I can lay your crew off. We're behind on a few jobs, and I need them working, not collecting unemployment."

This was not good news, especially with a strict timetable. The entire job depended on Noah's guys being willing to do something incredibly illegal. They had to be desperate enough to think it was a good idea. Brian's sudden change of heart was no doubt going to complicate things for Noah.

"That's not good," Noah muttered. "How else am I supposed to convince them? They're not going to be willing to do anything like this if they don't have a good reason."

"I know, I know," Brian agreed. "But laying you guys off right now is just not an option. There are things to do. Do you have any other ideas that don't involve a lay-off or furlough?"

"I'll have to think about it, ok?" Noah answered, cursing Brian in his mind. Screwing with the plan was not ok with something this delicate. "I'll talk to the guys today and judge how everyone's doing. If some guys are more desperate than others, it'll be easier. But don't count on it. You're going to have to be a dick about money to get them to do this, you know that right?"

"I'm well aware of that," Brian said, clearly annoyed with Noah's comment. "Listen, my kid is going to be on your crew for the rest of the week. I hope that's ok, but I know I can trust you to look out for her."

"Wait... her?"

Plenty of women worked for Omicron LLC and for the Local 12 Union, in fact nearly 50% of the upper management team at Omicron was comprised of females. Union Hall had several females in high positions too, but the number of females who worked on the actual job sites as laborers or operators was slim, although that trend was beginning to change. As part of their diversity outreach program, Omicron and the Local 12 had teamed up to promote diversity in the construction industry, encouraging minorities and women to get involved. Since then, there had been a fair number of women who'd joined the Union as operators or been hired at Omicron in a variety of roles. Those were all good things and promoted the inclusive values that both the Union and Omicron believed in. However, being responsible for the CEO's daughter was not something that Noah was looking forward to.

As with any job where men and women worked together, there was always the risk of someone saying something or doing something inappropriate. Noah had had to fire a handful of laborers on his crews for comments or unwanted touching over the years. He had no tolerance for that type of behavior and was never bothered by having to fire someone for doing that. They got what they deserved, as far as Noah was concerned.

"Yeah, her name's Alexa, but she goes by Lexi. She wants to get into the family business but has no desire to work in an office. She just wants to be an operator right now, I'm hoping you can train her for a while," Brian said. "And just between us, whatever happens with the crew, you'll be taken care of. I'm not going to lay you off or cut your pay or anything..."

"I appreciate that," Noah grunted. "I'll look after your kid."

"Thank you, Noah."

6

"You have got to be kidding me," Noah muttered out loud from inside the cab of his preferred Caterpillar 329F excavator. He gently set the bucket on the ground next to a pile of rubble on the 101; he was relieved to be back on the huge project since they were behind schedule now. Noah was hoping to get caught up within the next two weeks, but that was nearly impossible due to the lack of overtime allowed to him and his crew.

The cause of Noah's annoyance stemmed from two men on his crew being complete morons. From the cab, Noah would see EJ and Darren standing around Alexa Tyler, working harder than both of them combined. Noah had tasked her with torching through the rebar and metal debris in order to make it easier for Chandler to scoop it up with his skid steer. EJ and Darren were supposed to be working but appeared to be more focused on chatting with the new girl.

As a man, Noah couldn't necessarily blame them for wanting to talk to her. Lexi was a cool girl; Noah had liked her almost as soon as he met her. She was 24 years old and had recently graduated from Boise State with a dual degree in Construction Management and Business Management. In her free time, Lexi trained and showed a duo of horses that she'd had since a young age. They were kept on her dad's ranch, which was located almost an hour and a half away from Los Angeles in Temecula, California. Instead of going right into office work, she desperately wanted to work on the job sites and earn some wings before becoming a Project Manager or Project Engineer. Noah respected that immensely. Most people who were inheriting a business from their parents wouldn't have gone that route and put in the hours to understand the company from the ground up.

Climbing down from the excavator, Noah marched over to EJ and Darren, grabbing them both by the safety vests.

"What're you two knuckleheads doing?" Noah asked, using a calm enough tone to let them know he was only partially kidding. "Get back to work and stop flirting, she's not interested in your dirty asses."

Lexi flipped her welding helmet up and laughed loudly. EJ and Darren grumbled under their breath and walked back to their machines. Noah shook his head and looked at Lexi.

"Sorry about those guys," Noah said. "They're harmless, but they're annoying as hell."

"It's ok, I really don't mind," Lexi shrugged. "They weren't bothering me."

"No, but they were bothering me," Noah said, getting a laugh out of Lexi. "I just told your dad I'd keep an eye on you, so that's what I'm doing."

"Ugh, my dad," Lexi rolled her eyes. "He means well, but he's so overprotective it's annoying."

"He's gotta be," Noah answered. "He's doing his job as a father."

"I guess so," Lexi shrugged, taking off her welding helmet; her wavy blonde hair fell down to her waist. She took off her gloves and wiped her hands on her neon green Omicron sweater. Lexi was indeed a beautiful woman, Noah couldn't deny that. But as far as anyone was concerned, especially Noah, she was off-limits.

"Let me know if you need anything, ok?" Noah said. "One day this week, I'll get you in the hoe and get you some seat time."

"Really?" Lexi's face lit up.

"Yeah. I was told to turn you into an operator, and I'm going to. Just stay safe, ok? I can't risk anyone getting hurt or anything on my watch."

"I promise, I'll be safe," Lexi said, clearly excited about the prospect of becoming an operator. Noah grinned and stuck his fist out. Lexi banged her knuckles against his, and Noah walked back to his machine.

****

Noah's crew gathered around the excavator as the last few minutes of sunlight began dwindling. Sitting on the treads with his feet hanging, Noah watched as Lexi climbed into her white Ford F-250 pick-up truck - he'd excused her from the small meeting. It wasn't anything that concerned her.

"That is a woman right there, man," EJ said, watching her drive off.

"Tell me about it," Darren agreed. "Brian must hate us."

"You two need to keep your shit in your pants," Noah said, which got a hearty laugh from Chandler. EJ and Darren both laughed too. "The last thing I need is you two perving out over the owner's daughter. I do not need to be dealing with that right now."

"No promises, boss," Darren said with a grin.

"You go within a 10-foot radius of her and I'll break a crowbar over both your faces," Noah smirked at his guys and jumped down in front of them. He locked the door on the excavator and stuffed the key in the inside pocket of his jacket.

"Listen boys, I just wanted to check in and see how y'all are doing," Noah began. "I know this no-overtime thing is tough on us all, but I'm still responsible for you guys."

"Well, I'm getting hammered from Child Support," EJ admitted. "The ex is going crazy on me, I just can't afford it right now. I'm behind on my rent too, and it's just piling up. Haven't been able to get my feet underneath me since the divorce. Some overtime would be a big help. The holiday bonus will be a life-saver, but that's still a month away."

EJ had gone through a particularly nasty divorce and struggled financially ever since. Between Child Support, Alimony, and paying for the house he was no longer living in, EJ was the definition of down on his luck. Every Christmas season, the employees at Omicron were given a significant holiday bonus, and that might be all the leverage Noah needed.

"Yeah, I mean I agree," Chandler spoke up. "Medical bills are killing me right now, and Lyla's chemo is just getting more and more expensive. I need the overtime."

"I could use the overtime too," Darren muttered, not offering up more of an explanation, but Noah knew why. Darren's addictions were getting worse and more noticeable. His eyes gave away the constant drug use. Noah knew that Darren was a decent guy, but he was in so deep with gambling and substance use that he was destined for nothing but pain.

"I hear you guys, I'm trying to get us some more work," Noah paused. There was no turning back now. "But there are other ways of making some extra money..."

"You got some side jobs for us?" EJ asked, perking up instantly. Noah nodded, holding the attention of the three men. He looked around, making sure no one else was on the site aside from his crew.

"There are alternative ways to make some money," Noah said, choosing his words extremely carefully. "Just depends on what you guys are willing to do."

"I have no desire to be a prostitute," Darren said. EJ nodded in agreement.

"Not that, you idiots," Noah rolled his eyes. "I'm saying there are a few things we can do if we need money."

"What kind of things?" Chandler asked, clearly interested in hearing what Noah had to say.

"Things that can be... questionable. Legally speaking," Noah said quietly, keeping his gaze focused on his crew. EJ and Darren had almost no reaction to the suggestion, but Chandler appeared taken aback, as was expected.

"You're talking about taking it," Chandler said, crossing his arms across his chest.

"I am," Noah nodded. "We could all use the money."

"Why is that something you'd suggest?" Chandler asked. "Assuming you're being serious and not just jerking us around."

"I'm serious," Noah looked at Chandler. "Very serious."

"Why are you even thinking about something like that?"

"Because," Noah said, leaning on the tread of the excavator and crossing his feet. "I've done it before."

All three men in front of him exchanged surprised looks, although EJ looked more impressed than surprised.

"You've done what before?" Chandler pressed, wanting to hear Noah say the actual words. Noah looked at him seriously.

"You know what I'm talking about," was all that Noah said.

"Are we talking like banks?" EJ asked, lowering his voice significantly. Noah sighed audibly and shook his head.

"Yeah, I've done a bank before," Noah admitted.

"Holy shit," EJ breathed, looking at Darren with a wild smile. "I never had any idea you were such a badass, boss."

"Look, I'm just saying..." Noah began. "I've done it before, and it can be done. I care about you guys, and I want you all to be well-off. Upper Management doesn't give a shit about us. If we want our bonuses, it's up to us to go get them."

"Amen," EJ agreed. Noah had expected that he would be the first one to agree to the idea. "We deserve better, we're breaking our backs out here every day. We deserve better, we just do."

"I've always thought about doing a bank," Darren said. "Ever since I saw *The Town*, always wanted to try it."

"Banks are damn near impossible nowadays," Noah corrected. "Plus, the money isn't that good. You wanna hit something, hit a truck. That's where the big money is."

"I thought you said you've done a bank before?" Darren asked.

"I have," Noah nodded. "And I'm telling you, it's not worth the risk. Trucks are the way to go. Fewer people to deal with, and the payoff is much better than the haul you'd get at a bank."

"You've done trucks before then too?" EJ asked. Again, Noah nodded. "Then what the hell are you still doing working here? Shouldn't you be on a beach somewhere drinking Mai-Tais?"

"We all have our reasons," Noah said ominously. "I don't expect any of you to jump at the idea, but the offer is out there. I've done it before, and I'm still standing here. There are options. I need money too, you guys aren't alone in that. Just think about it, ok? That's all I ask. Think about it."

Without a word, EJ and Darren walked back to their trucks, talking in hushed tones to each other. Noah knew he had nothing to worry about with those two, they wouldn't rat him out or do anything like that. They needed their jobs too much to risk them. Noah turned to Chandler, who had his hands on his hips and was staring at Noah intently.

"I can't believe what I just heard from you," Chandler said.

"Well, what do you want me to say?" Noah asked.

"Why did you do it? The first time."

"I had to," Noah said. "If I didn't, my family probably would've been killed. That's why I did it. I had to."

"And what happened to the others? I'm guessing you didn't do that by yourself," Chandler said, an astute observation.

"They're not here, so what does it matter?" Noah responded. "I'm not forcing you to do anything, Chandler. I'm simply presenting an option. Lyla is sick, and she's not going to get any better without proper help. You look at me right now and tell me you're ready to let her leave this world, knowing you didn't do everything you could save her. Tell me that, and I'll find someone else. Plenty of guys need money nowadays."

Noah saw the reaction on Chandler's face and knew he had him. Lyla was Noah's ace in the hole, and he'd played it perfectly. Did it make him feel warm and fuzzy inside? Absolutely not. He felt like a scumbag for using Lyla as leverage, but he didn't have much of a choice. Chandler Bannington was perfect for the job, and Noah needed him to be a part of the crew. He was smart and loyal, and Noah could trust him; Noah needed that to pull the job off. EJ and Darren were both desperate enough to be stupid, Chandler was desperate enough to be smart. There was an important difference between the two. Chandler could help Noah keep the others under control. Noah saw it the first time around with the last crew he was a part of. Some guys get too desperate and too cocky and take unnecessary risks. The only place that led was six feet in the ground. Noah would do everything in his power to avoid that, for himself and for his guys. They needed to survive. And they needed money. Badly.

"You're a son of a bitch for bringing her up," Chandler muttered. "But you're not wrong..."

"I know I'm not."

"So... What's the job?" Chandler asked. Noah put his hand on Chandler's shoulder and smiled.

****

Pulling into his driveway and turning his truck off, Noah pulled out his phone and re-dialed Brian Tyler's number. Much to Noah's surprise, it didn't appear that Brian would have to do anything extreme to get his crew to go along with the plan. The only thing Brian had to do now was keep up his end of the deal and make sure Thomas Swaney did the same.

"Hey," Brian answered. "How'd Lexi do today?"

"She's going to do just fine," Noah said. "She's a hard worker."

"Glad to hear it. I know, she's a really hard worker. Got that from her mother."

"Tell me about it," Noah said. "Look, I talked to my guys, and shockingly enough, I don't think you'll have to do much. They need money. Badly."

"I mean, that's good to hear, but it also makes me feel like a shitty boss. My guys should be taken care of, not resorting to breaking the law in order to get by."

"Don't feel too bad for EJ or Darren, their problems are their own doing. Chandler needs all the support we can give him, his wife's cancer is a bitch," Noah explained.

"I'm sorry to hear that," Brian said.

"Yeah, we all are. Listen, I got the guys on board. At least, I think I do. Whatever happens, I need you to make sure that you and Thomas hold up your end of the bargain. Whatever I need, I expect you two to handle. Any hardware, equipment, vehicles, anything, you get it for me. I'm the one taking the risk here."

"I know, I know, I'll make sure Thomas honors the arrangement."

"I couldn't give a shit about Thomas, but when this is all done, you and I are going to chat."

"I know, Noah. I'm going to be in your debt."

"All of us will, Brian. I expect the guys to be taken care of."

"And they will be, I promise."

"Good," Noah nodded. "Listen, I'm going to give Joe a call. We're going to need him if we're serious about this."

"You think he'll go for it? He was pretty adamant after the last one that he had no desire to even speak to us again."

"He'll go for it if I'm asking him. I doubt he will if he finds out Thomas is the one calling the shots. I'll make sure that's kept a secret," Noah said.

"Alright, yeah give him a call," Brian agreed. "Joe's the best at what he does."

"Don't have to tell me that, Brian," Noah muttered. "I'm well aware of the man's talents."

7

In addition to its corporate headquarters in Downtown Los Angeles, Omicron LLC owned and operated four different warehouses in the Southern California area. Two in the greater Los Angeles area, one in Riverside, and another in Anaheim. The warehouses were used for storage of equipment, vehicles, dispatching, and a materials yard located at the Riverside location. Of the two in Los Angeles, the one on Jefferson Boulevard was the best for a low profile meeting; it was located right next to a Lutheran Church.

Noah had gotten there early and parked his truck inside the gates, not bothering to lock the gate behind him. As a Foreman, Noah had keys to all four warehouses. He unlocked the side door and set up a folding table inside the shop, between a pair of mid-sized Caterpillar excavators. Spreading out blueprints over the table, Noah began pacing the interior of the warehouse, checking his watch periodically. The last time he'd been to this warehouse on a Saturday morning was right before he'd taken part in the previous heist - a heist that had gone horribly, horribly wrong.

The door to the warehouse opened, and Noah heard heavy footfalls echo as a man entered. He wore a backward baseball hat, glasses, jeans, a pair of Vans sneakers, and a flannel shirt over a black Electrical Workers

Union T-shirt. His blonde hair was long - almost down to his shoulders - and unruly. The permanent smirk on his face was ever-present as he walked closer to Noah.

"As I live and breathe," he said with a smile. "Noah Riordan!"

"What's up, Joe?" Noah asked, holding out his hand. Joe and Noah clapped their hands together and hugged. "Been a long time, my man."

"Hell yeah it has," Joe agreed, patting Noah's shoulder. "I was surprised you called, especially considering how we left things."

"It wasn't our fault," Noah shrugged. "Don't see any reason for there to be hard feelings between us. You're one of my oldest friends."

"Agreed," Joe nodded. "So, what can I do for you? I have to admit, meeting here of all places is a little ominous..."

Noah stuffed his hands in the back pockets of his jeans and looked at Joe, shaking his head. Joe Kado was one of his oldest friends. They'd met in high school and had clicked almost instantly. After realizing that college wasn't for either of them, they both got involved with the trades. While Noah went into the Operators Union, Joe opted for the International Brotherhood of Electrical Workers Local 18. As an Electrical Worker, Joe specialized in everything involving electrical installation, water lines, and power. He worked mainly in Downtown Los Angeles and was extremely familiar with the power grid for the city, knowledge that was priceless to Noah.

"Joe, I'm not going to beat around the bush or lie to you..." Noah said. "I've got a job. Three, actually. And I need your help."

Joe's smile disappeared in a second. He shook his head in disbelief and lowered his gaze to his checkered sneakers. He knew by the way

Noah had phrased 'job' that it wasn't the kind of side work that Joe normally did in his spare time.

"Come on, man," Joe shook his head. "I told you last time, I'm done doing that. I barely walked away with my life, that's not something I'm willing to roll the dice on anymore."

"I know, Joe. I was right there with you," Noah responded. "But I wouldn't be asking if it wasn't absolutely necessary. I need your help."

"Don't do that," Joe groaned. "You're one of my best friends, don't make me say no."

"It's three jobs. Two trucks and one bank. You don't have to do anything other than sit in a truck and be my eye in the sky. I'm not asking you to carry a gun or anything like that. I just need your expertise so I don't get killed."

"I suppose it'd be pointless for me to tell you that this is crazy and complete suicide?"

"Yeah, unfortunately," Noah said with a smirk.

"Can I ask why? Don't you still have some cash leftover from the last time?" Joe asked.

"I do, but this isn't necessarily for me," Noah admitted. "The guys on my crew are struggling. Badly."

"Damn," Joe said quietly. "That sucks, I've been there. But there's got to be a better option that doesn't involve risking your life again, Noah. I don't want to see you dead or locked up for the rest of your life."

"That's not going to happen," Noah shook his head. "We did it before, and we're both still standing here."

"Barely," Joe scoffed. "And what about Jake or Cooper or Miles? Where are they? They're dead, Noah. Dead. And what for? A few hundred thousand dollars? It's not worth it."

"How about half a billion?" Noah asked flatly.

"Half a billion?" Joe gaped. Noah nodded, keeping his face neutral. "Where on earth are you going to steal half a billion?"

"I told you. Two trucks and a bank."

"Trucks don't carry anywhere near that amount of money, and neither do the banks. Not anymore."

"End of shift, after a day of pick-ups, filled to capacity, an armored truck can have anywhere from 500 to 600 mil on it," Noah explained. "The two trucks I want to hit *will* be loaded to capacity."

"Well, then that raises an entirely new problem," Joe said, putting his hands on his hips. "How are you and a couple of guys going to move that much money? The answer is, you can't. Not without attracting a ton of attention."

"Joe, you let me worry about that," Noah answered. "I have a plan, trust me. I just need you to get a tap on the police, that's it. You're the only guy I trust with that. I promise I will handle everything else."

"Fuck me," Joe grunted. "Fine, I'll help you."

Noah smiled and stuck his hand out. Joe laughed, shook his head, and gave Noah the middle finger. The two laughed and brought it in for a 'bro-hug'. Noah breathed a sigh of relief. The last time they had gone down this road, Joe had been absolutely critical in the success of their first couple of heists. He wouldn't dare consider doing another series of jobs without help from Joe Kado.

"I will make sure you are compensated for your services," Noah said. Joe waved off the comment.

"I know, don't worry about it. We can talk about all that crap later. But, from here on out, I want to be included in whatever planning sessions you're having. I need to know details, plans, routes, everything."

“Well, you're in luck,” Noah clapped Joe on the shoulder. “The rest of the guys will be here in a few minutes.”

****

After everyone got acquainted, Noah called the first meeting with his new crew to order. Standing at the head of the table, Noah looked around at Joe, EJ, Darren, and Chandler. He couldn’t help but think back to the first meeting he’d been a part of, listening to his old boss - Jake Tell - brief the crew on their first heist. Jake had been a great boss and mentor to Noah; he’d always respected and looked up to the man. Similar to how Noah had been recruited by the men he reported to, Jake had found himself at the mercy of Thomas Swaney. Noah, desperate to earn the approval of his superiors, had agreed to help with the heists. The promise of an insane amount of money didn’t hurt either; Noah had hoped his haul would be enough to retire young, but he couldn’t have been more wrong.

“Gentlemen,” Noah said, folding his arms across his chest. “From here on, everything you hear should be considered beyond top secret. There is a circle of trust amongst us. I’m not going to lie to any of you, we’re about to enter uncharted territories. What I am proposing to you all is both highly illegal and highly dangerous. The risk is great, but the reward is life-changing. That is a decision you all have had to weigh in your heads. No one can make that decision for you. You’re all sitting here because you’ve made up your mind. But, there is still a chance if you want out. If anyone has second thoughts, stand up, and walk yourself out. There will be no hard feelings.”

Noah paused and looked around, specifically at Chandler. He was the only one Noah thought might've considered leaving. All Chandler did was adjust his Los Angeles Dodgers baseball hat and lean back in his chair, clearly not going anywhere. No one else made any motion to get up and Joe - standing at the back of the group, leaning against a bulldozer - nodded in approval.

"Good," Noah said, a small smile on his face. "Going forward, we're gonna get a lot closer with one another. This only works if we all have absolute trust and faith in one another. I know you guys have not met Joe prior to this, but I vouch for the man, and that is all you need to consider. We all have our reasons for wanting to do this. Those are yours and yours alone. Is that clear?"

"Yes boss," the three men echoed in almost perfect unison.

"Joe, why don't you come help me brief them," Noah said, waving Joe to the front of the table. Reluctantly, Joe pushed away from the dozer and walked up next to Noah.

"We're not going to have to do a bunch of icebreakers, right?" Joe asked. "I hated that crap in high school."

The comment got a laugh from the guys.

"No, no kumbaya shit," Noah answered seriously. He picked up three black binders and set them on the table. "Over the course of four weeks, we're going to hit three different targets. Two armored trucks and one bank to finish it off, roughly nine or ten days between each job. In each of these binders, I have a collection of information that'll be crucial to pulling these off to perfection."

"Can I ask where you got all this information from?" EJ asked. Noah caught Joe's gaze; clearly, he'd been wondering the same thing. There was no way anyone could find out that Thomas Swaney had provided Noah with all of the information, especially Joe.

"You guys don't have to worry about that," Noah reassured them. "But trust me when I say that it's solid."

"Alright," EJ muttered, shifting in his seat.

"Joe and I are the only ones who have done this before, so the rest of you will need to get up to speed very quickly. For this to work, we need to work as a team, as a unit. We're going to train, we're going to practice, and we're going to make damn sure we know what we're doing before we go out there. Understood?"

"Yes, boss," Chandler nodded, looking oddly calm for a man who was in his situation. EJ and Darren were in agreement.

"Does anyone have any experience with firearms? Range shooting, hunting, anything like that?" Noah asked.

As expected, the three men raised their hands or nodded in the affirmative. He knew it was kind of a silly question. Most of the guys who worked for Omicron were known to have their Concealed Carry Licenses. Working out of the Los Angeles area meant sometimes working in extremely hostile neighborhoods. Carrying a gun was a necessity at that point. Noah had even kept a pistol in one of the excavators while doing an extended job in Skid Row - notoriously one of the most dangerous neighborhoods in the country.

"That's good. None of us are going to be using our personal guns, I'll handle getting the hardware. The guns are just a tool, ok? I don't want anyone killing or shooting anyone. If we get jammed up with the cops or something like that, shoot for their cars, no one needs to get hurt. Keep that in mind, these are regular people, just like us. They have families and kids of their own. They are not our enemy, just an obstacle."

Noah remembered hearing a similar speech from Jake Tell before their first heist. It was an important message that everyone needed to be 100% clear on. They were not murderers. Looking around the room, Noah could tell his message had been received.

"Alright. It goes without saying that you do not mention, speak of, or insinuate anything related to this. No texting or anything either. I'm gonna get my hands on some burner phones for us to communicate with. Other than that, go about your daily lives as usual. The circle of trust is real, do not make me regret trusting you guys. We're going to meet again in a few days once I get my hands on some hardware."

After a few more minutes of talking and answering questions, the guys got up and headed out of the warehouse, leaving Noah and Joe behind. Noah handed three binders to Joe, who started flipping through them and reading the various reports, delivery schedules, and routes.

"You really think there will be that much money on these trucks?" Joe asked.

"Would I be doing this if I thought otherwise?" Noah answered the question with a question.

"I don't know, man. I truly don't know," Joe said, snapping the binders shut. "I wonder what Jake would think if he could see us now."

"He'd wonder why we weren't going for four or five trucks," Noah said with a grin. Joe laughed and nodded in agreement.

"I miss that guy," he admitted. "Jake deserved better."

"They all did," Noah muttered.

"Do you ever feel guilty about it?" Joe asked, looking at Noah seriously. Noah cocked his head slightly.

"What do you mean?"

"I mean, we were the only ones who walked away last time. Miles and Cooper both had families. Jake... was about to be a father. You and I don't have that same kind of responsibility."

"We all have responsibilities, Joe," Noah said in a low voice. He said it a little more confrontationally than he intended, but Noah felt like the weight of the world was on his shoulders. Joe just couldn't understand that. "But yeah, sometimes I do."

"I don't want that to happen again," Joe shook his head and got quiet. "I've got a girl this time. I've got something on the horizon, I don't want to lose it."

"You're not going to," Noah responded. "If anything, you are setting yourself up for the best possible future. Same as the other guys, same as me."

"I hope you're right," Joe whispered.

****

As had become somewhat of a ritual for them, Noah Riordan and Tayler Palmer walked into Lucky's together and sat at the same booth in the back of the restaurant they had sat at so many times before. After ordering their drinks, they finally relaxed and began debriefing one another on the most recent happenings in their lives. There were times when Noah wanted to be honest with just one person. He wanted to tell someone what he was really up to, just to unburden himself from having to keep such a large secret. But who could understand? Who could understand that the labor union he was employed through was a modern-day mob and was involved in more criminal activity than Noah cared to think about? Tayler was the best, but even Noah doubted she'd be understanding if Noah told her he was planning to rob two armored trucks and a bank. More importantly, Noah could not risk telling Tayler anything about what he was planning. He wasn't about to put her in danger, and if she knew anything about what was really going on, she'd be a target that Thomas Swaney could exploit. There were just some things that were better kept to yourself, even if it made you sick to your stomach to bottle it all up.

"Your face is looking better," Tayler commented. "Or maybe you're just actually smiling tonight."

"I'm always smiling," Noah smiled overdramatically and rolled his eyes.

"Noah, I love you, but you're one of the crabbiest people I know," Tayler said honestly. Noah just shrugged; she wasn't wrong.

"Alright, you want to go first, or should I?" Noah asked. Tayler gestured with her hands for Noah to proceed.

"Well, I met a girl," Noah began, getting a big smile from Tayler.

"Oh really?" she asked. "Tell me everything."

Noah recalled the entire story to Tayler. Seeing Jessica and her boyfriend arguing, the ensuing fight, teaching her to operate an excavator, her asking for Noah's number, and the several texts they had exchanged since then. He watched Tayler's reactions carefully, trying to pick up on any subtle hints of doubt. For the most part, she maintained a pretty neutral expression - which Noah couldn't even pretend to try and read. He finished up his story just as the waiter put their drinks in front of them - two Long Island Ice Teas.

"Well, sounds like you've been pretty busy," Tayler commented. Noah shrugged and took a sip of his drink. "I have to ask, just because I know you, but doesn't this already kind of remind you of Paris?"

"What do you mean?" Noah asked.

"I mean you were always coming to the rescue with Paris. And you don't even know this girl, and you've already had to save her."

"Well, what was I supposed to do?"

"I think you did the right thing, obviously, but you already set a precedent and you don't even realize it," Tayler observed. "With Paris, all you did was be her knight in shining armor. She used you, Noah. And I know you know that."

"I'm not arguing that," Noah agreed. "But I don't even know this girl, we haven't even gone out yet."

"I know, I know, and I may be totally wrong," Tayler admitted. "But still, just once, I would love to see you be with someone who doesn't *need* you, but someone who *wants* you. Does that make any sense?"

"Yeah, it makes sense," Noah muttered. As much as he wanted to, there was no disagreeing with Tayler. She had had a perfect record in terms of predicting the future when it came to Noah's personal life. Most of the time, Noah figured he'd have better luck if he just let Tayler make any and all decisions in regard to his personal life. "I'm going to try and take her out, though. Guess we'll go from there?"

"I think you should, that's not what I'm saying," Tayler corrected. "I just think you should be aware that you definitely seem to attract a type of girl that needs a lot of rescuing. Sometimes, it's nice to not have to be a knight in shining armor and just be yourself."

"I know, I know," Noah said with a smile. "You're always right, you know you are."

"Well, as long as we've got that established," Tayler laughed. "As a matter of fact, I've got a date coming up too."

"Really?" Noah asked, suddenly very interested. It had been a while since the last time Tayler had a date to tell him about. By nature, she was quite private about her personal life, which Noah knew and understood. He never pried too much into it. "Tell me everything."

Tayler took a big sip of her drink and began telling Noah about another teacher at her school that had asked her out. His name was Reed Mattson, and he was a year older than her and Noah. He was recently divorced, had a young daughter, and taught history. According to Tayler, there had been some flirtatious dialogue for a while now, but nothing had ever come of it. Earlier that day, while in the teacher lounge, he'd approached her and invited her to a movie with him for the weekend. They were set to go out that Friday night after work. Tayler was clearly excited about it, Noah could tell just from the fact that she kept smiling as she told him about it. If anyone deserved to be happy, it was Tayler. Noah was glad that this Reed guy sounded like a genuinely nice guy, and the fact that Tayler was excited about going out with him was enough for him.

"Tayler, that's so awesome!" Noah said. "I hope you have a great time, he sounds like a good guy,"

"Thank you!" Tayler responded. "Yeah, I'm super excited. He's so sweet and very cute and yeah, I'm excited."

"You better tell me how it goes," Noah said. "If I need to scare this guy, just let me know. I'm free Friday."

"Oh my god," Tayler rolled her eyes. "I appreciate it though, you're like the brother I never had."

"And you're the sister I never had," Noah said, holding up his drink.

Tayler clinked her glass against Noah's and smiled at him. They ordered a few minutes later and enjoyed each other's company for the rest of the evening. Whenever he was with Tayler, Noah couldn't help but feel a million times more relaxed and calm. She was his confidant and one of his best friends. He knew he never had to worry about her judging him and vice-versa. Noah couldn't imagine a day without having Tayler as a friend. She was one of a kind, and Noah depended on her more than she'd ever understand. As usual, they split the bill, said their goodbyes, and headed on their separate ways. Once he was back in his truck, Noah checked his phone for the first time since he'd sat down with Tayler. He had several notifications, but the one that stood out was a missed call from Jessica. Turning his truck on, Noah redialed and put the phone to his ear.

"Hello?" Jessica answered a few rings later. The background sounded noisy, Noah guessed she must've still been at The Lamp.

"Hey, it's Noah. I saw you called..."

"Hey!" Jessica said. "Yeah, I was wondering if you were doing anything tomorrow night?"

"No plans. Why?"

"I'm off from the bar. Would you like to have a drink with me or something?"

"You know..." Noah said, blushing a little bit. "That sounds wonderful."

"Yay. How about 6:30 at 901?" Jessica suggested.

"That sounds perfect, I'll see you there," Noah agreed. He hung up and immediately called Tayler.

"Miss me already?" Tayler answered.

"What do I wear on a first date?" Noah blurted out.

****

Located right on the corner of 29th and Figueroa, 901 Bar and Grill was a much more relaxing environment compared to some of the other venues offered in Los Angeles. Extremely popular with the college community, Noah had first started going there when he attended the University of Southern California - 901 was a quick ten-minute walk from campus. Plus, it was relatively cheap and offered plenty of low-budget drinks and food to increase its popularity with the student body. Fortunately, it was pretty empty for a weeknight.

Noah hadn't been on a first date in so long. Because of that, he wasn't surprised that he was nervous. Tayler had coached him the night before during an hour-long FaceTime call in which she helped pick out his outfit for the night - a gray button-down, dark jeans, and a pair of leather boots. He had gotten there early on purpose, hoping to calm his nerves with a drink before Jessica arrived. Sitting at the far end of the bar, Noah could see the front door perfectly. He'd ordered a Johnnie Walker Black Label and waited. The drink calmed his anxiety a little bit.

It was funny how everything always seemed to happen all at once and without warning. Within a matter of weeks, Noah had gone from being ready to propose to sitting at a bar waiting for a woman he barely knew to arrive. Simultaneously, he was planning one of the most dangerous and illegal activities someone could attempt. The first job was set to take place in a week, which did not give Noah nearly as much time as he'd hoped to get the guys up to speed. They had spent a fair amount of time training at the gun range, and Noah was impressed that they all seemed to be fairly accurate. At least accurate enough that he felt comfortable with them by his side. Truth be told, no amount of training could prepare them for the real thing. There were so many variables and unknowns that could occur during the actual heist that Noah felt it somewhat pointless to even try to train them. But for his own sanity, the shooting drills and flanking formations he'd taught them would most likely come in handy. Noah always felt like he had a lot on his plate with work, but he'd have taken the daily stresses over what he was currently dealing with in a heartbeat. That was nothing compared to this.

Noah checked his phone and realized he'd been sitting at the bar by himself for over a half-hour. His mind had been wandering so much he hadn't even noticed the time going by. Jessica was late, which made him a little more anxious. Unfortunately, Noah was quite familiar with getting stood up on dates; Paris had been a professional at the art of standing him up. He thought about texting Jessica but decided against it. At this point, there was nothing he could do. She'd either show up, or she wouldn't.

"You want to order some food?" the bartender asked. He was younger than Noah, probably a senior at USC, if Noah had to guess.

"In a little bit, I'm waiting for someone," Noah said, hoping that last part was actually true. The bartender gave Noah a thumbs-up and went to tend to the other patrons seated around the bar. Noah sipped his whiskey and checked his phone again - still nothing from Jessica. Shaking his head, Noah stuck his phone back in his pocket and flagged the bartender down. "Can I get another drink?"

"Of course," he said. "What time was she supposed to be here?"

"What do you mean?" Noah asked, the question catching him off guard a little. The bartender chuckled.

"Do you have any idea how many guys I see get stood up on a weekly basis?" he asked.

"Fair enough," Noah muttered. "Supposed to be here at 6:30,"

"If she doesn't show by 7, your drinks and food are on us," the bartender said. "It's our policy."

"Who's idea was that?"

"Mine," the bartender said with a grin. He refilled Noah's glass with Johnnie Walker and slid the glass back toward him.

Almost as if on cue, Noah looked over toward the front door and saw Jessica walking in. He felt a massive sense of relief and smiled. Jessica spoke to the hostess for a brief moment before looking over to Noah and smiling brightly; she waved at him and walked over to the bar, sliding into the seat next to Noah. She was wearing a black knit sweater, blue jeans, and a pair of Vans. She'd straightened her blonde hair and had part of it falling across the right side of her face.

"I am so sorry!" Jessica said, wrapping her jacket and purse around the back of the chair. "My Uber took forever, I was waiting for like twenty minutes."

"Hey, no worries," Noah shrugged. "I'm just glad you're here, I was getting nervous for a minute."

"I'm so sorry, I should've texted you," Jessica admitted. "Just had a crazy day."

"Well, let's get you a drink, and then you can tell me all about it," Noah once again flagged down the bartender. He came over and gave Noah a subtle nod.

"What can I get for you, ma'am?" he asked.

"I'd love a Blue Moon, please and thank you," Jessica requested. The bartender nodded and fetched a tall Pilsner glass for the beer. He filled it to the top and popped an orange slice on the rim before setting the glass on a coaster and giving it to Jessica.

"You guys want to put in any food?" he asked.

"Few minutes would be great," Noah answered. Jessica nodded in agreement.

"Alright, just let me know," he said.

Noah held up his drink toward Jessica, and she tapped her beer glass against his. She smiled at him shyly before taking a sip.

"I'm sorry if I'm a little weird, I never do stuff like this," Jessica said. Noah raised an eyebrow.

"What do you mean?" he asked.

"Go on dates with people I barely know," Jessica responded. "It's just not something I normally do."

"So why are you here with me then?" Noah asked with a grin. She blushed.

"I just had a good feeling about you."

"And I'm sure that had nothing to do with me swinging a torque wrench on that asshole."

"Not as much as you'd think," Jessica winked. "Thank you for that, though. I was so shocked, he's never laid his hands on me like that before."

"Anyone who puts his hands on a woman is garbage," Noah shrugged. "End of story. No need to thank me."

"Well, it meant a lot to me," Jessica touched Noah's hand. Noah smiled at her.

"So, tell me everything there is to know about you."

"I mean, there's not much to tell. I feel like I'm super boring."

"Try me."

"Well, I graduated from UCLA with a degree in psychology. I just took my exams to be a counselor, and I passed, so I'm super excited about that."

"A counselor, huh?"

"Yeah, yeah, I want to be a clinical therapist. I'm hoping to go back to school once I've saved up enough money. That's kind of why I'm working at Lamp right now."

"That's so cool. Being a therapist has to be one of the most rewarding jobs in the world. I know I could never do that."

"I'm hoping. It's what I've wanted to do for a while now. I'm just ready to get my life moving on. Like, I'm still living with my parents and at their mercy, and it's just exhausting sometimes."

"Can't relate, man," Noah smiled. "I moved out as soon as I could."

"Lucky!" Jessica exclaimed, taking a sip of her Blue Moon.

"Yeah," Noah muttered, looking away as he drank his whiskey.

He didn't think it appropriate for a first-date conversation to tell her about his unique upbringing. In fact, Noah had never mentioned his father or brother to anyone other than his mom. And even then, they rarely spoke about them. Noah did, however, talk about his mom quite a bit. He told Jessica all about her, his grandpa Ron, and of course, Ivy. She asked questions about his job and seemed genuinely interested in what he did for a living after he showed her several pictures on his phone from various stages of the 101 job. He didn't go into too much detail for fear of boring her, but she asked more questions, and he answered them.

The conversation eventually shifted to more trivial things. What movies they enjoyed, the music they listened to, and podcasts they never missed. Noah felt himself feeling more and more comfortable being around Jessica with each passing minute. Unless he'd severely misread the entire situation, there seemed to be a connection between them - Noah could feel it. Granted, he hadn't been the best judge of that sort of thing in the past, especially with Paris. But sitting and talking to Jessica just felt normal. It felt comfortable, and it felt, in a word, nice.

"So, I have to ask," Jessica began, taking a sip of a freshly poured Blue Moon. "Are you currently seeing anyone? Talking to anyone?"

"Aside from you, nope," Noah said honestly. Jessica smiled inwardly and looked at her Vans.

"I just have to ask, you never know anymore," Jessica said. "I wouldn't care right now, but I was just wondering."

"How about you?" Noah asked.

"No, I broke up with Duke, like I told you," Jessica shook her head and rolled her eyes. "I can't believe it took me so long."

"Hard to be objective when you're in the relationship," Noah said. "Speaking from experience."

"Yeah?"

"Oh, yeah," Noah nodded. "I've only dated one other woman seriously, but it's been on and off for years. After a while, you get sick of the inconsistency. Plus, she just wasn't a good person at the end of the day."

"I understand that. I've got a few exes, only on good terms with one of them. The others I hope I never see again," Jessica said. "Relationships are just so hard nowadays."

"Only as hard as you make them," Noah responded. "I don't know, maybe that's the hopeless romantic in me."

"Can I ask you something?"

"Of course."

"What happened to your eye?" Jessica wondered, gesturing to the scar on Noah's eye. It was definitely healing but still extremely noticeable. Noah had gotten so used to it that he barely thought about it anymore. Instinctively, his hand went up to cover the scar. He looked away, more embarrassed than anything.

"I'm sorry, I shouldn't have asked," Jessica immediately spoke up, touching his arm softly.

"It's fine," Noah muttered. "How could you not? It's not like I was trying to hide it."

"You don't have to tell me," Jessica said. "It's not a big deal, I was just curious."

"That is from my ex," Noah sighed and folded his arms on the bartop, looking at Jessica and forcing a smile. Jessica's face warped into a combined expression of shock and horror.

"Are you serious?" she asked quietly. Noah nodded.

"Not something I really want to get into right now," he admitted.

"Of course not, I'm so sorry I had no idea."

"Don't worry about it," Noah said with a smile. Jessica nodded and rolled up her sweater sleeve. She had a nasty-looking scar on her bicep.

"This is from my ex before Duke," she whispered.

Noah leaned forward a little bit to look at the scar, which had clearly been inflicted by a knife or sharp object. He winced. It looked like it had to have been painful.

"My God," he muttered. Jessica put her sleeve down and smiled sadly.

"Guess we have a few things in common."

"Cheers to moving on," Noah held his glass towards Jessica.

The bartender came back over to them, pulling out his notepad and pen.

"Would you guys like to order dinner? The kitchen is about to close," he said. Noah looked at his phone and smiled. He and Jessica sat at the bar talking for almost three hours.

"I'd love some food, how about you?" Jessica answered.

"Food sounds great," Noah said, smiling at Jessica.

****

Noah held the door open for Jessica as they stepped out of 901 and onto the sidewalk. The night had been a lot more fun than Noah had hoped for. The only other first date he'd ever been on had been with Paris, so he had virtually nothing to compare it to. But, Noah felt genuinely happy, less stressed, and actually excited to see her again. He turned to her and smiled. Jessica had her phone out and was busy calling herself an Uber.

"I can give you a ride home if you want," Noah offered. "My truck isn't too far."

"Thank you so much, but I'm meeting up with some friends after this," Jessica said. "Don't want you driving out of the way for me."

"No worries, just wanted to offer," Noah shrugged.

"My ride will be here in like two minutes," Jessica said, slipping her phone into her back pocket. She looked up and smiled at Noah. "I had a really good time tonight."

"Yeah, so did I," Noah agreed. "Best first date I've ever been on."

"Oh, stop it," Jessica said, shoving his shoulder playfully.

"No, I'm serious," Noah said. "It was really great. I'm hoping there can be a second date..."

"Well... Me too," Jessica blushed.

A gray SUV pulled up alongside the curb; the Uber sticker was on the windshield. Jessica double-checked her phone to make sure it was the right one.

"Alright, that's me," Jessica said. "Thank you again for a great night,"
"Of course," Noah smiled. "Have fun tonight."

Noah leaned forward and hugged Jessica quickly. Not wanting to make her uncomfortable by holding her for too long, Noah pulled away quickly. Without a word, Jessica reached up, grabbed Noah's collar, and pulled him toward her. She kissed him passionately, slipping her tongue in his mouth as soon as Noah relaxed from the initial shock. Noah threw his hands around Jessica's waist and kissed her back, any thought he was having completely gone from his brain.

Jessica pulled away and gave Noah a quick hug before hurrying to the Uber; she climbed in the backseat, and a few moments later, she was gone. Noah stood on the sidewalk, still a little shocked. He knew he was blushing like crazy.

"Holy shit," he muttered, smiling widely.

****

Noah was still smiling by the time he got home to his house. He got Ivy's leash and collar and headed out with his companion, knowing she needed a walk just as much as he did. The long hours he'd been working had prevented him from taking her to the park or forest preserve where she normally got most of her exercise. Keeping a quick pace through the neighborhood, Noah pulled out his phone and dialed before putting the phone to his ear.

"Hey, what's up?" Brian Tyler answered almost immediately.

"The guys are going to be ready to go. Joe's on board. I need you to secure me some hardware. As fast as possible," Noah said, keeping his voice low, so it didn't carry in the night.

"You got it," Brian responded. "What do you need?"

"Armor, pistols, rifles, the works. Everything we had last time, I need it again," Noah listed off.

"Done," Brian said. "Come by the ranch on Saturday, and I'll have it all ready for you."

"See you then," Noah hung up and stuffed the phone in his pocket.

Ivy looked up at him, her tongue hanging out of her mouth with each pant. Her eyes, big and black, were filled with curiosity, almost as if she knew something was going on.

"Come on, Ivy," Noah encouraged, turning down his street to head home. "Let's go get some water."

Ivy barked excitedly, and they started jogging towards the house.

8

Dust kicked up all around Noah's truck as he drove down the long, winding gravel driveway. On either side of the driveway were massive pastures and corrals for horses. The ranch was almost a hundred acres of land, complete with a barn and large farmhouse right at the center. The barn had a small corral right outside where the horses were free to roam throughout the day. As he approached the house, Noah saw a horse running around in the corral. It was a beautiful brown horse - he had no idea what kind of horse it was though. He'd never been interested in horses as pets. They seemed like way too much work for a companion you couldn't snuggle up on the couch with.

Parking in front of the house, Noah climbed out of his truck and texted Brian Tyler to let him know he had arrived. Noah pulled on his Omicron baseball hat and walked toward the corral, curious to see the horse. As he got closer, he noticed Lexi Tyler in the corral, talking to the horse as it ran laps around her. She was wearing a pair of brown Ariat boots, light jeans, and a flannel shirt that she tied into a crop top, exposing her belly. Her blonde hair was contained under a wide-brimmed cowboy hat. Had Noah not seen her before, he'd have assumed she was a cowgirl right out of a Western movie.

"Hey!" Noah called, putting his right foot up on one of the horizontal fence posts. Lexi turned and squinted before smiling and waving. She walked over toward him. The horse came to a stop and watched Lexi intently.

"Hey!" Lexi said, folding her arms over the fence. "What are you doing here?"

"Eh, your dad asked me to pick up some tools," Noah lied, but only slightly. Technically speaking, he wasn't lying. "Got a few jobs coming up we're gonna need some special equipment for."

"Will I be working on those?" Lexi asked, pushing her hat up on her head slightly.

"We'll see, I guess, won't we?" Noah couldn't help but laugh. He decided to change the subject. "So, that's your horse?"

"Yep," Lexi said proudly. "That's my baby, Tucker. My dad got him for me for my twelfth birthday. I showed him a few times. We were a pretty good team."

"Looks like you got him trained pretty well," Noah said, nodding toward the animal. Lexi turned to look at Tucker and grinned.

"Yeah, he's a good boy," she nodded. "Have you ever ridden before?"

"Hell no!" Noah blurted. Lexi laughed loudly.

"Why so passionate?" she asked. Noah shrugged.

"I don't know. Horses kind of freak me out, I guess," Noah admitted. "Never felt comfortable getting so close to an animal that could trample me."

"Oh, come on," Lexi gestured for Noah to follow her. "There's nothing to be afraid of."

"I'm good, thanks," Noah didn't budge. Lexi put her hands on her hips and pouted her lip.

"Come on."

"Nope."

"Please!"

"No, thank you!" Noah shook his head, laughing at Lexi's persistence. Lexi shook her head and looked up at the sky.

"I never took you as someone who got scared off by anything," Lexi commented. Noah narrowed his eyes; she'd found his weakness. He was steadfast in his decisions unless someone challenged him or his bravery. It was all about maintaining his pride, and it definitely was his weakness; he recognized it and accepted it.

"Oh, come on," Noah groaned. "Please don't do that to me."

"Quit being a girly bitch and come ride the damn horse," Lexi said.

"Ugh, fine."

Sighing dramatically, Noah climbed over the fence and dropped into the sand. He could already feel his heart starting to beat a little bit faster as he and Lexi approached the horse. Lexi looked utterly delighted with herself, clearly enjoying how uncomfortable Noah was.

"I still need to meet with your dad," Noah grumbled. "I don't want to wake up paralyzed in a hospital."

"Calm down," Lexi rolled her eyes. She approached the horse and put her hand on his nose, petting him gently. Tucker snorted in approval. He already had a saddle on his back. "You'll be fine. Tucker's a good horse."

"Yeah, for you maybe," Noah countered, actually scared to climb atop the animal. "Look, how about I just watch? I don't need to ride him."

"Shut up and get on," Lexi said, flashing a smile at Noah to let him know she was only partially kidding. "Alright, put your right foot here in the stirrup and then haul yourself up and over. Got it?"

"I swear if something happens..."

"Nothing is going to happen!" Lexi reassured him. She grabbed hold of the reins. "I'll be right here."

Wiping his sweaty hands on his jeans, Noah slowly put his foot in the stirrup and pulled himself on top of the horse as gently as he could. Surprisingly, the horse didn't so much as twitch as Noah got situated on his back. Finally, after getting comfortable, Noah let out his breath. Lexi gave him a golf clap and bowed her head.

"Very funny," Noah rolled his eyes. "Can I be done now?"

"Not so fast," Lexi said. She clicked her tongue a few times. "Come on, Tuck."

With the reins in her hand, Lexi began guiding Tucker around the corral slowly. Noah held on for dear life as the horse picked up his pace to a gentle jog. Lexi couldn't help but laugh seeing Noah's look of total panic.

"See? It's not so bad," Lexi said, turning Tucker around and walking him in the opposite direction. Noah's teeth were clenched, and his fists were white-knuckled around the reins. He didn't even acknowledge Lexi's comment. He was too focused on not falling off and getting trampled to death.

After about five minutes of jogging around the corral, Noah gradually relaxed. He loosened his grip on the reins and felt more at ease. In all honesty, he could understand why so many people enjoyed riding. Noah didn't judge those people or think they were crazy. Riding horses was just not his thing. Robbing an armored truck in broad daylight was the kind of activity that Noah would rather spend his time doing.

"Alright, alright, you can be done now," Lexi laughed, noticing that Tucker seemed to be getting tired. "You did good, I'm very proud."

"Wow, thanks," Noah muttered, climbing off the horse as fast as he could. He gave Tucker a couple of gentle pats before putting distance between himself and the animal. Noah pulled his phone out and saw a text from Brian, letting him know he'd be back to the ranch shortly.

"He should be back soon," Lexi called, reading Noah's mind. "Sorry you had to wait."

"Oh, come on, are you kidding? I got to face my fears," Noah answered, pointing to the horse.

"That's worth something!" Lexi smiled. "I'm gonna go put Tucker in the barn, I'll be back in a few minutes."

"No worries," Noah waved. He climbed back over the fence and walked back to his truck, wiping his hands off on a dirt-stained rag he had.

Lexi Tyler came out of the barn a few minutes later, pieces of hay stuck to her jeans. She was carrying two beers in her left hand and two lawn chairs in her right. Noah jogged over to her and grabbed the lawn chairs from her.

"What a gentleman," she said sarcastically. Noah laughed.

"You give me a lot of shit for someone who wants me to train them," Noah observed.

"It's part of my job," Lexi said. "Gotta keep you on your toes,"

"Uh-huh. Where are we going with these?"

"Right here," Lexi stopped in front of the corral.

Noah set up the two chairs facing the driveway and sat down; Lexi dropped into the chair next to him and tossed him a beer. He was just about to pop the cap off when he saw Brian Tyler's truck come rumbling down the driveway. Standing up, Noah handed the beer back to Lexi.

"Sorry," he muttered. "Rain check?"

"Sure," Lexi said quietly. Noah almost detected a hint of disappointment.

Brian climbed down from his pickup truck and walked over to Noah and Lexi. He gave Lexi a hug and kissed the top of her head before shaking Noah's hand.

"Sorry I'm late," Brian said. "Had to get some of the extra tools you're gonna need."

"No problem," Noah nodded. Brian turned to Lexi and smiled.

"I'm gonna talk to Noah inside for a few minutes," he said. "How's Tucker doing today?"

"He's perfect," Lexi said, winking at Noah. She spun around and headed back to the barn.

"Come on, let's go inside," Brian said to Noah, leading the way back to the farmhouse. Noah followed close behind, hurrying inside as Brian held the door open for him.

The inside of the farmhouse was absolutely gorgeous. It looked like a log cabin and was decorated with hunting trophies, rustic memorabilia, and other knick-knacks to make it look like it was right out of an old-fashioned movie. Brian opened a sliding door to his personal office and ushered Noah inside. They sat down opposite each other in comfortable leather lounge chairs.

"Lexi loves working with you guys," Brian said, crossing his legs. "I've never seen her so happy."

"Glad to hear it," Noah smiled. "She's a hard worker, I like having her on the crew."

"She likes you, you know," Brian continued, giving Noah a mischievous grin.

"Excuse me?" Noah asked, furrowing his brow. Brain chuckled and ran his hands through his hair.

"She likes you, Noah," Brian repeated. "She'd kill me if I told you this, but every time she talks about you, she lights up. Last time she did that was with her old boyfriend, and I honestly thought they were going to get married. She had pretty much sworn off men after that, but the way she talks about you..."

That caught Noah off guard. He didn't really know how to respond to that information, and he couldn't understand why Brian would be telling him that. Brian seemed to pick up on the fact that Noah didn't know what to say and quickly changed the subject.

"Anyway, I've got everything you asked for and more. It's all in the bed of my truck, I'll give you a hand putting it in yours."

"Good. And I appreciate it," Noah nodded. "Few days until the first job..."

"I know. How are you feeling about it?"

"How the hell should I be feeling?" Noah retorted. "I've got a fifty-fifty chance I come back from it alive."

"Yeah," Brian muttered. "I wish there was another way."

"No, you don't," Noah responded. "Don't pretend, Brian. You guys get all of the rewards and none of the risk. It's the perfect deal for you."

"They didn't use to be like that, you know," Brian said. "Thomas and Larry were good guys. Stan's always kind of been a menace, though."

"Does it even matter?" Noah asked. "You're still in bed with them."

"I guess I am," Brain shrugged. "But everything I do, good or bad, is for Lexi. I want her to have the life she deserves. It's been hard on us both since her mother passed..."

"I can respect that," Noah admitted.

"Be careful, Noah," Brian said. "I really do not want to have to go to your funeral."

"Well, Brian," Noah sighed, standing up. "That makes two of us."

****

Joe Kado had already opened the gates to the warehouse off of Jefferson Boulevard by the time Noah pulled up. He spun the truck around and backed his truck into the warehouse; Joe closed the gates and locked them as soon as Noah was through. Once the truck was inside the warehouse, Joe reached up and pulled the large door down, kicking the bolt across the locking mechanism. Noah shut the truck off and hopped out.

"How'd that go?" Joe asked, hurrying over to the back of the truck.

"Just fantastic," Noah grumbled, jumping up into the bed of his truck. "I rode a horse."

"You what?" Joe asked, completely confused.

"Don't ask," Noah shook his head. He grabbed hold of one of the large gun cases. "Here, gimme a hand with all of this shit."

"Where do you want it?" Joe asked, heaving a duffle bag over his back.

"Put it all in that back office. Once we get everything in there, I want to inventory everything and make a list. We need to keep track of every single piece of equipment. None of this can come back to Omicron."

It took Noah and Joe every bit of ten minutes to move everything from the bed into the back office; Noah actually broke a sweat. Joe fetched two bottles of water from the fridge in the kitchen and tossed one to Noah. After taking a quick water break, Noah grabbed a notebook and pen before he and Joe went to work making a log of every single piece of hardware and equipment. It was painstaking work and incredibly boring, but it had to be done. One of the many things he had learned from Jake Tell - always know what you have. Jake had been a born thief disguised as a construction worker. It had come so naturally to him.

Close to an hour later, Noah tossed the notebook on the table, satisfied that he'd accounted for everything in the office. He sighed heavily and sat down in one of the office chairs.

"What's all here?" Joe asked, sitting down in the only other chair in the office. Noah picked up the notebook and began reading off items.

"A dozen AR-style rifles, two dozen pistols, fifty spare magazines for the guns, more ammo than I'd care to admit, half a dozen ballistic vests, eight tactical vests, ten smoke grenades, eleven concussion grenades, five gas masks, fifteen pairs of gloves-"

"Ok, ok, I get it," Joe rolled his eyes. "I don't need to know all of that shit."

"I can keep going, I got another page here," Noah said, tossing the notebook back onto the table. He rubbed his eyes and leaned back in the chair as far back as he could. "Are we crazy?"

"Absolutely, unequivocally, one-hundred percent, certifiably insane," Joe answered.

There was a moment of silence before Noah and Joe started laughing hysterically. It was amazing to Noah that even with something so serious on the horizon, he and Joe had always been able to laugh in the face of adversity. That's why they had been such good friends for so long. At the end of the day, they were simple men repeatedly put into extraordinarily complicated situations. And they had walked out alive every single time.

"We got this," Noah said with a nod of confidence.

"Hell yeah, we do," Joe agreed. "Are you nervous?"

"Could not be more terrified," Noah admitted. Joe smirked.

"Me too, brother. Me too."

"We've done it before," Noah said. "We know what we're doing. We just have to be smart and do our jobs."

"Couldn't have said it better myself."

Noah stood up and walked over to one of the gun cases. He popped it open and picked up a Glock 30, an easily concealable pistol chambered in .45 ACP ammunition. Grabbing a full 10-round magazine, Noah slipped the mag into the breach and racked the slide before tucking the gun into his waistband. Joe followed suit and armed himself with another Glock handgun. There was no need to discuss the thought behind this action. Both men knew it was necessary to arm themselves from this point on.

"Be ready on Wednesday," Noah said.

"I will be," Joe nodded. "You make sure your boys have their heads on straight. This is real life."

"I know. They'll be ready," Noah reassured him.

The two men locked up the office and the warehouse before heading back to their vehicles. Noah turned on the radio and waited until Joe drove away. The next few days were going to be some of the longest of his life, ripe with anticipation. In a few days, Noah would do something he swore he'd never do again. He despised Thomas Swaney for making him, but secretly, buried deep within his subconscious, Noah was excited. He wasn't good at many things, but he was great at two things - operating heavy equipment and executing a perfect heist.

Part Two: Sins of the Father

"Some go to prison for stealing, and others believe that a better system can be provided and maintained than one that makes it necessary for a man to steal in order to live" - Eugene V. Debs; Former United States Senator

9

Justin

He climbed the stairs, desperately trying to not make a sound behind his team of heavily armed SWAT officers. The tension in the rickety stairwell was palpable, each of the officers was itching to pull their triggers. None more so than Los Angeles Sheriff's Department Detective Justin Carter. If anyone was going to be pulling the trigger today, it was him. Over his 10-year career with the Sheriff's Department, Justin had gotten into his fair share of gunfights and had even killed two men in a brutal gun battle a few years ago. But this was different. This wasn't some drug bust that had gone south, and Justin had been forced to make a decision between his life and the lives of career criminals.

Two days prior, Justin and his team of five LASD Detectives had been conducting a raid on a house that was suspected of being a haven for human traffickers. Justin and his team had been surveilling a group of men associated with the Tijuana Cartel for weeks. The Tijuana Cartel had dominated the drug trade and human trafficking in Los Angeles for years. Against his superior's orders, Justin ordered his team on the raid as soon as they witnessed the men in the house unloading a van of kids, no doubt to be sold into some type of enslavement. Justin's Captain had been adamant that raiding the house was not the right move for fear of letting it ruin any chance of a bigger bust in the future. But Justin and his team unanimously agreed that they had to do something.

Armed to the teeth, the five Sheriffs kicked the front door in and raided the house, hoping to rescue the kids and arrest every single other person in the place. Unfortunately, as soon as they entered, the men inside began shooting wildly at them. Fernando Torrez, a 15-year veteran with the LASD and one of Justin's closest friends, caught a round through the neck - killing him instantly. Taking casualties that quickly ruined any chance the Sheriffs had of completing the raid, they hauled Fernando out of there and had to watch helplessly as the *mafiosos* escaped with their prisoners.

Since then, Justin had not even gone home. He and his now four-man unit had been searching nonstop for the men who killed Fernando. Thankfully, they found their secondary hideout - two old apartments in Boyle Heights. His wife, Karolyne, was also employed through the Los Angeles Police Department, working as a Crime Scene Investigator, and had been the one who located the apartment complex. Despite knowing that forwarding the information to Justin could run the risk of consequences, Karolyne did the right thing and made sure Justin knew where to hit next. From there, it was a phone call to a friend in the LAPD SWAT (Special Weapons and Tactics) Division to get everything set to raid the apartments.

"Eyes on the door," one of the SWAT officers whispered to the rest of the group.

"All units, be advised, we're moving in on the door," Justin said into his radio.

"Copy that," one of Justin's Sheriffs, Orlando Nicholson, answered over the radio. Orlando was waiting in the lobby of the apartment building with another squad of SWAT Officers.

"All units, I have eyes on four guys inside the apartment," another one of the Sheriff's, Dalton Dupree, whispered over their radio. Dalton and the last Sheriff in Justin's squad, Nate Murray, were positioned on the roof of the building across the street, armed with high-powered Remington Model 700 sniper rifles. "They look like our *eses*," Dalton continued, using Spanish slang.

"Understood," Justin responded. "Go loud on my breach."

"Copy, we have eyes on the door," Dalton answered. "You've got two on the couch, one in the kitchen, and one by the window."

"Nate, you got the kitchen. Dalton, you're on the window. We'll take the guys on the couch. Orlando, be ready in case shit goes sideways," Justin ordered. He turned to the SWAT Team and relayed the plan.

"Got it," Orlando answered.

"Copy that," Dalton and Nate said simultaneously. Both men adjusted their aim, centering their respective targets in the reticle of their rifles.

The SWAT Team stacked up on either side of the door in the middle of the hallway. Justin stepped up to the door and gripped his rifle. He took a deep breath before looking at the SWAT Officers; there was a collective nod amongst them.

"Nate, Dalton," Justin whispered. "Bust 'em."

Justin reared back and booted the door open - the door swung open, nearly breaking it off the hinges. Before the SWAT team rushed inside, two gunshots rang out, and the two gangsters in the kitchen and by the window were shot dead before they had a chance to draw their weapons. Rushing inside the apartment behind the first three SWAT Officers, Justin raised his rifle at the two remaining men sitting on the couch. They looked absolutely stunned and had their hands up in the air, not even bothering to reach for one of the many guns on the coffee table in front of them. The rest of the SWAT Team moved into the apartment, surrounding the two men in a semi-circle in front of them.

"There anyone else here?" Justin asked. The men on the couch shook their heads, indicating that there was not.

"It's your call..." the SWAT Team Lieutenant Capelli muttered to Justin.

"Here's what you two are going to do," Justin said. "Reach forward and pick up one of those guns on the table in front of you."

The two men looked at each other in confusion before looking back at Justin. They didn't move.

"Reach forward and pick up a fucking gun!" Justin screamed. They finally complied, reaching forward and both of them grabbing a weapon off the table.

As soon as their fingers touched the grips of the guns, Justin unloaded on them, shooting at least a dozen rounds into both men. Blood splattered all over the table and couch as the two gangsters fell over each other, their bodies riddled with bullets. The shooting stopped just as quickly as it had started. An uncomfortable silence fell over the room, smoke still escaping from the barrel of Justin's red hot rifle and the bodies of the two men. The SWAT Team looked at each other, avoiding eye contact with Justin. Collectively, they knew a line had just been crossed. Some were ok with that, and others were only pretending to be.

"Thank you," Justin muttered, lowering his rifle and flipping the safety switch on.

"It's a shame they had to draw on us," Capelli muttered with a smirk. "I would've much preferred to cuff them both."

"Amen, brother," Justin said, patting Capelli's shoulder. "Alright boys, let's pack it up."

****

It didn't take long for the Los Angeles Police to cordon off the entire building as a crime scene. Yellow tape and blockades of LAPD cruisers told the residents on the street that something was horribly wrong, drawing in a crowd of people eager to get a glimpse at the commotion. A few local newscasters were already up and running in front of their cameras, describing a brazen shootout between police and cartel affiliates. Witnesses were eager to give their much-exaggerated accounts to the hungry reporters.

All the while, Justin Carter and his Sheriff's stood off by Justin's truck - a monstrous Ford F-250 that was kitted out with police lights and a massive grill guard. They didn't consciously mean to isolate themselves from the rest of the Department. But no one could argue that Justin Carter, Orlando Nicholson, Dalton Dupree, and Nate Murray were just different than the other cops - bigger, stronger, louder, faster.

They were hotshots, cocky, and unabashedly themselves, no matter who was present. This, combined with their 'shoot first, ask questions later' approach to almost every encounter, drove a wedge between them and the rest of the LAPD personnel.

Forming a circle on the side of the truck, Justin produced a silver flask from the console of his truck. It was filled to the brim with Johnnie Walker, his personal favorite. He took a shot before passing it to Dalton. The ritual was repeated until the flask made its way back to Justin.

"To Fernando," Justin muttered, pouring a shot's worth of alcohol onto the ground between his team.

"To Fernando," they echoed.

"Make sure you give our thanks to Karolyne, J.C," Dalton said, clapping Justin on the shoulder. "Couldn't have bagged those motherfuckers without her help."

"I'll let her know," Justin nodded. "I know she wishes she could've been here too. She was pretty close with Fernando."

"Have you talked to his wife yet?" Orlando asked. Orlando Nicholson was the most physically imposing man Justin had ever met. He was six and a half feet tall, 250 pounds of rock-solid muscle, short black hair, a mustache, and wore glasses. His gigantic forearms were covered in tattoos.

"Not yet," Justin shook his head. "I'll have to later today. Let her know we at least got some type of justice for him."

"His kids though..." Dalton muttered, kicking a rock by his boot. "It's just a shame."

The Sheriffs fell silent, looking remorsefully at one another. There was a definite and noticeable gap in their team dynamic without Fernando Torrez. He was going to be missed. Dearly.

Before anyone could change the subject to something less mournful, a trio of ominous black SUVs came flying down the road, screeching to a halt before the blockade. The doors of the trucks swung open, and Los Angeles Police Captain Aidan Bingham stepped out, escorted by a pair of officers in black suits.

"Where are they?" he asked a wide-eyed patrolman. Bingham's voice was loud and angry. The young cop pointed over to Justin's truck, knowing exactly what Bingham meant. Bingham marched across the street toward Justin and the three Sheriffs. Justin swore he could see the smoke coming out of Bingham's ears.

"Someone else want to handle this shit for me?" Justin asked his Sheriffs.

"That's all you, brotha," Nate smirked.

"You guys are fucking useless," Justin muttered, getting a quiet chuckle from them. He stepped away from his team and met Bingham halfway. "Captain Bingham, it's a pleasure."

"Save it, Justin," Bingham hissed, keeping his voice low so it wouldn't be picked up by a nosy reporter. "Do you have any idea the absolute shit-storm you have created for us? I have an ICE Agent ready to rip me a new asshole because one of my Sheriffs just botched a two-year investigation into the cartels. I am only going to ask this one time, who gave you this address? You sure as shit didn't find this place without help."

"Which one of those do you want me to answer first?" Justin asked. Bingham was irate at the response.

"I do not like you, Justin," Bingham admitted. "In fact, I don't like you or anyone else in your little frat house. But those feelings aside, I need you to stop being an asshole and start being an actual cop for one second. Who told you?"

"Confidential Informant, sir," Justin answered with peak professionalism.

"Does that confidential informant have the same last name as you?" Bingham asked directly. Justin winced at the accusation. Bingham already assumed, correctly so, that Karolyne had helped out Justin by giving him the address, even if he had no way to prove that.

"Carter is a pretty common last name," Justin shrugged. Bingham actually looked like he could kill Justin.

"The Chief was screaming at me on the way here," Bingham growled. "He suggested I terminate you and Karolyne."

This changed Justin's whole attitude. His face dropped at the comment, and his facade dropped, even momentarily. In a low voice, Justin finally spoke to Captain Bingham with his version of respect.

"Sir, it was my call. Please do not punish Karolyne, she had nothing to do with this."

"We'll see about that," Bingham narrowed his eyes. "Until then, you're both riding a desk. Internal Affairs is going to need to do a thorough investigation. You're off any cartel cases until further notice, is that understood?"

Justin felt like he'd been kicked in the gut. Being pulled off the field and getting thrown behind a desk was a fate worse than death for cops. His team had been extremely effective, especially recently, in combating the ever-growing cartel activity. To pull him out now was both reckless and completely short-sighted. Although Justin doubted Captain Bingham would share his sentiments.

"This is understood, sir," Justin muttered, unable to meet Captain Bingham's eyes.

"Let me know who will be heading up your team until you return," Bingham continued. "I suggest Orlando or Dalton."

****

Justin was already halfway into a bottle of Johnnie Walker by the time he heard the door to his Downtown Los Angeles Apartment open. He hid the bottle in his liquor cabinet, maneuvering a few bottles of wine and champagne in front of it, and closed the cabinet before his wife had a chance to get in the kitchen.

"Hey, babe," Karolyne called from the foyer. Justin heard her kick off her shoes before she walked into the kitchen. She gave Justin a quick kiss on the cheek before going to the sink to wash her hands. "I hope your day was just as exciting as mine."

"Desk duty for the foreseeable future," Justin spat, collapsing onto the couch in their small but cozy living room.

"Yeah, me too," Karolyne admitted. "My boss is furious."

"Bingham actually came to the scene and reprimanded me in front of my guys. In front of them!"

"Bingham's a prick," Karolyne said, plain and simple. Justin couldn't help but crack a smile.

"I'm sorry," he said. "Didn't mean for you to get in trouble too."

"I knew very well what was going to happen if I passed that information along to you," Karolyne said. "But it had to be done. It was the right thing to do. No one is going to say it now, but everyone knows you did the right thing. When a brother is killed, you make sure the killer doesn't see trial. That's the way things are."

"I know, I know," Justin muttered. He changed the subject slightly. "I think we should go see Fernando's family tomorrow. Not like we're going to be busy with work or anything."

"I already talked to his wife," Karolyne nodded. "That's a good idea to go see them."

"You're always one step ahead of me," Justin smiled, holding his arms out for his wife. Karolyne gently moved onto the couch, resting her head on Justin's chest. He held her against his body for a few minutes, enjoying the warmth she brought with her.

"I'm gonna jump in the shower," Karolyne whispered in his ear. "Maybe I'll see you there?"

"Maybe..." Justin said with a wry grin. Karolyne rolled her eyes and headed into their bedroom.

Justin watched as she departed and reminded himself how lucky he was to be married to her. She was incredibly witty, smart, funny, and gorgeous. Her light brown hair was pretty much always kept in a tight bun or ponytail so it wouldn't get in the way. Both she and Justin enjoyed working out together and stayed in tip-top shape. Karolyne was almost a year older than him but looked several years younger. They had met during Justin's first year working as a Los Angeles Sheriff and had started dating shortly after. It didn't take long for things to get serious, and ever since then, they had been together. Many of Justin's fellow Sheriffs were both impressed and jealous that he'd been able to get her. But no one could deny that they were a good couple. Karolyne was a brilliant investigator with a knack for finding the most obscure clues and being able to put the jagged pieces together perfectly. On the other hand, Justin was a great Sheriff - strong and tough. They were two sides of the same coin and blended their different personalities very well together. Karolyne's family, both parents and three other siblings, had all taken a liking to Justin almost as soon as they met him. Her father was especially apprehensive about her getting involved with a fellow cop, but after meeting Justin, his worries had evaporated. Justin was closer with Karolyne's family than he'd ever been with his own, and he valued his relationship with her parents and siblings immensely.

Justin had been born into an incredibly toxic home life in San Francisco. An alcoholic and abusive father who had made his life a living hell. All throughout his childhood, Justin had endured more physical and psychological torture than most kids should ever have to go through. His mom, to her credit, tried her best to defend Justin and his brother, who was five years his junior. But eventually, the abuse and torment became too much for her to handle. When Justin was 21, his mom and younger brother made the decision to leave and head for Southern California. It was an impossible decision for Justin, he had just started at the Police Academy, and the abuse from his father had subsided, at least towards him. At the end of the day, Justin chose to stay behind - a decision that cost him his relationship with his brother. Justin was jealous that his brother had gotten to leave and despised him for it. He felt responsible for his dad and didn't want to abandon him, even if he was a form of the devil. It took years before Justin would answer his mom's calls even, but slowly over time, their relationship began to improve slightly. But Justin's brother hadn't acknowledged him in twelve long years. It hurt Justin greatly, considering that they had been pretty close growing up. The two brothers had been gifted athletes during their younger years and spent every day after school playing football together. It was a beautiful escape from the horrors inside their home. Not a day passed when Justin didn't miss his brother or his mom. But at the same time, his resentment and anger for them both were something he battled with. He was sure if he ever went to therapy, there'd be quite a few sessions on his pent-up feelings towards his family.

Karolyne and Justin did their nightly routine of eating dinner together before watching TV on the couch until Karolyne couldn't keep her eyes open any longer. They were in the midst of watching *The Boys*, a show on Amazon Prime that was a new twist on the superhero genre. Both Karolyne and Justin loved the show and were enjoying every second of it. When Karolyne was too tired to keep watching, they shut it off and went to bed. As always, Karolyne fell asleep as soon as her head hit the pillow. It never failed to amaze Justin how peaceful she could be. Sleep was never that easy for Justin; he was perpetually cursed with a form of insomnia. He didn't know whether it stemmed from his childhood or some of the things he'd seen during his time as a Sheriff, but sleep was just not something that came easy. His mind was always racing, and he had not been able to sleep a wink without his favorite vice, Johnnie Walker. Justin was very aware he had an addiction, much like his father. But, for the time being, Justin was able to control it. He'd managed to keep the extent of his alcoholism from Karolyne, which was difficult but not impossible. It scared him how much he relied on alcohol, knowing how easily he could turn into his father. They had many shared qualities and were so similar that it made Justin sick. But as much as he wanted to stop, when things got tough, Justin reached for the bottle. In that sense, he had come to understand his father a little more. While their relationship certainly wasn't anything to be proud of, they were at least on good terms.

Justin was just about to put the bottle back in his cabinet and call it a night when his phone started buzzing on the kitchen counter, where he kept it next to his badge, holster, and gun. He picked up the phone and answered without bothering to see who was calling.

"This is Justin," he answered quietly.

"Hey, boss," Dalton Dupree said, equally quiet. "Hope I'm not waking you. I just thought you should hear that I.A. came by the office tonight. They were asking a bunch of questions about you and Karolyne. Grilled myself, Orlando, and Nate pretty hard."

"Motherfucker," Justin cursed under his breath. Internal Affairs were the cops that investigate cops accused of crimes, a police force for the police. Just due to the nature of the job, many cops disliked the men and women from I.A. immensely, and Justin felt no differently.

"The boys and I didn't say anything. They'd have to kill me before I rat," Dalton said. Justin smiled. That was exactly why he'd put Dalton in charge of the team until Justin could come back. "I just wanted you to know that you should expect a visit pretty soon. Karolyne too. Get your stories straight, and then tell me what I should have the boys tell I.A."

"You got it, Dalton," Justin said. "Thanks again for the call. Let me know if you guys need anything until I'm back."

"I will," Dalton responded. "I'll try not to have too much fun without you."

"No gunfights or raids until I get back."

"No promises, my friend," Dalton laughed.

****

Dalton had been spot on in his prediction. Just after 10AM the next morning, Justin heard a knock on his front door. Groaning loudly, he got up off the couch and shuffled over to get the door. Before opening it, he peered through the peephole. Sure enough, two men in suits stood outside his apartment. They each carried a black leather briefcase. He saw the badges and guns on their belts; Justin sighed.

Internal Affairs.

Justin was glad that as soon as he and Karolyne had gotten up that morning, they'd prepared for such an occurrence. Their story was squared away.

"Is that who I think it is?" Karolyne asked from the kitchen, peering her head around the corner. Justin nodded. "Open it."

Justin unlocked the door and opened it, smiling politely at the two officers standing in front of him.

"Good morning, gentlemen," Justin said.

"Good morning, Detective Carter," the first cop said. "My name is Jim Wilson, and this is my partner, Greg Calhoun. We're with Internal Affairs."

"I figured," Justin muttered. "Care to come inside?"

"Thank you," Jim said. He and Greg filed into the apartment, marching into the home with authority.

"Hello," Karolyne said from behind the kitchen island, much less polite than Justin had been.

"That's my wife, Karolyne," Justin said after locking his front door behind the cops.

"Pleasure to meet you, ma'am," Greg nodded. He and Jim looked around the apartment before taking a seat at the kitchen table.

"Both of you can have a seat if you'd like," Jim said, gesturing to the two empty seats at the table. He was clearly in charge.

Reluctantly, Justin slid into the chair opposite the two Internal Affairs Officers. Karolyne, always defiant, stood in the kitchen, her arms folded across her chest.

"Well, let's just get right into it," Jim said once he realized Karolyne had no intention of sitting down with them. He and Greg pulled out large notepads and pens from their briefcases. "First and foremost, I want to give my condolences for Fernando, he was a great cop. I had the pleasure of working more than a few cases with him when we were both in the Gang Units."

"Thank you," Justin said quietly.

"Secondly, this is just going to be informal for now. You both are going to have to come down to the station later this week and give a full statement on the record, but given the circumstances, I thought it appropriate to just have a conversation first."

"We're not accusing either of you or anything," Greg chimed in. "We're just doing our jobs. Neither of us is going to lose any sleep about a cop-killer getting what he deserves."

"But..." Jim took over. "You do have a history of bending the rules for your Sheriffs and your family, especially when it comes to your father."

Justin clenched his fists and held his breath, counting to ten in his head to try and calm himself down. Whenever anyone brought up his father, it just brought out a different side of him.

"I don't really think that has any relevance to the current situation," Karolyne interjected. "Let's try and just keep this about yesterday."

"On the contrary," Jim glared at Karolyne. "It has extreme relevance. It shows a pattern of Detective Carter routinely using his power and influence as a Los Angeles Sheriff to manipulate the law in his favor. I've seen your father's rap sheet, a list of felonies and misdemeanors a mile long. He *should* be behind bars, but he isn't. And, Mrs. Carter, you're not clean in this either. If you provided your husband with information he wouldn't have been privy to, then that can make you an accomplice to murder,"

"Don't talk about my father," Justin growled. "You know nothing about that. If you want to ask me questions about yesterday, so be it. But leave my father out of it."

Jim looked at his partner and shook his head. They closed their briefcases and stood up.

"Clearly, this was a mistake," Jim said. "Detective Carter, Investigator Carter, I'm going to need you both to come down to the station."

10

Noah

The office was thick with anxiety and the sound of bullets being loaded into magazines. None of the five men spoke, each one dealing with their nerves in a different way. Noah had been here before, hyping himself up before he committed one of the most dangerous acts a man can commit. After loading up a dozen magazines for his rifle and half a dozen for his pistol, Noah got dressed. In addition to his tan boots and jeans, Noah threw on a black long sleeve compression shirt and a bulletproof vest. Then he began the tedious process of fitting all the magazines into his vest, pants, and other pouches. In his experience, it was better to be prepared for anything. The more ammo he could carry, the better. Noah Riordan turned around and looked at Joe, EJ, Chandler, and Darren. They were all dressed similarly and looked ready to go.

"Gentlemen, this is it," Noah said, speaking quietly and deliberately. "If all goes according to plan, we'll be back here in less than an hour and then at The Lamp shortly after to celebrate. I know you guys are probably nervous or apprehensive or whatever, but do not let that affect you. Yes, this is risky. Dangerous. Stupid. But we're going to do it anyway. Not because we can, but because we need to. We have to. Our families depend on our success. Keep that single thought in your mind, and everything will go smoothly. We're not out to hurt anyone, we just need the money. Everyone do your jobs, and we'll be alright. Any questions?"

No one said a word.

"Alright, Joe's gonna be positioned a few miles away where he can monitor police response and traffic routes. As far as we're concerned, his word is God's. If he says bail, we bail. We're not taking any unnecessary risks."

"I'll be able to talk to you all through the radio," Joe added on. "I'd leave your cell phones here, don't want them pinging anywhere close to the actual site."

"I was just about to say that," Noah agreed. He threw open a drawer in one of the desks and tossed his phone inside. One by one, the others followed suit.

"Lastly, no more using our names. The second we leave this place, codenames only," Noah pulled out a small drawstring bag and opened it up. He pulled out four masks - Jason Vorhees, Michael Myers, Freddy Krueger, and Ghostface. "EJ, you'll be Jason. Chandler can be Michael, and Darren is Freddy. I'm Ghostface."

"I hate that I love this," Darren muttered to himself, getting a snicker from EJ. They each grabbed their respective masks and weapons. Noah took one more look at his crew before he picked up his own mask and armaments.

"Let's go rob a fucking truck," Noah grumbled.

****

The white and black GARDA armored truck pulled into the parking lot of the Panda Express, stopping once it was taking up four entire parking spaces. As was standard for each and every armored car, the vehicle was occupied by two people - a driver and a courier. During their route, the driver would stay with the truck while the courier would make runs in and out of banks, restaurants, malls, and other businesses looking to move their money. It was mandated that the driver not leave the vehicle, even if their partner was in trouble. While they looked tough and impenetrable, armored trucks were huge targets for those who were gutsy enough to attempt a robbery.

From the Target parking lot across the street from the Panda Express, Noah watched the armored truck come to a stop. A few seconds later, a heavy-set man climbed down from the passenger side and waddled into the fast-food restaurant. Noah flexed his hands over the steering wheel and looked to his right, where Chandler was bouncing his leg nervously. EJ and Darren were in a separate truck, already in the Panda Express lot.

The plan was simple. Once the courier came back out with his lunch, Noah and Chandler would fly in and block the truck from backing out. Then, EJ and Darren would approach from the other side and surround the truck.

"Ghostface to Overwatch, the courier just went into the restaurant," Noah whispered into the mic around his neck.

"Copy," Joe answered immediately. He was in a Los Angeles Electric Company pickup truck almost two miles away, monitoring everything from two self-encrypted laptops.

"My heart is racing..." Chandler said quietly. "Is that normal?"

"Yes," Noah answered curtly, hoping that Chandler understood he didn't want to hear about anything other than the job ahead of them.

"Sorry..." Chandler muttered. "I'm nervous."

"So am I," Noah said. "It's ok to be nervous, just do your job, and we will be fine."

"Ok, ok," Chandler nodded. He looked down at the rubber Michael Myers mask. "Let's get this over with."

"Does anyone else really have a craving for Chinese food now?" Darren's voice came over the radio. Chandler looked over at Noah, appalled. But, after the comment hung in the air for a second, Noah and Chandler both laughed.

"Stay focused," Noah responded, only after his laughter subsided.

A full minute and a half later, the courier exited the restaurant with a plastic bag of food in his right hand. Noah took a deep breath and pulled the Ghostface mask over his head. Chandler did the same, adjusting the rubber mask so he could see through the poorly cut eyeholes.

"Go!" Noah barked into the radio, throwing the truck into drive and slamming on the gas. He turned the wheel and spun the truck out of the Target parking lot, across the busy road, and into the Panda Express lot in a few seconds. Screaming on the brakes, Noah threw the truck in park as he opened his door. He leapt out, his rifle aimed right at the courier with the bag of food. The courier's eyes went wide, and he dropped the bag of food, instinctively putting his hands up.

"Don't move!" Noah screamed, his voice slightly muffled by the mask. Chandler was already out of the truck and in front of the armored car, keeping his weapon trained on the driver.

"Driver, hands where I can see them!" Chandler hollered. "Do not touch your radio, and do not send a distress signal!"

"On your knees!" Noah shouted at the courier, who was all too willing to comply. $18 an hour was not enough money to risk losing his life. As soon as the courier's knees hit the ground, Noah moved around and cuffed his wrists and ankles with zip-ties.

The second pickup sped into the parking lot, pulling in right behind the armored car. EJ and Darren, wearing the Jason Vorhees and Freddy Kruger masks, jumped out and went to work, applying a small explosive device to the back of the truck. Since Darren had been the most familiar with demolition work, he opted to arm the device.

"Set!" Darren called out.

"Pop it," Noah ordered. Darren pressed the remote, and with a small explosion, the two rear doors of the armored truck swung open, and the locking mechanism completely disintegrated.

"Michael, keep your eye on the driver!" Noah shouted. "Jason, Freddy, on the truck."

"Got it!" Chandler answered loudly. He stood firmly and kept his rifle aimed right at the driver. The driver kept his hands on the steering wheel where Chandler could see them.

EJ and Darren climbed into the back of the truck and were instantly amazed at what they saw. The entire cargo hold of the car was filled with money, just like Noah had said it would be.

"Holy shit," EJ mumbled. Darren shook his head in disbelief.

"Come on, let's get to work," Darren said.

Noah checked his watch. Everything was happening right on time, just as he had planned it. He could see a few people from inside the Panda Express with their faces pressed against the windows, watching the robbery with a mix of amazement and fear. It was like a car accident; you couldn't look away. Seeing the prying eyes, Noah knew it was a matter of seconds before Joe would be informing him that 9-1-1 had been called and the cops were en route.

"Hurry up, boys!" Noah called out, hurrying to the back of the armored car. Darren and EJ and about two-thirds of the money transferred into the bed and backseat of their pickup, using large duffle bags to transport the sleeves of money. Noah smiled underneath the mask, seeing that the information he'd been given had been spot on. This was more money than he'd ever seen during his previous heists. Letting his rifle hang the harness across his chest, Noah grabbed two full duffles from the back of the armored car and tossed them into the bed of the truck.

"LAPD has been notified. Stand-by for response times," Joe's calm and collected voice came over the radio.

"Double time!" Noah hissed at EJ and Darren. They picked up the pace, forgetting the duffle bags, and resorting to just tossing the plastic sleeves of money into their pickup.

The hair on the back of Noah's neck stood up when he heard the wailing sirens of approaching first responders. It was a sound that most people were pretty familiar with, but it was different for Noah. To most, that was a sound that brought safety and protection. But when you break the law the way Noah had in the past - and was currently doing - that sound brought anxiety and a fight-or-flight sensation that every person possessed when pushed into a corner.

"Overwatch, where are those cops?" Noah asked into the radio, jumping out of the cargo hold of the armored truck.

"Right on top of you," Joe answered, his voice ripe with worry.

"Understood," Noah muttered. "Get out of here, we'll link up at the warehouse."

"Be careful," Joe whispered, fearing the worst. He ripped out his earpiece and began driving away just as the LAPD cruisers came barreling down the road, lights and sirens wailing.

Noah turned back to EJ and Darren; they were nearly done emptying out the contents of the armored truck. There was no way Noah was leaving without every single dollar they came for. If he came up even a little short, there was no doubt in his mind that Thomas Swaney would force Noah to even out the score in whatever way he saw fit. Noah could not and would not allow his life to be controlled by a man like Thomas Swaney.

"Finish up and get out of here," Noah growled, flipping the safety off his rifle.

"Wait, where are you going?" EJ asked as Noah took off.

"Cops incoming!" Noah screamed, giving a warning to everyone in earshot. He grabbed Chandler by the shoulder and gave him a nudge toward their truck. "Get in and get ready to go, I'm gonna buy us some time."

"What about him?" Chandler asked, gesturing to the driver.

"Least of our worries, man. Move your ass!" Noah yelled. Chandler did as he was told and ran back for the pickup truck. As expected, the driver immediately hit the alarm and radioed into his dispatch.

The first cop car came into view just as Noah dropped to a knee behind a parked sedan. He leaned across the hood of the car, took a deep breath, and yanked the trigger. In an instant, the entire plaza turned into a frenzy, terrified shoppers screaming and running in all directions. Noah kept the trigger down, blasting through the entire 30-round magazine as fast as the rifle would allow. He specifically aimed low, trying to take out the wheels and the engine on the cruiser. The police car came to a screeching stop, tires shot to shreds. Standing up, Noah reloaded the rifle, slapping a fresh magazine inside the breach.

"Right side, right side!" Chandler screamed from the truck. Noah adjusted and saw two more police cars flying towards them from the opposite side of the road.

"We're good to go!" EJ said, closing the liftgate and bed cap to his pickup truck. Darren and EJ jumped into their truck and took off, having memorized the escape route to perfection.

"Chandler, let's roll," Noah said, sprinting back to the truck. Before the door was even closed, Chandler stepped on the gas and spun the wheel, steering the truck out of the lot. They jumped in front of oncoming traffic and tore down the road, leaving the cops behind them. Once they got on the highway, Noah finally felt comfortable enough to take the Ghostface mask off. He tossed it in the backseat and took a deep breath. His hands were shaking, and his ears were ringing horribly. Not since the last time he'd been a part of a robbery had he shot at an actual person. It was a surreal and stomach-churning feeling.

"Are you ok?" Chandler muttered from under his mask, still driving well over the speed limit.

"Yeah, fine," Noah whispered. "Just get us to the warehouse as fast as you can."

****

EJ and Darren shut the gate as soon as Chandler sped into the warehouse lot. He drove the truck inside the garage and killed the engine, only then taking his mask off. Darren pulled the garage door behind them and kicked the lock into place. Chandler slowly stepped out of the truck, holding the Michael Myers mask in his right hand.

"You good?" EJ asked quietly, putting his hand on Chandler's shoulder. "That was a little intense."

"Yeah, I'm fine," Chandler nodded. "Seriously, I'm fine."

"You should see the back of the truck man," Darren said with a grin. "I've never seen so much money in my fucking life!"

"He's not wrong," EJ agreed. "Noah wasn't kidding, that truck was loaded."

"Well, at least we got something," Chandler kept his voice low.

Finally, Noah got out of the truck. He tossed his rifle on one of the tables next to the truck and slowly walked over to the rest of his crew. They looked at him, waiting for him to say something.

"Good job, guys," Noah said. He forced himself to smile, but his mind was racing, and memories from a life he thought he'd left behind were flooding back into the forefront.

"I can't believe we actually pulled it off," Darren said. "I mean, all things considered, it went pretty well."

"Enjoy the feeling while it lasts," Noah said ominously. "Next time is gonna be a lot harder, and the time after that will be damn near impossible."

"Christ, this guy should be a motivational speaker," Darren muttered under his breath. "I need a damn drink, anyone else with me?"

"Count me in," EJ said eagerly.

"I could go for a drink," Chandler chimed in.

"Good," Joe suddenly said, appearing in the offices. "You three idiots get out of here. Noah and I need to talk."

The warehouse fell silent immediately. Joe oozed a dangerous sense of anger, but he was so calm and collected it made everyone nervous, with the exception of Noah. He stared at Joe with a look of vague annoyance, not even appearing remotely concerned.

"Leave us," Noah said, his eyes locked on Joe.

In total silence, EJ, Darren, and Chandler retreated to the offices, where they changed back into street clothes before getting in their personal trucks and driving off to the nearest watering hole.

"What the fuck, Noah?" Joe asked in an accusatory tone. His hand was resting on the grip of the pistol holstered to his hip.

"What are you all mad about?" Noah shook his head. "We did the job."

"You opened fire on the cops!" Joe roared. "When Jake used to do that, it was out of sheer desperation, not a first option! What the hell were you thinking?"

"I was thinking EJ and Darren needed time that we didn't have," Noah said, keeping his voice even. He knew Joe well enough to know that yelling back would only escalate the situation. "The cops were closing in. I had to buy us some time."

"So you open up on the police?" Joe spat.

"I was aiming for the tires and the engine. I meant it when I told the guys, we're not in this to kill anyone," Noah answered. "We needed the extra time, and I got it for us. End of story. We got away, with the money, I might add, and everything is fine."

"No, it's not. Because now we left evidence. Shell casings, bullets, empty magazines. All evidence that can point right back to us!"

"The hardware was scrubbed before we left. And Brian assured me it is all untraceable. We're good, Joe. We're good. This is a success."

"Yeah right," Joe rolled his eyes. "Your version of a success needs some serious work."

"We all made it out alive," Noah shrugged. "Seems like a success to me."

"Alright," Joe sighed. "I just don't want to get into another situation like the one we got into with Jake."

"Can you stop bringing up Jake?" Noah asked. "I'm not Jake Tell. I'll never be Jake Tell."

Jake Tell was still, to this day, an incredibly sensitive subject for Noah. Joe could only understand parts of why that was the case. He hadn't had the relationship that Noah and Jake had.

"Yeah, I'm sorry," Joe finally said. "I know how much he meant to you. This whole thing just has me a bit on edge."

"Me too," Noah muttered. "Come on, let's go get a drink and call it a night. Like you said, the next one's going to be a bitch."

****

They sat at a table in the back corner of the bar, as removed from the crowd as they could be. A bucket of Modelos and a shot glass filled with slices of lime sat in the middle of the table. EJ and Darren stepped back inside, tossing their cigarettes out as the door closed. Chandler handed each of them a fresh beer. Overall, they were quiet, each man taking in his newfound career in different but similar ways.

Noah Riordan and Joe Kado had been here before, sitting at the same exact bar with a different crew of guys. It was almost surreal for them to be sitting here again. The crews were vastly different from one another, almost to a comical point. Jake Tell had assembled a crew based purely on skills and capability. There was no lighthearted humor or anything like that; it was strictly business. Noah, however, went the opposite way when putting together his crew. Skills meant little to him, pulling off heists required more than just technical expertise. These men all needed money, and for that reason alone, Noah knew he could trust them. In their own way, they were all relying on one another to secure a future for themselves and their families. Noah had to keep it that simple for them. If they knew what was really at stake, there was no telling how they'd react.

"Hey," Joe muttered, nudging Noah on the shoulder. "When are we going to head back for the money?"

"I'll handle it," Noah answered, keeping his voice low. He and Joe turned their backs on the rest of the crew so they could talk without being overheard. The noise and music from the bar helped drone out their voices.

"What do you mean?" Joe asked, narrowing his eyes.

"It means I'll handle it," Noah repeated.

"Someone else is getting a cut, right?" Joe ventured a guess. "Whoever gave you the intel for the heists."

"Yeah," Noah nodded. "He needs a cut."

Joe shook his head, and Noah knew in an instant that he knew it was Thomas Swaney. His eyes narrowed, and his lips pursed. Noah had seen that look from Joe a handful of times when he was too angry to formulate words.

"You son of a bitch," Joe swore under his breath.

Noah grabbed Joe's shoulder and pulled him outside, away from the rest of the crew. They pushed past a pair of overweight guys smoking and came to a stop on the side of the building.

"Joe, what was I supposed to do?" Noah hissed. "They came to me, I didn't seek this out!"

"You still should've told me we were working for the crooked old fuck!" Joe spat back.

"You wouldn't have agreed if I told you this was Thomas's job," Noah said.

"Goddamn right, I wouldn't have," Joe agreed. "After what happened last time, I'm shocked you agreed to this. And, to make matters worse, you got your own guys involved!"

"Joe, what was I supposed to do?" Noah repeated the same question. "Thomas threatened me, my family, everyone he could send Stan after. I didn't have a choice, man."

"Why didn't you tell me?" Joe asked.

"I already told you," Noah rolled his eyes. "I can't pull this off without you. I need you on the crew."

Joe lowered his gaze and put his hands on his hips. He kicked a small rock by his boot and watched it bounce across the pavement of the parking lot.

"I'm coming with you," Joe muttered, not taking his eyes off the ground. "There's no way I'm letting that piece of shit get away with this."

"You don't have to do that," Noah said. Joe finally looked up and relaxed his face into a small smile.

"I know I don't," Joe shrugged. "But you're my boy, and I'm not letting you go alone. I hate Thomas, and I know you do too. We gotta stick together, no matter what."

"Thanks man," Noah said, clapping Joe on the shoulder.

"But when this is done..." Joe said, looking off into the parking lot. "You and I are putting a bullet in Thomas Swaney and Stan Simmons."

"That's fine with me," Noah agreed.

They went back inside and finished off the rest of the beer at their table. A short while later, the bar started closing down for the night. Chandler was the first to leave, saying he had an early morning involving yet another doctor's appointment for his wife. EJ and Darren were the next to leave, inviting Joe and Noah on their next excursion to a local gentlemen's club. They respectfully declined the offer.

"I'm gonna settle up, and then I'm out of here," Noah said to Joe.

"Let me know when you're going to see Thomas," Joe muttered. Patting Noah on the back, Joe headed outside to his truck.

"That's it?" Jessica asked, sliding into one of the barstools at their table. Noah smiled and nodded.

"Yeah, that's it. Early morning tomorrow for all of us."

"Well, it was really good to see you," Jessica said with a shy smile.

"I was wondering..." Noah began as he finished signing the receipt. "Would you want to go out with me again? I had a really great time with you, and that kiss was..."

"Amazing," Jessica finished his sentence. Her cheeks blushed, and she looked down at her feet.

"Yeah," Noah said with a chuckle. "Amazing."

"Noah, I'd love to go out with you again," Jessica smiled. "Do you have anything in mind?"

"Hey, I'm game for anything. What about you? Do you have any ideas?"

"I'll think of something," Jessica looked behind her to make sure none of her coworkers or managers were looking. She leaned up and gave Noah a quick kiss on the lips. "See you soon, Noah."

"Yeah," Noah said stupidly. "See you soon, Jess."

****

Noah could tell Joe was uneasy. Everything about the man, from his body language to his facial expression, conveyed a clear and present message. They each carried two duffle bags, one in each hand. The bags were filled with Thomas's cut of the heist. With help from Joe, Noah had divided the money into separate bags for each man. Joe, Chandler, Darren, and EJ would be five million dollars richer by the end of the day. As much as Noah didn't enjoy having to lie to Joe yet again, he kept his cut of the heist out of sight. Right now, $75 million dollars in cash sat in the back of Noah's pickup truck, spread out between three duffle bags.

That alone was enough to make Noah's palms sweat. He was dying to get the money safe and sound inside his home.

The elevator chimed, and the doors opened. Joe led the way out and down the hallway of offices, breezing right past a formerly attractive secretary. She started to protest but stopped when she saw Noah Riordan.

"He's expecting you," she said with a stiff smile. The botox had greatly reduced her ability to smile naturally.

"Thank you, Stella," Noah returned the smile.

Joe hadn't even slowed down slightly. He marched right up to the door and shoved it open without bothering to knock. Thomas Swaney looked up from his computer, clearly surprised to see Joe Kado. Noah filed into the room behind Joe and gently set the two bags down before closing and locking the door to Thomas's office.

"I didn't know you were bringing company," Thomas said to Noah. Joe dropped the bags down at his feet and smirked.

"I didn't know you were still in the wannabe mob boss game, Tommy," Joe said with a smile.

"You certainly haven't changed much," Thomas commented, glaring at Joe.

"Sure I have!" Joe exclaimed enthusiastically. "I didn't put a bullet in your head the second I walked in here! I must be mellowing with old age."

Noah didn't think the situation could get any more uncomfortable, but he was horribly wrong. After hearing Joe's comment, Thomas opened a drawer in his desk and withdrew a two-toned revolver. He placed the gun on his desk without a sound and stood up, his eyes boring into Joe. To his credit, Joe didn't even flinch at the sight of the gun. Why should he? He and Noah were both carrying guns, but there was no point in letting Thomas know that. So, Joe did the only thing he could do to really piss off Thomas. He stood his ground and smiled at the man.

"Mr. Riordan, I would appreciate some warning next time before you bring an electrician into my office," Thomas drolled.

"Couldn't carry it all by myself, sir," Noah said, trying to sound genuine. He loved every second of Joe's antics, but he couldn't let Thomas know that.

"I'm surprised your lap dog isn't breathing down our necks," Joe looked around the office. "You let him off the leash?"

"Mr. Simmons is quite capable, as I'm sure you're both very aware," Thomas answered. It wasn't directly a threat, but Joe and Noah knew the subtext to that comment. Stan Simmons was a professional at making people disappear.

"Everything is here, sir," Noah said, changing the subject to avoid creating even more tension between Joe and Thomas. "With the exception of the cops showing up ahead of schedule, everything went according to plan."

"As I knew it would," Thomas said with an air of superiority that was infuriating. "Yes, the cops showing up was unfortunate. But you handled the situation well. The bank is in a few days, correct?"

"Nine days," Noah said. "We'll be good to go."

"Good," Thomas nodded. He reached into his desk and pulled out a small notepad before scrawling something on the paper. Ripping off the piece of paper, Thomas handed it to Noah. "In addition to the money, I need you to grab that specific safety deposit box. The bank manager will have a key to get into the vault."

"Got it, shouldn't be too hard," Noah stuffed the piece of paper in his pocket.

"I want you to bring me the entire box," Thomas continued. "Don't open it or anything like that, just bring the box."

"The bank's got nothing to do with the money then, right?" Joe chimed in.

"You're still as perceptive as ever," Thomas grumbled.

"Joe, give us a minute," Noah said. "I'll meet you down at the trucks."

"Sure thing," Joe spat, glaring at Thomas as he walked out of the office.

Noah sat down in one of the chairs in front of Thomas's desk, discreetly adjusting the pistol tucked in his waistband. He didn't really think Thomas had any intention of using the revolver on his desk, but Noah was still glad he was armed.

"I'm gonna get this done," Noah said, keeping his voice and tone as neutral as possible. "But I need you to guarantee me that Stan is going to stay away. I know you did some pretty icky shit to get Jake and the others on board last time. You don't have to with me. But Thomas, I swear to god..."

"Noah, you have my word," Thomas answered. "I have no desire to hurt anyone you care about. Contrary to what Joe thinks, I'm not a bad man. We need money, just the same as you and your guys. It's as simple as that."

"As long as we understand each other," Noah nodded. Thomas stood up and stuck out his hand.

"Of course."

Noah and Thomas shook hands before Noah spun on his heels and marched out of the office. He waved at Stella and hurried down the stairs to meet Joe out front of the Local 12 IUOE Headquarters. Joe was leaning against the hood of his truck, talking to someone on the phone.

"...Alright, baby. I gotta roll, I'll be home later," Noah heard Joe say. "Love you."

"You weren't kidding about having a girl, huh?" Noah commented, leaning on the truck next to Joe. "Are you ever going to introduce me?"

"Someday, my friend," Joe smiled. "Someday."

11

Justin

Justin was glued to the TV, watching the news coverage of the brazen armored truck heist that had taken place. While there had been no casualties sustained by the police, a total of four officers were being treated for injuries they sustained after one of the robbers opened fire at them. Bank and armored car robberies were fairly common in Los Angeles, but ones of this magnitude were rare. The newscasters were having a field day going into detail about the heist, especially focusing on the robber's choice of mask. A still of a man dressed as the Ghostface killer from the popular *Scream* franchise wielding a machine gun was on every news channel that Justin could find.

There was something oddly familiar about the heist to Justin, something that Justin couldn't quite identify. He'd worked a number of heist cases in his day. The most recent of which was a few years ago when a crew of guys knocked over several armored trucks and a few banks over the span of three months. Despite the fact that there were some discrepancies on the actual number of guys who had committed the robberies, three of the men had been killed in a shootout following their last attempted heist. Justin had actually been part of that fateful day. He'd exchanged gunfire with the robbers several times and nearly shot one. At least one of the robbers had gotten away that day, but Justin had been positive there had been a fifth man on the crew that day. The fourth robber disappeared during the gunfight, leaving Justin to believe that a getaway driver had to be involved. When the smoke had settled, there were three criminals dead, and all of the money had been recovered from the heist. As is the usual case with bank and armored truck heists, the FBI took over the case. They were never able to determine if there was a fifth man who'd been involved that day or find the fourth bandit.

"Are you still watching that?" Karolyne asked, walking into the living room. She was dressed like she was ready to go out. Justin turned around and raised an eyebrow.

"Wow, you look... phenomenal," Justin breathed. "What're you up to?"

"Thank you, baby," Karolyne blushed. "I'm just meeting my sister for lunch. She's got something she wants to talk to me about."

"Alright, have a good time," Justin smiled. He stood up and gave his wife a kiss before she left.

The second Karolyne left, Justin jumped off the couch and got dressed, throwing on jeans and a light blue button-down. Even though he and his wife were technically on Administrative Leave from their jobs until Internal Affairs concluded their investigation, Justin could still go to his office and meet with his team - just as long as it didn't pertain to any ongoing cases. He grabbed one of his personal handguns, a compact Sig Sauer P365. The beauty of the weapon came in its size. It was designed specifically to be an EDC, or everyday carry. Justin could easily conceal the gun in his waistband holster and be ready for action at a moment's notice. Grabbing his wallet, Justin left the apartment and got into his truck, eager to get back to the Sheriff's Department.

****

The Los Angeles Sheriff's Department was located right in the LA Hall of Justice off of Temple Road. Justin's team had their offices set up in a secluded hallway of the Sheriff's Department, with significantly less foot traffic. The fewer people interacted with them, the better. Justin and his team were quite simply a different breed. And that was why no one questioned Justin Carter as he marched through the Hall of Justice with authority.

"Look who's back!" Orlando Nicholson exclaimed as Justin walked into the large office. Orlando had his feet propped up on his desk and had been reading over some paperwork. He tossed the stack of papers on his desk and got up to greet his boss. "How's Leave treating you?"

"Not bad, not bad," Justin lied. He was losing his mind not being able to work in a normal capacity. "How're things here?"

"All good man," Orlando nodded, crossing his massive arms over his broad chest. The man was a behemoth to an almost comical degree. "Dalton and Nate won't be back for a while. They were meeting with some FBI chick about this heist."

"You guys looking into it?" Justin asked, taking a seat in one of the many open chairs around their office. Orlando dropped down into his chair and shrugged.

"I mean, kind of. But the FBI has the lead on it, we're providing support where we can," Orlando answered. "They're not having much luck, though. According to Dalton, these guys had to be pros. They were quick, efficient, and with the exception of the guy who started shooting, very disciplined. Not at all like the normal type of guys you see sticking up trucks."

"Remind you of anyone in particular?" Justin asked, curious if Orlando was thinking the same thing he was. Orlando smirked.

"As a matter of fact... yeah. That heist had Jake Tell written all over it. The way those guys swarmed the truck and popped the back with explosives, that was practically Jake's calling card. And the masks too, Jake loved using theatrical shit like that. Remember that one time they all dressed up like the Avengers and took down the bank in Montebello?"

"Yeah. Except for the fact that Jake Tell is dead," Justin muttered. "But that's what I was thinking too, watching it on TV. It was just so familiar."

"Well, unfortunately, I don't know much about what the FBI is looking into. Dalton hasn't shared too much info with us as of yet, but I'm sure he will once he knows more," Orlando admitted. He got up and walked over to one of the many file cabinets in their office. Orlando slid open one of the drawers and pulled out a large black binder. Flipping open the binder, Orlando skimmed the first couple of pages before returning to his desk. "Here, maybe this'll keep you busy until I.A. is done sticking a probe up your ass."

Justin took the binder and opened it up. All of the files, reports, crime scene photos, and evidence write-ups from the robberies Jake Tell had been linked to were compiled in the binder. Dossiers on Jake himself and his two known accomplices, Miles Dayne and Cooper Raynor, were also included.

"Thanks man," Justin said. "I gotta do something instead of sitting in front of the TV. Karolyne is at least going out and shit, but I don't know what to do with myself."

"Who says you gotta do anything? Take some time off man and rest." Orlando suggested. "Circumstances suck, but everyone needs a break every once in a while. Especially the big bad Lieutenant."

"Fair enough," Justin chuckled. "How about you? Are you all good?"

"Good as can be, my friend," Orlando smiled.

Justin was about to ask about Orlando's family when his phone rang. Pulling it out of his pocket, Justin checked the Caller ID before answering. He didn't recognize the number, but that wasn't shocking given his line of work.

"Detective Carter," Justin answered, hurrying outside of the office for some privacy. He normally wouldn't care if Orlando or any of his guys overheard his conversations, but with Internal Affairs investigating, it was better to be safe than sorry.

"Detective, it's Officer Bradford," a fellow police officer said. "Sorry to bother you, but I'm here at Rourke's Pub..."

"Goddamnit," Justin swore, interrupting the officer. He didn't need to hear the rest of what the officer had to say, Justin already knew.

"I'm sorry, sir," Officer Bradford said. "I figured it best to call you."

"Thanks, kid," Justin muttered. "Hold him in your squad car until I get there. I'll be there as fast as I can."

"Yessir."

"Everything ok?" Orlando asked, poking his head out of the office. Justin shook his head.

"No, it isn't."

"Want some help?" Orlando offered.

"Do you mind?"

"What are friends for?" Orlando smiled and returned a few moments later, his badge and gun on his waistband.

****

Justin and Orlando parked around the corner from Rourke's pub, an old-school Irish bar right in University Park. The LAPD squad car was parked on the street out in front of the bar, and two officers were speaking calmly to two women and a man. The three civilians, the man and first woman, probably in their late fifties, and the second woman who was significantly younger, were clearly very upset. Justin felt his stomach knot up, fearing the worst. Seeing how upset the three civilians were made his skin crawl.

"...That man needs to be arrested!" the older man said, jerking an angry finger toward the squad car. "That is the second time he's tried to grab my daughter!"

"We banned him from the bar last time," the older woman chimed in. She was just as mad. The younger girl wasn't saying much, but she looked absolutely disgusted.

"Officer Bradford!" Justin called, approaching the group. He shook Officer Bradford's hand and looked at the three people in front of the cops. They were all wearing Rouke's T-Shirts, giving them away as employees. "I'm Detective Carter," Justin introduced himself. "If you don't mind, I'm going to have Officer Bradford fill me in on what exactly happened here. Detective Nicholson will be happy to field any concerns you might have."

Justin pulled Bradford away from the group, stepping onto the street behind the parked cruiser; he avoided looking inside the cruiser. Bradford shook his head and chuckled as the older couple started right up yelling at Orlando.

"Alright, what's the damage?" Justin asked, rolling his eyes.

"Got drunk and made a move on the owner's daughter, who's also the bartender," Bradford said. "I guess it's not the first time he's done something like that. The dad came after him, and there was an altercation involving another employee, a busboy I think. Got the sense the kid was illegal, so probably didn't want to stick around for the cops to show up."

"Jesus Christ," Justin breathed, shaking his head in disgust.

"He should be booked," Bradford said, putting his hands on his hips. "They're probably going to want to press charges, so you're gonna be looking at..."

"You know I'm a fucking cop, right?" Justin snapped. "I know what he's looking at."

"Sorry," Bradford said quickly, feeling incredibly small. Justin kept shaking his head.

"Move him to my truck, it's parked around the corner," Justin muttered. "And then I want to talk to all three of them. Maybe I can convince them not to press charges."

"Whatever you say," Bradford shrugged. He looked over at his partner and waved him over. "Let's move him to Justin's truck."

Justin and Bradford's partner passed by each other with a nod of respect. Orlando seemed to have calmed the family down, which Justin was relieved to see.

"I am very sorry about what happened," Justin said. "I just want to personally guarantee you that he will not step foot in your establishment ever again. If there were any damages caused, I'll write you a check right here, right now. No questions asked."

"Why on earth would you do that?" the man asked, casting a strange look at Justin.

"Because," Justin sighed. He jerked his thumb behind him toward the cruiser. "That man is my father. And I know first hand what an asshole he is. I'm terribly sorry he caused you three so much grief."

Justin turned and faced the girl, who was probably in her twenties if Justin had to guess.

"You have my sincerest apologies," Justin offered. "And if you want to press charges, I'll fully support that. But, if you don't, I can promise you, I won't let him come near this place. The choice is yours."

The family of three exchanged looks that Justin had trouble deciphering. They were all still upset, that much was evident.

"He broke a few glasses and a barstool," the mother finally spoke up. "A few hundred dollars worth of damages."

"Will five hundred cover it?" Justin asked, reaching for his wallet. The mother nodded. Opening his wallet, Justin was relieved to find he had enough cash to cover. He thumbed out five hundred dollars and handed it to the father with a soft smile. The father accepted the money and gave a begrudging smile.

"We won't press charges," he said. "But if he comes near here..."

"He won't," Justin reassured them.

Satisfied, the family headed back inside to the bar. Justin took a deep breath and gave Orlando an exhausted expression. Orlando laughed, clapping Justin on the back.

"Go talk to him," Orlando said. "I'll chat up our fellow brothers in blue."

"Thanks buddy," Justin muttered. He waved at Bradford and his partner before hustling back to his truck.

Justin took a few deep breaths before climbing into the driver's seat. His nostrils were met with the repulsive smells of cigarettes and alcohol. Clearly, his father hadn't showered from the night before. Glancing in his rearview mirror, Justin stared at his father with disgust. Dave Carter's gray hair was ratty and disheveled, covering most of his drunken face, clothes just as tattered. He could've been mistaken for one of the thousands of homeless people wandering the streets of Los Angeles. And that was probably what made Justin so mad. His father was far from homeless, thanks to Justin and Karolyne, who made sure that his dad always had a roof over his head.

"What the fuck are you doing?" Justin growled. He didn't turn around to look at his father, knowing he wouldn't like what he saw. "It's barely one in the afternoon, and you're already shitfaced. You smell like shit, and you look like you've been sleeping in a dumpster for a week."

"It's nice to see you too, son," Dave responded, slightly slurring his words.

"Fuck you," Justin said. "It's one thing to get into bar fights with the other drunks, but feeling up a bartender? I mean, what the fuck?"

"She was hot. What do you want me to say?" Dave shrugged.

Balling his fist, Justin wheeled around and delivered a brutal punch to the side of Dave's face. Blood splattered onto the window of the truck, and Dave started coughing that horrible smoker's cough. Justin composed himself and took a deep breath, begging himself to have restraint. It didn't serve any purpose to beat up on an old drunk.

"You're gonna spend a few days in jail," Justin muttered, keeping his voice as calm as could be. "I'm not bailing your ass out this time. You're lucky they're not pressing charges,"

"Nice to see you finally have a backbone," Dave grumbled.

Justin Carter could've killed his father right then and there. That phrase had been something Justin had heard over and over again during his upbringing. Justin shook his head, trying to stop the floodgate of memories from his childhood. He closed his eyes and tried to think of nothing but good things; the day he married Karolyne, his first big promotion. But Justin's blood was boiling, but he knew that's what the old man wanted - to get a reaction out of him. He could not, would not, give him the satisfaction. Instead, he simply flexed his hands over the steering wheel and grabbed his radio.

"Orlando, let's roll," Justin said into the radio.

"Copy, falling back to you," Orlando answered.

"Maybe I was wrong," Dave muttered, staring blankly out the window.

****

Feeding the key into the lock, Justin opened the door to his apartment and immediately felt relieved to be home. He carried the large black binder underneath his arm, anxious to read it. There was something very relaxing to him about going over old cases and trying to look for new clues or leads.

"Hello?" Karolyne called out.

"Yeah, it's me," Justin said, kicking off his boots. He walked into the bedroom, where Karolyne was fresh out of the shower.

"Where'd you go?" Karolyne asked, drying her hair with a towel. "I was kind of surprised you weren't here when I got home."

"Went down to the office, talked to Orlando for a while," Justin said. He tossed the binder on their bed and opened the gun safe in his closet, unloading the pistol before placing it into the safe and locking it. "Then I got a call from some patrolman about a disturbance at Rourke's..."

"Oh no," Karolyne groaned. "Again?"

"Yeah, again," Justin shook his head and sat on the edge of their bed, staring at his feet. "God, Karolyne, I could've killed him. I swear the second he mentioned my fucking *'backbone'* I could've shot him right then and there. And the world would be better for it."

"Justin, I know you're upset," Karolyne consoled, crouching down in front of her husband. She held his head between her hands and smiled at him. "But he's still your father."

"Is he?" Justin asked. "I mean, when does he lose the right to get away with his shit just because he made me?"

"Never," Karolyne said firmly. "He's always going to be your father, and when he does pass, you're going to regret not having tried to mend things with him."

"No," Justin shook his head. "When he passes, the only regret I'll have is not being the one to have killed him."

"You don't mean that," Karolyne said, shaking her head. She stood up and went into their bathroom to get dressed.

"You didn't grow up with him," Justin called, speaking louder so his wife could hear him.

"You're right, I didn't," Karolyne answered, throwing the towel on the bathroom floor. She pulled on her bathrobe and plugged in her hairdryer. "But that doesn't mean I can't understand what you went through. You've told me enough stories, I know it was hell for you. All I'm saying is that you never consider how he's feeling, why he acts out the way he does."

"What on earth are you talking about?" Justin asked. He could feel himself getting more and more worked up. Talking about his father just brought out a rage inside of him that wasn't his normal self. Justin prided himself on being calm, cool, and collected. And for the most part, that held true, unless it involved his father.

"Well, think about it," Karolyne said, looking at her husband sympathetically. "His wife and son walked out on you guys. Has he talked to them since then? No. That must be horrible for him. I know it bothers you that you and your brother don't talk, try and imagine how he must feel."

"He probably doesn't even care," Justin shrugged off the suggestion. "Besides, it's his fault they left anyway. I don't blame them one bit. Had I not been in the Academy, I would've left too."

"When was the last time you talked to your mom?" Karolyne asked. "You might feel better if you talk to her about all of this."

"It's been a while," Justin grumbled. Karolyne grabbed Justin's hands and held them tightly.

"Justin, call your mom and have lunch with her or something. And when you're ready, you're going to have to talk to your dad," Karolyne said.

Justin knew her well enough to know that she wasn't going to let this go. But, he also understood that she knew it was for the best. That was part of why he loved her so much. She understood things in a way that he just never could. Karolyne saw the world in a much different light, and her different perspectives on almost everything were invaluable. As much as he didn't want to admit it, Karolyne was right. Even though Justin and his mother had come to an understanding and were on good terms, the fact that his relationship with his brother was nonexistent and his father was... well, his father was painful. It was a nagging pain, just a constant hurt that never seemed to go away.

"Ok," Justin said quietly. "I'll reach out to my mom."

"Good, that's all I ask," Karolyne smiled and kissed Justin on the cheek. "I'm gonna finish getting dressed."

"Take your time," Justin muttered, picking up the binder and heading out into the living room. There was a 50/50 chance he'd actually pick up the phone and call his mom, but Karolyne didn't need to know that.

He sat down on the couch and took a deep breath before setting the binder down on the coffee table and opening the first page. Hovering over the binder, Justin began reading. Something about the recent heist was too familiar to be a coincidence. For Justin's money, one or more of the guys who'd been a part of Jake Tell's crew had to be responsible. Or at least had been a part of planning the operation. All Justin had to do was find one clue.

The minutes turned to hours as Justin threw himself more and more into the case files. All together, Jake Tell and his crew had pulled off nine heists. In all of the heists, the crew ranged from four men to as many as six men - Justin's hunch was right. He now had confirmation that at least two more men had been involved with the heists. Whether or not they participated in the last heist when Jake and the others were killed was irrelevant. Two men had gotten away with the heists and had yet to be identified. After some searching, Jake found that the FBI Agent who'd handled the investigation was a man by the name of Owen Griffin. Jake wrote the name down on a notepad and made a note to reach out to this Agent Griffin.

After close to another hour of reading, Justin was staring at the three dossiers on Jake Tell, Miles Dayne, and Cooper Raynor. Their mugshots from previous arrests stared up at Justin. He rubbed his eyes and stretched his arms. And then that's when he saw the connection. Clearly stated on all three of the dossiers, Justin saw it.

All three men had been employed, at one time or another, by Omicron LLC.

Justin had seen their trucks and equipment all throughout the city over the years. Although he knew next to nothing about the company, they seemed to be a pretty big outfit. The connection had to have been investigated by the FBI, but there was no mention of it anywhere in the binder that Orlando had given him.

"Well," Justin muttered to himself, staring at the dossiers. "Gotta start somewhere."

12

Noah

The past few days of Noah Riordan's life were filled with long hours at the 101 job site. As was becoming a constant at work, Noah was bombarded with delays from city inspectors and other outside contractors. Still, his crew was making good progress at getting the new off-ramp constructed. Using the foot pedals, Noah walked the CAT 329F excavator toward another section of the ramp and began digging out the shoulder, loading up a dump truck that was driven by Scott. Directly in front of him, Lexi Tyler was expertly operating the D9 bulldozer. Much to Noah's chagrin, EJ and Darren had both called off of work early that morning, EJ claiming issues with his kids and Darren not giving an excuse. Chandler ran another excavator on a different part of the bridge, digging the foundation for what would be the new median.

Going in for another bucket of dirt, Noah noticed his phone light up in the cupholder of the machine. He paused for a moment and checked it. There were four missed call notifications, all from Brian Tyler.

"The hell?" Noah muttered to himself. Something had to be up if Brian was calling him more than once. Noah grabbed his radio. "Hey Lexi, you copy?"

"Yeah, what's up?" she answered almost immediately.

"Come down here and take over for me," Noah said. "Your dad is blowing up my phone right now, I gotta call him back."

"I'll be right there."

Lexi maneuvered the dozer back down the ramp and parked it close to Noah's excavator. As soon as she climbed down from the cab, Noah grabbed his phone and jumped out of the excavator, leaving the door open for her.

"Blueprints are in the cab if you need a refresher, just keep loading up Scott's truck. Hopefully, I'm not too long."

"I got it, I got it," Lexi said confidently. Noah smiled and watched her climb into the cab of the excavator and get right to work. It hadn't taken long for her to get the hang of being an operator. Noah hurried back toward where the vehicles were parked and jumped inside his truck so he could hear better. He connected his phone to the truck's Bluetooth system before he redialed Brian's number.

"Noah?" Brian answered immediately. He sounded panicked, which was completely unlike him.

"Brian, what's wrong?" Noah asked.

"We need to talk right now. In person. Where are you?"

"The 101," Noah said. Brian's tone was setting off all kinds of alarms in Noah's mind. Something was seriously wrong.

"Leave now. Head for the warehouse off Jefferson. I'll meet you there," Brian huffed. He was breathing heavily like he was running. "Call Joe and tell him to meet us there too. He needs to be involved."

"Ok, ok," Noah said and hung up.

Noah didn't even have time to think about what was going on. Brian Tyler didn't get panicked or worried. The fact that something had shaken him so badly told Noah all he needed to know. Grabbing his radio, Noah turned on his truck as he simultaneously switched channels to speak directly to Chandler.

"Chandler, you there?" Noah yelled into the radio.

"Go ahead," Chandler answered a few seconds later.

"You're in charge, I gotta go. Something's wrong with Brian," Noah said.

"Alright, I got it," Chandler answered. "Everything ok?"

"Not sure yet, I'll let you know," Noah responded. "Keep an eye on Lexi."

"You got it, boss," Chandler acknowledged.

Noah tossed the radio in his backseat and stepped on the gas, driving his truck out of the construction site and onto the highway as fast as he could. Weaving in and out of traffic, Noah pulled up Joe's contact on his phone and clicked on his number.

"This is Joe," he answered loudly. Noah could hear concrete saws in the background.

"Joe, you gotta go to the warehouse. Now," Noah said, speaking loudly to compensate for the insane noise on Joe's end.

"I'm working!" Joe yelled back.

"Me too! Brian Tyler just called me in a total panic. He said the three of us had to meet ASAP. I just left work, I'm on my way to the warehouse," Noah explained. "Something has him really freakin' worried, Joe."

"Damnit," Joe swore. "Alright, I'll be over there as fast as I can."

****

With typical Los Angeles traffic, it took Noah almost an hour to get from his job site to the warehouse in the Crenshaw neighborhood. He parked on the street across from the warehouse and reached into his glove box, producing the pistol he kept with him at all times. Stuffing the gun in the waistband of his work pants, Noah stepped out of the truck and jogged across the street to the front gate. Brian's expensive truck was already inside the gate.

"Hey!" Joe called, appearing from around the corner. He was covered in dust and concrete and was still wearing his Hi-Vis safety vest. "What's up?"

"No clue, man. But Brian's already here, let's go find out," Noah answered, pulling open the gate.

He and Joe slipped inside. Noah threw the gate shut and locked it. Since it was a typical workday, a handful of Omicron personnel was at the warehouse. However, they stuck to the shop, not going into the offices. Either way, Noah had locked the office containing all of their equipment and weapons. No one else, aside from Brian Tyler, could get in there.

They passed through the shop and stepped into the offices without incident, no one paying them too much attention. Brian Tyler was already inside, pacing nervously back and forth through the various offices. He looked like he was a few seconds away from a nervous breakdown.

"What's up, Brian?" Noah asked, concerned.

"Come on," Brian waved. The three men went into the back office with all of their equipment; Brian must've unlocked the door as soon as he got into the office. Once inside, Brian closed and locked the door, ensuring they wouldn't be interrupted just in case any Omicron employee got curious.

"You gonna tell us you're pregnant or something?" Joe blurted out. Noah put his hand over his mouth and fought the urge to burst out laughing. The situation was clearly serious for Brian to be this worked up, but Joe's comment was hysterical. Brian stared at Joe blankly for a few beats before he continued, wisely choosing to simply ignore the remark.

"I got to my office today, and two LA Sheriffs were waiting for me," Brian said, leaning against one of the desks with a stack of gun cases on top of it. He folded his arms and looked up at the ceiling. "And they were asking me about Jake and Miles and Cooper."

"What?" Noah gaped. The timing of that was far too perfect for it to be a coincidence. If LA Sheriff's were looking into Omicron LLC, then they had to suspect that someone at Omicron was involved with the recent armored truck heist.

"They were asking a lot of questions about those guys. How they met, how long they worked together," Brian continued. "They were really interested in the fact that those three guys worked together. But mostly, they wanted to know if there was anyone else who used to hang out with Jake and those guys."

"What the fuck?" Joe muttered under his breath.

"Well, hold on," Noah said, his mind working in overdrive. "Let's think this through. Those three were killed in the act of robbing a bank. The cops clearly went through old case files trying to find some connection to our heist. Surely they were going to see that Jake and Cooper and Miles all worked at the same place. And they're going to know that more than three guys were involved in that bank robbery. I mean, it's alarming, but it's not cause for panic yet. There's no reason for them to think the heists are really connected."

"But they do, Noah," Brian countered. "The one Sheriff basically said he thinks whoever got away from the bank job a few years ago has finally decided to give it another shot."

"Fuck," Noah swore. "That didn't take long at all."

"It must've been something we did that reminded them of Jake," Joe muttered. He chuckled to himself. "Shit, he taught you and me everything we know about taking down scores, of course there's gonna be some overlap."

"That's what I'm thinking too," Noah agreed. "But just because they *suspect* that someone at Omicron is involved doesn't mean they're on to any of us. How many guys at Omicron are ex-felons?"

"A lot," Brian said with a shrug.

"Well, they're going to look into those guys first," Noah said. "Joe and I have never had any legal trouble outside of a few speeding tickets."

"But what about the other guys?" Brian asked. "Chandler's clean, but I'm fairly certain EJ and Darren both have rap sheets."

"I'll talk to them and see," Noah said. "I'm not worried about EJ, but Darren is a wild card. He's probably the most likely to snitch if he gets cornered. And he's done some time."

"Well, then we have to make sure that doesn't happen," Joe said. The way he said it was so cold that it sent a chill down Noah's spine. He could tell by the facial expression and tone that Joe was implying removing Darren from the equation, should it come to that.

"Yes, we do," Brian nodded. "But first, I have to go talk to Thomas. He's not going to be happy about any of this."

"Leave Thomas out of this for now," Noah said. "Until there's real cause for concern, don't say a word."

"This isn't cause for concern?" Brian shouted. "The cops are onto us!"

"Keep your voice down!" Joe hissed. He jabbed an angry finger at Brian. "Noah and I are calling the shots. Not you. Until you go out there and risk your life, you don't get to tell us what to do. Not about this. Keep a lid on it until further notice. Thomas doesn't need to know anything for now."

There were a few moments of silence before Noah looked at Brian to turn the conversation back to the cops. Joe was right, Thomas didn't need to know anything right now. Until there was a clear and present threat to their future jobs, they wouldn't tell Thomas anything. There was no telling what he would do should he feel like he was in danger of being investigated by the cops.

"Did the cops leave you a business card or name or anything like that?" Noah asked. "If I knew who came to see you, maybe Joe and I could get some information on them."

"Yeah, they left a card," Brian said, opening his wallet. "The one guy was massive. I think he said his name was Nichols or something like that. Real scary-looking dude. Well they both were, actually. The second guy was in charge, you could just tell. He did most of the talking and seemed to know more than he was leading on to."

Brian thumbed the business card out of his wallet and handed it to Noah. Flipping the card over, Noah's eyes narrowed on the name.

Detective Justin Carter

Los Angeles Sheriff's Department

Noah closed his eyes and took a deep breath. When he reopened them, Joe and Brian were staring at him curiously.

"What's wrong?" Brian asked.

"Well," Noah cleared his throat. "We have a big problem."

"And what's that?" Joe said, crossing his arms.

"This..." Noah held up the card. "This is my brother."

Joe and Brian both looked at each other, wide-eyed.

"Wait... What do you mean?" Joe asked. "I didn't know you had a brother."

"I don't," Noah snapped. "I mean, I do, technically. He and I haven't spoken in like ten years. Probably longer, actually. My mom still talks to him every once in a while, and I knew he was a cop, but I didn't know he was in LA. I figured he was still up in San Francisco with my old man. When my mom and I left, my brother stuck around in SF, and that was the last time we talked."

"Well, you're right," Joe said, putting his hands on his hips. "This is a big fucking problem."

"He doesn't know anything about me," Noah responded. "But it does complicate things. Brian, you didn't give them a list of employees or anything like that, right?"

"No, not yet," Brian said. "They wanted me to email it over by the end of the day, though."

"Don't do that," Joe chimed in. "I'm not even an employee, and that's a dumb idea."

"The hell am I supposed to do, Joe?" Brian screamed, officially losing his patience.

"You should never have gotten in bed with Thomas in the first place, you dumbass!" Joe shouted back at him. Brian and Joe squared off like they were going to come to blows, but Noah put himself right in the middle of them.

"Shut up! Both of you!" Noah hollered. He grabbed Joe by the collar of his shirt and dragged him out of the office, throwing him outside and slamming the door shut. Spinning around, he marched up to Brian and lowered his voice. "Send them a list. Just leave EJ and Darren off of it. Chandler and I have no record, so he's not going to care about us. Joe doesn't work here, so no issue there. My brother and I don't have a relationship, and my guess is that he's not going to bother to talk to me, especially about this. Do not say a word to Thomas. Not until I've had a chance to look into all of this. Is that clear?"

Brian nodded. Noah was about to say something else when his phone buzzed. He pulled it out and swore under his breath. There was a text notification from Jessica; they were supposed to be meeting in a half-hour for their second date.

"I have to go," Noah muttered. "Just keep calm, and I'll figure this out."

****

Noah was met with an instant feeling of guilt the second he picked up Jessica from The Lamp. She'd just gotten off a long shift and was clearly excited for the date, but Noah's head was elsewhere. In the twelve years since he'd last spoken to his brother, he'd only thought about him a handful of times. There wasn't anything there to salvage anymore, at least not for Noah. Justin had abandoned him and his mom when Noah especially had needed him, it was that simple.

Their mom had come to Noah and Justin a few weeks prior and explained everything. She was done and was heading to live in Los Angeles with her father. Amy already had a job lined up and was actively looking for her own place; staying with her father would be temporary. Noah and Justin had agreed to go, eager to get away from their father. But a few days later, Justin received his acceptance into the police academy, and everything changed. Suddenly, he wasn't as eager to go. A couple of nights before they had planned on leaving, Justin had come to Noah and Amy and informed them he planned to stay in San Francisco. Amy, kind and understanding as always, had not been angry at all. She'd respected Justin's decision and acknowledged that he was old enough to make his own choices. Noah, however, had not been as understanding. The two brothers had gotten into a horrific fight, ending with them both trading punches. And that was the last time Noah had acknowledged Justin as his brother.

"...They were just so loud and so obnoxious. I swear every day is just more of a reason why I should quit," Jessica was saying. Noah nodded along and grumbled under his breath, trying to make it seem like he was listening. "Are you ok?" Jessica finally asked, turning to look at Noah as he drove.

"Yeah, I'm fine. Sorry, rough day," Noah answered, forcing himself to smile at her. "I'm happy to see you."

"I'm happy to see you too," Jessica said, touching Noah's hand that rested on the gearshift. "I'm sorry you had a hard day. I'm here if you want to talk about it."

"Do you have any siblings?" Noah asked. Jessica nodded.

"Older sister, she lives in Seattle."

"You guys close?"

"Yeah, I'd say we are," Jessica answered. "I mean, we were definitely closer when she still lived here, but we're still pretty close. We were inseparable as kids. Why do you ask?"

"Well, I've got a brother," Noah began, wondering how much he wanted to confide in Jessica. After all, he really didn't know her that well. "I haven't spoken to him in like twelve years. And I just found out that he's here in LA, and I don't know... I guess I just know I'm going to have to talk to him at some point, and that really, really bothers me."

"Oh, I'm so sorry," Jessica said. "That must be really hard on you."

"Eh, it's whatever," Noah shrugged, feeling awkward all of a sudden. He'd much rather talk about Paris or something like that than talk about Justin. He shook his head and put on a smile. "So, are you hungry?"

"Starving," Jessica said, understanding that Noah really did not want to talk about his brother. "I was hoping we could do something afterward too, as long as you don't have to wake up too early tomorrow."

"Honey, I'm always up early," Noah smirked. "What did you have in mind?"

"Oh, I'm sure we'll think of something," Jessica said with a smile. She rested her head on her hand and looked out the window. As they kept driving towards the restaurant, Noah spotted a billboard advertising a new gun range that had just opened up nearby. An idea suddenly popped into Noah's head.

"Have you ever shot a gun before?" Noah randomly asked. Jessica shook her head.

"Never."

"Well, I think I know what we're gonna do after we eat, then," Noah grinned at her.

****

After a quick yet enjoyable meal at a local Italian restaurant, Noah and Jessica drove to the city of Montebello. It was a relatively painless drive, considering how notorious all of Los Angeles was for having horrific traffic. Noah pulled into the parking lot outside of the recently opened gun range - Crackshot Sporting Range. There were only three other cars in the lot, which Noah was relieved to see. Nothing was worse than going to a crowded gun range. Throwing his truck in park and shutting off the engine, Noah looked at Jessica and smiled.

"Are you ready?" he asked. She nodded enthusiastically.

"I'm a little nervous, though," she said, getting out of the truck.

"Don't be, it'll be fun. I promise," Noah responded. He opened the back door and flipped up the bench seat to reveal a storage compartment. There were two gun cases and a backpack under the seat. Under normal circumstances, Noah only kept his pistol in his truck. But given his recent activities, Noah felt it necessary to be prepared. Grabbing both of the cases and throwing the backpack over his shoulder, Noah kicked the door shut and led the way into the range.

Soft country music played throughout the retail section of the range. Racks of camouflage shirts and pants, hats, gun cases, and gun bags filled the middle of the store. Along the perimeter of the store were clear display cases showcasing the plethora of weapons available for purchase.

At the back corner was a large sign that said "RANGE CHECK-IN". Noah headed over to the counter, where a man in his thirties stood watching something on his phone. He looked up at Noah and Jessica as they approached the counter and put his phone away.

"How can I help you today?" he asked.

"Hey, how much for an hour on the range?" Noah asked, setting the two cases down next to his boots.

"An hour is thirty, plus fourteen for an extra shooter," the man said. "I'll need to see your FOID card, too."

"Sounds good," Noah pulled out his wallet and handed over his credit card, along with his Firearm Owner's ID. "She'll just shoot on mine if that's ok."

"Yeah, that's fine. I'll just need to see her ID too."

Jessica pulled her ID out of her purse and handed it to the man. He scanned her ID and Noah's FOID card before handing both IDs back.

"Are you interested in renting anything for the range?" the attendant asked, gesturing to the wall of weapons behind him. Pistols, rifles, and shotguns were all available for rent. Noah looked at Jessica.

"Up to you, see anything you like?" Noah asked. Jessica stepped closer to the counter and looked over the wall curiously.

"How about that one," Jessica suggested, pointing to a tan rifle on the wall. The attendant smirked at Noah.

"She's got great taste," he said.

"You're telling me."

"Belgian made FN SCAR-L, shoots a 5.56 round," the attendant explained. "It's a great rifle, have you ever shot one?"

"Not yet," Noah admitted.

"Trust me, you're going to want to buy one after you shoot it. How many rounds do you want for the rifle?"

"Let's do sixty," Noah said. "You can put it all on that same card."

"I can pay for that," Jessica interjected, pulling her wallet out of her purse.

"Put your money away," Noah groaned, rolling his eyes dramatically. "You're not paying, this was all my idea. You can pay next time."

"Fine, fine," Jessica relented, putting her wallet back.

Noah smiled and grabbed both of his gun cases. The attendant handed a box of ammo to Jessica, along with the case containing the SCAR-L rifle.

"You guys can get set up out here before going into the range. Keep your eye protection on and earplugs in at all times while in the range."

"Got it. Thanks for your help," Noah said.

Stopping next to one of the small tables, Noah swung the backpack off and unzipped two different pouches. He pulled out two pairs of safety glasses and two pairs of large noise-canceling headphones.

"Glasses first, then the headphones," Noah said, slipping the glasses on before stretching the headphones over his ears.

"Got it," Jessica followed suit, adjusting the headphones to fit properly. Grinning, Noah gave her a thumbs up, and together, they walked into the range.

A single range employee stood at the back of the range. He nodded at them respectfully and held up three fingers, telling them to go to the third shooting bay. Only one other person was on the range actively shooting. Noah and Jessica set the cases down, and Noah retrieved a stack of targets from the back of the range. He clipped the first paper target onto the rail before opening any of the cases.

"We'll start small," Noah said, popping open the smallest case. It contained a compact nine-millimeter pistol. He grabbed a box of ammo from the backpack and opened it, setting the bullets, the empty magazine, and the weapon on the table. "You're gonna have to load it since you're shooting."

"I'm shooting first?" Jessica asked. Noah nodded. She was clearly a little apprehensive, but Jessica stepped up and gently picked up one of the bullets.

"Now, feed it into the magazine like this," Noah demonstrated. He snapped the first round into the magazine. "Just put like five or six rounds in, and we'll go from there."

"Ok," Jessica went to work, carefully loading the magazine. As she was doing that, Noah flipped the control switch in their bay and sent the target seven yards downrange. It was a good starting distance for a new shooter, especially with a pistol. "Alright, now what?" Jessica asked once she finished loading the magazine.

"The magazine goes in the gun just how you have it," Noah said. "Snap it in there and then pull the slide back. That'll load the first round, and you'll be good to go. Keep the barrel pointed downrange at all times, but once you're ready, go ahead and fire."

Jessica slammed the magazine into the breach and racked the slide, chambering the first round. She took a couple of deep breaths and gave Noah a nervous smile. Both hands on the gun, Jessica raised the weapon and aimed. After a brief pause, Jessica squeezed the trigger. The Glock bucked in her hands, but she did a good job of controlling the recoil.

Noah looked over to see where the first shot had hit. It was wide right, but a pretty decent shot for someone who'd never shot a gun before. Feeling relaxed after the first shot, Jessica squeezed the trigger again and again until the slide locked back and the gun was empty. Keeping the barrel aimed at the target, Jessica set the gun down and turned around. She was grinning.

"I love this!" she said excitedly. Noah flipped the control switch again and brought the target back towards them. The six rounds all went right, but Noah was impressed with her shot grouping.

"You're a natural," he said, pointing out where the bullets hit the target. "Let's do it again."

The next twenty or so minutes were spent with Jessica getting more comfortable shooting. Her shot group improved noticeably, and a couple of rounds even worked their way closer to a bullseye. Once Noah felt that she could handle the recoil, he opened his second gun case to reveal his favorite gun, a Springfield XDM .45. The gun was much bigger compared to the compact pistol and would have significantly more recoil. But Noah loved how sleek the gun looked and shot. For his money, the XDM was the pinnacle of weapons. He reached into the backpack and pulled out a box of fifty .45 caliber ACP bullets.

"This one's gonna have more kick to it, but it's my favorite," Noah explained, racking the slide a few times to ensure the gun was empty. He set the gun down on the table and stepped away, letting Jessica have the bay.

"Why don't you shoot first?" Jessica suggested. "I wanna see how you do it."

"Alright," Noah said, eager to shoot the XDM. "If you insist."

"I insist," Jessica said, winking at him.

Noah went to work quickly loading the magazine to its capacity at thirteen rounds. Once he finished, he snapped the magazine into the gun and racked the slide in one fluid motion. He'd done it a hundred times by now, but every time he heard the slide lock into place, he got excited. Noah took a deep breath, planted his feet, and raised the gun. He wrapped his finger around the trigger and exhaled, relaxing every muscle in his body.

As fast as he could, Noah blasted off the entire thirteen-round magazine. The slide locked back, and Noah dumped the empty magazine, the barrel still smoking as he set the gun down on the table. He turned around, and Jessica stared at him, her mouth slightly open.

"What the hell was that?" she asked.

"Not my first time," Noah shrugged casually. Jessica laughed nervously. "You want to try?"

"That's really all you're going to say?" Jessica asked. Again, Noah shrugged.

"I've been shooting for a long time," Noah said. "Once you get the hang of it, shooting fast is pretty easy."

"But you didn't just shoot fast..." Jessica said, flipping the switch to pull the target back to them. It swung back to them and came to a stop right in front of the bay. Every single round that Noah had fired had been within an inch of each other, all in the center circle of the target. "I mean, that's pretty freaking impressive."

"I got lucky," Noah said, brushing it off. "Come on, let's see how you do with the XDM."

Noah replaced the target with a fresh one and sent it back downrange. Jessica loaded up the XDM and aimed the pistol, focusing entirely on trying to fire a tight shot group. As she took her first few shots, Noah folded up his paper target and stuffed it in the backpack. He hoped Jessica wouldn't press anymore about his shooting ability. There wasn't exactly a great way to explain that to her without completely lying. When Noah had first been approached by Jake Tell to participate in the heists, Jake and Noah had spent a significant amount of time shooting together. Jake taught Noah everything from how to aim, proper form, and things of that nature. Since then, Noah made a point of going to the range as much as he could. There was something extremely relaxing about range shooting.

With only fifteen minutes left on their range time, Jessica and Noah switched bays to accommodate a longer distance. The pistol side of the range only went out to twenty yards. However, the rifle side went out as far as a hundred yards.

"Are you ready for the rifle?" Noah asked with a sly smile. "That's a lot of weapon right there."

"I can handle it," Jessica said confidently.

"That's what I like to hear," Noah chuckled.

Popping open the gun case, Noah marveled at the sleek-looking SCAR-L rifle. He set a box of rifle ammo on the table, gently picked up the weapon, and set it next to the ammo.

"You can shoot first," Jessica said. "I wanna see how good you are with a rifle."

"Ugh, don't put me on the spot like that," Noah grinned. "I get nervous."

"Uh huh, sure," Jessica smiled. She leaned in and kissed his cheek. "I'm having a really good time."

"Me too," Noah said, putting his arm around her and kissing the side of her forehead. Jessica pulled out her phone and opened the camera; she held the phone up and put her arm around Noah.

"Smile," Jessica said. And Noah did just that. He leaned in close to her as she snapped the picture.

"You're gonna have to send me that," Noah began loading bullets into the rifle magazine, hoping Jessica couldn't tell he was blushing.

Feeding the magazine into the rifle, Noah brought the stock into his shoulder and peered through the generic optic attached to the gun. He'd already sent the target out as far as it would allow. Steadying his aim, Noah flipped the safety off and pulled the trigger. The rifle barked, and the bullet tore through the target at the end of the range, a near-perfect shot. Noah grinned to himself. The salesman wasn't kidding. Noah had only fired one shot, and he was already in love.

"Damn," Noah muttered under his breath. He squeezed the trigger again, and his smile grew. After emptying the rest of the magazine into the target, Noah stepped aside and let Jessica finish up with the rifle. Noah watched, impressed by her natural ability to shoot. It wasn't a skill that everyone had. Obviously, it could be learned and honed, but Jessica was a natural. The way she effortlessly handled herself proved that. Noah had never been good at choosing dates, or so Paris had said. But, once he saw the smile on Jessica's face as she pulled the trigger on the badass rifle, Noah knew he'd done alright.

****

Following Jessica's directions, Noah drove back to her apartment building; it was a funky-looking building close to the USC campus. Noah parked on the street and turned to look at Jessica. He didn't even mind that he was out so much later than he ever was, especially on a work night. It amazed him how spending the night with her had made him almost entirely forget about his brother, the heists, and everything that was a mess in his life. When he was with her, that stuff ceased to matter.

"I had a really good time tonight," Jessica said. "That's the second time now you've outdone yourself."

"I live to impress," Noah said. Jessica laughed and smiled at him. She touched Noah's neck and pulled him in for a kiss. Their lips touched, and Noah swore he heard Jessica audibly sigh. It was adorable.

"When can I see you again?" Jessica asked in a soft voice.

"How about this weekend?" Noah suggested. "Maybe I could cook you dinner or something?"

"Noah Riordan can cook as well?" Jessica exclaimed. "Is there anything you can't do?"

"If you find out, let me know," Noah responded, again getting a laugh from Jessica.

"This weekend sounds great," Jessica said, touching Noah's face. "I'll see you then. Thank you for a great night."

"You're welcome," Noah smiled. "It was a great night."

"Bye, Noah," Jessica kissed him on the cheek and got out of the truck.

Noah waited until she got into the apartment building before driving away. As he sped back toward his home, he finally checked his phone. He had several emails from work, a few texts from Joe, a missed call from his mom, and a text attachment from Jessica containing the picture of them at the range. He made a mental note to call his mom back tomorrow before calling Joe to see what was up.

"Yo," Joe answered after a few rings. "It's late. I figured you were in bed for the night."

"Nah, not yet," Noah muttered. "What's up?"

"You know I know some guys in the department, right?" Joe asked, referring to a couple of old friends he had that were on the LAPD.

"Yep," Noah answered.

"Well, I asked them a few questions about your brother," Joe said. "And I think you'll be interested to hear what I found out."

"Oh yeah?" Noah asked, not at all in the mood to talk about Justin.

"Yeah. Let's meet up tomorrow and talk. We've got a few things you and I need to get situated before the bank job this weekend."

"Shit," Noah grumbled. He'd known the bank job was this weekend, and he'd still made plans with Jessica. Must've been a momentary lapse in judgment.

"What?" Joe asked.

"Forget it. Yeah, tomorrow after work meet me at the warehouse," Noah said.

"I'll be there."

****

The last Omicron employees were leaving the warehouse for the day when Noah sped into the parking lot. Most of them knew Noah's face and didn't bat an eye when they saw him coming and going at off-hours. It only took a few minutes for Joe's truck to appear in the lot; he backed in right next to Noah's truck. Noah rolled down his window and waved casually.

"Long day?" Joe asked after rolling down his windows too.

"Eh, not too bad," Noah answered. "You?"

"Oh, you know how it is. Just another day of keeping the city lit. Typical walk in the park for us electricians."

"Sure," Noah chuckled. "So what did you wanna tell me? I'm heading over to my mom's for dinner, so I'm kind of in a hurry."

"I'll keep it quick," Joe said. He tossed Noah a thin black folder. "You can read more in there, but basically, your brother is on administrative leave right now. He shot some guys or something, and he's still under investigation."

"If he's on leave, then there's no way he should be investigating anything involving Omicron," Noah commented.

"Exactly. Police procedure mandates that all cops on leave turn in their badges and guns."

"Any idea who was with my brother, then?"

"Yeah, info's all in that folder, but a Sheriff named Orlando Nicholson. He and your brother are apparently some bigshots in the Sheriff's Department. My guys gave me information on all the dudes on the team."

"Alright, I'll look into it," Noah said, rubbing his temple. "What do you think we should do about that?"

"Honestly, I think we need to keep an eye on your brother," Joe said. "If he's doing this all on his own without proper warrants and stuff, he's clearly bending protocol and procedure. And the only reason he'd be doing that is if he really knows something. Otherwise, why risk it? I don't know how all that shit works, but I'm guessing he could lose his job over that."

"I'm gonna see my mom tonight," Noah said. "I'll ask her what she knows about what he's been up to."

"That's a good idea. And, if it's ok with you," I'm gonna look into him a little."

"Explain that, just so we're clear," Noah looked at Joe seriously. Joe cocked his head slightly.

"I mean, I'm going to look into him. I'm gonna see where he lives, maybe tail him a little, and see what we get," Joe explained. "Dealing with the cops is one thing. Dealing with a Sheriff who wants to play vigilante is a different story."

"Alright, just don't do anything stupid, Joe," Noah shook his head. "I talked to my guys today. We're still on for this weekend."

"Good," Joe nodded. "I've got a tap in the security cameras around the bank, so we're good there. I'll just have to find a place to lie low so I can monitor everything while you guys go in."

"I'm sure you'll figure it out," Noah said. "I'll see you later, I gotta roll."

"See ya," Joe waved. "And tell momma Riordan I said hey."

"You got it," Noah nodded with a small smile.

Joe and Noah pulled out of the warehouse together. Noah stopped once he was past the gate and locked it. He climbed back into his truck and headed off towards his mother's house, his brother still weighing heavily on his mind. Noah had a sick feeling in his gut about all of this. Joe was right, there was no reason Justin should've gone to Omicron if he was on administrative leave. As he kept driving, Noah felt a wave of dread sweep over him. Justin's involvement and interest in his affairs had changed everything. One way or another, this was not going to end well.

****

As was routine before stopping by his mom's house, Noah went home to get Ivy. She had been cooped up in the house too much recently, and Noah felt bad for having to leave her all the time, but Ivy didn't seem to mind. Noah parked his truck in his usual spot on the street in front of his mom's house and opened the door for Ivy, who jumped out and darted up toward the front door, barking excitedly. Amy Riordan opened the door, and Ivy jumped up on her hind legs to greet her.

"Ivy, get down," Noah said, rolling his eyes. "Sorry, she's been locked up at the house all week."

"Oh stop it, you know I love this dog," Amy said, scratching Ivy's head. "She's more than welcome to stay with me for a few days if you're busy. Work giving you trouble?"

"Yeah," Noah nodded, giving his mom a hug. They went inside, and Ivy assumed her position on her dog bed, already worn out from all the excitement. "I appreciate it, I might drop her off then this weekend. Next week is going to be hectic."

"Please. I enjoy having her around," Amy said. "Can I get you anything to drink or eat? I've got chili on the stove."

"Yeah, that sounds great. Thanks," Noah sat down at the kitchen table. "Where's the old man at?"

"He's out with his friends, today's their golf day," Amy explained, grabbing a clean bowl and loading it with chili. She grabbed a spoon and set the food in front of her son. "It's good to see you."

"You too," Noah smiled and dug into the food. As usual, his mom's cooking was unrivaled to any food he'd ever tried. Amy sat down next to him and waited for Ivy to inevitably come over and rest her head on Amy's knee.

"So, work's been a pain?" Amy asked.

"Yeah, just a lot going on right now," Noah nodded. "I'm doing some side work with Joe too, and it's just taking up a lot of time. He says hi, by the way."

"Tell him I said hi, too," Amy smiled. "I always liked Joe, he's a good kid."

"Yeah, he's great," Noah said, taking another monstrous bite of chili. There was no real great way to transition the conversation to Justin. Noah just had to ask. He knew it would surprise his mom for sure, but she knew more about what he was up to than Noah did. "Have you talked to Justin recently?"

Amy froze and stared at Noah, narrowing her eyes at him. Noah continued eating, trying to remain as casual as could be.

"What?" Noah asked after Amy kept looking at him funny.

"Nothing, it's just... It's been years since you even said his name. Just caught me off guard is all," Amy said softly. "But yes, I have. As a matter of fact, he invited me over for dinner on Saturday."

"Really?" Noah cocked his head. This time, he was caught off guard.

"Yes."

"I didn't know he was here. Guess I thought he was still up north with..." Noah stopped himself before he said his father's name.

"They're both here, I think," Amy said, keeping her voice quiet. She and Noah hadn't openly talked about Justin or Dave in so long. It was strange in and of itself that Noah had even asked about Justin.

"Hmm," Noah grunted, going back to his chili. Unfortunately, it didn't appear that Amy had any relevant information on Justin. But perhaps she'd get some soon. "Are you gonna have dinner with him?"

"I don't see why not," Amy answered. "He is my son after all. Plus, I'd like to finally meet his wife."

"He's married?"

"Yep. Her name is Karolyne. She's a cop, just like him," Amy informed.

"Interesting."

"Why don't you come with me?" Amy suggested. "I'm sure Justin wouldn't mind, and it might be kind of nice for you two to see each other again."

"No offense, mom," Noah began. "But we've gone this long without talking. If he had something to say to me, he'd reach out. I got nothing to say to him right now."

"Just thought I'd ask," Amy said sadly. "I do hope you forgive him at some point. It's your life, I won't force you to talk to him, but it would mean a lot to me if you could give him a chance. He's not like your father, he's a good kid."

"This chili is great," Noah responded. Amy sighed and got up to pet Ivy.

Noah felt like a jerk, knowing his personal vendetta against Justin was hurting his mom more than it was hurting him. But he just wasn't ready. He had too much on his plate right now to worry about his so-called brother. The bank job was going to be much more complex than a truck, and he needed to focus solely on that. If Justin was inserting himself into the investigation, Noah had a feeling that their paths would cross anyway.

And that was a recipe for disaster.

13

Noah

Although Noah wouldn't exactly call himself a chef, he knew his way around the kitchen pretty well. However, he was especially talented when it came to the grill. Spending his teenage years around his mom and his grandpa had been crucial in his development as a cook. Amy was a culinary expert, and Ron had been a master on the grill. Ron had taught Noah everything he knew about grilling, and it still remained a fond memory for Noah.

Noah's backyard wasn't big at all, as was the case with most homes in his neighborhood. He had a brown fence around the perimeter and well-kept landscaping that made it look much nicer than some of the other yards he saw on his street. His patio, which he'd built himself, was the highlight. A table and set of chairs were positioned at the center of the small patio, along with a large umbrella for when it got too sunny. The grill sat right next to the door that led into his house. On the other side of the door was a large water dish for Ivy, who was running around in the backyard chasing a large exercise ball.

"She's a trip," Jessica commented, watching Ivy gleefully play with the ball.

"Yeah, I love her," Noah smiled as Ivy tumbled over the ball. He popped open the grill to flip the steaks he was grilling for dinner. Along with the steaks, Noah had mixed vegetables sauteeing on a sheet of tinfoil, perfectly seasoned.

"Dinner smells great," Jessica complimented, setting her glass of red wine down on the table. She came up behind Noah and wrapped her arms around him, resting her head on his back. "Thanks for having me over."

"Of course," Noah smiled, closing the grill and turning around to look at her. Jessica looked, in a word, incredible. Noah felt a little bad that she'd clearly gone to a lot of trouble to dress up for tonight. She wore a form-fitting green dress and matching high heels. Her makeup and hair were done up to perfection. "You look gorgeous," Noah commented, taking her hand and spinning her around in front of him.

"Why thank you," she laughed, blushing slightly. "It's a special occasion, I don't think a guy has ever offered to cook me dinner."

"I find that hard to believe," Noah smirked. Jessica rolled her eyes.

"Duke didn't know how to cook anything that didn't include protein powder," she said. "God, I don't know what I was thinking with him."

"Me neither, to be honest," Noah laughed. "I mean, don't get me wrong, he's got big muscles and all."

"And that's about it," Jessica shook her head. "In terms of goals and stuff, he had none outside of working out. I mean, he's still living with his brother. He's almost thirty and has never lived on his own. Barely has a full-time job..."

"Yeah, sounds like a winner," Noah said sarcastically.

"Oh, yeah," Jessica laughed. "So, if you don't mind me asking, did you get everything sorted out with your brother?"

"Nah, not really," Noah shook his head. He'd been expecting her to ask about it. "I'm sure I'll figure it out at some point but just haven't really wanted to address it yet."

"I get it," Jessica said. Noah could tell she was a little curious as to the history of Noah and his brother. He sat down in one of the chairs, and Jessica did the same.

"I didn't exactly have a great childhood," Noah began, rocking back in the chair as far as it would go. "So when my mom decided to leave my dad, I was all for it. My mom, my brother, and myself were supposed to leave together. And then I don't know what happened, but my brother got cold feet and stayed behind. That was twelve years ago and the last time I spoke to him."

"Wow," Jessica breathed. "I can't imagine how hard that must've been for you."

"Yeah, I mean I got over it," Noah shrugged, getting up to check on their food. "But that's why I wasn't overly excited to find out that he's here."

"I appreciate you telling me that," Jessica acknowledged that that couldn't have been easy for him to disclose. Noah smiled at her over his shoulder and popped the grill cover open. Much to his delight, the food looked perfect.

"Alright, dinner is served," Noah said, putting the steak and vegetables onto a large platter.

Noah and Jessica enjoyed a somewhat romantic dinner at Noah's kitchen table. He'd put a white table cloth down, lit a candle at the center of the table, and had soft music playing in the background. Ivy lay at their feet, hoping to catch any crumbs or scraps of food. For the first time in his life, Noah genuinely felt that his efforts had been appreciated. Paris had never had any interest in nights like this. If they weren't dining out at a restaurant Noah couldn't afford, it didn't count as a date. The more he thought about it, the more he kicked himself for not having dumped her sooner. Things that had been so much work and effort with Paris felt effortless with Jessica. The conversation was light and natural, no awkward silences or lapses. It felt good, and Noah recognized that he was happy. Happier than he'd ever been with Paris, which truly wasn't saying much.

Once they finished dinner, Noah quickly did the dishes and poured two more glasses of wine. Jessica had insisted on bringing dessert, and when it was time, she pulled out a delicious-looking apple pie.

"You're not the only one who's handy in the kitchen," Jessica said, proudly displaying the pie.

"Dang, you really outdid yourself," Noah said, sitting back down in the kitchen. "That looks delicious."

"I hope so! I had to call my mom and ask for help," Jessica laughed. Noah grinned and got two plates, two forks, and a bigger knife to cut the pie. Jessica took the knife and plates and delicately sliced two pieces onto the plates. Noah took a bite and was immediately impressed.

"Dude, this is freaking amazing!" he said, scooping another bite into his mouth. Again, Jessica blushed.

"Yay!" she grinned. "I was so nervous. I don't normally bake, if I'm being honest."

"Yeah man, you crushed it," Noah said, polishing off his plate with ease.

"So, what're you doing tomorrow?" Jessica asked. "Saturday's are usually my days off."

"Yeah, mine too," Noah muttered. But tomorrow was not a day off for Noah. Tomorrow, Noah would walk into a bank in Beverly Hills and rob it. "I'm doing a side job with some guys I work with tomorrow, just for some extra cash."

"Is that a good thing?" she asked. Noah chuckled at the irony of the question.

"No, not really," he admitted.

"Well, I'll get going then," Jessica stood up. "I don't wanna keep you up if you've got to be up early. Thank you for a really great night, Noah."

"You don't have to leave," Noah said with a soft smile; he stood up too. "I don't need much sleep anyways."

"No, it's ok," Jessica shrugged. She leaned over and gave Noah a hug. "I mean it, I had a really great night."

"So did I," Noah said. He moved his hand up Jessica's back and into her hair, pulling her in for a kiss. It was soft at first, respectful and tender. Jessica pulled away, and the look in her eye had changed. Noah grinned at her mischievously. "You're not going to leave right now, are you?"

"Shut up," Jessica rolled her eyes and pressed her lips against Noah's. He picked her up as she threw her arms around his neck and her legs around his waist. Carefully, Noah carried her to his bedroom.

****

Noah awoke the next morning with Jessica sleeping soundly on his shoulder. He smiled and gently ran his hand through her blonde hair. Reaching over to the nightstand, Noah grabbed his phone to check the time. It was just past five in the morning, around the usual time that Noah would be up and out the door for work. There was no chance he was getting back to sleep, not with what was in store for him today. Surprisingly, he didn't feel anxious or nervous. The biggest reason for this was that Noah knew what he was doing. Banks were a different beast altogether than trucks, but there were fewer variables to account for. He'd done enough banks with Jake Tell to know they'd be fine. If everyone kept cool and did their jobs, they'd be good. After today, Noah would be one step closer to getting out from under Thomas Swaney's thumb.

As gently as he could, Noah slipped out of bed, hoping he wouldn't wake Jessica. He wasn't thrilled about leaving her in his home alone, but he didn't have to leave right away. There were still a few things Noah had to square away before he left. Pulling on a pair of drawstring sweatpants, Noah walked across the hall to his spare bedroom, which was hardly ever used. There was a bed and dresser, but other than that, not much; at least that's what the naked eye saw. Noah quietly opened the closet to reveal a massive biometric safe. Putting his thumb on the scanner, the reader scanned his thumbprint. A small keypad appeared once the fingerprint was verified. Noah plugged in the code and the lock disengaged. He opened the safe, revealing his guns and stacks upon stacks of cash. While he kept a significant amount of money from his cuts of the heists in a secure lockbox at his bank, he stored a pretty large amount in his home. Noah wasn't a big spender, not at all. All of this was for his mom and his kids, should he ever have any. Although he didn't enjoy its politics, the Union paid him extremely well - to the point where Noah hadn't really ever had to worry about money. The money from his heists would allow his mom to retire wherever she pleased; it was the least he could do after everything she'd done for him.

Noah grabbed his compact pistol and slid the loaded magazine into the breach. He wrapped the gun in a rag and locked the safe, closing the closet door once he was done. As quietly as he could, Noah slipped out the front door and put the gun in the glove compartment of his truck. Once he got back inside, Ivy walked up to him, wagging her tail.

"How are you doing, girl?" Noah whispered, petting his dog. He let her out in the backyard and hurried back upstairs to get his clothes. Everything he needed for the heist was set aside in a large garment bag. Noah slipped into a pair of jeans and an old Omicron hoodie before grabbing the garment bag.

"Are you leaving?" Jessica suddenly asked. Her face was still buried in his pillows.

"Sorry, I didn't mean to wake you," Noah whispered, crossing the room to the side of the bed. He knelt down and kissed Jessica's cheek. "Yeah, I gotta get going soon. You're more than welcome to hang out here. I'll be back later today."

"Are you sure?" she asked, rolling over onto her side to look at Noah. She rubbed her eyes a few times, trying to adjust to the dark.

"Of course," Noah smiled, brushing her hair out of her face. "I don't exactly know when I'll be back, but you can chill here. I trust you."

"I feel really bad, but I don't want to get up at all," Jessica said sleepily. Ivy suddenly appeared in the doorway, done with her business outside. She sauntered over to the bed and casually jumped up into Noah's bed, making herself comfy next to Jessica.

"What do you think you're doing?" Noah asked incredulously. Jessica laughed and welcomed the dog with open arms, cuddling into her.

"I'll just hang out with my new buddy," Jessica said, scratching behind Ivy's ears.

"I'm jealous," Noah muttered. "Alright, her food is in the laundry room. "If you wouldn't mind feeding her one scoop of food when you guys get up, that'd be great. I'll text you when I'm on my way home."

"Sounds good," Jessica smiled. "Have a good day."

"You too," Noah leaned down and kissed Jessica on the lips. Noah grabbed the garment bag and headed out to his truck, dialing a number on his phone as he climbed inside.

"Yeah," Joe Kado answered.

"I'm on my way to the warehouse," Noah muttered, turning his truck on. "You got the van?"

"We're good to go. I'm on my way," Joe said.

"Good," Noah backed out of his driveway and headed toward the warehouse. "See you soon."

****

Located only about a half-hour west of Los Angeles, Beverly Hills was a hub for the rich and famous. Home of many celebrities, luxurious restaurants and hotels, and the famous Rodeo Drive shopping district, the city was less than six square miles but was one of the wealthiest cities in the country. Many people could only dream of being able to afford to live in Beverly Hills.

The bank was two blocks away from Rodeo Drive, creating a logistical nightmare for Noah and his crew. Getaway routes couldn't be strictly planned due to the unpredictability of traffic patterns. Noah didn't think it was possible for Thomas to pick a more complicated bank in the area for them to rob.

"My God, what is it with this place?" EJ asked from the backseat of the black Ford Econoline van. He was gawking at a pair of women walking on the sidewalk, shopping bags in hand.

"How much do you think it costs to live here?" Darren asked, craning his head to check out the women.

"More than you two make in a decade," Chandler said, unfortunately stuck in between Darren and EJ. Noah sat up front as Joe drove methodically down Wilshire Boulevard. They were packed into traffic, moving slowly from street to street.

"This is fucked," Joe muttered, gripping the steering wheel with both hands. He kept his voice low, so only Noah could hear him. The other guys on the crew were still unaware that Thomas Swaney was pulling strings behind the scenes. "I mean, could he have picked a more inconvenient bank for us to hit?"

"There's gotta be a reason, there's gotta be a reason," Noah said. He unfolded the slip of paper Thomas had given him.

City National Bank
Safety Deposit Box #338

"Whatever's in that box has got to be important to him," Noah set the piece of paper on the center console.

"And not his," Joe commented. "If it was his, we wouldn't have to hold a bank for it. The payout from this job isn't even worth the risk."

"Is he always this negative?" Darren asked from the backseat. Joe turned around and glared at Darren, who kept a remarkably straight face.

"Let's just focus on the task at hand," Noah stared at Joe. "We can argue about the details later."

"There it is," Joe said as they drove slowly past the bank.

"Alright, game time boys," Noah grunted. The mood in the van got serious in an instant. "Joe, drive around again."

"Got it," Joe made the next possible right turn.

They drove around the block once again before parking across the street from the bank. Joe threw the van in park but left the engine on. Noah Riordan lowered his sunglasses and stared at the bank. Reaching into the bag by his feet, Joe pulled out an iPad and pulled up security camera footage from inside the bank. Leaning over to see, Noah counted the number of people inside.

"16... looks like five employees and one guard. The rest are customers..." Noah said. He turned his attention back to the rest of his crew in the back of the van. Including Joe, they all were dressed in gray suits, white dress shirts, and matching gray ties. Additionally, they all wore black combat boots, black gloves, and sunglasses.

"That's a lot of ground to cover," Chandler said, staring at the bank intently. He looked intimidated.

"You're kidding?" Darren commented in mock surprise. "My god, Chandler you're a real sleuth."

"Fuck off, Darren," Chandler shot back.

"Can you both just shut up?" Noah asked. "You two are like little children."

"Sorry, Noah," Chandler said quietly.

"We went over the plan thoroughly," Noah said. "You guys all know what to do. Stick to the plan. Joe will monitor everything from the van."

"I hear you," Chandler nodded. "I'm not backing out... It is risky, though."

"The risk is what makes it fun," Darren muttered. EJ slapped him upside the head.

"It was a risk the first time we robbed the truck," Noah commented. "This is just a different degree."

"Let's just get it over with... The anticipation beforehand gives me the shits," Darren said. He pulled a black Ruroc motorcycle helmet over his head and reached behind him to the cargo hold of the van. He tossed three more identical helmets up to Chandler, EJ, and Noah.

"Thank you so much for sharing that," Chandler rolled his eyes before putting the helmet on.

Noah pulled his helmet on and grabbed the rifle he had resting next to him, an AR-15 carbine fitted with holographic optics and a foregrip. He yanked the charging handle back and slammed the bolt, priming the gun. EJ, Darren, and Chandler readied their own guns; they also carried simple AR-15 carbines. Noah grabbed a large black duffle bag, wrapping the straps across his shoulders. Chandler did the same with a second bag.

"Let's go," Noah said quietly. He opened the door and stepped out onto the sidewalk, concealing the rifle in his sport coat as best he could. The three other crew members followed suit, and they began walking toward the bank. They might've gotten strange looks at any other place on earth, but this close to Los Angeles, people didn't even seem to notice four men dressed in sharp suits and motorcycle helmets.

They crossed the street and marched toward the front of the bank just as a man and woman were approaching the front door. Noah pulled his sport coat aside so they could see the rifle and shook his head. For a few beats, the couple just stood there.

"Get out of here," Noah growled as he walked past them. The couple spun around and darted back toward their car. Noah swore under his breath, knowing they had just lost valuable seconds. Once they were in the safety of their car, the couple would no doubt call the police to report what they just saw. "We just made contact," Noah said into his radio.

"Understood," Joe's staticky voice answered. "No response yet."

The four men hurried over to the double glass doors, pausing before storming into the bank with their guns raised. There was a moment when the entire bank staff, the customers, and the lone guard stared at them in complete shock.

"Get down on the ground!" Noah screamed, brandishing his rifle. "Get down on the ground, right now!"

"What the hell?" one of the bank tellers gasped. The guard instinctively reached for his weapon, but Chandler swung his rifle and knocked the solitary guard unconscious. He reached down and picked up the guard's weapon, stuffing it into his waistband.

EJ and Darren swarmed into the bank, surrounding the group of customers and aiming their guns at them. Running full speed, Noah leapt over the counter to where the bank tellers were standing. Rising to his feet, he aimed his gun at them and waved them out onto the floor with the rest of the customers. The bank teller reached for the phone but froze once Noah stuck the barrel of his carbine mere inches from her face.

"Today is not the day to be a hero," he threatened. "Come on, on the floor with everyone else."

Reluctantly, the bank tellers complied. Reaching into his pocket, Chandler produced a zip-tie and immediately used it to lock the front door behind them. Chandler then hustled back to grab the branch manager from his office and returned a few moments later, manager in tow. He threw him to the ground next to the rest of their hostages.

"Ladies and gentlemen," Noah said, walking to the middle of the bank. The customers, being held at gunpoint by EJ and Darren, were frozen in fear. "I need you all to stay calm and stay on the ground. We are here for the bank's money, not yours. Keep your eyes down, mouths shut, and we'll all get through this without incident."

One by one, the customers dropped to the ground; they huddled together around the check-out counter. EJ corralled them together and held them at gunpoint.

"Get to work," Noah growled, nodding at Chandler. Methodically, Chandler unslung his duffle bag and began emptying the cash drawers, fanning through the stacks of money to eliminate any dye packs or tracers from their haul. Lowering his rifle, Noah marched up to the branch manager. "You, on your feet."

Slowly, the branch manager got to his feet. He was a middle-aged man with a beer belly and balding head. He was sweating profusely and looked like he was seconds away from having a panic attack. Noah rolled his eyes underneath his helmet and grabbed the manager by the shoulder. He walked him over to the vault located in the back corner of the bank.

"I need a safety deposit box out of your vault. You're gonna unlock it for me. Is that clear?" Noah growled, bringing his rifle up slightly to intimidate the man even further. The last part was unnecessary; the man was already scared enough to comply with whatever Noah wanted. Some men and women were braver than others in these types of situations, but not this man. The branch manager nodded profusely and went to work unlocking the vault.

"Call just went out," Joe's voice came through the radio. "Less than a minute."

"Less than a minute!" Noah screamed, so everyone was clear.

"Almost done!" Chandler echoed.

The lock to the vault disengaged, and the branch manager opened the heavy steel door. Noah shoved him inside at gunpoint. Safety deposit boxes lined the walls, and several carts of money were positioned at the center of the vault.

"338," Noah grunted, aiming his rifle at the branch manager. "Hurry up."

"Ok, ok," the branch manager panted. He found the correct deposit box and unlocked the hatch, pulling the lockbox out of the safe. Noah threw the duffle bag off his shoulder and stuffed the box inside, zipping it back up before hustling out of the vault.

"We're good!" Noah yelled. "Time to go!"

"You think you're really going to get out of here?" another bank teller scoffed, finally regaining some of his meek confidence.

"Yes," Noah said calmly. "Let's go, boys."

With their take in hand, the four ran out of the bank through the emergency exit door in the back. EJ held the door open as Noah darted outside onto the Beverly Hills streets. As soon as Noah turned left to head back toward the van, he ran full speed into a man. They toppled over each other and collapsed onto the sidewalk in a heap. Noah rolled back onto his feet and leapt up, just as the man he'd run into got back up. Noah's eyes bugged out underneath his helmet. It was like looking in a mirror, the man was astonished as he was. The only other thing Noah noticed was the large badge on his chest that identified him as a uniformed Beverly Hills police officer.

In an instant, the cop reached for his gun and held his other hand up.

"Beverly Hills PD!" he screamed. "Hands in the-"

Before he could finish his sentence or draw his service weapon, Noah launched himself at the officer, using his rifle to pin him against the building. He grabbed the officer's wrist and slammed it against the wall, trying to prevent him from pulling his gun. The two men struggled, each one trying to get the upper hand. Within seconds, they had drawn the attention of passers-by on both sides of the street.

"I don't have a shot!" EJ warned, trying to find an angle to shoot the cop without harming Noah.

"Get outta here now!" Noah screamed. He was straining against the strength of the cop but was keeping him pinned against the wall. "I'll catch up."

Chandler, Darren, and EJ took off running toward the van, knocking down a group of four shoppers in the process. Managing to get his left hand free, the cop delivered a solid strike to Noah's gut. Noah felt his legs buckle, but he didn't go down. He brought his knee up into the cop's stomach over and over, hoping that would incapacitate the cop long enough for him to make a break for the van. But whatever Noah did, the cop just absorbed and stayed standing. The cop wrestled back, fiercely trying to get at his gun. His eyes were filled with an intensity that Noah had never seen before. Twisting out of Noah's grasp, the officer managed to pull his service weapon out of its holster.

This was it, Noah thought to himself. He'd tried his hardest to keep the cop at bay but hadn't been able to. Without hesitation, the cop would surely shoot him and end this once and for all. Noah would die right there on the sidewalk of a city of superficial elitists. His mom would be without a son, his grandpa without a grandson. Tayler would be without her confidant and friend. And poor Ivy would be without her human companion. No, Noah couldn't let that happen. He couldn't let all of those people down. They needed him, and he needed them.

The cop adjusted his arm to aim at Noah, but there wasn't much aiming involved in such close-quarters. Noah did the only thing he could do to buy himself just a few more seconds. With all the strength he could muster, Noah jerked his rifle upwards, shoving the handrail across the cop's throat to cut off air circulation. With his left hand, Noah gripped the cop's wrist and held it at bay.

"Drop the gun!" Noah growled through gritted teeth, applying more pressure to the cop's neck. "Please... Just drop the gun. I don't wanna hurt you."

The cop's mouth was moving slightly, but no words formed. He was still fighting back as hard as he could against Noah. All of a sudden, the sound of police sirens blared. Noah angled his head and saw two squad cars approaching him and the cop. That momentary lapse in concentration was all the cop needed. He broke free from Noah's chokehold and raised the pistol. Moving as fast as he could, Noah grabbed the gun around the cop's hand and jerked the cop's entire arm.

The gun went off with a deafening blast, and everything seemed to stop. Instinctively, Noah flinched, knowing he'd been shot. He was surprised that he wasn't in immediate pain. Maybe that was the adrenaline helping him out. Noah couldn't even hear the police sirens anymore, which brought him a surprising feeling of peace. From behind the helmet, Noah looked up at the officer who had shot him and cocked his head.

The officer's stomach was bleeding profusely from a small bullet wound in his side; he collapsed against the building, a pool of blood began forming underneath him. Noah instantly looked down at himself, checking for any bullet holes; he couldn't find any. It took a moment before Noah realized he hadn't been shot. The officer looked up at Noah, his eyes glazing over as his life was expiring. Too stunned to move or say anything, Noah just stood there, watching the man die before him.

The pursuing police officers screamed on their brakes and leapt out of their cruisers, hollering orders at Noah. A second gunshot rang out, and that was what finally snapped Noah out of his daze. Shaking his helmeted head, Noah took off in the other direction, away from the police officers.

"Noah! Noah, where are you?" Joe was screaming over the radio.

"Heading East on Brighton!" Noah responded. The road was a one-way going in the opposite direction; the cops wouldn't be able to squeeze their cruisers and would have to pursue on foot. Hopefully, that would give Noah all the time he needed to link back up with Joe and the rest of the crew. However, he was running directly toward Rodeo Drive and the throng of people that was brought with it.

"Got it," Joe said, suddenly much calmer. "We haven't been made yet, I'll swing around and pick you up. Traffic is getting thick, you might have to come to us."

"We'll figure it out," Noah muttered, sprinting down the sidewalk as fast as he could. A group of women was in front of him, completely oblivious to what was going on behind them. "Out of the way!" Noah screamed, leaping over a bench to avoid running all four of them down.

Slowing for a moment, Noah turned around to see if the cops were on his tail. He could hear sirens in what felt like all directions but hadn't actually seen any more cruisers. Sure enough, a group of police officers were hot on his tail - their weapons already drawn.

"Son of a bitch," Noah grunted before picking up speed again. There was no way he could blend into the crowd even slightly. The irony was in the fact that the cheap suit was probably the first thing these elitists noticed and not that he was brandishing an assault rifle. Honestly, if he'd been wearing a suit that had been tailored by Gucci, he might've been able to just stroll through Rodeo Drive without a second glance.

****

"Joe, what the hell are we doing?" Chandler asked from the passenger seat of the van. He had the visor on his motorcycle helmet pushed up, but everyone, with the exception of Joe, was still wearing their helmets.

"Have to double back," Joe muttered. His eyes were locked on the car in front of him. The traffic was getting thicker and thicker around the luxury shopping strip. "There's no way to get to him without attracting a ton of attention. Once we get away from all the action, we'll pull over and wait for him."

"We can't wait, that's a great way to get killed or end up in jail," EJ commented.

"So we leave him?" Chandler snapped, turning around to look at EJ. Darren and EJ looked at each other and shrugged. "You two are fucking unbelievable. Noah's risking everything to help us out, and you two can't think of anyone other than yourselves."

"Shut up," Joe snarled. He looked in the rearview mirror at EJ and Darren. "And if you two say another word about leaving him behind, I'll pull over and kill you both. Is that clear?"

Creeping forward toward another busy intersection, Joe noticed the flashing strobe light atop the light poles, indicating emergency vehicles. He looked past the intersection and saw four police cars flying towards them from the opposite lane. It wouldn't take long for the cops to overwhelm Noah, especially in an area as congested as Beverly Hills. The only way for everyone to make it out alive and not in handcuffs was to get into the residential neighborhoods. But Noah would need time and cover. The decision was easy for Joe. Noah had been his best friend for years. There wasn't anything that Joe wouldn't do for him, and he was not about to let him down.

Reaching behind his seat, Joe snatched EJ's carbine out of his hands and flipped the fire selector switch to full-auto. Joe rolled down the window and stuck the carbine out of the van just as the first cop was speeding through the intersection. Using the side view mirror to level the weapon, Joe squeezed the trigger. His bullets smashed into the first cruiser, cutting through the windshield and engine blocks. The cruiser came to a screeching halt as the cops inside were shredded with numerous rounds from the rifle. That cruiser was rear-ended immediately by the cruiser that had been tailing it. The third and fourth police cars were unable to stop in time; the four cars were all smashed into one another. As expected, the cops who were still able to get out of their cruisers and began returning fire at the van.

Joe tossed the empty rifle back into the backseat and ripped EJ's rifle from his grasp, sticking it back out the window to continue firing at the police officers. He slammed on the gas pedal and bumped into the vehicle in front of him, the driver wisely pulled off to the right to let Joe by.

"Chandler, shoot those motherfuckers!" Joe screamed over the concussive hammering of the rifle. Rolling down the passenger window, Chandler angled his upper body around the van, steadying his rifle on the roof. He was surprised how calm he was doing it, but he aimed and started shooting back at the police officers. He wasn't a great shot by any means, but he did his job at forcing the officers down behind their cars for cover.

"What are we supposed to do?" EJ yelled.

"Pray I don't shoot you!" Joe screamed back, throwing EJ's empty rifle back at him. Drawing his pistol, Joe blasted off the entire magazine at the police officers before he rolled up his window and jerked the wheel to the right. Expertly maneuvering the entire vehicle through the intersection, he accelerated and sped down the road, blaring his horn wildly to get the slower-moving cars out of his way. Chandler swapped out the magazines on his rifle and sat back down in his seat, breathing heavily from the adrenaline pumping through his veins.

Joe swerved into the opposite lane to avoid a slight backup before turning left and flying past Beverly Gardens Park. He grabbed his radio from the cupholder and made another sharp right, zooming past rows of beautiful-looking homes.

"Noah, we're heading northeast down Carmelita," Joe said calmly. "I'm gonna find a place to hole up, and then we'll wait, alright?"

****

"Just get back to the warehouse!" Noah screamed, throwing his body aside as another barrage of bullets came down around him. "I'll meet you there, I've got a plan."

"No, we'll wait for you," Joe replied. Noah rolled his eyes and raised his rifle, returning fire at the cops chasing him.

"Just go!" Noah ordered. "I'll be fine. I'll meet you back later. Get out of here!"

Praying Joe would listen, Noah got back up and started running in a zig-zag pattern to avoid getting shot. He turned left and was now running right on Rodeo Drive; the fancy brand storefronts like Hermes, Gucci, Louis Vuitton, and Saint Laurent were filled with merchandise so expensive it might've made more sense to just hold up one of them instead of the bank. Noah wasn't entirely lying when he told Joe he had a plan, he did. Well, he had a part of a plan. Until this point, he'd been able to keep ahead of the cops, only having to stop twice to shoot back to buy himself more time. With all the gunfire, the foot traffic had disappeared as frightened shoppers ran into the closest building to avoid the crossfire. The people on the road, however, had less sense.

Suddenly, Noah saw his escape right in front of him. Coming his way on the road was a young man riding a Ducati Panigale motorcycle, a premier Italian-made bike. Noah knew the bike by heart, he'd always wanted to get one but couldn't justify spending close to $20,000 on a motorcycle. The bike also happened to be insanely fast, which would only benefit Noah. Reloading his rifle, Noah ran out into the road and aimed his rifle at the approaching biker.

"Stop the bike!" Noah screamed. The biker, who was only wearing sunglasses, squeezed the brakes and came to a stop less than ten feet in front of Noah. He flipped out the kickstand, put his feet on either side of the bike, and threw his hands up.

"What the hell is this?" he asked in a subtle Middle Eastern accent.

"Get off," Noah ordered, keeping his rifle aimed at him for emphasis. The man reluctantly did as he was told, realizing that his bike was getting stolen. "I'm sure you can afford a new one," Noah remarked, seeing the man's facial expression.

Mounting the bike, Noah switched the rifle into his left hand and kicked the stand up. He revved the throttle and took off down the road, soaring past the police officers who'd been chasing him. He saw another trio of cop cars coming after him as he flew through an intersection. Slowly applying the brakes, Noah raised the rifle with his left hand and blasted off the entire 30-round magazine at the cruisers. As he had been the entire day, Noah desperately tried to only aim for their engine blocks or tires. He didn't want to kill anyone. The visual of the cop he'd already killed was stuck in his mind, despite his best efforts to focus only on surviving.

Once the rifle was empty, Noah threw it on the ground, gripped the handlebars of the Ducati, and twisted the throttle. He launched himself forward, the front wheel of the bike popping up from the sheer velocity of the bike. Noah hit 100 miles per hour in seconds. In a matter of minutes, the chaos on Rodeo Drive was a small blip in his mirror.

****

Joe paced nervously back and forth through the warehouse. Chandler sat in the cab of a CAT skid steer with his feet propped up, trying to look somewhat relaxed. He was anything but relaxed. No one had heard from or seen Noah. The crew had already been at the warehouse for an hour; Noah should've been there by now. Chandler could tell that EJ and Darren were starting to get antsy. They kept checking their phones and muttering to each other. Every couple of minutes, Joe would step outside and look in either direction for any sign of Noah. Each time he came back inside shaking his head.

"So..." EJ muttered, looking at Joe carefully. "How long are we going to wait here?"

"Until he's back," Joe snapped. Darren looked at EJ and shook his head, silently telling EJ to not bring it up again. Neither Darren nor EJ liked feeling like they were in the dog house, but both were man enough to accept it for the time being.

"You two are really something else," Chandler scoffed, hopping out of the skid steer.

"Stop talking to us like we're fucking children," EJ shot back, glaring at Chandler. "This isn't like we're playing pick-up ball or something. We're criminals. I'm sorry, but a lifetime in jail is not something I want. Maybe I'm wrong, but I don't think you'd want that either, Chandler."

"I'm not disagreeing, but Noah is doing this all for us. To help us out. The least you two could do is have his back," Chandler said.

Joe stayed quiet, listening to EJ and Chandler carefully. He couldn't say anything. He knew why Noah was really doing all of this. Sure, some of it was to help his crew out. But the threat of Thomas Swaney was real, and that was something that Noah had to take seriously.

Before anyone could say anything else, they heard the rumbling of a motorcycle engine. Joe darted to the door and peered outside - Noah pulled into the warehouse lot atop the stolen Ducati.

"Thank god," Joe muttered, hitting the button to raise the garage door. Noah revved the throttle and carefully pulled the bike inside the warehouse, parking it next to the skid steer. Joe closed the door immediately and kicked the lock into place. "I was getting worried about you, dude."

"Are you ok?" Chandler asked.

Dismounting the bike, Noah stood up and pulled off the Ruroc helmet; he hung the helmet from the handlebars. Joe looked his friend over and grew instantly concerned. Noah had a vacant stare in his eyes and looked pale. Then Joe noticed the blood all over Noah's shirt, coat, and pants. Even his gloves had blood on them.

"I'm fine," Noah muttered, shrugging the duffle bag off his back. It dropped onto the concrete floor with a crash from the safety deposit box. He slowly took off his jacket and threw it over the bike before taking a seat at one of the mechanic's chairs; he put his head in his hands and fell silent.

"Guys, give us a few minutes," Joe said. He could tell something was horribly wrong with Noah.

"Can we go now?" EJ asked. Chandler shot him a look of disgust. Noah stood up and walked right up to EJ, getting far too close to him for comfort. Joe and Chandler waited for them to start throwing fists. But that never happened. Noah just stared at EJ, his eyes boring into him with such intensity that Chandler and Joe were both surprised nothing violent happened. EJ finally relented and looked away, defeated. In total silence, Noah returned to the chair and sat back down.

"Did we at least get everything we went there for?" Darren asked.

"Here, you wanna count it?" Chandler asked sarcastically. He threw the bag of money at Darren and EJ. "Do you even know how to count?"

"You know what, fuck you," Darren spat. He turned to Noah. "And fuck him."

This time it was Joe who snapped. He launched at Darren and grabbed him by the throat, forcing him up against one of the support pillars. Joe yanked out his pistol and jammed the barrel down Darren's throat. EJ and Chandler watched the entire spectacle unfold in front of them, unsure exactly what to do. The sudden threat from Joe was startling, and neither of them wanted to get in the middle of it, especially now that Joe had pulled out a pistol.

"Not so talkative now, are you?" Joe asked. Darren flailed his arms wildly, his eyes bugging out in panic.

"Joe, let him go," Noah said quietly, looking at the two men with nothing but annoyance.

"He wanted to leave your ass behind," Joe said, not taking his fiery eyes off of Darren. "If that's the kind of crew we're running where we don't have each other's backs, I'm out."

Noah got up and walked over to Joe, putting a friendly hand on his shoulder. He cocked his head, and after a few seconds, Joe put the gun away, letting Darren fall to the ground. Coughing and gasping for air, Darren scrambled to his feet and stood by EJ.

"Both of you should leave," Noah said quietly. "Right now."

Heads hung low, Darren and EJ walked out of the warehouse, slamming the door shut behind them. Noah grabbed his sport coat off the Ducati and went into the offices, returning a few minutes later in a change of clothes and carrying a full black garbage bag. He tossed the bag aside and picked up the duffle bag of stolen money.

"Here," Noah said, handing it to Chandler. "Go home. Tell Lyla I said hi and I hope she's feeling alright."

"What about the cuts?" Chandler asked, not taking the bag right away.

"Joe and I don't need it. Those two don't deserve it," Noah said. "Take it. Have a good weekend and relax. I'll see you next week."

"Thanks, Noah," Chandler said quietly. He threw the duffle bag over his shoulder and headed out. "See you later, Joe."

"Have a good one," Joe muttered, waving lazily at him as he passed by.

Once Chandler was gone, Noah and Joe went back into the offices and sat down in their respective chairs. Joe wheeled his chair over to the fridge and pulled out two cans of beer, tossing one to Noah. The two men cracked open their drinks and took a long sip, sighing in relief.

"What happened?" Joe asked. Noah stared blankly at the ground.

"I killed a man today, Joe," Noah spoke in barely a whisper. Joe took a deep breath and hung his head sadly. Noah would never be the same man he was just hours earlier. He was a changed man, forever. Very few men, relatively speaking, experienced that.

"It's the eyes, isn't it?" Joe spoke in a quiet, calm voice. He leaned against the skid steer, looking at Noah sympathetically. Noah looked up at him, almost a little confused. "When the eyes go blank, that's what you see. At least, for me, that's what I see. More than anything, it's the eyes."

"Yeah," Noah nodded slowly. He looked like he was on the verge of breaking down. "You've killed someone before?

"I think I killed a few more today if I'm being honest," Joe muttered, shaking his head. Noah had never, ever seen this side of Joe. The killer hidden underneath the normal-guy persona. "But yeah, my first was a few years ago, before Jake and all of that. I was dating this girl, and her ex came after me with a knife while we were leaving a restaurant. I have valid CCL and all of that bullshit, and I was defending myself, but I still killed him. He was closer than you right now when I blasted him. You don't forget something like that,"

"I just can't get it out of my head. I didn't mean to kill him, Joe. I didn't, I just..."

"Noah, you can't do this to yourself. Otherwise, you'll never be able to move on," Joe said sternly. "You took a life, there's no coming back from that. But the reason you did it wasn't just because you wanted to or some psychotic shit like that. No, you were just trying to get home. Focus on that and you will be ok, I promise."

Noah's hands were shaking while he listened to Joe. Everything Joe was saying made sense to him in a dark and twisted way. Even though

Noah had broken the law many times and was admittedly a criminal, he'd never thought of himself as a horrible person. He was doing what he was doing in order to protect and help people, as backwards as it sounded.

"What's in the box?" Joe asked, gesturing to the bag that contained the safety deposit box. Noah had brought it into the offices with them.

"Thomas told me not to open the box, just deliver it to him," Noah shrugged. "I'm not gonna ask any more questions than I have to,"

"You aren't at all curious about what's in there?" Joe inquired. "I don't know about you, but I'm curious what was worth shooting up Rodeo Drive."

"Well, when you put it like that..." Noah muttered. Joe had a point. Noah had killed a man in order to get whatever was in that box. It only seemed fair that Noah and Joe should know what they had in their hands.

Noah grabbed the bag and set it on the desk. He unzipped it and pulled the steel lockbox out, tossing the bag back on the floor before setting the box down.

"We're gonna need some tools," Noah commented, testing the lock.

"I'll be back," Joe said, walking out of the office and heading back out into the shop. Noah took the opportunity to check his phone, seeing a few texts from Jessica. She was leaving his place, had locked everything up, and had let Ivy out. He sent a quick response, letting her know he was still at work.

Joe returned, carrying a red toolbox. He pulled out a small chisel and a hammer; he went to work carefully hammering around the lock to jar it loose. When he finally got it loose enough, he took a crowbar from the toolbox and snapped the lock with relative ease.

"I feel like we're going to be really disappointed," Noah muttered. "But open it up, let's see what's in there."

They both took a deep breath before Joe slowly opened the lockbox. Noah and Joe stood over the box and were instantly confused. The first thing they saw was a 4x6 picture. It was of Jake Tell and his then-girlfriend.

"What the hell?" Joe muttered. He gently reached inside and removed the picture, setting it next to the lockbox. There was only one other item in the lockbox - a small flash drive with the Omicron LLC logo on both sides of it.

"This belonged to Jake," Noah stated. Joe nodded in agreement. "Why would Thomas want us to steal Jake Tell's lockbox?"

"I think the answers are right here," Joe said quietly, holding up the flash drive.

Joe sat down behind a computer and powered it up, tapping his hand on the desk nervously as the computer booted up. Once it was ready, Noah entered his Omicron log-in information so they could get on the computer. When the home screen popped up, Joe inserted the flash drive and waited for it to pop up. He clicked on the icon and opened the drive; there were exactly five files on the drive. Noah leaned down so he could see the file names. Nothing stood out to him as overly suspicious; the entire thing was just weird. Why would Thomas Swaney want them to steal a box that had belonged to Jake Tell? Why would Jake Tell have a box with nothing more than a picture and a flash drive in it? Nothing about it made sense.

"Click on the first one," Noah said, pointing to the first file on the drive. Noah moved the mouse over and double-clicked. The file opened to reveal it was password protected.

"Got any ideas?" Joe asked, looking up at Noah. He merely shook his head, there was no way to guess what the password would've been.

"Any chance you can get it without it?" Noah asked.

"I doubt it," Joe said. "Even if I had the proper equipment, these files are heavily secured. I'd need some NSA-type shit to get this unlocked without the password."

Noah was about to just give up and bring the drive to Thomas when he saw the picture sitting next to the box. He picked up the photo and flipped it over. There was a single word written on the back in the smallest print Noah had ever seen.

Jacqueline

"Hold on..." Noah muttered, taking over for Joe. He clicked on where he could enter a password and typed in the name before clicking ENTER. The computer froze for a second, but the file opened.

"Well, I'll be damned," Joe said, nodding his approval. "How'd you figure that out?"

"Why else would there be a picture?" Noah asked. Joe took control of the mouse and began inspecting the file. It was a spreadsheet containing various addresses corresponding with a dollar amount. Hundreds of thousands of dollars were attached to the different addresses.

"What the hell are we looking at?" Noah asked. Joe shrugged but kept looking through the spreadsheet, seeing more addresses and more money. "Click on a different file."

"Yeah," Joe agreed, exiting the file to open the second one. Again needing the password, Joe typed it in, and the file opened. This time the file contained pages and pages of pictures. Joe clicked on the first picture, which popped up an image of Thomas Swaney and Stan Simmons talking to a pair of men in suits. The next several pictures were from that same conversation, zooming in on the two men that Thomas and Stan were talking to. It was clear that whoever had taken these pictures was doing so without the knowledge of the men being photographed.

"Man, what the hell is this?" Noah asked, getting more and more confused by the second.

"Hold on..." Joe muttered. He pointed to one of the men that Thomas and Stan were talking to. He opened a new tab in the browser and paused, wondering what exactly to type in. "I'm positive I've seen that face before."

After a few Google searches, Joe pulled up a news article from a few years ago and turned the monitor so Noah could see. The article detailed an operation conducted by the DEA (Drug Enforcement Agency) that ended with the arrest of Marcos Guzmán, a powerful member of the Sinaloa Cartel in Los Angeles. Attached in the article was Guzmán's mugshot - it was the same man who'd been talking to Thomas.

"When the DEA busted him, my crew had been working a block away installing some wires in a new apartment building. We heard all the gunshots and shit, so I remember being pretty interested in the case," Joe explained, leaning back in his chair.

"Well, why would Thomas be talking to guys in the cartel?" Noah asked.

"I have no idea, but I think one thing is crystal clear..."

"Jake was gathering evidence against Thomas," Noah finished Joe's sentence. Joe nodded slowly.

"Clearly, Thomas is involved with more than just organizing bank robberies. He must've found out that Jake had all of this and that's why he wanted it back."

"Make a copy of this," Noah spoke in a deadly serious tone. Joe nodded and grabbed an extra flash drive that was sitting in one of the desk drawers. He quickly copied all of the files onto the second drive.

"They're still going to be password protected, but that's not an issue now," Joe said, handing Noah the second flash drive. He took it and stuffed it in his pocket. Noah grabbed the first flash drive from the lock-box and held it in his hand.

"I'll give this to Thomas myself," Noah muttered. He picked up the picture with the name written on it and gave it to Joe. "Burn this or shred it or something. Thomas can have the drive, he's on his own trying to figure out what's on it."

"Good man," Joe nodded.

"If he tries to screw with us, now we've got leverage," Noah pat the drive in his pocket. "Get rid of the lockbox too."

"Will do," Joe nodded. "I'll melt it down at work on Monday, shouldn't be a problem. Also, we're gonna need to talk about Darren and EJ. When you're ready," Joe said, crossing his arms.

"What do you mean?" Noah asked, glad Joe changed the topic of conversation.

"I don't trust them. They're not reliable, and I think if push comes to shove, they'd sell us out in a heartbeat to save their own skin. Cooper, Miles, and Jake were the exact opposite. Those guys you could've buried a body with."

"I guess I don't really trust them either," Noah muttered. "But what are we supposed to do? We've involved them this much already..."

"Maybe we don't have to do anything," Joe shrugged. "All I'm saying is we need to keep an eye on them. And if it were me, I would not have them on the last job. It's too critical to risk them fucking it up."

"We need the bodies, though," Noah countered. "Chandler and I can't take down a truck by ourselves."

"No, you can't," Joe agreed. "But the three of us can."

"No," Noah shook his head. "I already got you in enough trouble. I can't ask you to do that. When we first started this..."

"Stop it," Joe shook his head. "I know what you said, and I don't care. We take down this last score. You, me, and Chandler split it three ways, and then the three of us take an early retirement."

"You're serious?"

"Of course I am," Joe nodded. "My girl's got family in London, we're heading there once this is all done. That's the good thing about working in the trades, man. You can do it anywhere in the world."

"I'd like to meet this girl sometime," Noah said, smiling half-heartedly. He was still in a world of pain, confusion, and guilt. It would take time to process it all, he already knew that. Perhaps investing in a good therapist would be a good way to spend some of the haul.

"You will. When we're done," Joe said. "But before we go, we'll have to take care of any loose ends, just to be safe. I don't wanna get extradited."

"Loose ends?"

"Darren, EJ, and Mr. Thomas Swaney," Joe listed off. Noah narrowed his eyes a little bit.

"Thomas will get what's coming to him," he grumbled.

"Go home, dude," Joe said, clapping Noah on the shoulder. "You'll be ok, I promise. Take a few days and just wind down. If you need anything, give me a call. It's not a good idea to be alone right now and let yourself dwell, go see your mom or something."

"I know who I need to see," Noah smiled softly. There wasn't any way he could face his mom, not after today. But, fortunately, there were others that Noah could count on.

14

Noah

The streets around the University of Southern California were crowded with college students flocking to the bars and restaurants. It was a Saturday night, a night reserved for fun and letting loose, especially if you were in college. Noah navigated through a couple of crowded blocks before parallel parking across the street from a strange-looking building only a few blocks from the campus. It had been recently renovated and turned into modern apartments. Grabbing the two grocery bags he'd brought, Noah jumped out of his truck and headed for the apartments. He was feeling a little better overall, but the entire day had utterly exhausted him. Nothing sounded more appealing than going home, crawling into bed, and sleeping for a week. But Joe had warned him about being alone, and the truth was that Noah didn't want to be alone. He wanted to be with someone who made him feel like a good person.

Entering the building through the revolving door, Noah headed up to the second floor, eager to surprise Jessica. He'd stopped at the store to quickly grab all the things needed to make a great taco dinner, including a bottle of tequila. She'd texted him a few times throughout the day to let him know she locked up at his place and was heading back home. Jessica had even sent a picture of her and Ivy on a walk. That picture had been a bright spot on an otherwise horrific day.

Noah came to a stop in front of the apartment marked '2C' and switched both grocery bags into his left hand. He knocked on the door three times and waited to see her reaction. The door opened, and a man stepped into the doorway. He looked Noah up and down with a vague look of recognition. The man was wearing a tank top and shorts. And Noah recognized him instantly.

Duke.

It took a few seconds longer for Duke to realize that the man who'd beaten him with a torque wrench was standing outside of his apartment, carrying two bags full of food.

"You!" Duke's eyes went wide as he fully recognized Noah.

"Babe, who's that?" Jessica asked, coming into view.

Her face fell when she saw Noah standing there.

Noah looked down at the food in his hands and felt like a complete and total idiot. He was so busy wondering what in the hell was going on that he didn't see the fist flying toward his face until it was too late. The left side of his face absorbed most of the blow, and Noah fell to the ground, dropping the food onto the carpeted hallway. It took him a second to orientate himself, but Duke was already coming in for a second attack. Noah could sort of make out Jessica begging him to stop, but it sounded distorted to an annoying degree. A second fist connected with Noah's face, this time splitting his lip open. He tasted his own blood, which thankfully snapped him back to reality. Noah knew how to fight, after all. And he was armed, which he knew Duke didn't know.

As Duke raised his fist for the third time, Noah rolled to his feet and grabbed the pistol tucked in his back waistband. Purposefully keeping his finger well away from the trigger to avoid an accidental discharge, Noah swung the gun as hard as he could towards Duke's head; he heard the satisfying *crack* and knew he'd hit his target. Duke stumbled against the wall, bleeding from a fresh laceration on his forehead - he dropped to a knee, panting heavily.

Jessica stood in the doorway, watching the entire incident with her hands over her mouth. She was too shocked to say anything. Noah looked at her sadly and slipped the gun back into his waistband. He swiped his hand across his lip and came back with blood.

"Damnit," he muttered, wiping the blood on his jeans.

"Noah, I..." Jessica began, trying to formulate the correct words.

But Noah wasn't in the listening mood. He'd had enough bad things happen for one day. He barely acknowledged her or Duke as he walked back toward the staircase, leaving the two bags of food sprawled out in the hallway.

He got back to his truck without further incident and grabbed a bandana from his glove box, standing in front of the side view mirror to examine the damage done to his nose and face. His lip was already swollen and bleeding. It could've been much worse, Duke far outweighed Noah and was clearly stronger than he was. But both times, Noah walked away feeling he'd won the altercation.

"Noah! Noah, please wait a minute!" Jessica called, running across the street from her apartment building to his truck. He didn't even look at her as he tossed the bloody bandana on the floor of his truck and walked back around to the driver's side. "Noah, please I just want to talk."

"I have nothing to say," Noah shrugged. He opened the door and climbed inside.

"I'm sorry," Jessica said, blocking Noah from closing his door. Tears were falling from her eyes, ruining her makeup. "Look, it's not what it looks like. He just came over to grab some stuff that he'd left here."

"Do you think I'm dumb?" Noah looked at her and almost had to laugh. He tapped his ears. "I may have shitty hearing, but I still heard you call him '*babe*'! Or is that 'not how it looks' either?"

Jessica hung her head and didn't try to defend herself anymore. She was caught, and she knew it. Noah shook his head and turned his truck on, the engine rumbling to life.

"Noah, please don't go," Jessica said. She looked up at him sadly. "Can I come with you?"

"No," Noah shook his head. "I have nothing to say. You made your choice already."

"It's not like that!" Jessica protested. Noah turned toward her and stared at her.

"Really?" he asked. "You're still trying to defend yourself?"

"I'm not, but you don't..."

"Understand?" Noah finished her sentence for her. He shook his head. "No, what I don't understand is how I could've been so dumb as to think you were actually different. I should've known. I've been treated like absolute shit by the people I let in, but I seriously thought you were gonna be different."

Noah shook his head again in a mix of disgust and sadness. He wasn't going to lie, after the day he'd had, all he had wanted was some affection from Jessica. It stung in more ways than one to see she'd clearly never gotten over the ex-boyfriend.

"Guess I was wrong," Noah muttered. His words looked like they instantly hurt Jessica. And it was the most bizarre thing that Noah almost felt bad for a second. But there was nothing to feel bad about, he hadn't done a damn thing wrong. Well, at least with her. He slammed his door shut and threw the truck in gear, carefully pulling out of his parking spot. Jessica watched him as he pulled away, standing still on the sidewalk. Noah stepped on the gas and rumbled off into the California sunset.

****

It was still early, and Noah couldn't bring himself to go home just yet, knowing Jessica had spent most of the day there by herself. He morbidly wondered if she'd had Duke over the second he left for work. There was a small local bar near his house called The Hollywood; it was fairly popular for a local bar, offering an outdoor lounge area, dance floor, and slot machines. Noah swung his truck into the parking lot. He'd never been a real heavy drinker, mostly because of his father. But a beer and a greasy sandwich felt like the best remedy at the moment. Then he'd finally go home and call it a night. The thought of seeing Ivy all excited to see him, as she usually was, made him order almost as soon as he sat down at the bar.

The loud music from the dance floor was a good distraction from everything going through his head. Only a few people, mostly drunk guys, were out there dancing. The girls they were with sat off on the side, laughing hysterically as the guys moved without any care in the world. Noah yearned to be that carefree.

His whole life had been one big mess after another, with brief periods of steadiness in between. He hadn't really ever known what it was like to be truly happy. Things with Paris had been alright for a while, but something had always felt off with that entire relationship, probably because it was insanely toxic. Outside of her, Noah had never really had a serious relationship. That in and of itself was pretty sad, Noah thought to himself.

The bartender set his plate of food in front of him a few minutes later, along with a fresh beer. Noah polished off the food and beer quickly, suddenly in a hurry to get home. He drank the rest of the beer and slapped some cash on the bartop, leaving a generous tip for the bartender. Eager to get home, wash the day off, and see his dog, Noah got up and headed for the exit, pushing past a large group of people lingering around the bar. The concept of personal space ceased to exist in bars.

"Noah!" a voice called from off to his left. Noah tilted his head around the annoying group in order to see who was calling his name. He actually smiled when he saw Lexi Tyler sitting at the bar, waving at him.

She got up and maneuvered through the crowded bar over to him. Even as she walked over to him, Noah noticed a few heads turn. She wore faded jeans, a pair of cowgirl boots, and a flannel shirt that she had tied in a knot just above her belly. Noah couldn't blame anyone for checking her out. She was beautiful and carried herself with such confidence that it was incredibly intimidating.

"What're you doing here?" Lexi asked, giving him a quick hug.

"Just had dinner," Noah said, shrugging. "Long day."

"It's nice to see you," Lexi smiled at him. "Are you leaving or...?"

"Was about to, yeah," Noah nodded.

"Well, if you want to stay for a drink, you're more than welcome to. I'm buying this round," Lexi offered. She then looked at him more closely in the dimly lit bar, finally seeing his bruised and battered face. "Oh my god, Noah! What happened to you?"

"It's a long story," Noah muttered, feeling awkward by the attention. Lexi gave him a concerned look.

"I'm not going anywhere," she said. "I'm just here with a few friends. Come on, come say hi and have a drink with us."

"Nah, I don't wanna interrupt," Noah said. "Plus, I don't wanna make things weird with work."

"Oh, come on, Noah," Lexi groaned. "It's just a drink, you're not going to make anything weird. I want to hear what happened,". She pointed at Noah's face. Noah sighed and chuckled a little bit. Lexi was persistent and clearly wasn't going to take no for an answer.

"Alright, I'll stay for a drink," Noah relented.

"Yay!" Lexi exclaimed. "Come on, I'll introduce you."

She led Noah back over to where her two friends were sitting at the bar, Lexi's open chair in between them. There were a pair of guys chatting with them, clearly trying to see what their chances were of going home with the girls.

"Guys," Lexi said, getting the two girls' attention. "This is Noah."

The two girls turned around and looked at Noah excitedly, completely forgetting about the conversation they had just been having.

"No way, you're Noah?" the girl on Noah's right asked, flashing Lexi a look that Noah couldn't even attempt to decipher.

"That's me," Noah shrugged. He stuck his hand out awkwardly. "Noah Riordan."

"Hannah Winters," the girl introduced herself with a smile and a firm handshake. "And that's Terri."

"Nice to meet you," Terri said. "We've heard so much about you,"

"Really?" Noah asked, giving Lexi a look. Lexi got red instantly and looked away, but the smile on her face didn't go anywhere.

"Lexi talks about you all the time. You're her boss, right?" Hannah asked.

"I think she's actually my boss," Noah said.

"Oh, shut up," Lexi said. "Come on, let's do a shot."

Lexi ordered four shots of tequila for them. The bartender set out four shot glasses and poured them all in one fell swoop before passing them out. Holding her shot glass in front of her, Lexi winked at Noah.

"Cheers!" she said. They held up their glasses before throwing them back. The tequila burned something awful, and Noah tried his best to conceal his discomfort. He couldn't remember the last time he'd done a shot of anything.

"God, that was terrible," Noah groaned. He flagged down the bartender and ordered himself a beer to wash down the shot.

"Not into shots, huh?" Lexi asked. She was turned all the way around in her chair so she could talk to Noah.

"Not really my thing," Noah said honestly. "I don't drink too much anyway, but I prefer beer."

"I respect that," Lexi nodded, taking a sip of the blue drink she already had. "So, when are you gonna tell me what happened to your face?"

"You probably don't want to know," Noah said, kind of pathetically.

"I do," Lexi insisted.

"Alright, fine," Noah said. "You win."

"I was kind of seeing this girl," Noah began. Hannah and Terri leaned in closer so they could hear too. "And we were doing pretty good, at least I thought. Anyway, she spent the night at my place last night, and then today I had to get up and go do this side job, so I left her at my place."

"That's a horrible idea. Continue," Lexi said bluntly. Noah couldn't help but laugh at her sheer honesty. Yes, it had been a horrible idea.

"I know, I know," Noah agreed. "But yeah, today turned out to be kind of a terrible day, so afterwards I thought I'd surprise her at her place and make her dinner. Stopped at the store to get everything, and then I went over to her place."

"Wait, I thought she was at your place?" Lexi commented.

"We texted a little, and she said she was heading back to her place," Noah clarified. "Anyway, so I get there and knock on her door, and I'm all excited. And this guy answers the door."

"No!" Lexi exclaimed. Noah nodded, clearly feeling defeated. "Please tell me it was like her brother or something."

"Ex-boyfriend, actually," Noah said. The girls looked absolutely appalled. "That's not even the worst part."

"How?" Terri asked. "That sounds pretty bad to me."

"The first time I met this girl, she was with him, and he knocked her down; intentionally, I might add. And I may or may not have kicked his ass. So when he saw me tonight, it was just an on sight brawl."

"I hate to say it, Noah," Lexi began, inspecting his injuries. They were mostly superficial, more damaging to Noah's pride than anything else. "But I think he might've won this round."

"Nonsense, you shoulda seen him when I left," Noah grinned, although it was painful to do with a split lip. Lexi and the girls laughed, which did a lot for Noah's spirits.

Although Noah had wanted to go home early, he spent the next hour talking with Lexi and her friends. They had all known each other since grade school, had similar interests, but had gone into extremely different career fields. Terri was studying to be a veterinarian, Hannah was in the beginning stages of her career as a lawyer, and then there was Lexi, who was on her way to taking over a massive construction company. The company and conversation had been just what Noah needed. He was honestly surprised at how much better he felt as more time passed.

The dance floor got to be more and more crowded as the night went on, and the patrons got more drunk and more confident. Noah had never really seen the place that lively, it was very amusing.

"You dance?" Lexi asked, catching Noah looking over in that direction. He laughed and shook his head.

"Hell no, I don't dance," he said. Lexi grinned and stood up, holding out her hand towards him. He looked at her apprehensively.

"Come on, it's just a dance," she insisted. "It'll be fun, I promise,"

"You're not gonna take no for an answer, are you?" Noah groaned.

"Not a chance," Lexi smiled at him.

Noah again relented and took Lexi's hand, letting her lead him out onto the dance floor. They settled into a spot towards the back corner, at least giving themselves some space. Lexi naturally fell into whatever song was playing, moving in rhythm; her long, wavy blonde hair swayed back and forth. She was smiling the entire time, having a total blast. Not at all musically inclined, Noah tried his best to not be awkward about it, but he had none of the natural ability that Lexi did. He bopped back and forth, though, trying not to look as uncomfortable as he was. Give him an armored truck or a bank to rob any day of the week over dancing in a public setting.

"Alright everyone!" the DJ announced with a microphone. "Last call at the bar, so go get your orders in. We're gonna finish the night like we always do with a slow song. Here is Chris Stapleton's '*Tennessee Whiskey*'. Have a good night everyone, and thanks for coming out."

Lexi looked up at Noah and smiled shyly. As the song started up, she put her arms around his neck, clasping her hands together. She started swaying slowly to the beat of the song.

"You can put your hands on my hips," Lexi said quietly. "You don't have to stand there like an idiot."

"Dude, I told you I don't dance," Noah laughed. He put his hands on either side of Lexi and swayed with her. The song was actually one of his favorites.

As the song went on, Lexi rested her head on his chest, still moving in rhythm with the music. Noah Riordan couldn't explain what he was feeling. He thought back to his conversation with Brian Tyler, his boss and Lexi's father, when he'd told Noah that Lexi liked him. He hadn't given it much thought, largely because of who she was. But Noah wasn't thinking like that anymore. He was a hopeless romantic at heart and, more than anything, didn't want to end up alone and miserable. The example set for him by his parents had been horrible, but for whatever reason, Noah was still a believer in finding the right person. Paris had been a mistake, and Jessica had clearly been a lapse in judgment. He had initially been upset about Jessica, but what was the point? There was nothing he could've done differently. She wasn't worth the time and effort.

"Hey, thanks," Noah said quietly, leaning closer to Lexi so she could hear him. "I had a really good time tonight."

"Me too," Lexi smiled softly, looking up at him. "Thanks for staying, I know you didn't want to."

"I'm glad I did," Noah smiled at her, holding her a little close to him. The song began winding down, and the patrons on the dance floor began heading out. The fun was over.

Living with regret was not something Noah Riodan enjoyed doing. He deeply regretted ever getting involved with Thomas Swaney. He regretted staying with Paris for so long when she'd been borderline abusive to him. It made absolutely no sense at all, but Noah didn't want to regret not having done something. Sometimes it was better to just wing it and hope for the best. There was nothing to lose on his end; he'd already had an awful day, there wasn't much that could make it worse.

Noah leaned down and gave Lexi a quick peck on the cheek, not wanting to freak her out. She leaned back, clearly taken aback by that. Her cheeks were red almost immediately. There was a moment of awkward silence, and Noah thought he had royally messed up.

"I'm sorry," he said, shaking his head.

"Why?" Lexi asked.

"I shouldn't have done that."

"Noah," Lexi whispered, scratching the back of his neck. " I have been wanting you to kiss me for about three hours."

This time it was Noah's turn to blush. He looked away from her, trying to contain the stupid grin that was making its way onto his face. Lexi laughed and hugged him, holding onto him tightly. They stayed like that for the last verse of the song, letting most of the other people on the dance floor retreat back to their tables or spots around the bar top. When the song finally ended, Noah looked back toward their spot at the bar.

"Hey," Lexi whispered to get his attention. Noah turned back toward her, and she slowly pulled him down to her, closing her eyes before she kissed him. It was a slow and sensual kiss, both of them dragging it out as long as they possibly could before their mouths parted to take a quick breath. In an instant, everything from that day ceased to exist. Kissing Lexi again was the only thing that mattered. She held him around his neck, pulling him in as close as she possibly could. Noah ran his hands through her hair, gently touching the back of her head.

They separated, and Lexi looked down at her boots, her cheeks as red as could be; Noah felt like he probably looked the same. His heart was racing with the rush of sudden emotional heat. Lexi didn't say anything, but she didn't need to. She took his hand and led him back to her friends.

"You guys are absolutely adorable," Terri said, her tone just the right amount of sarcastic to be hilarious.

"Oh, shut up," Lexi responded, still smiling from ear to ear.

"I paid the tab," Hannah said, standing up to put her jacket on. "Let's go, they're closing the place up."

"Thank you," Noah said to Hannah. "Do you want cash or anything?"

"Dude, you had one shot and a beer. No, I don't need anything," Hannah laughed. Lexi and Terri put on their jackets and headed outside. "Hey, hang back for a second."

"What's up?" Noah asked, leaning on the bar top.

"I've known her my whole life," Hannah said, referring to Lexi. "I doubt she'll ever tell you about it, but she's been hurt a few times. Badly. It's not my place to tell you specifics, but I can tell you that I've never seen her light up the way she does when she talks about you. I'm protective of her, I just wanna make sure you know that."

"I appreciate it," Noah nodded. "I get it, I really do. But she's... She's something else."

"I know," Hannah agreed. "Don't break her heart."

"I don't think that'll happen," Noah said, longingly looking outside at Lexi.

15

Justin

The kitchen table was set to perfection, the food was cooking nicely in the oven, and Justin finally felt like everything was ready for his mom. He hadn't ever had her over to his apartment, and it was the first time he'd be physically seeing her in quite a long time. Also, his mother hadn't ever met Karolyne, so tonight was a night of firsts.

Justin had been anxious about the meal for days now. He was glad that it was finally the right day so he could stop worrying about it, but there was still that feeling of the unknown. There was no way of knowing how he or his mom would react to each other. Sure, they'd talked over the phone and had reconciled their relationship. But they had not been in the same room together in years.

On top of that, Justin had still yet to be cleared to come back to work. Internal Affairs was being extra diligent in their investigation, which was a good thing but bad for Justin. He didn't think there was any real shot he'd get charged, but not being able to work was driving him nuts. The bank robbery in Beverly Hills had been plastered all over the news. Images depicting the brutal heist were being shown on every station Justin checked.

"Don't be nervous," Karolyne said, giving her husband a warm hug. She knew he needed it right now, she could tell he was anxious about the dinner. While Karolyne didn't know the entire story, she knew about his upbringing enough to understand the pain associated with Justin's family. Karolyne also understood the regret he'd feel later in life if he didn't try to mend the fence, at least with his mother.

"Babe, I love you so much. But that is easier said than done," Justin said, adjusting the collar on his shirt. "I haven't seen this woman in I don't even know how many years."

"She's still your mother," Karolyne said. "I'm proud of you for reaching out to her."

"Thanks," Justin muttered. He shook his head and smiled. "Alright, what else needs to be done?"

"I think you've got everything ready to go," Karolyne said. "Lasagna is in the oven, garlic bread is in the oven. Once she gets here, I'll make sure the salad is ready."

"You are an angel on Earth," Justin said, giving his wife a kiss. "Thank you for this."

"You do not have to thank me," Karolyne waved off the comment. "I encouraged it, I'm glad we're doing this."

"Honestly, me too," Justin admitted.

As if on cue, there was a knock on their apartment door. Justin took a deep breath and smiled to himself. He couldn't pretend he wasn't excited to see his mom. For the longest time, he thought he'd be angry or upset, but he didn't feel anything of that nature. More than anything else, Justin felt relieved. Relieved and excited to see his mom, it had been far too long.

Justin opened the door with a smile on his face. His mom, Amy, looked equally thrilled to see him. As soon as she laid eyes on him, she couldn't help but start to cry. She covered her mouth with her hands as tears began to fall from her eyes. There wasn't anything that either of them needed to say, at least not at that moment. At first, Justin fought the urge to get emotional. But seeing his mom start to cry was what made him start to cry. He threw his arms around his mom and hugged her so tight he hoped he didn't hurt her. Amy didn't seem to mind, hugging him back just as tight. Karolyne stood in the doorway, wiping away tears from her eyes as well. It was a beautiful moment.

Amy finally got herself composed again, wiping her eyes with the back of her hand. She smiled at Justin and then looked past him to Karolyne.

"You must be Karolyne," Amy said, her voice a little hoarse. Amy and Karolyne embraced. "It's so nice to meet you finally."

"It's nice to meet you too, Ms. Riordan."

"Oh, please," Amy said. "Call me Amy."

The three of them went inside the apartment, Justin with his arm around his mom. Words couldn't describe how good it felt to finally see her again. In-person. He didn't hold any ill feelings toward his mom, not at all. If anything, he felt bad about not having reached out sooner. Justin wished more than anything for his family to be whole again, but having his mom back was a tremendous start. Hopefully, someday, his brother would come around.

"You guys, this place is beautiful," Amy commented, looking at both the view from their balcony and the interior of the apartment.

"Thank Karolyne," Justin said. "She did everything."

"You have excellent taste," Amy complimented. Karolyne smiled and nodded humbly.

"Thank you, I try."

"Care for a glass of wine?" Justin asked, handing his mom a glass of red wine. She accepted, smiling graciously. Justin passed out another glass to his wife before grabbing his own. "Mom, it's great to see you and great to have you here."

"And it's great to be here," Amy grinned.

The three of them clinked their wine glasses together and sat down in the living room, catching up on everything while dinner finished cooking. Amy talked about her job and about her dad; Justin loved hearing that his grandpa was still doing good. He hadn't seen him in years too, that would have to change soon. But mostly, Amy just wanted to know about Justin and Karolyne. She asked questions and loved hearing everything about what they had been up to. Justin and Karolyne both wisely excluded their recent lay-offs from work, not wanting to talk about that with Amy. The conversation was filled with humor, levity, and kindness. Karolyne and Amy instantly liked each other, and when the conversation turned to things that Justin couldn't contribute to, he went to check on dinner.

A few minutes later, everyone was seated around the dining room table. Justin portioned out three plates of lasagna and garlic bread while Karolyne finished preparing three bowls of salad.

"The food looks delicious," Amy said. "I'm so used to cooking for everyone, I can't tell you the last time someone actually cooked me a meal."

"Well, thank Justin," Karolyne chimed in. "He's the cook of the family. Without him, we'd be having carry-out every night."

"Thank you, Justin," Amy acknowledged, smiling at her son. "I hope you didn't go to too much trouble."

"No trouble at all," Justin returned the smile. "I hope you enjoy it. Karolyne and I are so happy you're here."

"Yes, this'll have to be a regular thing," Karolyne said. Amy smiled and took a bite of lasagna, nodding her approval at Justin.

"Very good," she complimented. Justin smiled to himself and took a bite. She wasn't lying, he had done a good job with dinner.

The conversation at dinner was much more lighthearted as the group compared movies and TV shows they were keeping up with, celebrity drama, and other current events. Throughout the meal, Justin was waiting for a good time to switch the conversation to his brother. He was dying to know more about what he'd been up to but didn't want to risk any awkwardness during the meal. When everyone was finished, Karolyne got up to clear the dishes to the sink. And that was the best opportunity Justin would get to inquire.

"Hey mom, how's Noah doing?" Justin asked. His mom's entire mood changed visibly.

"He's ok," she said quietly. "I invited him to come tonight, I was really hoping he'd show up."

"Oh," Justin nodded. It didn't surprise him that Noah didn't show up, but it felt bad just the same. "I was just wondering about him, is all."

"He's been going through a rough time, I think," Amy said. "I don't really know, though, I don't see him as much as I'd like to anymore. He's been so busy with work and all of that, but I still see him for dinner every once in a while. He's got this beautiful golden retriever, she's just the sweetest."

"That's cute," Justin smiled, trying to picture his little brother with a big dog like that. "Where's he working now?"

"He's in construction; he's a foreman or something like that for Omicron. Your uncle Corey works there too, that's how he got the job. He's been running all of the construction on the 101."

"Noah works for Omicron?" Justin asked.

He'd spent the last week investigating the Omicron connection to the recent bank and truck heists. Justin had gone over the list of employees and hadn't seen his brother's name. At least, he didn't think he had. But the fact that Noah worked at Omicron gave Justin a strange feeling. Maybe he knew something or had known Jake Tell.

"Yes," Amy answered. She gave him an odd look. "Why? What's wrong? You got all weird when I said Omicron..."

"Oh, nothing," Justin shook his head. "Just made me think of something from work."

Before Amy could respond, Justin's cell phone started ringing in the kitchen where he had it plugged in. He got up and hustled over to see that Orlando was calling him.

"I'm sorry, it's work," Justin said, stepping out into the hallway to answer. "Hey, what's up?"

"Are you watching the news?" Orlando asked.

"No, we're having dinner. What's up?" Justin answered.

"Turn it on."

"Hold on," Justin muttered, walking back inside his apartment.

He went over into the living room and switched the TV on, flipping to the first news channel that he could get. A reporter stood near Rodeo Drive, in front of a massive amount of police cars and yellow tape that blocked off the entire shopping strip.

"...We are still awaiting confirmation from the Beverly Hills Police Department, but at least seven cops are said to have been shot and wounded here today during the robbery. As of right now, one of the cops has been pronounced dead, with two more in critical condition. The suspects entered City National Bank this morning and are believed to have made off with well over $300,000 in cash, as well as a safety deposit box. During their escape, one of the suspects hijacked a motorcycle belonging to fashion model Rafat Muhammad..."

"Oh my god," Justin muttered into the phone.

"I just got a call from Dalton. The FBI wants our support on this," Orlando explained. He lowered his voice. "I talked to Bingham. As long as I.A. doesn't get too nosy, you can come back. We're gonna need you here."

"I'll be there tomorrow morning," Justin said. "And I think I know who we should talk to."

"Copy that," Orlando said. "We'll see you bright and early. Get some rest. I have a feeling we're not getting days off any time soon."

"10-4, see you tomorrow," Justin said, ending the call.

"What's up?" Karolyne asked, walking over to the living room. Justin pointed to the TV and turned the volume up a little more. The reporter began describing the shooting that had occurred in the intersection, where the suspects ambushed four squad cars. "Oh my god," Karolyne whispered.

"They just said one cop is dead," Justin muttered. "Orlando called, the FBI wants our support on this. Captain said I could come back as long as I stay away from Internal Affairs."

"I should check my phone," Karolyne whispered. "I have a feeling I'm going to start getting calls now too."

"Is everything ok?" Amy asked, walking into the living room. Justin shook his head and gestured to the TV.

"Not really," he said. "I'm so sorry, but I think I'm gonna have to go to work."

"Don't apologize," Amy said with an understanding smile. "Thank you both so much for having me over. I had a great time."

"I did too," Justin gave his mom a hug. "I'll call you soon, we'll do this again."

"I'd like that."

After Amy said her goodbyes to Karolyne, Justin walked her down to her car and made sure she was safe. Once she was gone, Justin ran back upstairs and went straight to the file on his nightstand. He flipped to the Omicron employee list and started scanning. His eyes stopped on the name he was looking for; he couldn't believe he'd missed it the first time.

"Son of a bitch," Justin muttered, staring at the name - Noah Riordan.

****

Justin Carter and Orlando Nicholson drove in relative silence on the 101 highway. They were both wearing street clothes, with the addition of their heavy tactical vests with the word 'SHERIFF' on the back of the vest. Both men had their service weapons holstered on their hips and a pair of spare magazines on their opposite hip. Orlando knew Justin well enough to see that he was visibly anxious about what they were going to do.

"You ok?" Orlando asked. Justin shrugged.

"Yeah, I guess," he grumbled. "I mean, not really, though. I haven't talked to him in years, and now I have to go and be a cop, not an older brother."

"I can talk to him, man," Orlando offered. "You don't have to say a word to him."

"No," Justin shook his head. "If anyone is going to talk to him, it's going to be me. It just has to be. It's been long enough."

"Whatever you say, boss," Orlando nodded.

After a few more minutes, Justin spotted the construction equipment with the Omicron logos all over. He turned on his truck's flashing lights and pulled over onto the shoulder, behind a pair of Omicron pickup trucks. Justin waited for a minute before he stepped out of the truck. With Orlando right behind him, Justin marched toward the heavy equipment and construction workers. A young-looking woman in a hard hat and safety vest met them halfway.

"What's going on?" she asked, looking skeptically at the two cops. "Is everything ok?"

"Hello, ma'am," Justin said in a neutral voice. "I'm looking for Noah Riordan. Any idea where I can find him?"

"Noah?" the woman repeated. She looked concerned. Justin nodded. "Um, yeah. Give me one second."

The woman took a few steps away from the police officers and gripped the radio on her jacket.

"Hey Noah, it's Lexi. You got a copy?" she said.

"Go ahead," Noah answered.

"Hey, there are some police guys here looking for you," Lexi informed. There was a long pause before Noah answered.

"I'll be right there," he grumbled. The way Noah answered her made Lexi extremely uncomfortable. Something about this entire situation was giving her bad vibes. Why on earth would a duo of Los Angeles Sheriffs be looking for Noah? Lexi turned back toward the cops.

"He'll be here soon," Lexi said.

"Thank you," Justin nodded respectfully.

After about five minutes, Justin and Orlando noticed the CAT excavator rumbling toward the duo of police officers. Justin took a deep breath and put his hands in his pockets, waiting patiently as the slow-moving machine got closer to them.

"I'll handle this," Justin said to Orlando, watching the excavator come to a stop. The operator set the bucket on the ground before turning the machine off and throwing open the door. Even though he hadn't seen Noah in over a dozen years, Justin recognized his brother instantly. Noah climbed out of the excavator and tossed his hardhat back into the cab before he closed the door behind him.

Justin scratched his chin and started walking toward his brother, having absolutely no idea how the inevitable conversation was about to go. Noah and Justin locked eyes, and both men came to a stop when they were about ten feet away from each other. Noah Riordan didn't say a word, looking utterly disgusted.

"How's it going?" Justin asked, looking at his brother. Even though he looked so familiar to Justin, he had no idea really who the man was standing before him. Noah didn't even blink as Justin spoke, his gaze completely stoic.

"Look, I just want to ask you a few questions," Justin continued. "I don't want to bother you if you're busy, we can schedule a better time to talk."

"You got a lot of fucking nerve," Noah finally addressed his older brother. "After twelve years, you're gonna come here and play cop instead of big brother?"

"I didn't think you'd want the big brother routine. Truthfully, I wasn't sure which one would be the better approach," Justin admitted. "Trust me, I didn't want to do this either, but you and I need to talk. About a lot of things. It's been long enough."

"You think?" Noah asked sarcastically. "I don't know. Personally, I think I could've gone another twelve years without talking to you."

Noah's words stung. Justin wasn't exactly expecting his brother to be overjoyed to see him, especially given the circumstances. But to see his brother so displeased - no, that wasn't a strong enough word. To see his younger brother still so angry at him made him feel horrible. It had never been his intention to hurt Noah. The fact that Noah had held onto a grudge for so many years was mind-boggling to Justin.

"Let's leave our personal feelings out of this if that's at all possible," Justin suggested. "I just want to ask you a few questions, that's all."

"Let's get one thing straight," Noah growled, marching right up to his brother. Noah wasn't all intimidated by Justin's bravado or police gear, not in the slightest. That by itself didn't sit right with Justin. Jabbing an angry finger at his estranged older brother, Noah lowered his voice to a growl so coated in anger it made Justin regret having come to talk to him.

"You do not get to march back into my life and ask me anything," Noah snarled. "You lost that right the day you stopped being my brother. I have no idea why you'd show up all of a sudden, but do us both a favor and stay away. If I wanted to talk to you, or interact with you, or even look at you, I would've reached out."

"Noah..." Justin said hesitantly. He took a step back and put his hands up, hoping to diffuse the situation so he and Noah could talk like civil adults. "I just want to talk..."

"Find someone else to talk to," Noah interrupted. "Go find a therapist if you wanna talk to someone. I ain't got anything to say to you."

Noah Riordan turned on his heels and marched back toward the excavator. He hopped back into the machine effortlessly, and a few seconds later the excavator roared to life. Noah swung the cab around, and the machine began crawling back the way it had come.

Feeling somewhat defeated by his brother's pent-up anger, Justin kicked a rock with his boot and strolled back to his truck. Orlando was leaning against the hood, scrolling through emails on his phone. He looked up as Justin got closer and gave him a sympathetic look; he could tell by Justin's gait that things didn't go well.

"How'd that go?"

"About as well as we expected, I guess," Justin muttered. "Come on, let's get back to the office. We can start by diving into everything we know about Jake Tell. We've got a few pieces to the puzzle, we just need to start figuring out how they all fit together."

"Sounds good," Orlando agreed. "Dalton and Nate are out with the FBI, I'll tell them to meet us back at the office."

Justin and Orlando jumped into the truck and carefully pulled back onto the 101. They made a U-Turn the first possible chance they could and headed back toward Downtown Los Angeles.

****

While waiting for Dalton and Nate to get back to the Sheriff's office, Justin and Orlando went to work setting up the large cork and dry-erase boards at the front of their office. On the corkboard, Justin put up three enlarged mugshots of Jake Tell, Miles Dayne, and Cooper Raynor - along with their coroner images. Additionally, he added two generic male caricatures with question marks over their faces. Also on the corkboard, Justin pinned up images from the heists that the crew had orchestrated a few years ago, most noticeably the downtown bank job that got the three men killed during the escape. On the dry-erase board, Orlando wrote out the three men's names, along with the job titles they held at Omicron LLC. He also put up pictures from the recent armored truck heist and the Beverly Hills bank job.

"Hey, hey!" Dalton Dupree exclaimed as he and Nate Murray strutted into the office. They had their tactical gear on, complete with AR-15 rifles hanging from their harnesses. "Good to see you, boss."

"Good to see you too, D," Justin waved, giving Dalton and Nate a thumbs-up.

"Yeah, glad you're back," Nate chimed in. "I was going to quit if Dalton was in charge any longer. I think the newfound responsibility went to his head."

"Shut up," Dalton laughed, shoving Nate. "Boss, let me unload my gear, and I'll be right back."

"Same here," Nate said.

"Take your time," Justin nodded.

Dalton and Nate headed back into their lockers and bathrooms to remove their gear and put their weapons away. A few minutes later, they came back - minus the tactical gear and assault rifles. Nate reached into the mini-fridge under his desk and grabbed four bottles of orange Gatorade; he tossed a bottle to his fellow Sheriff before he twisted open the cap and took a long, refreshing sip.

"Alright," Dalton said, taking a seat at his desk. He leaned back in his chair and propped his feet up on the desk. "Let's hear it, boss."

Justin cleared his throat and stood up next to the two large boards at the front of the office. He opened the binder of information provided by Orlando and set it down in front of him on his desk.

"A few years ago, these three men committed several armored truck and bank heists in the Los Angeles area," Justin began, pointing to the three mugshots. "Jake Tell, Miles Dayne, and Cooper Raynor. All three of these guys were killed during their last heist following a pretty significant shootout with law enforcement. It has been officially confirmed that there was a fourth accomplice that day who managed to get away. And while it has never been confirmed by the Bureau, I suspect that there was a fifth man involved with at least some of these heists. Probably a wheelman, if I had to venture a guess.

"Now, this fourth man has never been identified, arrested, or anything. But, given what we know about our three suspects, I think it's safe to say that this guy was, or still is, an employee at Omicron LLC. Tell, Dayne, and Raynor were all employed through Omicron and were affiliated with the Local 12 labor union. Apparently, this connection was investigated by the FBI, but nothing ever came of it. While it's not necessarily relevant, it is worth noting that the Local 12 is currently battling a trio of extremely expensive and damning lawsuits. Two sexual harrassment cases and one wrongful death for an operator who died on a site last year."

"This recent armored truck heist was just a little too familiar for me," Justin continued. "The way the bandits used two trucks to swarm the vehicle, the way they swarmed the truck, and used explosives commonly used in construction demolition. To me, all of this screams a clear connection to that fourth and possibly fifth guy. But..."

Justin paused, giving his team a chance to grasp everything he was saying and explaining.

"This bank job has me puzzled. Jake Tell's crew never killed anyone. They injured and shot a bunch of cops during that shootout I mentioned, but no fatalities. This new crew dropped a brother cop, and that means this is personal for all of us now. So, we need to find out who that fourth guy was. That is our first priority. Find him. I want to start surveilling Omicron's warehouses and offices. Just to see if anything out of the ordinary pops out at us. I have a connection to someone at Omicron, which I'm going to try and use to get some more information, but I can't promise anything."

"We're going to split into two teams and take shifts checking out Omicron," Orlando took over for Justin, giving him a moment to breathe. "Whoever isn't out on surveillance is going to be digging deep into Omicron's employees. We've got a master list, and we're going to do a deep dive into every single employee. That fourth bandit is out there somewhere, and we're going to find him."

Justin, satisfied with the briefing, sat back down behind his desk and sighed. He knew he'd have to go and confront Noah again, which was something he was not looking forward to. But, Justin was a police officer at the end of the day, and he had a job to do. There was no way of knowing if Noah knew anything that would help his investigation, but the connection was there nonetheless. He set a timer on his phone, knowing he'd have to allow for traffic if he was going to be able to catch his brother at a better time.

16

Noah

At the end of the day, Noah did his usual routine of parking the excavator next to the rest of their equipment and cleaning out the cab of any loose garbage or excess dirt. Noah tried to keep the cab of his machine meticulously clean, otherwise it would distract him to no end.

Climbing down from the excavator, Noah stretched out his back and legs, stiff from a long day of operating. He ignored EJ and Darren, who were already walking to their respective trucks. They hadn't even acknowledged Noah or Chandler since the bank job, only getting their instructions for the day from Noah.

"Hey," Lexi said, coming over to Noah with a smile on her face. She wiped her dirt-covered hands on her stained blue jeans. Lexi hadn't really stopped smiling since running into Noah at the bar over the weekend. "What was up with that cop?"

"Well, that is a long story," Noah muttered, not wanting to talk about his brother at all, especially with Lexi. "You alright?"

"I'm fine," Lexi said, getting the hint that whatever had transpired, Noah did not want to talk about it. She respected his privacy enough to not pry. "I just wanted to make sure you were ok. You looked pretty upset..."

"Yeah..." Noah muttered, closing and locking the door to his machine. "I'm alright, I promise. Just some personal issues."

"I'm here if you need anything just so you know," Lexi said, touching Noah's hand discreetly. Noah grinned at her and pulled her behind the excavator and out of sight of the other Omicron employees. He kissed her quickly, savoring the little moment.

"Your father is going to fire me and then kill me," Noah shook his head, kissing Lexi again.

"No he won't," Lexi giggled. "I promise he won't. I'll protect you."

"Well, that's reassuring," Noah rolled his eyes sardonically. "I'll see you tomorrow, ok?"

"Sounds good," Lexi smiled, leaning up and kissing Noah's cheek. She turned and headed back to her truck, tossing her red and white cooler in the bed. Noah was usually the last one to leave the 101 site and tonight was no different. He made sure everyone was offsite before he climbed into his truck and began the journey back home, fighting the urge to doze off to sleep as he drove slowly through the traffic.

Noah had absolutely no idea what he was doing with Lexi. He hadn't the slightest clue if she was just looking for a fling or what, although he wasn't entirely sure that he cared. Lexi was a phenomenal woman, and the unattainability of her was extremely enticing to him. But most importantly, Lexi was a genuinely kind and caring person. That was something that Paris, and evidently Jessica too, had been severely lacking. As much as he wanted to just relax, calm down, and take things one day at a time, that wasn't Noah Riordan. He was an all-or-nothing type of guy.

The flashing blue and red lights snapped Noah out of his daydreams. He looked in his rearview mirror and saw a Dodge Charger police cruiser tailing him, obviously looking to pull him over. Noah instinctively looked at his speedometer and noted that he wasn't even close to speeding.

"Oh, what the hell?" Noah grumbled, snapping his turn signal on. Carefully, Noah pulled over onto the shoulder and came to a stop. The Charger did the same, coming to a stop right behind Noah's truck.

Feeling the hair on the back of his neck stand up, Noah slowly reached into his glove box and grabbed his pistol, cocking it before pressing it against the driver's side door. His eyes were glued to the side view mirror, watching the cop car intently. The door opened, and the police officer stepped out of the car, shutting the door to the Charger. Noah held his breath and gripped the pistol, praying that the cop was pulling him over for some minuscule traffic violation and not for something relating to Noah's side job. As the police officer got closer, Noah rolled his window down.

Justin Carter leaned down and looked at the utterly shocked look on his younger brother's face. Noah immediately hid the pistol under his leg.

"How you doing?" Justin asked, oblivious to the fact that Noah was armed. Noah was still so surprised to see his brother that he didn't respond right away.

"Uh, fine," Noah finally muttered, shaking his head. "What... What're you doing?"

"I want to talk to you," Justin said. "I just want to have a civil conversation."

"Jesus Christ, Justin," Noah shook his head in total annoyance. "Fuck it, fine let's talk. You wanna talk on the side of the 101 or what?"

"There's a Starbucks after this exit. Meet me there?" Justin suggested.

"Sure," Noah grumbled.

Justin patted Noah's truck a few times and strolled back to his Charger, jumping inside and finally shutting off the flashing lights. Noah wasn't getting out of this one. If Justin had resorted to pulling him over on the side of the damn highway, Noah was going to have to talk to him. His blood boiling, Noah drove back onto the highway and took the next exit. All the while, Justin followed closely, making sure Noah actually did what he was supposed to do.

****

They ordered their drinks in silence; a black coffee for Noah and a caramel mocha for Justin. Neither man spoke or looked at the other man as they paid and received their drinks, which was just fine with Noah. The longer he went without having to talk to his brother, the better. Noah wasn't an idiot. He figured there was only one real reason why Justin would want to talk to Noah after all these years. And it wasn't about their relationship or their broken family. The two men settled into a table in the back of the coffee shop. There was only one other table occupied by a couple clearly on a first or second date.

"So," Justin said, taking a sip of his coffee.

"So," Noah muttered, not even making eye contact with Justin. He stared out into the parking lot, a look of faint disgust on his face. But, he sipped his coffee and remained seated, surrendered to the fact that he was stuck in this situation.

"It's good to see you, Noah," Justin said. And he meant it. It was great to see his brother in one piece. Granted, it would have been better had Noah reciprocated those sentiments. But Justin was still happy to see him.

"Sure it is," Noah scoffed, rolling his eyes. Justin cocked his head.

"Why do you say it like that?" Justin asked. Noah looked like he was going to say something, but he bit his tongue and shook his head, taking another sip of coffee. "Please talk to me, Noah."

"Trust me, you don't want to hear what I have to say," Noah spat.

"I do," Justin responded. "I haven't spoken to my little brother in ten years, of course I want-"

"Twelve years," Noah interjected. "Twelve years. Almost thirteen."

"Ok," Justin lowered his head. "Twelve years."

"Who's fault is that, Justin?" Noah asked, finally looking at his brother. "Who's fucking fault is that?"

"You're still so mad at me about that?" Justin couldn't comprehend why Noah was still holding on to all of that anger. Noah's eyes went wide as if Justin had said the moon was made of cheese.

"Please tell me you're joking," Noah said. "Tell me you didn't seriously just ask me that?"

"Noah, I don't get it," Justin said honestly. "I made a decision to secure a better future for myself. I'll never understand how it cost me a relationship with my brother and my mother. When I was ready to talk to her again, Mom wasn't angry or bitter at all. She understood."

"Good for Ma," Noah growled. "I'm not her."

"Why are you so mad at me, Noah?" Justin asked again.

"Because you fucking abandoned us," Noah finally admitted. "You left us. We needed you. I needed you. You're supposed to be my big brother. And you chose yourself over me and mom. I'll never forgive you for that."

Justin fell silent, unable to think of a response that would assuage Noah's seething anger.

"But I'll bet you never thought of it like that, huh?" Noah continued. The dam had burst. The years of pent-up anger toward his brother were finally at the surface, and Noah wasn't sure he'd be able to control what he said. And that was a bad scenario. "You were always too busy thinking of yourself."

"How can you even say that?" Justin asked, dumbfounded. "Noah, it wasn't like I stayed behind to party or something. That was my future, I had an opportunity I couldn't pass up. I don't regret it at all, it was the best decision I ever made. I set myself up with a great job, I met my wife-"

"I, I, I," Noah shot back. "That's all that comes out of your mouth, you self-centered jackass."

"Ok," Justin nodded, realizing there was no hope in trying to get his brother to understand. "I need to ask you about Jake Tell."

"Oh, do you?" Noah rolled his eyes and laughed. "You've got a lot of balls."

"I tried to be a brother, Noah," Justin shrugged. "Now, I'm being a cop. I need to know about Jake Tell. I know he worked at Omicron with you..."

"I've worked with a lot of guys over the years," Noah said. "Not everyone leaves a lasting impression."

"Is that so?" Justin pressed. He could see it in Noah's eyes. Noah was lying. Every single person had a tell when they would lie, some little twitch or movement that would give them away. For Noah, it was his eyes. He either made too much eye contact or didn't look at you at all when he was lying. Right now, he was staring at Justin with such unwavering focus that Justin knew there was something he wasn't telling him.

"Omicron's a big company," Noah muttered. "I don't know everyone there."

"But you'd hear things, right? People gossip at work, it's human nature. I'd imagine if three employees at the same company all conspired together to rob banks and armored trucks, and then those same three employees were killed in a shootout with police, someone would say something."

"We don't work in an office, sitting in a cubicle 9-5 every day, waiting for the right opportunity to jump out the window. We've got shit to do."

"I find that somewhat hard to believe, Noah," Justin shook his head. This conversation wasn't going anywhere. "I don't want to have to bring you in for questioning, Noah. You have to give me something to go on."

"No, Justin," Noah shook his head. "I don't. You want to arrest me, go ahead. But I don't have to give you anything."

"You know that makes you look incredibly guilty right? If you have nothing to hide, why lie to me?"

"Who said I had nothing to hide?" Noah said with a sneer. The comment took Justin by surprise.

"What did you just say?" Justin asked quietly. He narrowed his eyes on his younger brother. Noah kept his mouth shut and shrugged. "Goddamnit, Noah!" Justin slammed his fists on the table.

Noah lunged forward toward Justin. From under the table, Justin felt something jammed into his stomach. He looked down and saw the pistol pressed against his abdomen. Justin heard the familiar *click* as Noah disengaged the safety. The couple on the date looked over, concerned with the sudden commotion. They couldn't see the gun from where they were sitting.

"Oh my god," Justin whispered, looking at his little brother's steely gaze. "It's you... You're the fourth guy..."

Noah did not say a word or move a muscle. It was like he was frozen solid, pressing the gun into his brother. Justin and Noah stared at each other for a while, each one holding their breath. Finally, Noah flicked the safety back on and tucked the gun away in his waistband. He scooted his chair back and sighed heavily. Justin was stunned, unable to formulate words.

This entire time, that fourth bandit had been living in plain sight, right under everyone's noses. As Justin looked at his brother, he finally understood that he truly did not know the man sitting before him. That Noah was not the Noah that he'd grown up with.

"What... What happened to you, Noah?" Justin asked. Noah's face contorted.

"Same thing that happened to you, big brother," Noah said, emphasizing the sarcasm with the words '*big brother*'.

"What is that supposed to mean?"

Noah took a deep breath before he spoke, his eyes looking suddenly empty and sad. Justin hadn't seen that look from him yet; he looked like a sad puppy that had been kicked one too many times.

"Do you remember that night a few weeks before mom and I left?" Noah asked in a small voice.

"Which one?" Justin asked. "You'll have to be a little more specific."

"You and I were playing *Halo* in our room. And we heard him come home. Both of us panicked when he started screaming at mom, so we shut everything off and jumped into our beds, pretending to be asleep."

Justin bit his lip. He knew exactly where this was going.

"He comes in and sees us..." Noah's voice started cracking a little bit. "Looks at you and doesn't do anything. He looked at me and grabbed one of the controllers..."

Noah shook his head, his lip was quivering.

"I still have the fucking scars on my arm and back," Noah whispered. "He beat me so badly I could barely walk the next day. And you... You just sat there and let him."

Justin looked up, and the sadness in Noah's eyes had been replaced with a rage so real and vivid it unnerved him. He thought for a second that Noah was really going to attack him.

"That was the last straw for me. That was the day I realized that I couldn't count on you. You didn't have my back. When you told mom and I you were staying behind, I wasn't even surprised. So when you talk about not understanding why I'm still angry..." Noah continued. "I want you to remember that night. I want you to remember mom and I driving off without you. And then you're going to ask what happened to me? You're a detective, aren't you? Figure it the fuck out."

Noah stood up and downed the rest of his coffee, setting the empty cup back down on the table. He adjusted his shirt, purposefully flashing the gun at his older brother one more time.

"Do not get in my way, Justin," Noah warned cryptically. "I don't care who comes after me. I won't let them get in my way. You have no idea what you're getting involved in."

"Noah..." Justin began, standing up. He couldn't arrest his brother right here and right now. There was no solid proof he'd done anything, and an ominous discussion wasn't going to hold up in any court of law.

And with that, Noah walked out of the coffee shop, not turning back even once. He got into his truck and peeled out of the parking lot as fast as he could. It wasn't until Noah was far away from the coffee shop and almost home that he finally broke down and actually cried for the first time in years.

Part Three: Blood Brothers

"In this world, goodness is destined to be defeated. But a man must go down fighting. That is victory. To do anything less is to be less than a man"
- Walker Percy; Writer

17

Noah

Noah Riordan was constantly looking over his shoulder, waiting for his brother to pop out of nowhere with an entire SWAT Team. It was only a matter of time until Justin would come after him. While Noah had not explicitly stated that he'd been involved with the heists, he'd implied enough to know that Justin already knew the truth.

The black SUV pulled up along the street, and Stan Simmons hopped out of the passenger seat. He opened up the back door for Thomas Swaney, who stepped out and buttoned the front of his jacket. With Stan flanking him, Thomas walked toward the middle of the little park - only a few blocks away from IUOE Headquarters.

Noah Riordan walked toward them from the opposite direction. He had the flash drive from the safety deposit box in his front pocket and his pistol in his waistband, just in case. Thomas looked thoroughly displeased with him, which infuriated Noah to no end.

"Mr. Riordan," Thomas said ominously, coming to a stop about ten feet away from Noah. Stan Simmons stood behind him like the bodyguard he truly was. "You've made an exceptional mess of things."

"That's how it's gonna be, huh," Noah commented. He shook his head and scoffed.

"It's all that's been on the news," Thomas continued. "That brings a ton of unwanted attention. The exact opposite of what I wanted."

"Well, pick up a gun and mask and go do it yourself," Noah offered. "As far as I'm concerned, unless you come out with us, you have no room to bitch at me."

"Did you bring it?" Thomas asked, ignoring Noah's disdain.

"No, I forgot it at my place," Noah rolled his eyes. "Of course, I brought it."

He reached into his pocket and tossed Thomas the flash drive. It fell to the ground; Thomas made no effort to even attempt to make the catch. Stan dropped down and picked it up instantly. He stuffed the drive in his coat pocket and resumed his position.

"You got him trained pretty well," Noah commented. Stan looked at him, eyes narrowed, like an angry pitbull.

"I thought I said specifically to not open up the deposit box," Thomas said.

"Yeah, well, shit happens," Noah shrugged. "I'm not dragging a safety deposit box across town. You got what was inside."

"And that was the only thing inside the box?"

"Yeah," Noah answered immediately.

"And I think it goes without saying that you didn't look at what is on this drive?"

"No, I don't give a shit," Noah lied. Thomas nodded, seemingly satisfied with the answer.

"I assume the plan for the third and final job remains the same?" Thomas inquired.

"It may be smart to wait," Noah answered honestly. "With this much attention, it could be a disaster."

"Waiting is not an option," Thomas responded. "There's not going to be another truck carrying that much cargo for a long time. This has to happen on schedule. Otherwise, this was all for nothing."

"I figured," Noah grunted. "I'll make it work."

"Good," Thomas said with an emotionless smile. "I knew I could trust you to get the job done. I didn't have to convince you the same way I did with Jake..."

"Yeah," Noah mumbled, knowing exactly what Thomas was talking about. "If you come near anyone I care about..."

"There's no need for threats," Thomas held his hand up. "I'm a man of my word."

"Yeah, alright," Noah stuffed his hands in his pockets. "I'll be seeing you, Thomas."

Noah turned and walked back through the park, leaving through a side entrance. His truck was only a block away, but once he was out of the park, Noah checked his phone. Sure enough, the miniature tracking device he'd installed in the flash drive was emitting a signal. Grinning, Noah put his phone away and jumped into his truck. It was Joe's idea, and it had been a damn good one. The more leverage they could get over Thomas, the better. Having the spare flash drive of incriminating evidence was huge, but knowing where he slept would be even better. That was assuming he'd take the drive home with him. As he started driving back home, Noah called Joe, waiting a few moments for an answer.

"This is Joe," Joe answered. It was his standard answer to let Noah know he either had an audience or was at work.

"I gave Thomas the drive. Let's meet with the entire crew later this week to discuss the last job."

"Good. Let me know when. I'll be there," Joe said. "What are you doing tonight?"

"I got some personal stuff to take care of," Noah muttered. "I gotta make sure some things are squared away before we do this."

"Yeah, I feel ya," Joe lowered his voice. "We might not be able to walk away from this one so easily."

"That's what I'm afraid of," Noah admitted.

****

Noah pulled into the parking lot at The Lamp and immediately regretted driving there. But, it was the right thing to do. He needed closure with Jessica before anything further could happen with anyone else. She'd tried to call him a few times, but Noah repeatedly sent the calls to voicemail. They needed to talk in person, not on the phone. He got out of the truck, locked it, and leaned against the liftgate.

It only took a few minutes for Noah to spot the white car, drive into the lot, and park closer to the bar. Jessica and her friend, Maggie, stepped out of the car. Maggie hurried into the bar, leaving Jessica to gather a duffle bag and a pair of boots. Hands in his pockets, Noah jogged over toward the car. Hearing the footfalls, Jessica turned around to see who was running toward her. Noah slowed to a walk as she closed the door to the car and took a few steps toward him.

"Hey," Noah said quietly.

"Hi."

"I just wanted to talk for a minute," Noah admitted.

"I've been trying to call you," Jessica said. "I wanted to talk too."

"Yeah?"

"Yeah," Jessica lowered her gaze. "I'm sorry, Noah. I really am. You're an awesome person, and I really care about you..."

"You know I find that hard to believe, right?" Noah responded. "Especially now."

"Yeah, I know," Jessica said sadly. She looked back up at Noah's face, which was healing fairly well considering the damage Duke had done to it. "God, I'm so sorry."

"I don't want an apology," Noah shrugged. "I really just wanted to know why..."

"I don't know, Noah," Jessica shook her head. "I don't have an answer for you. I wish I did."

"Well then..." Noah was almost surprised at how aloof she seemed to the entire situation. He stuffed his hands back in his pockets and started backing away. "Guess there's nothing to talk about then."

"Wait, where are you going?" Jessica asked as Noah turned to leave.

"Home," Noah shrugged. Jessica looked hurt.

"When... When will I see you again?" she asked.

"You won't."

"Noah, please..."

"No," he shook his head. "You made your decision. Live with it. I hope you're happy. Genuinely, I do."

Noah Riordan marched back to his truck, a proud smile on his face. He had never stood up for himself when it came to relationships. He never pushed back against Paris and all of the crap she put him through.

Those days were behind Noah, and that made him feel incredibly happy. But more than that, Noah felt that he was in the process of opening a new door. Once Thomas was off his back, Noah would be truly free to start his life. He didn't really know what that would entail yet. Maybe he'd stay with the Union, or maybe he'd go do something else. But whatever he did, he had a feeling that he'd be happy. For once in his life, Noah didn't feel alone. He had someone.

****

For only the second time in his life, Noah Riordan sped down the dirt road that led up to Brian Tyler's extravagant farmhouse. There were no horses in the pasture, and he didn't see Lexi training any horses in the corrals. The ranch was quiet and relaxed. Unlike the last time Noah was here, he wasn't here to pick up weapons and equipment for a heist; he wasn't as anxious as he'd been last time either. This time was different.

Parking in the same spot of the circle drive he'd utilized last time, Noah climbed out of his truck, straightened out his Omicron Polo shirt, and walked toward the front door. The front of the house had a beautiful and rustic wrap-around porch, adding to the overall homey feeling that the farmhouse exuded. Noah could definitely picture himself settling down on a ranch or a farm.

Knocking on the door a few times, Noah took a few steps back and waited patiently. The door opened, and Brian Tyler manifested in the doorway. He gave Noah a confused glance at first.

"Noah?" he asked. "Is everything ok?"

"Yeah, yeah, everything is totally fine," Noah said with a genuine smile. "I'm sorry, I guess I should've called ahead, just had a busy day."

"No worries at all," Brian said. Even though Brian was somewhat responsible for this entire mess Noah found himself in, Noah didn't blame him. Noah knew that Brian was a good man at heart, even if he'd made some mistakes. But who hadn't?

Lexi Tyler poked her head around the door frame, and her face lit up to see Noah standing there; she waved at him.

"So, what can I do for you?" Brian asked.

"Actually, sir, I'm here to see her..." Noah said, nodding toward Lexi. Brian turned and saw Lexi standing behind him.

"Oh, uh, of course," Brian said awkwardly. "Sorry, I'll just be in the kitchen."

"Thanks dad," Lexi said, her cheeks getting a little red. Brian disappeared into the house, and Lexi stepped outside onto the front porch, closing the door quietly behind her. "Hey. What're you doing here?"

"I wanted to see you," Noah whispered. "I hope that's ok."

"Of course it is," she said, snuggling into his arms and against his chest. "I'm glad to see you."

"Me too."

"Do you wanna sit down?" Lexi asked, pointing to the wooden rocking chair on the corner of the porch. Noah nodded, and they sat down in the rocking chair. Lexi pulled a blanket off from the back and wrapped it around them. She curled her feet up underneath the blanket and rested her head on Noah's broad shoulder.

"It's so peaceful out here," Noah muttered. "I'm jealous."

"It is," Lexi agreed, sighing happily. She looked up at Noah and smiled. "This was a nice surprise."

"I'm glad," Noah said, kissing the top of Lexi's head.

"Are you ok?"

"No, not really," Noah decided honesty was the best way to go. For whatever reason, he hadn't had much issue lying to Jessica about what he was up to. The thought of lying and deceiving Lexi made Noah sick to his stomach. He couldn't start another relationship on the same terrible foundation as he had before.

"What's wrong?" Lexi asked.

"That cop that came to the site yesterday..." Noah spoke in a quiet voice. "That was my brother."

"Oh?" Lexi said, unsure exactly how to respond. She didn't know Noah had a brother, but they'd also really never had an in-depth conversation about their families.

"I hadn't seen him or talked to him in almost thirteen years. Same with my dad," Noah admitted. Lexi could almost hear the pain in his voice as he spoke. It wasn't sorrowful, more a mix of pain and anger. His eyes looked more angry than pained.

"What happened?" Lexi looked up at him, hoping she wasn't being pushy or anything. Under the blanket, she felt Noah's hand and gently intertwined her fingers with his.

"I grew up in a really abusive home," Noah said, his gaze focused on the horse pastures. "My dad was a raging alcoholic... It was just a horrible situation. It took a while, but my mom finally had enough. We left him, and my brother was supposed to come with."

"But he didn't?"

"No," Noah shook his head. "He didn't. He stayed behind. And, I don't know, I guess after that I just kinda wrote him off. My mom still has tried to have a relationship with him. They're ok, I guess, but I just am not there yet. I don't think I'll ever speak to my father again if I'm being honest. I know it's not exactly the most mature thing to do, but my brother still abandoned us, and I just don't know if I can get over that."

"Oh my god, Noah," Lexi said sympathetically. "I'm so sorry, that must've been so hard."

"You don't have to be sorry. It is what it is," Noah shrugged. "I just didn't want to pretend I was alright or lie to you. Just seeing him brought back a lot of stuff I've tried to ignore."

"Speaking from personal experience, no matter how long you try and push down the bad stuff, it always comes back up. It's better to try and talk about it and process it, whatever that may look like."

"I know, you're right," Noah nodded. "It's just hard. I guess I didn't really realize how much it was still bothering me."

"Well," Lexi said, holding him a little tighter. "I'm here for you."

"Why?" Noah blurted. Lexi's face contorted into a look of confusion.

"What do you mean?"

"I've only ever seriously been with one woman," Noah had no idea why he was openly admitting that. "And she was never there for me. It was all about what I could do for her. I guess I'm just not used to someone giving a shit about what's going on with me."

Hearing that made Lexi's heart break just a little. In five minutes, her entire opinion of Noah had changed. Not in a bad way at all, but he clearly wasn't the man that he portrayed to the outside world. It was becoming very clear to Lexi that the face Noah Riordan put on at work was not the real Noah. She had seen the real Noah that night at the pub. And since then, Lexi had been hard-pressed to think of much else. If anyone looked at Noah while at work, you'd see an impenetrable man. A calm and collected man who was completely immune to anything. That had been Lexi's first impression, that nothing could bother Noah; he was rock solid. And that was true, but hearing Noah admit his personal issues somehow made Lexi understand that on a whole different level.

He was strong, but not because he was emotionless or cold. He was strong because he was actively dealing with trauma, and no one was any the wiser.

"Then that wasn't a real relationship," Lexi said, trying to choose her words carefully. "A relationship is a two-way street, based on mutual care, love, and interest for each other. Without that, it's not a relationship."

"And here I thought you were all about construction and horses. When did you turn into an expert on love?" Noah teased, his tone playful.

"I've been watching *The Bachelorette* for fifteen years," Lexi admitted. "You learn a lot, trust me."

Noah laughed out loud and squeezed Lexi's hand a little tighter.

"I'm serious!" Lexi said, taking a mock offense. "It's admittedly terrible TV, but there is some merit to it. A relationship is hard work, and it takes both parties putting in the same effort in order to work out."

"So, that's what you want, then?" Noah asked. "A relationship?"

"With the right person, yes," Lexi nodded. "Everyone has had their fair share of heartbreak, myself included. I just know what I want and need, and I'm done settling. I did that last time, and I got burned pretty badly."

"Yeah, I feel that," Noah scoffed. He looked down at her intently. "Look, I want to make a change. People talk about wanting to change their lives, and that's all it is. Talk. But I'm serious. I want to change mine. And... I don't know, this just feels right to me. I've thought that before, but sitting here with you... It feels right."

"I know," Lexi smiled. "It feels right to me too."

"There're just some things I have to do first," Noah admitted. "Some things I have to square away before. Would you... Would you wait for me?"

"I understand, Noah," Lexi whispered. "Everyone has their baggage, I get it. But yes... Of course, I'll wait for you. It's crazy and it's fast, but in a weird way, I feel like I've known you a long time."

Noah smiled and wrapped both of his arms around Lexi, hugging her with everything he had. She hugged him back, burying her face in his shoulder. He had to finish this last heist and set himself - as well as Joe and Chandler - up for the rest of their lives. He'd have to deal with EJ and Darren. He'd have to deal with Thomas and Stan. And lastly, Noah would have to deal with his brother. Only time would tell what exactly that would entail. But, sitting there on the porch, with Lexi in his arms, Noah knew it would be worth it.

18

Justin

He sat in the Sheriff's Office, lights off, blinds open to let some of the light from the city in. The glass was nearly empty, the ice cubes melting and mixing with the blended Irish whiskey. Popping the cap off the green Jameson bottle, Justin refilled his drink and took a huge gulp.

On his desk, he had two pictures. One was a surveillance camera image from the armored truck heist of the man in the Ghostface mask. The second image was of Noah, an ID picture from the Operating Engineers Union. Justin had been borderline obsessing over who could be that fourth bandit from all those years ago. He'd had a hunch, call it a cops intuition, that that same bandit had to have been involved with these recent crimes. And he was right on all accounts. Justin just never in a million years expected that Noah would be that bandit.

As much as he tried to come to terms with reality, Justin just couldn't make sense of it all. Noah hadn't grown up in a poor family, quite the contrary, actually. Sure, their dad had been abusive and a drunk, but Noah left that environment with their mom, one of the kindest, most thoughtful women Justin had ever encountered. By all accounts, Noah made good money and had benefits and a pension that made Justin jealous. None of it added up. But Justin had heard Noah's words, felt the gun against him, and seen the look in his eyes.

His brother Noah was that fourth bandit. And the man responsible for the armored truck heist and the Beverly Hills Bank job.

Taking another sip of Jameson, Justin grabbed both pictures and walked to the corkboard. He stared at one of the blank male profiles that were next to the mugshots of Jake, Miles, and Cooper. Justin grabbed a spare push-pin and placed Noah's picture on top of the blank image. Directly underneath it, he pinned up the image of the Ghostface bandit.

It felt oddly satisfying to finally be able to put a face to one of the bandits. But at the same time, it made Justin want to throw up. He couldn't tell the FBI about his revelation, no way. They'd bust down Noah's door and probably shoot him. The mystery would end right there. Many questions remained open: Who were the other bandits? How did they choose their targets? Where did they acquire all of the equipment? Who else was helping them? And most importantly, why? Why was Noah doing this?

"Hey," a small voice snapped Justin out of his trance. He whirled around and saw his wife standing in the doorway to the large office. She was still wearing her blue CSI jacket and khaki pants, her standard work outfit.

"Hey," Justin muttered, his voice a little hoarse. He'd maybe had a little too much Jameson. "How'd the doctor go?"

"Fine, fine," Karolyne said. She'd had a late doctor's appointment after her shift.

"Are you ok?" Karolyne asked. He hadn't said much of anything since his conversation with his brother. Karolyne didn't even know what they'd talked about that night. Once Justin got home, he grabbed a bottle and passed out a few minutes later.

"No, I'm not," Justin said. He pointed to the corkboard, not sure if he could bring himself to start talking about Noah. Karolyne walked up to the board and studied it, her eyes landing on the picture of Noah. Justin didn't have to tell her that it was his brother; she could tell. They had similar facial features, but their eyes were so alike it kind of freaked Karolyne out. Seeing his picture up there told Karolyne everything she needed to know about what Justin suspected.

"Are you sure?" she asked in a voice that was barely audible. Justin gulped down the rest of his drink and nodded slowly.

"He practically admitted it to me," Justin said, his eyes feeling like they weighed a ton. He slowly shook his head as he continued. "You should've seen him, Karolyne. He hates me. He's so angry, so bitter. I barely recognized him. I just don't understand..."

"Which part?" she asked.

"We had virtually the same upbringing..." Justin observed. "Yeah, our dad was a real asshole, still is. But we still came from a decent family... I mean, you met my mom. She's an angel. How does he... How does he turn into someone who kills cops? Who breaks the law so willingly? What makes someone turn into that?"

"I wish I knew the answers," Karolyne said softly. "But the fact that you're thinking all of this leads me to believe that you think something else is going on here. That maybe your brother is not the 'mastermind' behind all of this..."

"I just don't see it," Justin admitted. "He wouldn't have hurt anyone when we were younger. Even when we played football, he never could hit hard 'cause he didn't want to hurt the other kids. That guy doesn't hold up a bank and shoot at the police for no reason."

"No, you're right," Karolyne said. "If he wasn't your brother, I don't know if I'd be saying this. But, he deserves some benefit of the doubt. We can't just assume he's something when that might not be the case. He's still your family. You owe him that much."

Justin let Karolyne's words sit for a minute. She was always right about this sort of thing. And Justin did not want to assume the worst about Noah. There had to be something else going on, some other piece to the puzzle that he was still missing. He'd gotten all of the edges and the middle put together. But there were still a few missing pieces, which were always the hardest to find and put together. Even if it killed him, Justin was going to find out what those pieces were. He had to. He owed his little brother and his mom that much.

But those thoughts were put on hold the second his phone started ringing.

****

The home was nothing special, just four walls and running water. Even from outside, Justin could smell the alcohol and cigarettes. Normally, Justin probably would've ignored a call from Dave Carter. But for whatever reason, he'd answered. A decision he was already regretting.

"Dad! It's me," Justin called from the rickety front porch. He banged on the front door a few times and waited. Justin heard a bottle crash on the ground from inside the house, and a few moments later, his father opened the door. His eyes looked sunken and had dark circles underneath them. He reeked of alcohol and cigarettes.

"Son..." Dave slurred. "Come on in."

"I'm fine out here," Justin answered. "Why'd you want me out here? I got other shit to do today. Contrary to what you might think, my job doesn't only involve getting you out of trouble."

"Oh, ok," Dave said quietly. "Do you want some coffee?"

"No, I don't," Justin shook his head. "Look, is there a problem here, or are you just coming down from a bender?"

"Justin, I just wanted to talk..." Dave muttered, sounding surprisingly sober all of a sudden. "I just wanted to talk."

"Ok, let's talk," Justin grumbled, rolling his eyes slightly. He was running out of patience with his father already. It was bad enough he constantly had to worry about what kind of trouble his dad was getting into; now, he had to worry about Noah as well.

Dave, still somewhat unsteady on his feet, stepped outside of the house and plopped down in one of the old, rusty chairs that he had on his porch. Reluctantly, Justin sat down in the chair next to him, looking out at his truck to avoid having to look at his father. It was sad to see him in this state constantly, clearly unhappy with his life. But the routineness of it had long grown old for Justin to the point where he no longer felt so bad.

"Your mother and I used to sit out on the porch every night before we had you and your brother," Dave muttered. Justin shook his head.

He couldn't remember the last time his dad had talked about Amy or Noah.

"Yeah?"

"Yeah," Dave nodded sadly. "It was years before things started to go so bad. We'd just sit here and talk about our days, what we wanted to do that weekend, plans for the future. Stuff like that."

"Sounds nice," Justin commented.

"It was," Dave looked at his son, a deep sadness in his eyes. "I am sorry, Justin. I know you might not believe me, but I am. I've been a shit father to you."

Justin didn't know what to say. He and his dad avoided these types of emotional, heart-to-heart conversations at all times. He was surprised to be hearing the words out of his dad's mouth, but he could tell it was genuine.

"Things got hard once you kids came around," Dave admitted. "I never knew my dad, I didn't know how to be a dad. I wasn't sure I really wanted to be one either. But your mom wanted kids, and I wanted to be with your mom, so we had you and then Noah. I was out of my depth, and I felt incompetent... And that's when I started drinking..."

"Am I supposed to feel sorry for you?" Justin asked. He knew his tone was harsh, but he didn't like where his dad was steering this conversation. "You know, I don't blame mom or Noah for leaving. I blame you. One-thousand percent."

"I know," Dave mumbled. Justin went silent but then asked a question he'd wanted to know for a long time.

"Why did you never try to reach back out to mom? Or to Noah?" Justin asked.

"They wouldn't have wanted to hear from me."

"But you didn't even try," Justin pressed. "You didn't try to change once they left. You didn't try and improve yourself and realize *why* they left. I stayed and watched you just drown yourself in a bottle. And you made that my problem."

"I don't know," Dave grumbled, not having any answer that would satisfy Justin.

"You know what's crazy? You couldn't even sober up enough to come to my wedding, and Karolyne still asks when she's going to meet you. And you know what, she never will, as long as I have anything to say about it. I don't want her to be around you for a second."

"I know. It's my fault," Dave said through gritted teeth and a lot less genuine than he had been minutes earlier.

"Well, then don't make it seem like you're the victim here," Justin spat. "You should consider yourself lucky that I still answer your calls at this point or even refer to you as my father."

"I'm sorry, Justin," Dave said. "I just wanted you to know that. I'm sorry I've caused you so much grief over the years."

"Yeah, sure," Justin grumbled, looking away from his dad. He thought about telling him about Noah but decided against it. It would just make things worse. Dave already felt guilty enough, he didn't need to know that there was most likely some correlation between his treatment of Noah and his current side hustle. Justin stood up and brushed the rust off his jeans.

"Look, next time you get sentimental, call someone else," Justin reached into his wallet and thumbed out the business card for a therapist that he knew. "I don't get paid enough to be your therapist. You wanna talk, give her a call."

"Justin..."

"Don't," Justin put his hand up. He tossed the business card at Dave. "And don't call me again for this kind of shit. You need professional help. And that's not what I do."

Justin clambered down the wooden steps and walked to his truck, barely noticing the utility truck that drove passed Dave's house. He climbed into his pickup and took off, just in time to see Dave stumble back into the house.

The utility truck made a 3-point turn and began following Justin's truck from a distance. Joe Kado had managed to snap a few photos of Justin and the old man on the porch during his first pass of the house. He assumed it was Justin and Noah's father, but there was only one way to know for sure.

****

It was well into the morning by the time Justin woke up the next morning, lying on his stomach. He moved his hand over to Karolyne's side of the bed but didn't feel her lying next to him.

"Baby!" Justin groaned loudly. He rolled onto his back and saw light coming from the kitchen. "Karolyne?"

"In the kitchen!" Karolyne called back. Justin sighed and rolled out of bed, throwing on a baggy pair of sweatpants and a t-shirt. Barefooted, Justin rubbed his eyes to wake himself up and trudged out to the kitchen, already wishing he was back in bed.

He walked into the kitchen to find a stunning breakfast spread set out on the table; eggs, bacon, french toast, and orange juice. Karolyne stood by the stove, flipping two steaming hot pieces of french toast. She was wearing a pair of running shorts and a t-shirt and had Justin's apron on that said '*Kiss the Cook*'. Turning around to see Justin's surprised look, Karolyne giggled to herself.

"Good morning, Detective Carter," Karolyne said.

"Detective Carter?" Justin repeated, laughing to himself. "You remember what happened the last time you called me that?"

"Oh, I sure do," Karolyne said, giving Justin a knowing wink. She plated the french toast and walked over to the table, setting the plate down and taking her seat.

"This looks incredible," Justin commented, grinning at his wife. "What's the occasion? Please don't tell me I forgot something I shouldn't have."

"We're celebrating," Karolyne said, barely able to contain her excitement. She picked up a small gift bag that was resting by her seat and passed it across the table to Justin. "I got you something."

Justin accepted the bag and looked at her skeptically. It was well known that Justin didn't enjoy getting gifts; he always felt awkward about it. But Karolyne looked so excited, he couldn't help but be excited too.

He reached inside and pulled out a few sheets of thin paper, dropping them onto the floor next to him. Justin pulled out a small box and set the bag on the ground, making room for the box on his lap. Slowly opening the box and enjoying Karolyne's obvious excitement, Justin looked inside.

A tiny baby onesie stared back up at him. There were words across the chest of the onesie that read '*Future Police Officer*'. Justin's eyes bugged out, and he looked across the table at Karolyne, who was grinning from ear to ear. Tears were forming in her eyes.

"No way!" Justin exclaimed. Karolyne nodded enthusiastically. Justin jumped up from his chair and rushed over to embrace his wife.

"We're going to be parents!" Karolyne cried, hugging her husband with every ounce of her strength.

"We're going to be parents!" Justin repeated, just as excited as Karolyne was. It was a surprise, to be sure, but Justin was thrilled. "How long have you known?"

"Yesterday," Karolyne said. "That's why I went to the doctor."

"Oh my god," Justin breathed. Karolyne laughed and wiped her eyes. Justin threw his arms around her once again and just held her. "I can't believe it. We're having a baby. Oh my gosh, Karolyne. We'll have to make room for the baby. I'll have to make sure this place is 100% safe..."

"Justin, slow down," Karolyne laughed. "We'll figure all of that out. Let's eat, foods getting cold."

With a reignited fire in their relationship, Justin and Karolyne sat down and dug into the delicious meal that Karolyne had prepared. They talked excitedly about every aspect of what they had to do in order to prepare for their child. Justin and Karolyne couldn't stop smiling as they discussed it in detail. Nothing else mattered to Justin; not his father, not Noah, and not the heists. The only thing that mattered now was the baby. It was crazy how in just a few minutes, his entire worldview had shifted. But that was what being a parent was all about, or so he suspected.

"When are you going to tell everyone?" Justin asked, chewing noisily on a piece of bacon.

"Today," Karolyne smiled. "When would you like to tell your parents?"

"I guess as soon as I can," Justin said. Immediately, he wondered how his mom and dad would react to the news. "I'll go see my mom later today and tell her."

"*We* will go," Karolyne corrected.

"Alright, perfect," Justin grinned.

****

The couple was completely exhausted by the time they both crawled into the bed, Karolyne wrapping Justin's arms around her body. She snuggled into him as tightly as possible and sighed. Justin's mom, as expected, had been absolutely delighted to hear the good news. His grandfather, Ron, had been equally happy to see Justin and to finally meet Karolyne. As much as Justin didn't want to get his hopes up, it did feel really nice to know that his family was starting to normalize. It was a shame that he'd waited so long to reach out to his mom and his grandfather; they were fantastic people. But in the back of his head, Justin couldn't help but worry about Noah. There was no way that was going to have a good ending, and Justin felt existential dread about that. One way or another, he and his brother were going to come face to face again. And when that time came, it would not be for a friendly cup of coffee. Noah was still a criminal, and Justin was still a cop. Cops chased criminals. It had been that way forever.

"You're thinking about your brother," Karolyne said sleepily. Her eyes were shut, but she squeezed Justin's arm.

"Yeah," he muttered. "I don't know what to do, Karolyne. I just don't know what to do."

"Justin, I can't tell you what to do," Karolyne said, rolling over to look at her husband. Even though it was dark, she could still make out his distinct facial features. "It's your brother. I have my opinions as a cop. And I have my opinions as your wife. This man and his crew *may* have been responsible for the death of a cop. That's not something to take lightly at all. But he's still your brother, and I know you. If you had to be the one to arrest him, the guilt would eat you alive."

"I just wish things were different," Justin muttered, gently touching the top of his wife's head. "I'll have to be the one to bring him in. It's the right thing to do."

"If that's what you decide, I'll support you always," Karolyne reassured him. "And while we're on the more serious subjects, once the baby comes, there's no more alcohol in this home. Is that clear?"

"What do you mean?"

"I'm not an idiot, Justin," Karolyne said firmly. "I love you so much, and I never want to live a day without you by my side. But the drinking needs to stop."

And in that moment, right then, Justin couldn't stomach the thought of ever taking another sip of alcohol. He would not turn into his father. Never.

"Tomorrow morning, it's gone," Justin said, feeling proud of himself.

"And that's why I love you," Karolyne whispered, falling asleep in his arms.

19

Noah

There was a noticeable rift in the warehouse. EJ and Darren stood off together, purposefully away from Chandler and Joe. Neither side had exchanged pleasantries, greetings, anything of the sort. As was to be expected, EJ and Darren were pissed about not having received their cut from the bank job. The money they'd made off the first armored truck heist had proven to not be good enough.

The door to the warehouse creaked open, and Noah slipped inside, closing it behind him. He locked the door, tested the lock, and then turned to his crew; he was holding two paper cup carriers with coffee.

"Brought some coffee if y'all want," Noah said, setting the two carriers on a toolbox. He grabbed one of the coffees and pulled over a chair, sitting down comfortably. Somewhat hesitantly, EJ and Darren each grabbed a coffee before Chandler and Joe did as well. Finally, they acknowledged one another, nodding respectfully at each other.

"Thank you all for coming," Noah began, speaking casually to his crew. The last thing he wanted to do was to continue the hostility from last time. "There are several things we need to discuss. Things went awry last time."

"That's putting it mildly," Chandler commented. EJ and Darren nodded in agreement. "I've just been thinking a lot, and I've got a lot of people who I care about counting on me. I can't go to jail or get shot down in the street."

"Chandler's right," EJ agreed. "I've got kids. I think I'm the only one here who has kids. That's a big, big responsibility. I can't let them down. I won't let them down. They're going to need me in their lives later on. I have to be there."

"I mean, I don't have kids, but I'm still trying to take care of my girl," Darren said. He looked sad. "She needs rehab desperately, I just can't bring myself to be the one to have to bring her there. She's going to hate me..."

It was a lot for Noah to take in right away. All of their concerns were valid; this was heavy stuff. They all made good points, and Noah had no idea how he could convince them that doing another armored truck would be a good idea. The amount of heat the crew had already was enough to make Noah want to forget about the job. But Thomas wouldn't allow that. No, there would be dire consequences if the crew should refuse to do the job.

"You guys are all right to be concerned," Noah said. "We got a lot of unwanted attention last time. But one more job and then we can all retire wherever we want to."

"I'd believe you, Noah," EJ began. "But you screwed Darren and me out of the money last time. I understood at first, we were dicks. But we still stuck our necks out for you guys. And I'm sorry, but the amount of money we got away with the first time is not at all close to what I received. So either you and Joe are taking the majority of the money for yourselves, or something else is going on here."

Noah and Joe looked at each other. There was a huge risk involved with telling the guys the truth about these heists. The more people knew Thomas was involved, the more chance there was for someone bad to find out. And that could prove dangerous for everyone involved with the plot. But the guys needed to understand. Noah couldn't risk them walking away, not before the job was done.

"The majority of the money went to the man who hired us," Noah admitted. "We all got cuts significantly smaller than the total haul, but I knew that going in."

"Why was that not told to all of us?" Chandler asked, surprised to hear Noah admit that. He looked almost offended. "We're all here because we trust you, Noah. Not some random guy."

"The less you guys knew, the better," Joe came to Noah's defense. "The unfortunate reality is that this guy is not someone any of us want to cross."

"Well, then fuck it," Darren shrugged. "I'm out. This guy can do his own dirty work, I'm no one's errand boy. He gets to sit on the sideline and take the majority of the money? What is he, a politician?"

"Sorry, Noah," EJ shook his head. "I'm gone too. That's not a good deal for any of us."

"You guys don't want to do that," Noah warned. "Trust me. This guy isn't going to just let us walk away from this. I know, I've tried before."

"What do you mean?" Chandler asked.

Noah sighed and made a decision. These guys needed to know the truth about what had happened all those years ago. What happened to Jake Tell and the others.

"A few years ago, this guy approached my boss at the time. Jake Tell," Noah began, crossing his arms over his chest.

"I remember Jake," EJ commented.

"Yeah. Well, Jake had fallen on hard times. He had a new wife and was upside down in his mortgage. He needed money, desperately. So he agreed to work for this guy. Recruited myself, Joe, and three others. Just like us. We did the first couple of jobs without too much incident. But Jake had a bad feeling, this gut feeling that things were going to go bad. And by that point, he'd stolen enough to be comfortable with. So, Jake goes to this man and tells him we're done, we don't need the money anymore."

Joe was listening closely now. He had heard a version of this story, but not the entire thing. And certainly not Noah's version.

"Jake came home from work to find his wife beaten within an inch of her life," Noah muttered, shaking his head in disgust. "This poor woman had nothing to do with anything... And she survived, but she had to learn to walk again, learn to talk again. She needed years and years of therapy and rehab, all of which would cost a fortune. And that was done solely to give Jake a reason to need to keep doing jobs. Jake did just that, and he ended up getting killed by the police."

"My god," Joe muttered. He hadn't known what had happened to Jake's wife. It made his stomach sick knowing that Thomas would order such a violent act against someone's spouse, someone who was completely innocent in all of this.

Chandler, EJ, and Darren exchanged looks, reeling from the story they'd just heard. Their immediate thoughts were of their loved ones. Keeping them out of harm's way is their first priority, as it should be.

"Are you saying that this guy is going to come after our families?" Chandler asked, his mind only thinking of his wife, Lyla. Noah didn't say anything right away.

"Noah, what are you telling us?" Darren yelled.

"I'm saying this guy has a capacity for violence that the rest of you do not," Noah snapped. "I'm saying that this guy is a lot more dangerous than I was initially led to believe. I'm saying that walking away is not an option. It just isn't. I've got loved ones I'm trying to keep safe, ok? This man has already threatened my family, I don't want him to threaten yours."

"What do you mean we don't have a capacity for violence?" EJ asked. "We've helped you every step of the way so far. If this guy is threatening our families, fuck him."

"It's not that simple," Noah shook his head.

"Why?" Darren pressed.

"It just is not that easy," Noah repeated. "There's a lot going on here that you guys don't understand."

"Then tell us!" Chandler screamed. "Goddamnit, enough with the secrets and the bullshit! Just be honest with us. These are *our* families, Noah."

"Because the guy who hired us is Thomas Swaney," Noah blurted out, instantly regretting it.

"Fuck," Joe muttered, knowing that was a giant mistake.

Chandler, Darren, and EJ had similar reactions. Initial confusion, then the realization that the man who had hired them was their Union boss - a man with an impeccable reputation and who was known to have a ton of connections in the government. Thomas was powerful, and everyone knew it. Although it sounded crazy to them, it also made sense for someone that powerful to be involved in something illegal.

"Thomas Swaney?" Chandler said the name aloud. He couldn't believe it.

"That two-faced scumbag," EJ shook his head. Darren, much to Noah's surprise, didn't have a smart-ass comment for the group. He was silent. Then it occurred to Noah. Darren's family was highly involved with Union. Thomas had probably been someone that Darren had looked up to his entire life.

"I didn't want to tell you guys that for obvious reasons," Noah said. "But Thomas, Stan Simmons, who knows who else, they're all involved in some pretty sketchy shit. And that is why we cannot walk away until we finish the job."

Again, silence overtook the warehouse. Noah was having a hard time reading the room. Chandler looked concerned. EJ was acting as if the news wasn't that surprising. And then there was Darren, who had a vacant stare on his face, almost as if he didn't want to believe what he was hearing.

"I'm sorry I didn't tell you guys," Noah finally spoke again. "But I know what those guys are capable of."

"Yeah," Darren spoke up. "I do too. I've heard things from my family, people my family knows. It's been talked about that Thomas and those big union bosses were involved with some stuff. I always just thought it was an exaggeration, like old mob stories and stuff. Things were different twenty years ago when a lot of those guys were starting out. I guess I just didn't understand the extent of it."

"So, what do you think?" Chandler asked Darren. "Are we smart to be afraid of these guys? To worry about our families?"

"You'd be an idiot to not be," Darren muttered, shaking his head in disbelief. He looked up at Noah. "We have to finish this. Permanently. Thomas can't keep getting away with this kind of shit."

"We can't go up against those guys," EJ said. "We don't stand a chance. We'll lose our pensions, our benefits, everything we worked all those years for."

"We'll lose our lives if we don't," Darren responded. "There's no way Thomas is going to let us walk away from this knowing what we know."

"He makes a good point," Joe chimed in.

Noah was relieved that the crew seemed to be back on the same page. That was one less thing he had to worry about. He needed these guys to all understand what was at stake, and they now seemed to. One of the only good things about their current situation is that the crew had options. The hard part would be choosing the right one for all parties involved.

"Guys, the choice is yours," Noah said calmly. "We're not pushed into a corner right now. The way I see it, we've got a few options. First, we can do this last job, give Thomas his cut, and go on with our lives. There's always the risk that the cops will come after us. Thomas will still be around, and he could always try this again on us. Second, we don't do it. We risk retaliation from Thomas against us and our families. Third, we do the job and take the money for ourselves. We permanently remove Thomas Swaney from the equation, and then we take an early retirement. The cops will no doubt be after us, but we can disappear before they figure out what's been really going on. If anyone has any other ideas, please speak up."

"I don't like the idea of having to look over my shoulder for the rest of my life," Chandler said. "But I guess we're going to have to, no matter what. That being said, we've all taken enough of a risk. I'd like to walk away knowing I'm set for life."

"I agree," EJ nodded.

"I'm with them," Darren gestured to Chandler and EJ. "It's the best move for all of us."

"Joe?" Noah asked, looking to his friend. After a moment, Joe cracked a smile.

"The boys are right. We do the job, split the take, and remove Thomas from his office."

"Alright," Noad nodded. "Then it's settled. The truck will be loaded to maximum capacity. Split five ways evenly, we're looking at anywhere from a hundred to one hundred and twenty million dollars apiece."

There was a collective breath taken among the crew. EJ and Darren grinned at each other, both imagining what it would be like to have that much money. Chandler smiled too, knowing that would alleviate him from ever having to worry about medical bills ever again. Even Joe cracked a smile.

"I think it's safe to say if we pull this off, our union days are over," Joe said, speaking for the entire crew. The crew shared a laugh.

"The truck will be making the route on Wednesday. We hit it on the way back to the depot, and then we're gone," Noah said. He folded his arms and looked at his crew, nodding in approval. "We've got this, boys."

"Hell yeah we do," Chandler said. He checked his phone and then looked at Noah, giving him a nod of respect. "I gotta go get Lyla. I'll see you guys around, alright?"

"Be safe brother," Darren said. "Give my best to Lyla."

"Same here," EJ added. Noah walked Chandler out to his truck, waiting until they were out of earshot before he said anything to him.

"You sure you're ok with all of this?" Noah asked. "No offense, but I feel like you got the most to lose."

"I do," Chandler agreed. "But that's why I'm doing it. Lyla's getting better. Slowly but surely. If I can get ahead and be there for her, that's the best move."

"Alright, I just wanted to check," Noah said. "Be careful, man."

"You too, brother."

****

Ivy barked with excitement as soon as Noah grabbed her collar and leash, the universal indicator that they were going for a walk. Once outside, Noah let Ivy lead the way down the sidewalks and through their neighborhoods. She pulled on him, wanting to explore everything she could. Whenever life got crazy, Noah relied on a good, long walk with Ivy to clear his head. There was something so peaceful, so natural about spending time with Ivy. No matter what he did, Ivy would never judge him. As long as he fed her consistently and petted her, she would love him as long as she could. It was a special bond.

They got back to the house an hour later, Ivy panting up a storm. She flopped over to her water dish and lay next to it, resting her head on the bowl and lapping up water effortlessly. Within minutes, she was snoring, her head still resting on the water dish.

Noah went over to the counter to check his phone, having left it at the house during his walk. He noticed a missed call from Brian Tyler and immediately called him back, putting the call on speakerphone while he fetched a Gatorade from the fridge.

"Noah?" Brian answered. Noah stood up straight and immediately was concerned. Something about Brian's tone was off.

"What's wrong?" Noah asked.

"Have you seen Lexi?"

"No, why?"

"She never came home last night," Brian said. "She was going out with some friends, so I didn't think anything of it, but I haven't been able to reach her today."

"Do you know if she was at work today?" Noah asked. "I wasn't at the site today, handling some things at the warehouse."

"I talked to Corey," Brian's voice was breaking. "He said she was a no show."

Noah shook his head and cursed. Something was terribly, horribly wrong. That wasn't like her at all.

"Have you called the police yet?" Noah asked.

"No, not yet," Brian admitted. "I don't know what to do. I don't want the attention on us, especially since..."

"Don't worry about that," Noah interrupted. "Look, my brother's a cop. I'll get him involved, alright? I'll tell him what's up."

"Are you sure that's a good idea?"

"Doesn't matter right now. Only thing that matters is finding Lexi."

Noah hung up and ran out to his truck, jumping in the driver's seat and tearing out onto the road without even putting his seat belt on. After connecting his phone to his truck, Noah dialed Tayler, praying she'd answer.

"Hey, hey!" Tayler said, her usual cheerful self. "What's going on?"

"Hey, look I got something I need to handle. I left Ivy at the house. Is there any way you can go feed her tonight? I don't know when I'll be back."

"Of course, Noah," Tayler responded. She heard how upset he sounded. "Is everything ok?"

"I don't know yet," Noah said bluntly. "Trying to figure it out."

"Ok. Yeah, I'll go get Ivy after I leave work. Can she spend the night at my place?"

"Totally fine. I'm so sorry."

"Don't be. Let me know if I can help."

"Will do," Noah hung up and made a sharp left, accelerating past an intersection.

He didn't have his brother's phone number, but he knew where he could get it. Scrolling through his contacts, he clicked on his mom's name. The call went straight to voicemail. That was weird; his mom always picked up unless she was working, but it was well after she would have gotten off of work. He redialed and again went straight to voicemail.

"What the fuck?" Noah muttered. His grandpa didn't even own a cellphone, so no luck there. He sped up, weaving in and out of traffic. Noah had a horrible feeling in his gut; there was something really wrong, Noah could feel it.

****

Slamming on the brakes in front of his mother's Thousand Oaks home, Noah looked at the front door and felt his stomach drop. The door was open, it looked like it was barely hanging on to the hinges. Forced entry. Noah reached into his glove box and pulled out his pistol, racking the slide back to prime the weapon. Tucking the gun into the front of his waistband, Noah leapt out of the truck and hustled to the front door. He looked around for any nosy neighbors. The last thing he needed was someone calling the cops on a suspicious man with a gun entering a home. Drawing the pistol, Noah stepped into the home past the broken door.

"Hello?" he called. There was no response. His heart started beating a little faster. He knew something was wrong, he could feel it. Moving through the living room, Noah kept his gun in front of him, scanning the entire room. A coffee table was knocked over, and a chair had been thrown across the room. Whatever had happened here, it looked like it had been violent. His hands were sweating horribly, fearful of what he'd find if he kept moving into the house.

Noah was holding his breath as he wrapped around the corner into the kitchen, leaning around with his gun. The kitchen was in complete disarray; the table had been flipped over, the chairs were scattered, and there were several broken glasses on the floor. Trying his hardest to keep calm and quiet, Noah took another step into the kitchen. And that was when he saw a body lying behind the kitchen island.

"Oh, fuck. Fuck!" Noah said, his voice breaking. He dropped to the ground next to his mom, setting the pistol on the floor. There wasn't a massive pool of blood or any gunshot wounds, which was a relief. But Amy had clearly gotten hit. Hard. The side of her face was bruised, but other than that, she looked to be in one piece. Frantically, Noah felt for a pulse, still holding his breath. He nearly started crying when he felt a pulse on the side of her neck.

"Mom? Mom, can you hear me?" Noah asked. His eyes were welling with tears. Amy moved her hand slightly, her eyes starting to flutter. She tried to sit up but was still extremely disorientated.

"Noah?" she asked, her voice hoarse.

"I'm here, momma," Noah said, wiping his eyes. "Are you ok?"

"I... I think so," she said, leaning against one of the cabinets. She winced in pain. "My face hurts."

"What happened?" Noah asked. "Where's pop?"

"This man, he just came through the front door..." Amy whispered. "Oh my god, where's my dad?"

"Stay here," Noah said. He picked up the pistol and headed further into the house. "Pop! It's Noah. If you can hear me, let me know!"

"Back room," Noah's Grandpa Ron responded in a low voice. Noah hurried into the back room, which served as Ron's office; it had been ransacked just like the kitchen and living room. Ron lay on the ground in a heap, he looked less beaten than Amy, but his Vietnam Veteran shirt was ripped. Noah helped his grandpa onto the couch.

"What the fuck happened?" Noah asked, slipping the gun into his back pocket.

"Some guy..." Ron muttered, clearly distraught with what had happened. "Is Amy ok?"

"Yeah, she's alright," Noah reassured him. "Look, stay put, ok? I'll be back in a minute."

Noah rushed back into the kitchen. Amy was standing now, pressing a frozen box of vegetables against her head.

"Where's your phone?" Noah asked her. She pointed to the counter next to the fridge where her phone was plugged in. Noah grabbed it and unlocked it. He found Justin's number and dialed it, putting the phone to his ear and walking into the living room.

"Hi Mom," Justin answered. Noah paused for only a second.

"Mom and Grandpa were attacked," Noah said bluntly.

"Noah?" Justin asked.

"Did you hear me?"

"What happened?"

"I don't know, but they're both in bad shape. The house looks like it was ransacked."

"Oh my god," Justin breathed. "Ok, I'm on my way. Stay there and wait for me, I'll have to get your statement."

"Yeah, ok," Noah grunted. He hung up and set the phone back on the kitchen counter. "Mom, Justin will be here soon, ok? I just need to ask you one question."

"Ok," Amy said, sitting down in one of the kitchen chairs.

"The man who did this..." Noah began, kneeling in front of his mom. "What did he look like?"

"He... He was big. Wore a suit. I'm sorry, I didn't really get a good look at his face," Amy muttered.

"If I showed you a picture, would you be able to tell me if it was him?" Noah asked.

"Yeah, I think so," Amy nodded. Noah got out his own phone and scrolled through his photos, looking for one that would be useful. He zoomed in on a picture of Thomas Swaney.

"Is this him?" Noah showed Amy the picture. She shook her head.

"Not him."

"Ok," Noah scrolled to a picture of Stan Simmons. He turned the phone back around. "What about him?"

Amy's eyes locked on the picture. She looked up at Noah and nodded.

"That's him."

****

Noah was positive he looked absolutely psychotic as he stormed through the Union Hall, literally pushing people out of his way. Joe Kado was right behind him, giving hideously dirty looks to anyone who got in their way. Once ensuring that his mother and grandfather were ok, Noah got out of there. He was sure he'd hear about it later from his mom, but he couldn't interact with any form of police right now. After he left his mom's house, he called Joe, and the two met outside the Union Hall. Noah didn't need to say anything. Joe saw the look on his face and knew something serious was about to go down. Noah and Joe stepped off the elevator and marched down the hallway, getting a few dirty looks from some Union employees in suits.

Stella, Thomas Swaney's secretary, looked up and seemed surprised to see them. Noah and Joe didn't even acknowledge her. They simply advanced through the office with grave seriousness.

"Noah, Mr. Swaney is busy right now," Stella said, standing up to block their path. Noah and Joe came to a stop as the woman put herself between them and Thomas's door.

"Stella... Move," Noah growled. He had no idea whether or not Stella had any idea what Thomas was really up to, but he guessed that she knew more than she'd let on. It wasn't likely that she worked so closely with him and didn't know.

Lowering her eyes, Stella slowly stepped out of the way. With one forceful motion, Noah threw the door open and flew into the office; Joe was right behind him. Thomas was on the phone and looked visibly surprised to see Noah and Joe barging into his office. Reaching behind his back, Noah yanked out his pistol and aimed it at Thomas, waiting just long enough for the door to swing shut.

"Gun!" a voice called from behind Noah and Joe. Wheeling around, Joe saw Stan Simmons reaching into his sport coat to draw his weapon. Moving quickly, Joe launched himself at Stan, driving him against the wall. Pinning his wrist up against the wall, Joe drew his own pistol with his free hand and jammed the barrel under Stan's chin. Thomas Swaney slowly set his phone down and stood up, staring calmly at Noah and Noah's pistol.

"What the fuck are you doing?" Noah asked, his voice strained. "We're doing the job... We're doing the goddamn job."

"You lied to me, Noah," Thomas said, his voice sending chills down Noah's spine. He grabbed the flash drive from his desk and held it up. "You made a copy of this drive, which tells me you looked at what was on it. And the only reason you would make a copy of what is on this drive is to try and fuck me over in the future. Steps had to be taken, I'm sure you understand."

"You sent your errand boy after my mom, you motherfucker!" Noah snarled, jerking the pistol toward Thomas. His hand was shaking, barely able to steady his aim.

"To send a message, Noah," Thomas said. Noah was disgusted at Thomas's justification.

"Lexi Tyler," Noah swallowed. "Where is she?"

The second his mom confirmed that Stan Simmons had been the man who attacked her and Ron, Noah knew that he had to be behind Lexi going missing. That was an insanely risky move, considering how much Brian Tyler knew about Thomas. Noah guessed that Thomas had enough leverage against Brian to know he wouldn't retaliate.

"She is quite safe, I assure you," Thomas said. "You see, it's quite simple, Noah. You do this last job, you bring me every single dollar, and the second flash drive. And in return, I'll give you Lexi. Fair trade, don't you think? You two seem to be fond of each other, which is adorable."

"Fuck you," Noah spat, still not lowering the pistol. He was fighting the urge to blast him right then and there, but Thomas knew where Lexi was. Noah couldn't risk anything happening to her.

"I'm being patient with you, Noah," Thomas continued. He didn't seem fazed at all that Noah was aiming a weapon at him. "When Jake started trying to compile evidence against me, I made sure he was dealt with. In fact, you two shouldn't even be standing here right now..."

"What... What are you talking about?" Noah asked.

Joe, who still had Stan pinned against the wall, perked up at that comment. He looked over at Thomas and Noah, furrowing his brow in confusion.

"Jake stood right where you're standing and threatened my life after I had Stan pay his wife a visit. He told me he had evidence of my personal business dealings and was going to ruin me. Naturally, steps had to be taken. I called in an anonymous tip to the police just before you guys took over that bank. How do you think the cops were able to respond so fast and surround you? It worked pretty well, but... You and Joe weren't supposed to survive."

Noah and Joe couldn't believe what they were hearing. They both knew Thomas was a horrible person, but hearing that he'd tried to have them killed, especially after they'd done all of his dirty work, just showed them a whole new side to his evil.

"Are you going to shoot me, Noah?" Thomas asked, almost bored with the conversation.

"I swear to god, Thomas," Noah growled, lowering his gun. "I'm gonna kill you."

"Good luck, my friend," Thomas smirked. He put his hands on his desk and smiled emotionlessly. "Bring me the money and the drive. I will return Lexi to you. That's the deal."

Noah tucked his gun back into his waistband. He glared at Thomas for a few seconds before turning around and walking back toward the door.

"Come on, Joe. We're done here," Noah muttered.

"See you soon, Stan," Joe growled. He hit Stan directly in the throat with his pistol, dropping him instantly. Stan fell to the ground, gasping desperately for air as his throat closed up from the hit.

They walked back out of the building the way they came, hustling back to their trucks.

“What’s the plan?” Joe asked. “Is your mom ok?”

“She’s fine,” Noah said. He lowered his voice and leaned in closer to Joe. “We’re gonna kill him.”

“I’m with you. Just say the word,” Joe nodded.

“You’ve been tracking that drive?” Noah asked.

“Yeah, but it hasn’t left the office, unfortunately. It’s still transmitting, though.”

“How the hell did he know we cloned it?”

“I don’t know,” Joe shrugged. “I’m good, but not that good.”

“Ok,” Noah muttered. “Just be ready. We’re hitting that truck, and then we are putting an end to this. Once and for all.”

20

Justin

Justin Carter sat at his mother's kitchen table, listening to his mom and grandfather give a report to another LAPD Detective. Orlando Nicholson, Dalton Dupree, and Nate Murray stood guard outside of the house, openly carrying their rifles and tactical gear. A duo of Crime Scene Technicians were dusting for fingerprints but weren't having any luck.

"...And you're sure you didn't get a good look at who did this?" a female detective asked Amy and Ron. They both shook their heads.

"He was wearing a mask," Amy said.

Amy felt conflicted about lying to the police and to Justin. But Noah had insisted that she didn't say a word about the attacker. Noah had clearly known the man, and that made Amy concerned. What was Noah involved in that a man would come after her and her father? It didn't make any sense to her. Noah was a construction worker. This felt like something out of a mobster movie.

Throughout the entire interview, Justin remained silent, listening carefully to every word his mother or grandfather spoke. They conveniently left out the part about Noah having been there. Justin wasn't about to speak up. If anyone looked at his phone, they'd see he'd received a call from his mom, not from his estranged brother. Amy confirmed that she did indeed call Justin from her phone once she regained consciousness.

"Well, Ms. Riordan," the detective sighed, folding up her notepad. "Thank you for your time. I will get in contact with you if I need any more information or have any more questions. If there's anything we can do for you, feel free to reach out to myself or to Justin. I'll leave you my card."

"Thank you very much," Amy said with a genuine smile. The side of her face still stung, but the throbbing pain had subsided. She was left with a nasty bruise, but nothing was broken or damaged.

The cops and crime scene technicians packed up their gear and were out the door about ten minutes later. Justin escorted them outside and walked over to his team, where they were still standing guard at the front of the property.

"Are they ok?" Orlando asked. Justin nodded.

"Yeah, they're fine. Little shaken up, but they'll be ok."

"Anything for us to go on?"

"I'm not sure yet," Justin admitted. "They both said the guy who attacked them wore a mask, and CSU couldn't find any fingerprints."

"Shit."

"Look, between you and me," Justin lowered his voice. "There's something going on here. My brother was here, he's the one who called me."

"Really?" Orlando looked at him curiously. "So what're you thinking? This had something to do with your brother?"

"I didn't tell you this part..." Justin whispered. "But after you and I went to see him at work, I went back after. Pulled him over. We grabbed coffee and talked. And..."

"What?"

"Dude, he practically admitted to me that he's behind these heists." Justin revealed.

"Oh shit," Orlando exhaled. "That complicates things."

"I know," Justin agreed. "Look, we need to get back to the office and find out where my brother is. We need to bring him and talk to him. I don't have any solid evidence against him right now, but we need to get him in a room. Something is going on here, and I don't know what it is. That's scary."

"Alright, I'll bring the guys back," Orlando said. "Finish up here and meet us back at the office."

"See you there," Justin walked back inside to his mom's house as Orlando and the rest of his team climbed back into their vehicles.

Amy and Ron were putting the furniture back where it should be. Justin was relieved that they were both ok, but the murky circumstances over what actually had transpired were bothering him to no end.

"Mom, what was Noah doing here?" Justin asked, standing in the living room. Amy looked at him sadly and sat down on the couch.

"I don't know," she said. "I woke up and he was here."

"You don't think that's weird?" Justin inquired.

"Justin, what are you asking me?" Amy was clearly not happy with the questioning. "I don't know what you want me to say. I don't know what's going on. I don't know who attacked us. I do not appreciate the insinuations."

"Ok, ok," Justin relented. "I'm sorry, I was just asking. It's my job."

"I know it is," Amy softened her voice. "But I don't know what to tell you, Justin. Noah was here, and he seemed to know something that he didn't feel inclined to share with me. I don't know where he is or what he's doing. I just don't."

"Alright, mom," Justin nodded. "I'm sorry."

"Don't apologize," Amy said. "We're ok. I'm sure you have police stuff to do."

"I just want to make sure you're ok," Justin said.

"I appreciate it, honey. I promise we're ok. I'll let you know if we need anything."

"Thanks mom," Justin made to leave. He stopped before reaching for the door. "I love you, mom."

"I love you too," Amy answered with a warm smile.

****

The Sheriffs were all anxiously awaiting Justin's arrival, still wearing their tactical gear. Orlando hadn't been specific, but he did tell Dalton and Nate that they have a possible suspect. Whatever Justin decided to do, they were ready to go on a moment's notice.

Orlando heard the door swing open and saw Justin, looking more tired than he usually did. The entire team was still unaware that Justin was going to be a father; he'd been waiting for the right time to break the news but hadn't had a good opportunity since finding out himself.

"What's the plan, boss?" Orlando asked. Justin marched right to his desk and threw open the top drawer, pulling out his stash bottle of Jameson. He popped the cap open and took a swig straight from the bottle.

"Get me an address for Noah Riordan," Justin muttered, taking another sip.

"On it," Nate said, quickly opening up the database on his computer. "Gimme a few minutes, I'll find a current address."

"Are we kicking his door down?" Orlando asked.

"No," Justin answered firmly. "Not yet. But we're gonna watch him like a fucking stalker and wait until he screws up. I know he is involved, we just need to gather proof. He's got to have a crew, so we need to find out who they are too."

"Got it!" Nate exclaimed. "He's got a house in Pasadena. I'm sending all of you guys the address right now."

"Good," Justin nodded. "Alright, Dalton and Nate, take one of the pickups and park your asses outside his home. Orlando, you're with me. We're gonna check out the other Omicron locations. I'm sorry to do this to you guys, but we're going around the clock until we put this guy in a cell. I think he had something to do with my mom getting attacked, and we're not letting him get away. Is that understood?"

"10-4," Orlando acknowledged.

"If you see Noah, don't engage. Call it in and wait for me. We're gathering information. This is strictly surveillance."

"You got it," Dalton said. He grabbed the keys to one of their unmarked trucks before following Nate out of the office.

Justin hurried into their locker room and donned his heavy tactical vest. He changed out of his loafers in favor of a pair of black boots.

Lastly, he strapped a thigh holster onto his right leg and slammed his service weapon into the holster. Snagging a spare rifle from the weapons rack, Justin grabbed a few extra magazines and an ammo box.

"Ready?" Orlando asked.

"Let's do this," Justin growled.

21

Noah

Noah Riordan had been exceptional at keeping certain parts of his life extremely private. He'd kept secrets from everyone with relative ease. Not one person in his entire life knew everything. One could argue that it was deceitful or lonely, but Noah knew it was the safest thing for him. There was no denying the things he'd done in the past. Even though his actions had been to keep the people he cared about safe, Noah had broken every major law in the book. Noah had taken a life, the life of a police officer. It hadn't been intentional, but that wouldn't matter, not in a court of law.

One of the best-kept secrets Noah had was the condo in Northridge, California. When Noah had bought the condo almost seven years ago, he originally planned on renting it out. And he did, for a while. But when his most recent tenants moved out, Noah decided not to rent it out again. It was a bit of an ordeal, but Noah chose to renovate the entire place himself. It gave him something to do, someplace to escape to. When his relationship with Paris was falling apart, Noah would spend days at a time at the condo, working on fixing the floors, painting the walls, or putting granite countertops in. No one, not his mother, Joe, or even Paris, had known about the apartment. It was the one safe place that Noah had where no one would bother him.

He had been laying low the last two days, barely leaving the condo at all. After heading home from Union Hall, Noah spotted the unmarked police truck outside his home. While most people probably wouldn't take notice, Noah was not most people. Jake had taught him very early on in their criminal careers how to spot unmarked police vehicles. Knowing that his house was being watched, Noah doubled back before the cops noticed him. A few hours later, he'd received a phone call from Joe, letting him know that a similar unmarked vehicle was watching one of the warehouses in Los Angeles. Thankfully, not the one that the crew had been operating out of. As soon as Noah heard that, he went straight to their warehouse and loaded up his truck with as much equipment as he could fit before heading to his condo to hunker down until the last job. Fortunately for him, Tayler was perfectly ok with watching Ivy for a couple more days. He kept things vague but explained that he was dealing with some things and wouldn't be back home for a few days.

There wasn't much he felt like doing. He couldn't sleep and could barely eat. All Noah seemed to be able to focus on was his mom and Lexi. They were both put in danger because of him. There was no one Noah could ask for advice on how to handle this situation. Alone in the condo, Noah found himself wondering how Jake Tell handled it when he found his wife beaten within an inch of her life, courtesy of Thomas Swaney and Stan Simmons. Noah yearned for Jake's wisdom and friendship now more than ever.

But the day had finally come. At exactly 3:15PM, the GARDA armored truck would make its way back to the depot, filled to capacity with money. Noah and his crew would have to hit the truck out in the open, not knowing the driver's schedules by heart like they had on the first job. It didn't matter this time. Noah didn't care. He was too angry at the whole situation to care. He wasn't going to let anyone get in his way. Not Thomas, not the cops, not even Justin.

Noah stepped out of the shower and dried himself off before walking into the master bedroom - he had all of his clothes and equipment laid out on the bed and floor. At the foot of the bed was the Ghostface mask. Noah picked up the mask and stared at it. He'd worn that mask for every truck heist he'd ever been a part of. In a very strange way, the mask felt like a good luck charm. He set the mask down and went to work getting dressed; dark boots, black jeans, a black long sleeve compression shirt, and a red/black flannel over it. Then, Noah went to work meticulously preparing the vest and bandolier, filling every available pouch with spare magazines for his rifle and pistol.

The rifle and pistol lay on the floor, on top of a thin throw blanket. Noah was methodical in his inspection of both weapons, making sure they were cleaned and ready to go. Everything already had to go perfectly today. He couldn't waste time dealing with a gun jamming on him should it come to that. Once he was satisfied, Noah placed both guns into a large case and closed it, snapping the clips down to secure the lid. He carried the case, along with two massive duffle bags, to the front foyer of his condo.

Grabbing his phone from the counter in the kitchen, Noah sent a quick text to Joe, letting him know he was leaving. The crew couldn't risk meeting at the warehouse; Noah assumed the police were still watching the locations. Instead, the crew would meet up in an industrial park and go from there. All Noah had to do was get there without drawing the attention of any police officers; a relatively easy task.

"Alright," Noah muttered to himself. He walked back into the bedroom and grabbed the Ghostface mask. "Time to go be a criminal."

****

The industrial park was busy; semi-trucks, box trucks, and cargo vans drove all around the intertwining maze of side streets. Forklifts and industrial workers moved throughout the large lots, prepping goods to be loaded onto the trucks. With so much activity, Noah and Joe had agreed it was a great place to hide in plain sight. Just to be careful, Joe tampered with all of the security cameras, having them play on a loop so that the crew would never once show up on the monitors.

Turning his truck in the back lot of a massive warehouse, Noah saw the blue cargo van and black GMC Denali, both of which were recently acquired by Joe. Noah flashed his brights, and the crew stepped out of the vehicles, dressed, ready for action. Noah parked his truck and got out, grabbing the gun case and duffles from the back of his truck.

"It's a great day for a robbery, huh?" Darren commented as Noah transferred his equipment into the Denali. Noah was less inclined to make jokes.

"Let's keep our eyes on the prize, alright?" Joe suggested, sensing the tension from Noah.

"This one is going to be more difficult," Noah said flatly. "No way around it. But if we pull this off, we'll be set for life. That should motivate you guys."

"We got your back, Noah," Chandler said. EJ and Darren both nodded in agreement. Noah checked his watch.

"Alright, let's get moving. We're gonna get one shot at this," Noah said. "Joe, find a place to lay low and monitor everything, same as last time. When we're ready, come pick us up."

"Sounds good to me."

"Everyone else with me in the Denali. Chandler, you're driving."

"Got it," Chandler jumped into the driver's seat. They all loaded up into the van and truck, Noah sliding into the passenger seat alongside Chandler.

"You ok?" Darren asked Noah. Noah shook his head.

"No, not really," he admitted. "But I will be. We've got this. No one's gonna stop us today."

"That's what I like to hear," Darren smirked.

Chandler and Joe navigated their way out of the industrial park and headed toward Downtown Los Angeles, where the armored truck was most likely making a pick up at one of the banks on its route.

****

The truck was parked on the street right in front of the bank, engine running, hazards flashing. The driver was visible, sitting behind the wheel of the vehicle, as procedure dictated. The messenger was finishing up inside the bank; he had a dolly loaded with cash sacks to be transferred.

"There it is," Noah muttered as Chandler drove the Denali slowly past the armored truck. "Overwatch, this is Ghostface. We've got eyes on the truck."

"Understood," Joe answered immediately. "In position."

"10-4," Noah responded. He turned to Chandler, EJ, and Darren. "We'll hit here when they're just about to leave."

"You sure?" Chandler asked, making a right turn. "This area is pretty residential."

"Which is why we gotta do it here," Noah said. "Less congested, less traffic. We can use the neighborhoods to skip back over to the highway and get back to the warehouse."

"Got it," Chandler nodded. "That's why you're in charge."

"You two ready?" Noah asked EJ and Darren. They sat in the back of the Denali, gripping their masks and weapons in their hands.

"Always," Darren said with a wink.

"Good to go, boss."

"Alright," Noah muttered. "Let's do this. Masks on."

Once he stopped at a red light, Chandler pulled on his rubber Michael Myers mask. EJ and Darren both donned their Jason Vorhees and Freddy Krueger masks, respectively. Noah took a breath before he gently slipped into the Ghostface mask, adjusting it so he could see clearly. Halloween masks notoriously had poor vision, but Noah had long ago cut out slits in the mask so he could see much better.

The light turned green, and Chandler accelerated down the road, making another right to circle back toward the armored truck. As they neared the truck, Noah saw the messenger coming out of the bank - dolly of cash in hand. The driver moved around inside the truck, going to the cargo hold to help load the money.

"Chandler and EJ, you guys got the guards. Darren with me, we'll clear the truck," Noah growled.

"You got it," Chandler responded, driving closer to the truck.

"Here we go," Darren whispered.

Chandler sped up, cutting in front of a minivan, before slamming on the brakes when he was parallel with the armored truck. Noah leapt out and rushed out toward the cargo hold, with Darren and EJ moving in from the opposite side.

"Hands up," Noah said calmly, aiming his rifle at the two guards. The guards were stunned and instantly threw their hands up in the air, doing exactly what the man pointing a gun in their faces ordered. "Stay there. Michael, watch them!"

"On it," Chandler answered, leaping into the back of the cargo hold. "Alright, gentlemen, let's move it forward. Give my associates some room to work."

"Freddy, let's go!" Noah barked at Darren. "Jason, form a chain. Michael's got the guards."

"Copy!" EJ echoed.

Noah began grabbing the cash bags and passing them off to Darren, who passed them off to EJ, who loaded them into the Denali. They moved quickly and precisely, not even slowing down or breaking rhythm once. Moments like this, Noah knew he'd chosen the right crew. Doing this sort of work that needed rhythm and precision was exactly what his crew excelled at. Whether it was on the construction site or in the back of an armored truck, they just fell into a rhythm and got it done.

Chandler didn't have to do much in order to keep the guards subdued. They both looked young and clearly weren't about to risk their lives for someone else's money. Once again, things seemed to be going their way. He couldn't even think about what pedestrians were seeing or thinking as they drove past.

Noah cleared out the entire right side of the cargo hold and shifted to the left, grabbing two cash bags at a time. He was moving as fast as possible, but there was just so much money. They couldn't leave a single dime behind, not if Noah had anything to say about it.

"Alright boys, call just went out," Joe's voice came over the radio.

"Shit," Noah muttered. One of the passersby must've called 9-1-1 already. "Double time it, let's go!"

He started grabbing three or four bags, throwing them out to Darren as fast as he could. To his credit, Darren didn't stumble or pause at all. Whatever Noah threw at him, he gathered up and made sure EJ got it cleanly. The gradual sound of police sirens started getting more and more frequent as the cops swarmed to the call.

"How many are responding?" Noah asked Joe over the radio.

"Looks like you got five cruisers converging on your position," Joe reported. "Get out of there, now! Take your first right and lose them down Beverly."

"We're outta time, boys," Noah called out. "Let's move it. Michael, grab the rest of these."

Between the two of them, Noah and Chandler were able to grab the rest of the cash sacks, successfully clearing out the entire truck. They threw their haul in the trunk of the Denali and rushed around to get in. EJ closed the trunk and jumped in alongside Darren. Just as Noah was about to jump in, the two guards came clamoring out of the cargo hold, their guns drawn. They'd either had a change of heart or regained some of their courage. Either way, it was bad news for Noah and the crew.

"Gun!" Noah warned, raising his rifle at the guards. He flicked the safety off the rifle, ready to engage should it come to that. Not a single bone in Noah's body wanted to pull the trigger. The guards didn't need to be risking their lives, it just wasn't smart. "Put the guns down guys, we don't have to do this."

"Fuck you!" one of the guards yelled, gripping his pistol with his hands. His entire body language told Noah that he intended to shoot him. "You're never going to get away,"

"Yeah?" Noah asked. "Watch me."

He adjusted his aim and squeezed the trigger two times, shooting both guards in the arm. They instantly dropped their weapons and fell back onto the ground, screaming in pain. Noah lowered his rifle and jumped into the truck. Chandler slammed on the gas, and the Denali jerked forward.

Noah looked behind him and saw the first two cruisers responding to the truck and the downed guards. They were still far enough away not to have identified them as the getaway vehicle. Yet. He doubted that it would stay stagnant.

"Drive normal," Noah said, pulling his mask off. The others did the same, not wanting to draw any unwanted attention to themselves. "Joe, I need you to tell me the exact locations of these cops. I think we're clear right now, but I don't want any surprises."

"Yeah, I'm monitoring their radio chatter," Joe responded. "They haven't ID'd you guys yet. Standby… Looks like two have stopped at the truck. One is coming up on Arden, and two more are on Rossmore. You should be clear on Beverly. Take that all the way to Silver Lake and keep going. I'm heading back to the industrial park. I'll monitor your progress."

"You got all that?" Noah asked Chandler.

"Yeah, yeah," Chandler nodded. "I'm good."

"There's no way that went as smoothly as it just did," Darren muttered from the back of the Denali. Noah looked at him, and a smile slowly spread over his face.

"You know what, I think it did."

"Don't jinx it, we still gotta get back to the park," Chandler muttered.

"Well, hurry the fuck up," Darren said. "Get a move on!"

****

Chandler pulled the Denali right up to Noah's pickup and shut the vehicle off. Each man in the truck breathed a sigh of relief. They'd made it back without even the slightest of incidents. That was a miracle in and of itself.

"Holy shit," Chandler said. He looked at Noah with a wide grin. "We did it."

"Yeah, we did," Noah said quietly. There was a little part of Noah that wanted to celebrate, but he couldn't. He had to deal with Thomas. And make sure Lexi was safe. That took priority, it had to. Noah pulled his cell phone out and stepped out of the truck, dialing Thomas's number.

"Mr. Riordan," Thomas answered formally. "I was hoping to hear from you today."

"I've got it. All of it," Noah snarled into the phone. "I'll bring it to your office as soon as I know Lexi's safe."

"I can assure you, she is safe. It'd be bad for business if I harmed Brian's daughter."

"But kidnapping her is nothing, right?"

"Now you're catching on," Thomas sneered. "She is safe, you have my word, Noah."

"You can understand why that doesn't mean much to me," Noah responded. He paused. "I'll be at your office in an hour."

"No, not here," Thomas said. "Can't have you and Joe causing a storm like last time. We'll meet in public. Somewhere busy, so you're forced to be on your best behavior."

"Where?" Noah growled, clenching his fists. He wasn't in the mood for any of Thomas's games. Thomas took a deep breath, drawing out the conversation as long as humanly possible. It was totally infuriating for Noah.

"How about that bar you guys go to? The Lamp? I've heard you're familiar with it."

"Yeah, I'm familiar," Noah grunted.

"Wonderful," Thomas said pleasantly. "I'll see you there. How about one hour from now?"

"I'll be there."

22

Justin

Los Angeles Sheriff Justin Carter was getting angrier and angrier by the second. He stood on the corner in front of the bank, staring inside the empty cargo hold of the armored truck. Everything that he was being told was making him more and more enraged. And on top of that, no one had any correct answers to any of the questions Justin had.

How did the guards get ambushed? They weren't paying attention. Why did they not make a distress call? Both men were corralled in the cargo hold and held at gunpoint. What were the suspects driving? A black SUV, but not positive what kind. Is there at least security camera footage? No, cameras were down throughout the entire block.

"This whole thing is fucked," Orlando muttered to Justin, bumping his shoulder. Both men looked intimidating in their heavy tactical gear and bearing assault rifles.

"How did we miss them? We had the warehouses and Noah's home under surveillance," Justin hissed.

"I honestly have no idea," Orlando shrugged. "We were watching like hawks, I don't know how we didn't see anything."

"Unless..." Justin wondered aloud. "Unless Noah made us right away and had a second location to hunker down in."

"I mean, it's possible," Orlando responded. "It would explain how we missed them."

"But how did they get away? I mean, none of the responding officers saw anything?"

"They're one step ahead of us," Orlando spat. "But if you're asking my opinion, these guys definitely have had help. I mean, they've hit three extremely specific targets. It doesn't feel random. And, there's been almost nothing in terms of security camera or traffic cam footage."

"So, what? They've got someone who knows electrical shit?"

"Probably," Orlando nodded. "And if our guys are some union, blue-collar motherfuckers, I'd say we look for an electrician. Almost certainly union. I don't know any self-respecting union man who'd associate with a non-union."

"Fair enough," Justin nodded. "It's not much, but it's a start. Damn, I thought we had 'em."

"Me too, boss," Orlando consoled. "Come on, let's get going. There's nothing for us here."

"Yeah," Justin agreed. "Dalton, Nate! We're rolling."

"On it," Dalton called back, leaving his conversation with a few patrolmen.

The Sheriff's walked back to their respective vehicles parked on the opposite side of the yellow tape the LAPD Patrolmen had used to cordon off the crime scene. The sea of police officers, technicians, and news reporters parted for the heavily armed Sheriffs.

"What's the move?" Dalton asked Justin. "We rolling back to the warehouse or what?"

"I don't know, man," Justin said honestly. "If I'm being real, I want to go home, make love to my wife, go to sleep, and forget the last two months."

"That makes two of us," Dalton grumbled.

"You want to go home and make love to Justin's wife?" Orlando asked.

"Yes, Orlando. That's exactly what I want to do."

"Yikes, good luck. Karolyne scares me."

"Fuck you."

"Karolyne scares me too," Justin laughed. "You can try, Dalton, but I don't think you'll have much luck. She's been all over the place since she found out she's pregnant."

"Hold on!" Dalton yelled. The Sheriffs all stood still. "Boss, did you just say Karolyne is pregnant?"

"Yep," Justin nodded. Dalton, Orlando, and Nate all grinned.

"Dude! That's awesome!" Orlando exclaimed, walking over to hug his boss.

"Congratulations, Justin," Nate said. "That's so cool, good for you guys."

"Well, screw going back to the office! We're celebrating, let's go grab a drink. I'm buying," Dalton proclaimed.

"I'm not gonna say no to that," Justin accepted. "I'm gonna give Karolyne a call, and then I'll meet you guys wherever. Shoot me a text where we're going."

"Will do, boss," Orlando gave a thumbs up.

Starting his truck, Justin pulled his phone out of his back pocket and was about to dial his wife's number when the phone started ringing.

Justin raised an eyebrow, not recognizing the number. But that wasn't too weird, especially for a man in his profession.

"Detective Carter," Justin answered, putting his truck into drive and pulling away from the crime scene.

"Hello Detective," the voice on the other end said. It was a man's voice.

"Uh, hi," Justin said back. "Who is this?"

"Who I am is not relevant. It's what I can do for you, that's what's relevant."

"Ok, I'm hanging up now," Justin rolled his eyes. "Please don't call this number again, or I'll have you tossed in a cell."

"Your brother and his crew will be at The Lamp in approximately one hour," the voice said.

Justin slammed on the brakes, coming to a screeching halt in the middle of the road.

"What did you just say?"

"Your brother, his entire crew, and the money taken from the armored truck. They will all be at The Lamp. Do with that what you want."

And then the call was disconnected, leaving Justin stunned. That wasn't some phony tip being called in to waste the time of the police. No, Justin could usually tell the fake tips from the ones that were worth investigating. But whoever had called him knew that Justin and Noah were brothers. And knew that Noah was behind all of this. Justin grabbed his radio.

"Boys, let's meet at The Lamp."

23

Noah

The crew stood or sat at a large high-top bar table. They'd changed back into their work attire, wearing a various assortment of work boots, dirt-covered jeans or khakis, and Hi-Vis jackets or vests. They all wore various colored bandanas around their necks, a common practice to keep dust, dirt, or shale out of their mouths while working. To everyone else in The Lamp, they were just another crew of ditch diggers who'd gotten off work and gone for a ritualistic beer. Little did they know that the crew had enough money to buy the entire bar plenty of times over. EJ and Darren sat on the stools, resting their elbows on the table. Noah kept watching the front door, waiting anxiously for Thomas or Stan to come waltzing in. He refused to have a drink, although the others tried to insist. They didn't, couldn't know about Lexi. This was Noah's responsibility to finish once and for all.

"What's bothering you?" Joe whispered to Noah. Noah shook his head.

"Nothing, I'm fine," he muttered, shrugging off Joe's concern.

"Tell me."

"Joe, I'm fine."

"Jesus, Noah," Joe grunted. "Just tell me. We've been through enough together, what's the point of keeping secrets?"

"Thomas had Stan attack my mom and my grandpa," Noah said quietly. He maintained a steely look, but his eyes gave away his worry. "And they have Lexi..."

"Lexi... Who's Lexi?"

"She's on our crew. Brian Tyler's daughter," Noah shook his head. "Thomas knows we made a copy of the drive, and he wants that and all of the money in exchange for Lexi."

"And he told you to meet him here," Joe finished the rest of Noah's thought. Noah nodded. "Good. Let him come then."

Joe pulled back his orange vest to show Noah the pistol he had in a shoulder holster. He nodded slowly at Noah, letting Noah know that Joe was ready for absolutely anything.

A couple of vehicles entered the parking lot, catching Noah's glance. He looked out the window, watching them closely. Three dark-colored pickup trucks, tinted windows, and large light beams on top. At first, Noah thought it was Thomas and Stan. But when he saw his brother climb out of one of the trucks, Noah felt his heart skip a beat. He knew in that instant that they had been set up. Thomas had set them up and ratted them out to the police the same way he'd done to Jake Tell.

"God fucking damnit," Noah cursed.

"What?" Joe asked.

"We've been made."

****

Justin hurried around his truck, out of sight of anyone inside the bar. Dalton, Orlando, and Nate got out, unaware of the call that Justin had received. Waving them over, Justin opened up the bed of his truck and grabbed his gear, pulling it back onto the liftgate. He yanked out his pistol and made sure the magazine was topped off before slamming it back into the breach.

"Yo, what's going on?" Dalton asked. "We're just going for a drink. We don't have to kick the door down if we're paying customers. No need to load up, boss."

"They're in there," Justin said simply. "My brother, his crew, they're in there right now."

"Wait, are you serious?" Orlando asked. "How do you know?"

"Guys," Justin looked at his team seriously. "Just trust me."

That was all Justin had to say. His team trusted him implicitly. If he said the crew of bandits were inside that bar, then they were inside that bar. In half a second, their relaxed demeanor shifted into the hardened cops they all were.

"What's the plan?" Dalton narrowed his eyes. This was no longer fun and games.This was serious business.

"I am going to go try and talk to him," Justin said. "If that doesn't work, we go in there and drag them out in cuffs if we have to."

"Haven't you tried to talk to him already?" Orlando asked. "I know he's your brother, but I just don't want to risk the safety of everyone else in there..."

"He's my brother," Justin said clearly. "I'm going to go talk to him."

"Yessir," Orlando nodded respectfully, understanding this was something that Justin had to do. Alone. "We'll wait out here for you. Good luck."

"Thanks boys," Justin said. "If you see shit go sideways, you know what to do."

Justin left his tactical vest behind but tucked his pistol into the front of his waistband, using the front of his shirt to conceal it from view. The rest of the Sheriffs got back into their trucks, watching their leader closely. None of them had a good feeling about the situation, but Justin wasn't going to be talked out of going in there to try and communicate with his brother, even if it was futile.

"Be ready to get in there," Orlando muttered into his radio.

"Yeah, copy that," Dalton agreed.

****

EJ, Darren, and Chandler were rather oblivious to what was happening around them. Noah wanted to keep it that way as long as he could, praying Justin wasn't going to do anything stupid. They hadn't made eye contact yet, but Justin sat at the end of the bar, keeping a watchful eye on his brother and the crew. Noah had watched Justin and his team of Sheriff's talk before Justin came in solo. He guessed it was either to see how many guys Noah had with him or to try and talk this through. But Noah had no desire to talk. And he sure as hell wasn't going to jail today. Now, Noah had to figure out a way to get to Thomas and evade his brother, at least until he made sure Lexi was safe.

"What do you want to do?" Joe asked in a low voice so that the others couldn't hear him.

"I'll let you know," Noah grumbled. He picked up a fresh bottle of beer from the bucket at the center of the table and shouldered his way to the bar. Justin didn't look at him, his gaze focused on what was directly in front of him; although Noah knew better, Justin had already seen him get up and walk over. The steely look of concentration was a show, an unsuccessful intimidation tactic. There was one open bar stool to Justin's left, and Noah sat down in it, setting his beer on the bar top.

"Hello Noah," Justin said, finally turning his head to acknowledge his brother. Before Noah said anything, the bartender placed a coaster and a cold can of Coors Light in front of Justin. Justin picked up the drink and took a sip.

"What're you doing here?" Noah asked. "Got a tip or something?"

Justin tried his absolute best to contain his surprise at Noah's comment. If Noah knew, or figured, that Justin was there based on an anonymous tip, then there was someone else pulling a lot of strings in this entire thing.

"Something like that," Justin nodded. "Clearly don't have as good of friends as you thought."

"The man who called you, told you where I was, he's the one who attacked Mom," Noah lowered his voice. "You have no idea what you're doing. Listen to me, walk away. Now."

"You killed a cop. Left several others critically injured."

"And that's something I'll have to live with," Noah shook his head, knowing it would be a long time before he'd be able to truly process that.

"But if you get in my way right now, people are going to die. People that I care about. Just let me handle this, Justin. Please."

"Why should I believe you?" Justin narrowed his eyes. "No, you don't get to ask for anything. Now, we can do this quietly, or I can have my team barge in here and make a big production. Which would you prefer?"

Noah shook his head. He picked up his beer and guzzled the rest of it down, gently setting the beet on the bar top. Looking over to his table, he made eye contact with Joe. Noah nodded at Joe once, and Joe seemed to understand. This was not going to end well.

"Yeah, well..." Noah muttered, grabbing Justin by the back of the neck. "I told you I wasn't going to let you get in my way."

"Don't make me do this, Noah," Justin pleaded with his brother, ignoring the pain in his neck. "I don't want to do this."

"You should've thought about that before you waltzed in here, big brother," Noah said.

With that, Noah left the bar and walked back to his table. By now, his entire crew was looking at him, concerned. Taking a seat between Joe and Chandler, Noah took a deep breath. EJ and Darren polished off their beers, tossing the empty bottles into the bucket.

"What's up?" Chandler asked. He looked over them and saw Justin leaving the bar, heading back out toward his truck. Noah took the time to look at each of the guys at the table. Chandler Bannington, Edward James, Darren Lock, and Joe Kado.

"I'm proud of you guys," Noah said. "Proud of us. I know all of us haven't seen eye to eye on everything, but we did it. You are good guys, risking it all for the betterment of your family's future. That's the kind of men we are, I don't give a fuck what anyone else tries to paint us as. We were those same guys before any of this. Busting our asses daily so that our kids, spouses, families will have what they need. So that the people we care about are taken care of. This is the most selfless thing a person could do for someone. It is. We are the last of a dying breed, guys. Look around this place, how many guys in here do you think could do what we did?"

The four men took a quick glance around the bar, looking at the mix of guys in suits, guys in sweatpants who were way too into working out, and the misfits. A large melting pot of guys without backbones. At least, that's what the crew saw.

"But right now, you guys have a decision to make. Right now, there is a team of Sheriffs out there who would love nothing more than to drag us into a cell. I can't let that happen. But you guys walk out there with your hands up, you might not get the book thrown at you. I certainly won't judge..."

"What's the other option?" Darren asked, speaking for everyone except Joe. Joe knew what the second option was.

"We fight," Noah said simply. "Fight our way out of here. Grab our families and go underground. That's it."

Silence. Each of the men contemplated, weighing the options in their heads.

"You're gonna fight?" Chandler asked Noah. Noah nodded slowly.

"I have to."

"And you?" Chandler looked to Joe. "You too?"

"Whatever Noah does, I do," Joe answered.

"I got your back," Darren chimed in, nodding at Noah and Joe. "I'm with you guys."

"Me too," EJ said. "You guys know me, I'm not gonna back down from a fight."

"Are you sure?" Noah asked, making sure the guys knew what they were getting into. "There's no guarantee we will walk away from this one."

"There was no guarantee we'd walk away from the first job," Darren offered. "Way I see it, I'm already on borrowed time."

"Chandler?" Noah looked at the only man at the table who hadn't voiced his decision yet. Chandler looked at Noah and then looked out into the parking lot at the trucks, where Justin was talking to the other Sheriffs. Without a word, Chandler pulled his Carhartt jacket aside, flashing the grip of a pistol. There was nothing else to say.

"Ok," Noah said softly. He looked at Joe. "You got a few spares?"

"You know me, Noah," Joe said, reaching into his vest. "I'm always prepared."

Making a circle around the table to block anyone from seeing what they were doing, Joe pulled out the spare guns he had on his person, either in a shoulder holster or tucked into his waistband. Like Chandler, Darren was carrying his own pistol, along with spare magazines in the pockets of his work pants. EJ accepted one of Joe's spares and quietly racked the slide, chambering the first round. He made sure the safety was on before he tucked in the back of his waistband. Joe handed Noah a Glock, along with four extra magazines. Noah took hold of the magazines, stuffing them into his back pockets before he grabbed the gun. It felt heavy, like all of the weight of what they had decided had been transferred into this one inanimate object. Regardless, Noah racked the gun and slipped it into his jacket pocket. The last thing he did was pull the bandana up over his nose. The rest of the crew followed suit. Noah looked outside and saw his brother and the rest of the Sheriffs donning their tactical vests and weapons.

"Alright, boys," Noah said. "Get ready."

****

They worked in silence, strapping on their tactical vests, bandoliers of ammunition, and weapons harnesses. It was a quick process, getting ready to conduct an arrest like this. Justin stressed to the entire team that they should expect the men inside to be armed and not want to come quietly. The first priority was to make sure that none of the patrons at the bar got killed or injured. That had to stay the priority. Justin and his Sheriffs were cops, after all. They were the good guys.

"You guys ready?" Justin asked, attaching his rifle to the harness around his shoulder and chest. Dalton, Nate, and Orlando nodded - hands on their weapons. "Then let's do this."

Justin leading the way, the Sheriffs marched toward the front entrance, earning a few confused looks from some people who were also walking in.

"Stay in your cars," Justin said calmly, addressing their looks of concern.

"What's going on?" a middle-aged man asked.

"Stay in your car," Dalton repeated, not going into further detail.

As they got closer to the door, Orlando rushed ahead to open the door, letting the team file in before him. The large group of people at the entrance waiting for open seats at the bar or for a table hid the Sheriffs, even momentarily. Justin peered around the throng of bodies toward the back of the bar, where he'd seen Noah's crew sitting just moments before. They were gone. Looking around, Justin tried to find the group of men in Hi-Vis gear, but the crowd was too thick.

"Shit," Justin muttered. He leaned back to his team. "Follow my lead."

"You got it," Dalton nodded. Justin took a deep breath before marching forward through the group of waiting customers.

"LAPD Sheriff's Department!" Justin screamed, raising his rifle. "Everyone on the ground, now!"

As if everyone was possessed by the same unseen power, most of the entire crowd dropped to their knees. But not Noah Riordan. He stood across the bar from Justin, a red bandana pulled up over the lower half of his face. It took Justin all of half a second to see Noah reaching for a pistol.

"Gun!" Nate screamed, facing the other side of the bar.

And that's when it all exploded into chaos.

Joe Kado drew down on the Sheriff a few beats before Nate Murray called out the warning. He didn't hesitate either, squeezing the trigger just as the shout left Nate's mouth. The explosion from the gun was followed by an immediate and eerie silence that swept over the bar, most of the patrons and employees too terrified to move after a gun had just been discharged inside the place.

Justin wheeled around in time to see Nate Murray fall onto his back, his lifeless eyes staring up at the ceiling as blood flowed out from a ghastly head wound. Once his body hit the floor, the bar erupted into blood-curdling screams and cries.

"No!" Justin Carter screamed, drawing his rifle on Joe. He squeezed the trigger, firing at Joe, who ducked behind a booth before blasting off two more rounds at the cops. At that moment, Justin only saw red. He leveled his rifle and started firing round after round at the booth.

"Boss, on your left!" Dalton screamed, raising his rifle and firing across the bar top as EJ and Darren leapt up, shooting wildly at the cops. Noah gripped his pistol and moved alongside EJ and Darren, keeping low to avoid getting shot. He ducked below the bar top, ready to engage if need be. If he was being completely honest with himself, the last thing Noah wanted was to get into a gun battle with his brother. He had to get to Thomas and Lexi; wasting time here with his brother was not something he wanted to be doing.

The restaurant had evacuated in a hurry; as soon as the shooting started, people had dispersed immediately. There was a mass exodus of customers fleeing through the front entrance or the back kitchen. Some even smashed out the windows with chairs in order to escape. Justin knew it wouldn't be long before the entire LAPD would be swarming the building. He had to end this entire situation now, or he knew he'd be relieved of duty by the end of the day.

EJ and Darren were doing a solid job of keeping the cops at bay, shooting as fast as they could. They weren't exactly accurate, but the constant barrage forced the cops to seek cover. Rolling back up to his feet, Noah searched the bar for Joe.

"Where's Joe?" Noah yelled up at Darren.

"Right here!" Joe hollered, diving toward them. He leaned against the bar and reloaded his pistol, tossing the empty magazine away. "What's the plan?"

"I need to get the hell out of here!" Noah said to Joe.

"No shit, we all do," Joe muttered, getting to one knee. "I'll draw their fire, head for the exits. We are screwed if we stay here, the entire fucking force will be on us in minutes."

"I got your back, Joe," Darren nodded, reloading his weapon.

"Go!" Joe screamed.

Joe and Darren leapt to their feet and rushed away from the bar, bombing rounds at the Sheriffs. Taking cover behind two large support pillars, Joe dropped to one knee and fired until his gun ran dry. He spun back around cover and reloaded.

"You got any ammo?" Darren asked, dumping the empty magazine from his own pistol.

"Catch!" Joe yelled, tossing Darren a fully loaded magazine. Darren caught the clip and slapped it into the gun, snapping the slide forward to prime the weapon.

Justin reloaded his rifle, took cover behind the hostess table, and started shooting back at Joe and Darren. His high-powered rifle was cutting through the wood support pillars with ease, but he hadn't been able to hit any of the bandits.

"Justin! Behind the pillars!" Orlando yelled over the gunfire.

"Moving," Justin said, popping off three rounds before jumping over a table, trying to get a shot on Darren or Joe.

With Joe and Darren drawing the Sheriff's attention away from the bar, Noah and EJ kept low and began moving toward the exit, weaving around the tables and booths. They were closing in on the exit door when Noah looked to his left and froze. Jessica and two other waitresses were cowering in the corner, shuddering in absolute terror.

"Goddamnit," Noah muttered under his breath.

"What the fuck are you doing?" EJ asked. "Keep moving."

"Go, I'm right behind you," Noah said, waving EJ ahead of him.

Shaking his head, EJ stood up and made for the exit door. Before he could reach the door, Dalton squeezed off a single round with pinpoint accuracy. The bullet hit EJ in the back of the head, right at the base of his spinal cord. His body went limp, like a robot that had been powered down, dead before his body collapsed to the ground. Jessica and the two waitresses screamed in terror as EJ's lifeless eyes stared at them. Eyes wide, Noah crawled over to EJ's body, feeling for a pulse. It didn't even take a second for Noah to see that EJ was dead. Noah felt like he was moving on autopilot, grabbing EJ's pistol and extra ammo. He couldn't even process what was happening.

"Jessica," Noah said, pulling down his bandana so she could see his face.

"Noah?" Jessica asked, her voice shaky. She stared up at him with a look of faint confusion.

"Come on, we gotta get out of here," Noah said, reaching out for Jessica's hand.

And that's when Noah noticed that Jessica was clutching her leg, blood seeping through her fingers. Noah slid on his knees to Jessica's side. Blood had pooled around her; her entire thigh was covered in the red plasma. Her breathing was shallow, but she was hanging on. With the amount of blood Noah saw, he ventured a guess that an artery had been hit.

"Motherfuck," Noah snapped. He ripped off his bandana and wrapped it around her leg, tying it as tight as he could. "Hang on, Jess."

"Am I going to die?" she whispered, tears falling relentlessly down her cheeks.

"No, of course not," Noah shook his head. "Come on, it's not safe here for you guys. Jess, you gotta get outside, ok?"

"Noah..." Jessica began, bringing a bloody hand up to his face. She touched his cheek, leaving a handprint of blood behind. "I'm sorry..."

"Don't be sorry. Everything is ok..."

Noah was cut off when a bullet smashed into his shoulder, the force of the bullet throwing him off Jessica and against a chair.

"Noah!" Jessica shrieked. Dalton Dupree stepped over to Noah and the three waitresses, smoke curling around the barrel of his pistol. Noah writhed in pain, trying to find his gun.

Joe heard the shouts and immediately started looking for Noah. He saw Dalton stepping menacingly toward the injured Noah.

"Darren, Chandler, cover me!" he yelled to Darren and Chandler, who both continued blasting rounds at the Sheriffs. Joe began moving towards Noah, trying to avoid getting shot by Orlando, who'd taken cover near Nate's body. He dumped the magazine of his pistol and slapped a fresh mag in, loading the gun.

Running as fast as he could across the bar, Joe launched himself into the air and tackled Dalton, throwing the Sheriff across the restaurant; Dalton crashed into a table, the wind knocked out of him. Joe knelt by Noah and frantically checked the gunshot wound in his shoulder. Noah was bleeding badly, but the wound wasn't life-threatening.

"You're alright, dude," Joe reassured Noah. "You're going to be fine."

"Jess..." Noah muttered, pointing at the three waitresses huddled in the corner.

"Snap out of it, Noah!" Joe yelled, shaking Noah. "You're fine, ok? Now get up, and let's get the fuck out of here."

"Where's my gun?" Noah grunted, getting to his knees. He winced as he tried to move his left arm, the pain excruciating. Joe kicked over Noah's gun to him. As soon as Noah picked up the gun with his good arm, the gunfire kicked up again, forcing Joe to take cover next to Jessica and the waitresses.

"Darren! Chandler!" Joe screamed over the gunfire. He stuck his gun up above him and blindly popped off seven rounds. "Move to us!"

Justin came sprinting out of the dining room, gun drawn. He saw Orlando and hurried over to him, kneeling down next to his partner.

"Where's Dalton?" he asked, blasting a round off in the general direction of the bar.

"Right here," Dalton said, appearing from behind a booth. His upper lip was split open and bleeding profusely. He looked dazed and was continually shaking his head.

"You ok?" Justin asked.

"Nah, I think I got a concussion," Dalton muttered, blinking his eyes a few times. "Can't see straight."

"Get back out to the trucks," Justin ordered Dalton. "If PD shows up, hold 'em off as long as you can until we can get this situation under control."

"Yeah, ok," Dalton nodded.

"We'll cover you, but haul ass, ok?" Justin urged. "Get your ass checked out when this is all over."

"Will do, boss," Dalton nodded.

"Alright, three... two... one. Go!"

Justin and Orlando jumped up and began shooting at the bandits, providing cover while Dalton escaped out the front door. Justin sprinted toward the bar and leaped over the counter, crashing into the rack of beer and liquor. Chandler and Darren fired multiple rounds into the bar before turning and seeking cover in the kitchen of the bar, desperately trying to work their way over to Joe and Noah. Orlando reloaded his rifle and moved around the side of the bar, trying to get an angle on any of the men shooting at him.

Standing to his full height, Noah raised his pistol and started fighting back against his brother. He saw Chandler and Darren shooting from the kitchen. Joe, oblivious to his own safety, moved openly toward the bar, blasting off every single round in his gun. Once the gun was empty, Joe ducked into a booth to reload.

"Kitchen!" Noah yelled to Joe.

"Got it," Joe acknowledged. Vaulting over a downed table, Noah kept up his rate of fire, only pausing to duck behind cover when Justin or Orlando shot back at him. His pistol locked back, indicating that it was empty.

"Reloading!" Noah called out to his team. Reloading his gun, Noah signaled for Joe to move toward the kitchen. Before ducking behind a video slot machine, he jumped over the bar, firing four rounds toward Justin and Orlando. Noah blasted off another series of shots before turning and running back behind Joe; his hope now was to keep his brother pinned down long enough to escape through the back of the kitchen. He glanced over across the bar and saw Jessica and her two friends crawling toward the side exit.

"What's the plan, guys?" Darren asked, looking at Noah. "As much fun as this is, I'm running out of places to hide."

"Noah needs a distraction," Joe said simply. "Darren, you and I need to keep the cops occupied as long as we can. Are you good with that?"

"Oh, yeah," Darren rolled his eyes. He reloaded his pistol.

"What about me?" Chandler asked.

"Get them out of here, ok?" Noah said, pointing to Jessica and the two waitresses. "Hospital. She's lost a lot of blood. Just drop her off and then get the fuck out of there."

"I got it," Chandler nodded, slightly relieved he wasn't tasked with the distraction.

"You're not going after him alone," Joe argued. "Come on, man. That's suicide."

"I have to finish this," Noah shook his head. "This is my doing, I'm going to finish it."

"We'll meet up later then," Joe said.

"Yeah, sure," Noah nodded. The way he said it, Joe could tell Noah didn't think that was going to happen. But Noah looked at his remaining crew, and despite everything, he smiled.

"We got it," Darren said, looking at Noah. "Go kill that sonofabitch."

Joe and Darren leapt up and once again started shooting back at the Sheriffs. Chandler and Noah darted for the side door; Noah fired two rounds, shattering the glass door. Running full speed, Noah broke through the glass door and sprinted toward his pickup truck. Chandler knelt down beside Jessica.

"Come on," he said, gently reaching under Jessica to pick her up. She was obviously fading. Chandler nodded to the two other waitresses, and all three of them rushed Jessica out the door toward Chandler's vehicle.

Noah fired up his truck and flew out of the parking lot with Chandler on his tail. Turning onto the main road, Noah saw a mass of emergency vehicles rushing toward the bar. Chandler sped off in the other direction, heading for the nearest hospital. Slamming on the gas, Noah accelerated down the road, flying right past the convoy of first responders. Thankfully, none of them seemed to pay him any attention.

Once he was far enough away from the bar, Noah texted Joe just to let him know he was good. He prayed that Joe and Darren had been able to get away, although he doubted it. Turning the wheel, Noah reached into his backseat, fetching a roll of electrical tape from his toolbox. As quickly as he could, Noah wrapped it around his wound as tightly as he could. There was only one place Noah thought Thomas would be. And if Noah was going to get Lexi back, he'd need to be able to use both arms.

24

Noah

The sun had set by the time Noah Riordan stood across the street from the Union Headquarters. Most of the employees had gone home for the night, but there was enough light on inside to let Noah know someone was still there, Thomas Swaney most likely being one of them. There wasn't a better place for him to hide out with Stan Simmons by his side. It was the most logical place for Thomas to be holding Lexi, at least Noah hoped it was.

Reaching into his waistband, Noah drew his pistol and crossed the street. He didn't enter through the front door, instead sneaking in through a side door that he knew was on an automatic time lock. Once inside, Noah kept the gun hidden behind his leg, just in case he ran into someone who wasn't Thomas or Stan. Ignoring the throbbing pain in his left shoulder, Noah opened the door that led to the staircase and closed the door behind him without sound. Moving as quietly as he could, Noah climbed the stairs to the top floor of the building.

Stepping out of the stairwell, Noah drew his gun and moved toward Thomas's top-floor office. The door, usually open for Thomas's secretary to see who was coming, was closed. That wasn't too surprising. Noah assumed that Stella had already gone home for the night. He moved silently across the hall toward the office, gently testing the handle once he got to the door. The door opened slowly, unlocked. Noah took a deep breath and raised his weapon before stepping into Thomas's office.

The lights were off, the only source of light coming from the lights bleeding through the blinds over the windows, allowing just enough light in for Noah to at least see the waiting room was clear. He stepped forward toward the double doors behind Stella's desk - Thomas Swaney's office was on the other side. Noah could see from under the doors that the lights were on in the office. Steadying his breath, Noah stepped up to the door. He was about to kick the door in when he was hit in the side with a massive pipe wrench.

Falling to his knees, Noah felt the air get sucked out of his lungs. The pistol fell away from his grasp, clattering on the floor. He looked up and saw Stan Simmons standing above him, the pipe wrench in his equally massive right hand.

"Thomas said you'd be here," Stan said with a cruel grin. "Glad to see he wasn't wrong."

"Fuck you," Noah gasped. Stan set the wrench down on Stella's desk and reached into his jacket, pulling a pistol and a suppressor out. He made a show of screwing the suppressor onto the barrel, trying to intimidate Noah. Stan reached down and grabbed Noah by the collar, hauling him up to his feet.

"Come on," Stan grunted. "Boss doesn't want me spilling your blood inside the office. Too many questions."

Spinning Noah around so he was in front of him, Stan poked Noah in the back with the gun, forcing him to walk out of the office. Despite still reeling from the knockdown blow, Noah knew he had to make a move immediately. If he didn't, Stan would surely kill him as soon as they left the premises. Noah saw his gun on the ground and took his chance.

Jerking his elbow back as hard as he could, Noah caught Stan in the stomach, momentarily stunning the man. Noah grabbed Stan's pistol and yanked it out of his hand as hard as he could, simultaneously kicking his own gun on the ground back so Stan couldn't reach it. Before Noah could aim the pistol, Stan rushed him, tackling him with perfect form.

In an instant, Stan was on top of Noah, raining punches on Noah's face. Noah threw up his left arm to defend himself, determined to not let go of the pistol. When Stan reeled back to hit Noah again, Noah adjusted his aim slightly and pulled the trigger. The gun jumped in his hand, and Stan hollered in pain, the round tearing across the side of his abdomen. Noah jerked his knee upward, catching Stan in the groin. Roaring in pain, Stan fell off of Noah. Jumping to his feet, Noah swung his leg as hard as he could, kicking Stan in the face; blood and teeth flew across the floor.

Groaning in agony, Stan rolled onto his back, one hand clutching his groin while the other was pressed against the flesh wound. Noah racked the gun and aimed at Stan, surprisingly not feeling anything other than the headache from the barrage of fists from Stan.

"Goodbye, Stan," Noah muttered.

He squeezed the trigger, and the gun did its job; the bullet snapped Stan's head back, coating the carpet with gore.

Noah turned his attention to Thomas's office and marched ahead, barely slowing down before he planted his foot right above the lock. The door virtually shattered on impact, collapsing in on itself. Stepping over the splintered wood, Noah raised the suppressed pistol in the direction of Thomas Swaney's desk.

He sat behind his obscenely large desk, hands folded politely on the table. His hair, his suit, ironed and pressed, were both immaculate. Given the circumstances, Noah was off-put by how utterly and completely calm Thomas looked.

And then there was Lexi, sitting in a chair in front of Thomas's desk. Her makeup was streaked down her cheeks, and her lip was a little swollen. Her ankles were shackled to the chair by a pair of handcuffs.

"Noah!" Lexi exclaimed as soon as she saw who had burst through the door. He was relieved to see that she was ok, but he kept his glare at Thomas.

"Is Stan dead?" Thomas asked quietly.

"Yep."

"I see," Thomas nodded slowly. He didn't appear to be sad or scared, more disappointed than anything else. "And I suppose you plan on killing me too?"

"What would you do, Thomas?" Noah asked flatly. He lowered the pistol slightly. "I did everything you asked of me. Just like Jake did..."

"You do not understand everything that is at stake here," Thomas said. Noah saw a shift in Thomas. He was scared, not of Noah, but of something else. "You do not understand the severity of your actions, the people you're upsetting by doing this."

"That sounds like your problem, Thomas," Noah said. "I just came here to get my girl."

"I respect that," Thomas admitted. With his free hand, Noah reached into his pocket and pulled out the flash drive, showing Thomas so he could see what exactly it was.

"I did everything you asked," Noah repeated. "I don't care who you're involved with. I just don't care. It's not my problem."

"It will be if you do something with that drive other than give it to me," Thomas explained. "Please, Noah, just hand it over and we can forget all of this. I'll leave you be, you have my word."

Noah was silent, staring at Thomas thoughtfully. He acted as if he was thinking this over, but in reality, Noah was just drawing out the inevitable. Lowering his gun to his side, Noah took a step toward Thomas's desk, holding the flash drive out in front of him. A smile creeping across his face, Thomas stood up and stuck out his hand, ready to accept the drive.

"You know, Thomas," Noah said casually. "I could look past a lot of things, I honestly could. But you know where you fucked up?"

"Where?" Thomas asked, still smiling stupidly.

"You fucking hurt my mom," Noah narrowed his eyes.

Before Thomas could react, Noah raised the gun and squeezed the trigger, blowing a hole through the center of Thomas's face. Thomas Swaney dropped to the ground, dead. Noah lowered the gun and stepped over Thomas's body, firing two more rounds into his gut just for insurance's sake. An unceremonious death for an unceremonious man.

Noah walked over to Lexi and looked at the manacles around her ankles.

"Hold still," Noah whispered.

"Ok," Lexi whimpered.

Noah fired two hushed rounds through each of the chains, breaking them apart. Lexi stood up instantly and threw her arms around Noah's neck, thanking him over and over again. Ignoring the pain in his shoulder, Noah hugged her back and smiled softly. The tender moment was interrupted by the blaring sounds of police sirens; flashing red and blue lights bled through the drawn blinds in Thomas's office.

"Shit," Noah groaned, dragging out the curse for a few extra syllables. He let Lexi go and ran over to the window, bending the blinds with the barrel of his gun so he could see through. About two dozen emergency vehicles were out front of the Union Hall.

"Noah, what's going on?" Lexi asked, scared.

"It's ok," Noah reassured her, not really believing the words himself. "I'll explain everything later, I promise."

"Noah..." Lexi looked at him, her voice breaking. "Thank you."

"Come on," Noah urged. He kissed her on the forehead. "We gotta go. Like right now."

25

Justin

The blaring sirens and flashing lights were incredibly disorientating, and the street was filled with them. Cruisers, ambulances, and fire trucks all amassed in the lot with enough personnel to occupy a small town. Justin Carter leaned against his truck, blueprints spread out over the hood. SWAT officers, all geared up, surrounded the truck as well. Orlando stood next to Justin, eager to get inside.

Neither of them had managed to apprehend the other bandits at the restaurant. They both had vanished almost into thin air, which nearly sent Justin into a fit of rage. There wasn't even time to process that Nate had been killed. All of that would come later once the criminals were finally behind bars or six feet beneath the ground.

"Entry points are here and here," Justin said, pointing to two separate entrances of the Union Hall. "We're gonna go in quick and carefully, ok? We've got no idea who's in there, so check your lines of fire if it comes to it. I don't need to remind you all that I want these guys *alive.* Understood?"

"Yessir!" the squad of SWAT officers called out in unison.

"Lock and load, boys," Justin ordered. He pulled out his own pistol and racked the slide, chambering the first round.

"Justin, I got someone on the phone for you!" Karolyne yelled from the front seat of her unmarked Dodge Charger. Justin looked at her quizzically.

"Who?" he asked.

"He says he's your brother," Karolyne said quietly.

Time stopped. The noise, the flashing lights, the sheer commotion of the situation evaporated. The SWAT officers were staring at Justin, waiting for him to give the order for them to move in. They had no way of knowing that, in an instant, they had ceased to exist in Justin's mind. Slowly, he walked toward Karolyne's outstretched hand, his eyes glued to the phone. His hands were sweating by the time he reached out and touched the device.

"Hello?" Justin answered, his voice hoarse. He wasn't sure if that was from all of the yelling and screaming he'd been doing or if it was because of who was on the other line.

"Hey," Noah said in a low voice. "You out there?"

"Yeah," Justin grunted, looking up at the building. "Are you still inside?"

"Not for long," Noah responded.

"Noah, I'm gonna ask you one last time, man. Just come out with your hands up, and we don't have to do this. Please, man. I don't want to have to bring you in."

"You ain't bringing me in, brother," Noah said, almost with a chuckle. "When this is all over, you'll understand why."

"We got reports of gunshots inside the building," Justin sighed.

"The men who hurt mom..."

"You killed 'em?"

"I certainly did," Noah said matter-of-factly. Justin took a deep breath. His brother was just padding his criminal stat sheet at this point.

"Noah, I don't want to have to chase you..."

"Then don't," Noah countered. "Just for once, be a brother to me. Just let me walk away. You want to come after me in a few days, go ahead. But let me finish what I need to finish."

"You know I can't do that," Justin shook his head. Noah fell quiet. Justin could hear him breathing heavily.

"Alright, Justin," Noah finally spoke. "Good luck, brother."

Justin hung up and tossed the phone back to Karolyne, ignoring the concerned look on her face. He slapped each side of his face to clear his head and stormed back toward the SWAT team.

"Babe!" Karolyne called. "Baby, are you ok?"

Justin ignored her. He felt bad for a second, knowing she didn't deserve his coldness. But this was not the time for integrity. This was the time for action. Grabbing a bullhorn from his Suburban, Justin stepped out from cover and pressed the 'Talk' button.

"Come out with your hands up and no one needs to get hurt!" Justin screamed into the horn. "You got ten seconds or we're coming in!"

The SWAT guys stepped up behind Justin, brandishing their menacing assault rifles, shotguns, and riot shields. Justin counted in his head, slowly.

"Come on, come on, come on," he kept repeating to himself. "Please don't make me do this, man."

Ten seconds felt like an eternity, but it came and went just the same. Justin had no choice, no other options. He looked back at the team and nodded his head.

"Let's move."

****

Justin was overwhelmed with an increasing sense of dread as he moved through the main floor of Union Hall. As soon as they entered the building, the SWAT Team fanned out and began clearing the rest of the floor. A few paces behind Justin was Orlando, covering the back of his boss. Although he wasn't about to ask Justin, Orlando figured Noah had been the one who Justin had been on the phone with. The look on Justin's face was all Orlando needed to see.

"First floor offices clear," one of the SWAT officers said over the radio. "Moving up to the second floor."

"Copy that," Justin answered, speaking quietly into the radio mounted on the shoulder strap of his vest. He looked back toward Orlando. "Come on, let's move upstairs. He's gotta be here somewhere."

"Ok, boss," Orlando nodded. "I got you."

The two LA Sheriff's stepped into a corner stairwell and ascended to the second floor; they began moving through the maze of hallways and offices, clearing every room for any sign of Noah. Justin constantly felt that he was going to turn a corner and walk right into Noah. His palms were getting sweaty, and he constantly had to wipe his right hand on his jeans to keep a solid grip on the trigger of his rifle.

"Are you ok?" Orlando asked, darting into an office and clearing it quickly before rejoining Justin in the hall.

"Yeah, I'm fine," Justin grunted. He grabbed the radio on his shoulder and squeezed the 'Talk' button. "All units, second floor is clear. Move on."

"Understood, moving up. I'm splitting the team in half, well hit three and four," the same SWAT officer said. "You and Orlando wanna hit five?"

"We'll take five," Justin acknowledged.

He and Orlando re-entered the staircase and climbed the next two flights to the fifth floor as fast as they could. Orlando grabbed the door handle and pulled the door open, letting Justin out first. As soon as Justin stepped foot into the hall, he was kicked in the knee so hard his leg buckled. Justin fell to the ground and felt his rifle get ripped from his grip.

"Freeze!" Orlando screamed, coming out of the stairwell with his weapon raised.

Justin looked up and saw Noah standing in the hallway, aiming Justin's rifle at the two Sheriffs. There was a young woman behind him, holding onto his arm; she looked like she'd been beaten up pretty good.

Racking the charging handle, Noah looked down the rifle calmly, his finger bent around the trigger.

"What should I do?" Orlando yelled, keeping his own weapon aimed right at Noah's head.

"Put the gun down and walk away," Noah said calmly. "I just want to talk to Justin."

"You're insane if you think I'm gonna walk away," Orlando spat. Lexi shuddered behind Noah.

"Justin, just you and me," Noah said, looking at Justin, who was still on the ground.

"Drop the gun and get down on the ground!" Orlando screamed, jerking his weapon toward Noah.

"I can't do that," Noah shook his head. He and Lexi both took a step back, away from Justin and Orlando.

Wincing in pain, Justin got to his feet. His knee was throbbing in pain, but he ignored it for the most part. Keeping most of his weight on his right foot, Justin steadied himself. He drew his pistol but kept it at his hip, not raising it in his brother's direction. Justin took a painful step toward his brother, keeping his gaze locked in on his brother.

"Orlando..." Justin muttered. "Lower your weapon."

"Wait... what?" Orlando asked, dumbfounded.

"Lower your weapon," Justin repeated. He didn't even look at Orlando, who was thoroughly shocked at the request. But, Orlando followed orders. He engaged the safety on his rifle and lowered it, letting it hang from the harness around him. Slowly, Noah lowered Justin's rifle, casually holding it with one hand.

"We can't keep doing this, Noah," Justin began, taking another step away from Orlando, trying to separate himself from his fellow Sheriff. "This has gone on long enough."

"Justin, you don't understand!" Noah said, sounding almost as if he was begging the Sheriff to listen to him. "You never have."

"Then explain it to me," Justin responded. "I'm here, I'm listening to you. Just talk to me."

"The men I killed..." Noah pointed above them. "They attacked mom. They kidnapped Lexi..." Noah cocked his head toward Lexi. "All to get me to do something that I didn't want to do. That's what he did last time, too."

"What do you mean?"

"Thomas, he blackmailed our boss the last time around," Noah explained. "Used the threat of violence against his family, same as he did to me. I didn't want any of this. This isn't me."

"Whether you wanted to or not," Justin tried to keep his voice neutral. "You still killed a cop and that is not something I am going to ever look past."

"And that's something I'll have to live with as long as I live. But, it was an accident," Noah said sadly. "I didn't mean to. It wasn't intentional. He went for my gun and it just went off, I wasn't trying to kill him. I promise I wasn't."

"Is that supposed to make it better?" Justin spat.

"No, not at all," Noah shook his head. He took a deep breath. "Look, I don't blame you, Justin. I really don't. You found a job you love and a woman you love. Mom told me that you and Karolyne are having a kid. I'm happy for you, truly. You grew up with me, and I know you're gonna be a good dad. You're not gonna make the same mistakes he made. Me? I don't have any of that. But I want that. This life is not mine, it's someone else's. I'm asking for a chance to start over, clean. I'm asking for a chance to find a job that I love... With the woman that I love."

Justin was utterly stunned by his brother's words. Justin couldn't move, he couldn't even find words to speak. Seeing his brother, his younger brother, surrendering before him made him feel about as small as possible. He didn't feel the usual pride he felt when he made an arrest. This was his little brother, someone he was supposed to protect. He'd failed earlier in life. Justin had never been able to protect Noah from his father's wrath. He hadn't been able to protect Noah from Thomas Swaney. And now, he was still unable to protect him. For the first time in a long time, Justin looked at Noah through the eyes of a brother, not the eyes of a cop.

"Ok," Noah hung his head sadly after Justin didn't say anything. He looked tired, defeated. Justin finally noticed that he was bleeding from the gunshot wound in his shoulder. Noah turned and whispered something to Lexi. She looked horrified by whatever he was saying. He gave her a kiss before taking a step away from her, toward Justin and Orlando. Slowly, Noah set Justin's rifle down on the ground. Standing up, Noah looked at his brother with a resigned look on his face.

"Alright, Justin," Noah held his wrists out toward Justin. "I'm not gonna fight you anymore. If you have to take me in, then take me in. But let Lexi get out of here. She's done nothing wrong."

"I'll cuff him," Orlando muttered after Justin didn't initially react. Orlando reached to his belt and grabbed a pair of silver handcuffs. He unlocked the cuffs, making sure they were good to go. But before he could approach Noah, the door to the stairwell burst open.

Joe Kado and Darren Lock burst into the hallway. Grabbing Orlando in a chokehold, Joe pressed the barrel of his pistol to Orlando's forehead. Darren raised a rifle, aiming it right at Justin. Orlando struggled beneath Joe, trying to free himself. Despite Orlando being a massive physical being, Joe was surprisingly strong and wasn't budging at all.

"Sorry to break up the family reunion," Joe said with a wry smile. "But I do believe we have worn out our welcome here."

Darren and Joe looked absolutely fatigued. They had sweat through their shirts, their hair was a disaster, and Joe had blood all over his face, courtesy of a nasty gash on his forehead. But there they were, ready to protect their boss. Noah gave them a nod and a small smile. How they had managed to get into the building without raising any alarms was beyond comprehension, but Noah was relieved to see them nonetheless. He turned back to Justin, who didn't even look surprised.

"Come on," Darren said to Lexi, reaching his hand out toward her. "We'll get you home."

After Noah gave her a soft nudge, Lexi hurried over to Darren, who put his arm around her and hurried back into the stairwell.

"Your turn, boss," Joe said, cocking his head toward the stairwell.

Noah and Justin just looked at each other, each of them coming to a silent understanding of the other. Strangely, Noah felt at peace. The anger he'd held onto for so long suddenly didn't feel so heavy. He felt free from the burden, knowing he could get an opportunity to start over.

"You better get going," Justin finally said. "SWAT's gonna be wondering where I am. They'll come looking."

"Thank you," Noah whispered. As he walked past Justin, Noah put his hand on his brother's shoulder. With his other hand, Noah placed the flash drive into Justin's hand. His brother would know what to do with it. "Thank you, brother."

Noah and Joe rushed back into the stairwell, disappearing as the door swung shut behind them. Orlando, gasping for air, didn't even ask whether or not he should relay what happened to SWAT. He knew the answer. And while he did not agree with it, he at least respected it. Justin was doing what any older brother would do.

26

Noah

Keeping his arm securely around Lexi, Noah turned the wheel of the truck and pulled onto Brian Tyler's property. He drove carefully down the winding dirt road leading up to the farmhouse. Lexi had slept most of the drive back to her father's house, which was fine with Noah. There would be undoubtedly many questions on her end. Truth be told, Noah knew she would see him differently when she inevitably found out what he really had been doing this entire time.

Parking the truck right out front of the house, Noah turned the vehicle off and slowly got out. Lexi stirred when he removed his arm and blinked her eyes awake. As soon as Noah got out, Brian rushed out of the farmhouse, leaping off the front porch toward the truck. His eyes went wide when he saw Noah; the thick bandage on his shoulder, the blood stained on his arms and hands, the black eye.

Noah opened the passenger door, and Lexi jumped out, running to embrace her father. Lexi threw her arms around Brian, crying softly into his shoulder while Noah watched, leaning against the hood of his truck.

Everything in his body hurt but seeing the reunion numbed the pain, just slightly. After a few minutes, Brian whispered something in Lexi's ear, and she went inside without looking in Noah's direction. Wiping his eyes, Brian walked up to Noah and gently wrapped his arms around the man.

"Thank you," Brian said, his voice hoarse. "Thank you so much."

"Yeah," Noah grunted, wincing in pain. "Don't mention it."

"She's just going to clean up, she'll be back out in a few minutes," Brian said, taking a step back.

"Don't worry about it," Noah shook his head. "I'm taking off."

"She'll want to talk to you," Brian said. Noah sighed and nodded.

"Ok, I'll wait."

Lexi came out of the house and found Noah sitting on one of the front steps, leaning against the wood railing. He really did look like hell. She sat down next to him and put her arms around him, trying to be careful not to hurt him.

"Thank you," she said in a quiet, small voice. "I don't even know how to thank you."

"You don't have to thank me," Noah said, painfully putting his arm around Lexi's shoulder.

"Are you ok?" she asked. Noah nodded.

"Yeah, I'll be alright," he muttered. He turned and looked at Lexi, sadness in his eyes. "Look, I understand if you feel differently about everything. I don't blame you at all. No hard feelings, ok?"

"Oh, Noah," Lexi whispered, touching his face. "No, not at all. I mean, I have questions, but that doesn't change how I feel about you."

"Well, here's what happened," Noah began, deciding being preemptive was the best way to approach this.

27

Noah

18 Months Later...

Noah Riordan couldn't believe how nervous he was, it was almost hysterical to him. He'd done some pretty insane things, but this was by far the most insane and nerve-wracking thing he'd ever done. He was constantly fidgeting with the tie or the buttons on his black suit.

"Calm down, brother," Joe Kado whispered, leaning in so his voice wouldn't carry. He was also wearing a black suit. "You look fine."

"I feel like I'm going to throw up," Noah muttered back. Joe sniggered and resumed his position in between Noah and Chandler.

The music started up again, and Noah held his breath, looking out into the small crowd of people. His mom and grandpa were in the first row, smiling brightly at him. Ron looked at Noah and winked at him.

Brian Tyler appeared first around the corner. He was also dressed in a crisp black suit and was beaming with pride. Taking another step, Lexi

Tyler came into view, her arm wrapped tightly around her father's. Noah grinned, seeing his soon-to-be bride walk down the aisle. She looked stunning.

Lexi was equally grinning at Noah as she and her father stepped up to him. Brian gave Noah a quick hug before taking a seat in the front row, across from Noah's mom. Taking Lexi's hands in his own, Noah admired her, still smiling brightly.

"You look gorgeous," Noah whispered as the Pastor began speaking to the audience.

"So do you," Lexi said with a wink.

They said their vows, heard a reading from one of Lexi's friends and exchanged rings.

"And by the power vested in me," the Pastor said. "I pronounce you husband and wife. You may kiss the bride."

Grinning from ear to ear, Noah leaned forward and kissed Lexi. The audience erupted with applause and cheers as Noah and Lexi shared their first kiss as a married couple.

****

The reception was beautiful and easily one of the best nights of Noah's life. Although he and Lexi had both decided to keep the wedding small, it was a terrific night. Noah and Lexi spent the majority of the night on the dance floor, enjoying their night. Many of Lexi's friends let

Noah know that he was insanely lucky, which he already knew. But by the end of the night, when the music had lulled, and the small crowd began to disperse, it was Joe and Noah who sat off by themselves - each of them clutching an ice-cold beer. Joe, admittedly drunker than Noah, struggled to keep his eyes open.

"Tonight was a good night," Joe said, patting Noah on the back.

"Yeah," Noah nodded. "It was."

"You pay for this by yourself?"

"What else am I gonna use all that fucking money for?" Noah said with a wry grin.

Noah had confessed everything to Lexi. Much to his pleasure, she hadn't been scared off by anything that she heard. The only stipulation was that most of the money had to be given to charity; Lexi did not want to live off of the stolen money, which Noah understood. But, Noah hadn't been entirely truthful about the amount of money he had saved. There was still a significant amount that he had kept for a rainy day, knowing there'd come a day when he'd need it. He certainly gave a lot of it away, even setting a generous portion aside for the family of the cop who he'd accidentally killed. It wouldn't bring him back, but at least Noah could feel like he had tried to make amends.

"Who are they?" Joe asked, cocking his head toward two men who were walking toward them. They both were in suits, minus the ties. Noah had seen them earlier during the reception; he'd assumed they'd been from Lexi's side of the family.

"No idea," Noah shrugged.

The two men approached Noah and Joe, the taller of them taking a step forward and sticking out his hand toward Noah. With a nod, Noah shook his hand.

"Great night," the tall man said. He was probably in his thirties, short brown hair and a neatly groomed beard and mustache. His suit was crisp, clean, and perfectly ironed. "You guys make a lovely couple."

"Thanks," Noah said with a sincere smile. "You know Lexi?"

"I know her father," the tall man said somewhat ominously. "He speaks rather highly of you."

"Yeah? Brian's a good guy," Noah nodded. Joe was nodding off to sleep, leaning against the wall.

"So, I hear you're looking to move away from here," the taller man continued. This caught Noah off guard. He and Lexi hadn't specifically stated their plans yet, but they had been thinking of relocating.

"Uh, yeah..." Noah said, raising an eyebrow. "Thinking about it."

"Ever thought about Chicago? It's a great city, lots of building going on. You won't struggle looking for a job."

"Good to know," Noah said quickly, hoping these men would get bored of the conversation and move along.

"You know..." the man said, leaning in closer to Noah. "If you're looking for something a little more up your alley, I think I can help with that."

Noah looked up at the man. The implications of his statement were alarming to Noah. With a soft smile, the tall man pulled his jacket aside, revealing a Chicago Police Badge on his hip. In an instant, Noah got tense. He balled his fists, ready to burst out of the reception hall should it come to that.

"Relax," the man said, clapping Noah on the shoulder. "I'm not that kind of cop. Besides, I think you could help me."

"Help you?" Noah asked. The man nodded. "With what?"

"Oh, a few things," he said. "My associate and I are looking to expand our little team. You and Mr. Kado fit certain requirements we're looking for,"

"Is that right?" Noah asked, suddenly very intrigued.

"Certainly," the man nodded. "Should you be interested, here's my number. Call anytime."

The tall man handed Noah a blank card with ten digits on it. Noah accepted the card and slipped it into his pocket. Sticking his hand out, the man shook Noah's hand once again.

"I hope to hear from you soon, Noah," the man said.

"What's your name, anyway?" Noah asked. It seemed to be the most logical question, despite Noah having close to a thousand.

"It's Klint. Klint Kavanaugh," the tall man said, flashing his perfect white teeth.

Noah looked to the second man. He was slightly shorter than Klint but was built solidly. His brown hair was short but slightly unkempt. He was clean-shaven and had very rugged features compared to Klint, who looked more like a model than a cop. The shorter man had unwavering, intense eyes that made Noah slightly uncomfortable. But nonetheless, Noah stuck his hand out toward the man.

"Noah Riordan," Noah introduced, even though he figured both men already knew that. The shorter man gripped Noah's hand.

“The name’s Shannon,” the man said in a deep voice. “John Shannon.”

Author's Note

Writing this book was definitely a passion project for me as it combined two of my favorite things - bank robbers and construction. Since I was able to speak, I've always been enamored with heavy equipment. By the time I was four years old, I knew the names of every piece of equipment out there and could spot a CAT machine from a mile away. As I got older, that love grew and grew. I take immense pride in being able to jump in the cab of anything from an excavator to a small skid steer or a crane and know how to run it. While I certainly haven't had the stereotypical "blue collar" upbringing, I like to consider myself a part of that community. The work ethic, the values, and the camaraderie among the men and women in the trades is something I'll always admire. Working in the trades doesn't get enough credit anymore, with so much emphasis being put on going to college. Without the trades, our country's entire infrastructure would grind to a halt, and it's important to remember that. Our country was built by the trades and will continue to prosper because of them.

My fascination with bank heists started when a 12-year old me first saw *The Town*, a film about Boston bank robbers. This book, and its two sequels, are a love letter to those types of stories. I love the thrill, the excitement, of a good heist movie or book. Movies like *Heat, Den of Thieves, Wrath of Man,* or *Ocean's Eleven* are some of my absolute favorites. I never tire of watching them and only hope to one day write something as compelling as those movies.

I want to start by thanking my publisher, Tyler, for once again letting me publish a book with him and his company - Boxhead Books. It's been a great experience working together and I'm very proud of the three books we've been able to publish together. I'm super excited to keep publishing through him and continue to produce exciting stories for everyone to read.

Next, I want to give credit to my good friend Taylor Piggott for another terrific job done on the cover design. Her work on all of my books so far has been invaluable in capturing the tone and atmosphere of each book. Taylor has been an incredible friend throughout this entire process, always happy to discuss my crazy ideas for books. I absolutely love the look of the cover for this book and pray I never have to find another artist.

A special thank you to Mr. Ryan Schuetz for editing *The Last of A Dying Breed.* Ryan and I met back in 6th or 7th grade when I first started writing short stories. This hobby was started largely out of boredom, but Ryan and I would casually talk about plotlines, characters, stuff like that. As it turned out, we ended up having several English classes together in high school. He's read a lot of my early writing and being able to connect again through this book was awesome.

Not enough can be said for the work my mother did on perfecting this book. She has read every book I've written since *Phantom* and gone over it with a fine tooth comb. The manuscript I printed off for her is covered in his signature pink pen, making comments, suggestions, or corrections when needed. Being able to sit down, discuss, and work on my books with her has been a really meaningful experience. My mom is my rock and keeps me humble, but is also my biggest supporter when it comes to being creative. I've enjoyed every second of working on my books with her.

The only other person who has read all of my writing to date is my grandpa, Richard "Dick" Kasper. I don't even know where to start. My grandpa has been an irreplaceable figure in my life. My grandpa is the type of man who'll give you the shirt off his back. He would move mountains for any of his kids or grandkids and that is something I admire greatly about him. His work ethic is second to none and I only hope I have that same dedication throughout my life. Being the oldest grandson, he and I have always had a special bond, but over the years it's grown into much more. My grandpa showed me all of the classic movies that helped form my love for storytelling: *The Godfather, Heat, Black Hawk Down,* to name a few. Going to the movies or just watching a movie on Netflix has become a ritual for us. Every time I write a new book, my mom and my grandpa are the first ones to get a copy. I always look forward to the call I get from my grandpa to tell me he's done with it (which usually comes a day or two after I give it to him). Those little 30-second conversations mean more to me than he'll ever know. My grandpa, and my grandma Marilyn, are the best people I know. They are the definition of unconditional love and I know I speak for my entire family when I say we all feel safest when we're in the presence of them.

Lastly, I want to mention two people who've had a tremendously positive influence on my life. When my family first moved into our house, it was one of the first homes to be built in the subdivision. I spent a good majority of time with my nose pressed against the window watching the construction of the house next door to us. That became the house of Jim and Kathy, our next door neighbors. I still have very vivid memories of sitting on Jim's lap while he mowed his lawn with the infamous John Deere tractor. Over the next 15 years, Jim and Kathy became like another set of grandparents for me and my sister. Jim helped teach me how to drive, went car shopping with me, and helped me test drive a few different muscle cars when I was looking to get my first car. We've spent many days together working on his yard, spreading mulch, leveling the patio, or working in the garage. Jim is a retired Operating Engineer and also taught me how to operate a skid steer and an excavator. Everything I know about that stuff, I learned from him. It's been an honor to not only learn from him, but to still have a great relationship with him and his wife. Together, they're the best surrogate grandparents I could have ever asked for.

About the Author

Carl Michaelsen is a graduate of North Central College in Naperville where he studied Small Business Management. It was during college when he wrote his first book. His love for writing stems from elementary school where creative free writes were the best part of his days. Since publishing his first book, *Phantom,* Carl has gone on to write four more books and plans to keep writing. In addition to writing, Carl enjoys reading, going to the movies, collecting comic books, and spending time with his three dogs.

Also by Carl Michaelsen

The Phantom Soldier Series

Book One - Phantom

The Wolf's Empire Series

Book One - A Love Story

Book Two - The Crimson Wedding (Coming Soon)

The Union Brotherhood Anthology

Book One - The Last of A Dying Breed

Book Two - Cowboys of the Sky (Coming Soon)

Contact

Instagram - @cmmichaelsauthor

E-Mail - @cmichaelseniv@gmail.com

CPSIA information can be obtained
at www.ICGtesting.com
Printed in the USA
LVHW021546270523
748232LV00009B/457